APPRENTICE IN DEATH

J. D. ROBB

LARGE
PRINT

First published in Great Britain 2016
by
Piatkus
an imprint of Little, Brown Book Group

First Isis Edition
published 2017
by arrangement with
Little, Brown Book Group
an Hachette UK Company

A catalogue record for this book is available
from the British Library.

ISBN 978–1–78541–426–8 (hb)
ISBN 978–1–78541–432–9 (pb)

APPRENTICE IN DEATH

The shots came quickly, silently, and with unerring accuracy. Within seconds, three people lay dead at Central Park's ice skating rink. There's a sniper loose on the streets of New York City, and Lieutenant Eve Dallas is about to face one of the toughest and most unsettling cases of her career. She knows that only a handful of people could have carried out such a professional and audacious hit. Even more disturbing, this expert in death has an accomplice. Someone is being trained in the science of killing — and they have a terrifying agenda of their own. With a city shaken to its core, Eve and her team are forced to hunt not one but two killers. Worse still, this talented young apprentice has developed an insatiable taste for murder . . .

One impulse from a vernal wood
May teach you more of man,
Of moral evil and of good,
Than all the sages can.

WILLIAM WORDSWORTH

Are God and Nature then at strife,
That Nature lends such evil dreams?

ALFRED, LORD TENNYSON

Prologue

It would be the first kill.

The apprentice understood the years of practice, the countless targets destroyed, the training, the discipline, the hours of study, all led to this moment.

This cold, bright afternoon in January 2061 marked the true beginning.

A clear mind and cool blood.

The apprentice knew these elements were as vital as skill, as wind direction, humiture, and speed. Under the cool blood lived an eagerness ruthlessly suppressed.

The mentor had arranged all. Efficiently, and with an attention to detail that was also vital. The room in the clean, middle-class hotel on Second Avenue faced west, had privacy screens and windows that opened. It sat, unpretentiously, on a quiet block of Sutton Place, and offered a view of Central Park — though from nearly a mile away.

The mentor had planned well, booking a room on a floor well above the trees. To the naked eye, Wollman Rink was only a blob of white catching glints from the strong sun. And those who glided over it were only dots of moving color.

They'd skated there — student and teacher — more than once, had watched the target skimming, twirling, without a care in the world.

They'd scouted other areas. The target's workplace, the home, the favored shops, restaurants, all the routines. And had decided, together, the rink in the great park offered everything they wanted.

They worked well together, smoothly, and in silence as the the mentor adjusted the bipod by the west-facing window, as the apprentice attached the long-range laser rifle, secured it.

Cold winter air eked in the window as they raised it a few inches. Breath even, hands steady, the apprentice looked through the scope, adjusted.

The ice rink jumped close, close enough to see blade marks scoring the surface.

All those people, the brightly colored hats, gloves, and scarves. A couple, holding hands, laughing as they stumbled over the ice together. A girl with golden-blond hair, wearing a red skin suit and vest, was spinning, spinning, spinning until she blurred. Another couple with a little boy between them, their hands joined with his as he grinned in wonder.

The old, the young, the in-between. The novices and the show-offs, the speedsters and the creep-alongs.

And none of them knew, none of them, that they were caught in the crosshairs, seconds from death. Seconds from the choice to let them live, make them die.

The power was incredible.

"Do you have the target?"

It took another moment. So many faces. So many bodies.

Then the apprentice nodded. There, the face, the body. The target. How many times had that face, that body been in the scope? Countless. But today would be the last time.

"Have you selected the other two?"

Another nod, as cool as the first.

"In any order. You're green to go."

The apprentice checked the wind speed, made a minute adjustment. Then with a clear mind, with cool blood, began.

The girl in the red skin suit circled in back crossovers, building speed for an axel jump. She began the rotation forward, the move from right skate to left, arms lifting.

The lethal stream struck the center of her back, with her own momentum propelling her forward. Her body, already dying, struck the family with the little boy. Like a projectile, that already dying body propelled them back, down.

The screaming began.

In the chaos that followed, a man gliding along on the other side of the rink slowed, glanced over.

The stream hit him center mass. As he crumpled, two skaters coming up behind him swerved around, kept going.

The couple, holding hands, still tripping along, skated awkwardly to the rail. The man gestured toward the jumble of bodies ahead of them.

"Hey. I think they're — "

3

The stream punched between his eyes.

In the hotel room, in the silence, the apprentice continued to watch through the scope, imagined the sounds, the screams. It would have been easy to take out a fourth, a fifth. A dozen.

Easy, satisfying. Powerful.

But the mentor lowered his field glasses.

"Three clean hits. Target's down." A hand laid on the apprentice's shoulder signaled approval. Signaled the end of the moment.

"Well done."

Quickly, efficiently, the apprentice broke down the rifle, stored it in its case as the mentor retracted the bipod.

Though no words were exchanged, the *joy*, the pride in the act, in the approval spoke clearly. And seeing it, the mentor smiled, just a little.

"We need to secure the gear, then we'll celebrate. You earned it. We can debrief after that. Tomorrow's soon enough to move on to the next."

As they left the hotel room — wiped clean before they'd begun and after they'd finished — the apprentice thought the next couldn't come soon enough.

CHAPTER
ONE

When Lieutenant Eve Dallas strode into the bullpen of Homicide after an annoying appearance in court, she wanted coffee. But Detective Jenkinson had obviously been lying in wait. He popped up from his desk, started toward her, leading with his obnoxious tie of the day.

"Are those frogs?" she demanded. "Why would you wear a tie with piss-yellow frogs jumping around on — Christ — puke-green lily pads?"

"Frogs are good luck. It's feng shui or some shit. Anyways, the fresh meat you brought in took a pop in the eye from some chemi-head down on Avenue B. She and Uniform Carmichael hauled him and the dealer in. They're in the tank. New girl's in the break room with an ice patch. Figured you'd want to know."

Fresh meat equaled the newly transferred Officer Shelby. "How'd she handle it?"

"Like a cop. She's all right, LT."

"Good to know."

She really wanted coffee — and not crap break-room coffee, but the *real* coffee in her office AutoChef. But she'd brought Officer Shelby on board, and on her first full day she'd taken a fist in the eye.

So Eve, tall and lanky in her black leather coat, walked to the break room.

Inside, Shelby sat drinking crap coffee, squinting at her PPC while wearing a cold patch over her right eye. She started to get to her feet, but Eve gestured her down.

"How's the eye, Officer?"

"My kid sister hits harder, Lieutenant."

At Eve's finger motion, Shelby lifted the patch.

The bloodshot white, the black and purple raying out from it had Eve nodding. "That's a nice one. Stick with the patch awhile."

"Yes, sir."

"Good work."

"Thank you, sir."

On the way to her office, she stopped by Uniform Carmichael's cube. "Run it through for me."

"Detectives Carmichael and Santiago caught one down on Avenue B. We're support, just crowd control. We spot the illegals deal going down, five feet away. Can't just ignore it, but since we've got a body coming out, we're just going to move them along. Dealer? He's hands up, no problem. Chemi-head's jonesing some, and he just punched her. Sucker punch, sir. She took him down, and fast, I'll give her that. A little bit on the reckless side, maybe, but it's her eye his fist punched. We hauled them both in, with assaulting an officer added to the doper.

"She can take a punch," Uniform Carmichael added. "I'll give her that, too."

"Keep her tight for a few days, and let's see how she rolls."

Before somebody else wanted her for anything else, Eve cut straight through to her office. She programmed coffee, black, without bothering to take off her coat.

She stood by her skinny window drinking the coffee, her whiskey-colored cop's eyes scanning the street traffic below, the sky traffic above.

She had paperwork — there was always paperwork — and she'd get to it. But she had just closed an ugly case, and had spent the morning testifying over another ugly case. She supposed they were all ugly, but some twisted harder than others.

So she wanted a minute with her coffee and the city she'd sworn to protect and serve.

Maybe, if she was lucky, a quiet night would follow. Just her and Roarke, she thought. Some wine, some dinner, maybe a vid, some sex. When a murder cop ended up with a busy, billionaire businessman, quiet nights at home were like the biggest, shiniest prize in the box.

Thank God he wanted those quiet nights, too.

Maybe sometimes they did the fancy bits — it was part of the deal, part of the Marriage Rules in her book. And more than sometimes he worked with her over pizza in her home office. The reformed criminal with the mind of a cop? A hell of a tool.

So maybe a quiet night for both of them.

She set the coffee on her desk, took off her coat and tossed it over her deliberately uncomfortable visitor's chair. Paperwork, she reminded herself, and started to rake her hand through her hair. Hit the snowflake hat she tried not to let embarrass her. After tossing that on top of the coat, she finger-combed her short, choppy cap of brown hair, sat.

"Computer," she began, and her desk 'link sounded. "Dallas."

"Dispatch, Dallas, Lieutenant Eve."

Even before the rest, she knew the shiny prize would have to stay in the box for a while.

With her partner, Eve walked from Sixth Avenue where she'd double-parked her DLE.

With a scarf of purple-and-green zigzags wrapped around her neck, Peabody clomped along the path, shooting unhappy looks at the snow blanketing everything else.

"I figured, hey, we'll be in court, and we got temps in the forties, I can wear my cowgirl boots no problem. If we've got to go tramping through the snow — "

"It's January. And what cop wears pink to a murder trial?"

"Reo had on red shoes," Peabody pointed out, referring to the APA. "Red's just dark pink when you think about it."

When Eve thought about it, she wondered why the hell they were talking about footwear when they had three DBs on tap. "Suck it up."

She flashed her badge when they came to the first police line, kept walking — ignored reporters who pushed against that line and shouted questions.

Somebody had their head on right, she decided, holding the media hounds back out of sight of the rink. That wouldn't last, but it kept what was bound to be complicated a little simpler for the time being.

She spotted more than a dozen uniforms coming or going and at least fifty civilians. Raised voices, a few edged with hysteria, carried clearly.

"I thought we'd have more civilians, more witnesses."

Eve kept scanning. "Bodies drop, people run. We probably lost half of them before the first-on-scene got here." She shook her head. "Media doesn't need to get within camera range. They're going to have dozens of people sending them vids."

Since nothing could be done about that, Eve set it aside, flashed through the next barricade.

As she did, a uniform peeled off, lumbered toward her. She recognized the thirty-plus-years vet, and knew the relative order established was due to his experience and no-bullshit style.

"Fericke."

He gave her a nod. He had a dark bulldog face on a broad-chested bulldog body. And eyes of bitter chocolate-brown that had seen it all, and expected to see worse at any moment.

"Hell of a mess."

"Run it through for me."

"Got the first dispatch at 'round fifteen-twenty. I'm baby-walking a rook, and had him doing some foot patrol on Sixth, so we hotfooted it. Had him start a line back aways, keep people out. But Christ on a crutch, you can't block the whole freaking park."

"You're first-on-scene."

"Yeah. Nine-one-ones started pumping in and so did cops, but people were already running from the scene when I got here. Had to work with park security to hold what we could. Had some injuries. We got MTs in to treat the minors, but we had a kid, about six, broken leg. The way the wit reports shake out — once you cut through the crap — is the first vic collided with him and the kid's parents, and the kid's leg got broke in the fall. Got their contact info, and the hospital for you."

"Peabody."

"I'll take that information, Officer."

He reeled it off without pulling out his notebook.

"Sweepers aren't going to be happy about the state of the crime scene. People all the fuck over it, and the bodies've been moved around. Had a medical on the ice, and a vet — an animal doc — and they worked on the vics, and the injured.

"First vic took it in the back. That's the female out there, in red." He turned, gestured with a lift of that bulldog chin. "Wit statements aren't clear about which got hit second, but you got two males, one gut shot, one between the fucking eyes. Looks like a laser strike to me, LT, but I don't wanna tell you your job. And you're going to hear from some of these wits about knives and suspicious individuals, and the usual crap."

You didn't make lieutenant without wading through, and learning to cut through, the usual crap.

"All right. You got the doctors on tap?"

10

"Yeah. Got them inside the locker room, got another couple in there, too, who claim they were the first to reach one of the male vics. And the wife of one of the male vics. She's firm he was the last hit, and I lean toward that."

"Peabody, take them, and I'll start on the bodies. I want the security discs, and I want them now."

"They got them ready for you," Fericke told her. "Ask for Spicher. He's rink security, and not altogether a dickhead."

"I'm on it." Peabody headed off, careful to avoid the snow.

"Gonna want some grippers for your boots," Fericke told Eve. "Pile of them up there. Hotshot murder cop face-planting on the ice wouldn't inspire confidence."

"Hold the line, Fericke."

"It's what we do."

She walked around to the rink's entrance, strapping on a pair of the toothy grips before opening her field kit and sealing her hands and boots.

"Hey! Hey! Are you in charge? Who's in fucking charge?"

She glanced over, locking eyes with a red-faced man of about forty who was wearing a thick white sweater and black skin pants.

"I'm in charge."

"You have no right to hold me! I have an appointment."

"Mister . . . "

"Granger. Wayne Granger, and I know my rights!"

11

"Mr. Granger, do you see the three people lying on the rink?"

"Of course I see them."

"Their rights trump yours."

He shouted after her as she worked her way across the ice to the female victim, something about police states and lawsuits. Looking down at the girl in red — couldn't have been more than twenty years old — Eve didn't give him another thought.

Blood pooled under her, spreading more red on the ice. She lay on her side, and Eve could clearly see bloody marks where other skaters, and the medicals, had gone through.

Her eyes, a bright, summer blue already glazed with death, stared, and one hand lay, palm up, in her own blood.

No, Eve didn't give Granger and his appointment another thought.

She crouched down, opening her field kit, and did her job.

She didn't rise or turn when Peabody came out.

"Vic is Ellissa Wyman, age nineteen. Still lives with her parents and younger sister, Upper West. TOD, fifteen-fifteen. ME will determine COD, but I agree with Fericke. It looks like a laser strike."

"The doctors — both of them — agree. And the vet? He was an Army corpsman, so he's seen laser strikes. They didn't do more than look at her — she was obviously gone. One tried working on the gut shot, and the other examined the head shot — but they were all gone. So they focused on the injured."

Eve rose with a nod. "Security discs."

"Right here."

Eve plugged one of the discs into her own PPC, cued it to fifteen-fourteen, and focused first on the girl in red.

"She's good," Peabody commented. "Her form, I mean. She's building up some speed there, and — "

She broke off when the girl shot through the air, form gone, and collided with the young family.

Eve rewound it, backed up another minute, and now scanned the other skaters, the onlookers.

"People are giving her room," Eve murmured, "some are watching her. I don't see any weapons."

She let it play through, watched the second victim jerk back, eyes widening, knees buckling.

Ran it back, noted the time. Ran it forward.

"Less than six seconds between strikes."

People skated to the first vic and the family. Security came rushing out. And the couple skating — poorly — along the rail — slowed. The man glanced back. And the strike.

"Just over six seconds for the third. Three shots in roughly twelve seconds, three dead — center back, gut, forehead. That's not luck. And none of those strikes came from the rink or around it. Tell Fericke, when he's got all names and contacts, that anyone who has given a statement can go. Except for the medicals and the third vic's wife.

"Get a full statement from all three of them, and contact whoever the vic's wife wants. The female's cleared for bagging, tagging, and transpo to the morgue. And we need park security feeds."

"Which sector?"

"All of them."

Leaving Peabody gaping, Eve crossed the ice to the second victim.

When she finished with the bodies, she went inside.

The two medicals sat together on a bench in a locker area, drinking coffee out of go-cups.

Eve nodded to the uniform, dismissing her, then sat on the bench across from them. "I'm Lieutenant Dallas. You've given statements to my partner, Detective Peabody."

They both nodded, the one on the left — trim, close-shaven, mid-thirties — nodded. "Nothing we could do for the three who were killed. By the time we got to them, they were gone."

"Doctor?"

"Sorry. Dr. Lansing. I thought, I honestly thought the girl — the girl in the red suit — had just taken a bad spill. And the little boy, he was screaming. I was right there, that is, right behind them when it happened. So I tried to get to him, first. I started to move the girl, to get to the little boy, and realized she wasn't hurt or unconscious. I heard Matt shouting for everyone to get off the ice, to get clear."

"Matt."

"That's me. Matt Brolin. I saw the collision — saw that girl go into her turn for a jump, saw her propelled forward into the family. I was going to go help, then I saw the guy go down, saw him drop. Even then I didn't

14

put it together. But I saw the third one, I saw the strike, and I knew. I was a corpsman. Twenty-six years ago, but it doesn't leave you. We were under attack, and I wanted people to get to cover."

"You two know each other."

"We do now," Brolin said. "I knew the third guy was gone — hell of a sniper strike — but I tried to do what I could for the second one. He was still alive, Lieutenant. He looked at me. I remembered that look — and it's a hard one to remember. He wasn't going to make it, but you've got to do what you can do."

"He shielded the guy with his own body," Lansing put in. "People panicked, and I swear some would've skated right over that man, but Matt shielded him."

"Jack had his hands full with the little boy, and the parents got banged around some, too. Right?"

"They didn't have time to break their own fall," Lansing explained. "The father's got a mild concussion, the mother's a sprained wrist. They'll be all right. The boy, too, but he got the worst of it. Security had a first aid kit. I gave him a little something for the pain. The MTs were here inside of two minutes. You have to give them credit. I went to help Matt. And we had to try on the last one. But like Matt said, he was gone. Gone before he hit the ice."

"Nothing to do but perform some basic first aid on people who'd taken falls or cut themselves on blades — skates," Matt added. He scrubbed a hand over his scruffy gray beard. "It wasn't until they put us in here that it came back to me. You've got to put it away when you're working."

"Put what away?"

"The fear. The fear you could take a strike in the back of the head any second. Whoever shot those people? They've got skills. It came from the east. The strikes."

"How can you know that?"

"I saw the third hit. Saw the angle, the way the guy was turned. From the east." His eyes narrowed on Eve's. "You already knew that."

"I reviewed the security discs. We'll reconstruct, but at this point I agree with you."

"His wife's in the office over there, with your partner. Her parents just got here." Brolin heaved out a breath. "This is why I went to veterinary school when I got out of the Army. Dogs and cats? Easier to handle than people."

"You handled people just fine. Both of you. I want to thank you for what you did here today. We have your contact information if we need to talk to you again. You can reach me at Cop Central if you need to talk to me. Lieutenant Dallas."

"We can go?" Lansing asked.

"Yes."

"How about that beer?"

Brolin managed a weak smile. "How about a couple of them?"

"First round's on me." Lansing pushed to his feet. "People come here to enjoy the park, to take their kids for a little adventure. Or like that girl, for the joy. She was a pleasure to watch. And now . . . "

He broke off, shook his head. "Yeah, first round's on me."

As they went out, a man and a woman with security badges on lanyards stepped in.

"Lieutenant Dallas. I'm Carly Deen, rink security, and this is Paul Spicher. Is there anything else we can do. Anything?"

"Who's head of security?"

"That would be me." Carly, no more than five-two and a hundred pounds, lifted her shoulders. "People assume it's Paul. He's the muscle." She said it as a joke, struggling to smile.

"Okay. We're going to have to keep you closed down until further notice."

"We've already taken care of that. The media's bombarding the main 'link, but we've put it on record — just your standard 'The rink's closed.' One of them managed to get my personal number, but I've blocked it."

"Keep doing that. I need you to keep off the ice. You and any of your staff, until that's cleared. Crime Scene techs will come in shortly. Did you know any of the victims?"

"Ellissa. Ellissa Wyman. She's here almost daily during the season. She was going to try out for this skating troupe." Carly lifted her hands, dropped them. "She was nice. Friendly. She'd bring her kid sister sometimes."

"I knew Mr. Michaelson, a little," Paul added.

Second vic, Eve thought. Brent Michaelson — doctor — age sixty-three, divorced, one offspring.

"From here?"

"He liked to skate, would take an afternoon. Every other Tuesday. Nothing fancy, nothing like Ellissa, but he was a regular. Once in a while he'd bring his grandkids — evenings or Saturdays for that. He liked the solo in the afternoons. I never saw the other guy before."

Paul glanced toward the office.

"The one whose wife's in my office," Carly added. "Your partner's with her. She's good with her. Is there anything we can do for you, Lieutenant?"

"Give us your office for a little while more."

"As long as you need."

"I'm sure my partner asked, but so will I. Have either one of you noticed anyone coming around, either to skate or to watch, anyone who seemed too interested in Ellissa or Brent Michaelson?"

"Not like this. A lot of people hang around longer when Ellissa's skating. And there've been a couple of boys off and on who hit on her. But nothing over the top. We keep an eye out," Carly continued. "We don't have a lot of trouble. Pushy-shovies, your basic collisions."

"More trouble at night, but even then." Paul shrugged. "You get an asshole who starts a fight. Sorry about the *asshole*," he added.

"I'm rarely sorry about assholes," Eve commented. "We'll be in touch when you're clear. I'd advise your brass to coordinate with the police liaison on a statement. Timing and content."

18

"They're — the brass — they're going to be in a spin about lawsuits."

"The brass always is," Eve said, moving to the office.

Inside, a woman in her early thirties sat in a folding chair, flanked by a man and a woman. Each had an arm around her while Peabody crouched on the floor, talking softly.

Peabody took the woman's hand when Eve entered. "Jenny, this is Lieutenant Dallas."

Jenny looked up with devastated eyes. "We saw the vid. Alan really liked it. You look like you did in the vid. I mean like the actress did. I don't know what to do."

"I'm sorry for your loss, Mrs. Markum. I know Detective Peabody has already talked to you. If I could just have a few more minutes."

"We were skating. We're terrible skaters. And we were laughing. We were taking the whole day together, and tonight, too. It's our anniversary. Five years today."

She turned her face into the man's shoulder.

"They had their first date here." He cleared his throat, but it didn't clear the faint Irish accent that made Eve think of Roarke. "I'm Liam O'Dell, Jenny's father. This is Kate Hollis, her mother."

"It was my idea, the skating. Let's do everything we did on our first date. It was my idea to come here, like we did that day. We both took off work, and we were going to get pizza afterward, just like we did on our first date. That's when I was going to tell him why I wasn't having wine like we did then. I was going to tell him I'm pregnant."

"Oh. Oh, baby." Her mother drew her in close so they clung and shuddered together. "Oh, my baby."

"I was going to tell him, then we were going to tell you and Daddy and Alan's mom and dad. But we were going to have today, all day."

As Peabody had, Eve crouched so she was eye level. "Jenny, who else knew you'd be here today?"

"Sherry, my friend, and I think her guy — Charlie. They're our friends. I told Mom. We really just decided a couple days ago. I pushed for it when I took the test and it was positive."

"Did Alan have any enemies, anyone he had trouble with?"

"No. No. Detective Peabody asked, and just no. People like Alan. He's a teacher. We're teachers, and he helps coach soccer, and, and volunteers at the homeless shelter. Everyone likes Alan. Why would anyone hurt him? Why?"

"We're going to do everything we can to find out. You can contact me or Detective Peabody anytime."

"I don't know what to do."

"You should go with your mom." Liam leaned over, kissed her head. "Go home with your mom now."

"Daddy — "

"I'll come. I'll be there." He looked over her head to Kate, got a teary nod. "Go with your mom, darling, and I'll be coming right along."

"Peabody."

"Come with me. We'll have an officer take you home."

Liam sat where he was as Peabody led them out.

20

"We're divorced, you see, and Kate, she's married again. Eight years. Or is it nine?" He shook his head. "But such things don't matter a bit now, do they?" As he rose, he cleared his throat again. "He was a good man, our Alan. A good and stable man who loved my girl with his whole heart. You'll find who took him from her, from my girl and from the baby inside her."

"We'll do everything we can."

"I saw the vid, and read the book as well. That Icove business. You'll find who took the life of this good young man."

Eyes blurred with tears, he hurried out.

Eve sat, took a moment to clear away the grief that hung so thick in the air. Then pulled out her 'link.

"Lowenbaum." SWAT commander — the best she knew. "I need a consult."

"I'm getting rumors about Central Park."

"I'm confirming them. I need an expert consult."

"And to think I was going off tour. I can be at the rink in — "

"Not the rink, not yet. I've got security feed, and I need a good screen. My place isn't far from here. Can you come there?"

"The Dallas Palace?"

"Bite me, Lowenbaum."

He laughed, then just grinned at her. "Yeah, I can come there." The grin faded. "I get conflicting numbers on vics."

"Three. And it's my sense it could've been a hell of a lot worse."

"If it can get worse, it usually does."

"That's why I need the consult. I think it could get worse. I have to do the notifications. Can you be there in an hour?"

"Can do."

"Appreciate it."

She clicked off as Peabody came back.

"I need you to go to the hospital — or check and see if the kid with the broken leg and his parents are still there. Wherever they are, go there. See what they saw, write it up. I'll do the notifications."

"I'm still working on the security feeds. It's a big park."

"Have them sent to my home and office units. We can start with sectors east of the rink. Have them sent to your home and office units, too. I want you to study them — get McNab to study them. You flag anything or anyone that looks off. If this came from inside the park, we're looking for an individual with some sort of bag or case."

"If?"

Eve stepped out of the office, scanned the empty locker room. "Because I'm betting it came from outside the park. We're going to be looking at buildings with west-facing windows, starting with Sixth, working east until Lowenbaum tells me to stop."

"Lowenbaum?"

"He's coming in to consult. I want this rink feed on my screens at home, with equipment that doesn't argue with me."

"Lowenbaum. He's so cute." At Eve's steely stare, Peabody hunched her shoulders. "I'm with McNab

22

through and through, but I can see cuteness through my eyes and my Cute-O-Meter. You have to admit, he ranks high on the Cute-O-Meter."

"Cute's for kids and puppies — if you're into kids and puppies. I'll give you he's frosty enough."

"Completely. I'll push on the security feeds, and see if I can find anything new from the kid and his parents." As she spoke, Peabody began to rewind her long scarf. "We're going to be wading through piles of wit statements."

"Take the first ten. I'll start on the rest. Let's see if we can find anything that connects the three vics other than a visit to the skating rink. And let's hope we do. If this was pure random, it's already gotten worse."

As she stepped outside, Eve looked over the heads of the sweepers busy working on the scene, and stared east.

Again she thought: It could get a lot worse.

CHAPTER
TWO

Hard to say, Eve thought as she finally headed home, if notifying next of kin was worse in person or over the 'link. Either way, she had just sliced Ellissa Wyman's parents in two, face-to-face, and had done the same to Brent Michaelson's daughter, who was in Philadelphia on business, via 'link.

Their lives would never be the same. Death changed everything, she knew, and murder added a bloody smear to the change.

She had to cut through the grief — it blurred focus.

No enemies, no threats, no trouble. No bitter exes, no big piles of coveted money. At this point, it appeared the three victims had been ordinary, law-abiding people.

Wrong place, wrong time.

But why those three — two of them regulars to the rink? Out of the dozens and dozens there, why *those* three?

There was always a reason, she reminded herself. Even if the reason was bat-shit crazy.

She toyed with reasons as she turned through the gates, started down the winding drive toward home.

Lowenbaum's remark broke through her theorizing.

24

Dallas Palace? Seriously? Is that how some of the cops saw it?

Maybe it did look something like a castle (was that the same thing as a palace?) with its grand stone walls catching the first glints of winter's bright stars. It had towers and turrets, and with the white expanse of snow, the ice shimmering on denuded branches of trees, maybe it looked like something out of another time.

Another world.

But that was Roarke's doing. He'd built it — his personal fortress in the heart of the city. And maybe it had impressed and intimidated the crap out of her at first — and for a while after. But now?

It was home.

Where fires would be burning, where the man she loved would look at her in a way that showed her, in an instant, she mattered. Where a cat would rub against her legs in greeting.

Where, she thought as she parked at the front entrance, Summerset would loom in the foyer like a ghoul.

Like he expected her to trail mud and blood over the pristine floors. And, okay, maybe she had, more than once. But not today.

She checked her boots as she got out of the car, just in case.

Today she didn't have time to give or receive any shit.

She stepped in, and there he was — bony, black-suited, stone-faced, with the pudgy cat sitting at his feet.

"Save it," she said before he could lead with whatever insult he'd devised for the day. "I've got a cop coming in. Lowenbaum. Send him straight up."

"And will your guest be joining you for dinner?"

She figured the silky tone took the place of the insult — though the question itself threw her off. "I . . . "

What the hell time was it? She had to force herself not to check her wrist unit, wouldn't give him the satisfaction.

"He's not a guest, he's a cop. It's work."

To get some of her own back, she walked around the cat rubbing against her legs, shrugged out of her coat, and tossed it over the newel post.

"Naturally."

Ignoring him, she started up the stairs, the cat running behind her.

She headed straight to her office, stopped short when she saw Roarke, leaning back against her desk.

The man could stop her heart, then send it into full gallop. Just a look at him. They'd been married more than two years, she thought. Shouldn't that ease off? Where was that in the Marriage Rules?

But a man who looked like Roarke broke every rule.

That absurdly beautiful face set off with the wild blue eyes of some Irish god, and the perfect poet's mouth. The black hair, silkier than Summerset's tone, tied back in work mode. The tall, lean length of him all in black — no tie or suit coat, the sleeves of his shirt rolled to the elbow.

So he'd been home, and working, for some time.

Yeah, the look of him broke the rules, stopped the heart. But it was that instant, just that instant when those amazing blue eyes met hers that sent it into the gallop.

In them lived love. Just that simple, just that extraordinary.

"You're just in time," he said, the Irish sliding through the words.

"I — for what?"

He simply held out a hand.

She walked to him, and the first thing he did was draw her in, his clever hands skimming up her back as he brushed his lips to hers.

Home, she thought again, and the last few hours dropped down on her, had her wrapping around him, leaning in. Knowing she could, here she could lean and not lose what she was.

"You caught one," he murmured. "It's the murders at Wollman Rink, isn't it? I thought of you as soon as I heard the bulletin."

"Yeah. I just left the first victim's parents and her fourteen-year-old sister smashed to bits."

"The most brutal part of a brutal job. I'm sorry for it."

"Me, too."

He tipped her face back, brushed those lips over her forehead. "You'll tell me. I think a glass of wine first — there'll be plenty of coffee later, but a moment to settle for now."

"Don't really have one. Lowenbaum's on his way over. I need him to look at the security disc. I need a consult. He's SWAT," she began.

"Yes, I remember him, quite well, from the Red Horse investigation last year. Why him, particularly?"

"They were laser strikes, one strike for each vic, and each one lethal. And I think they came from outside Central Park."

"Outside? I see."

Because he did, because he could, it relieved her of long explanations.

"Maybe one of them was a specific target, the other two cover. Maybe I'll find a connection linking the three of them. But . . . " She shook her head. "I need to set up my murder board, start the book."

"I can help you with that."

"Yeah, thanks. Maybe if you — " She turned, and once again her heart stopped. But not in a good way.

On her wall screen lived a pink and purple nightmare.

Pink walls with purple squiggles framed a room filled with worse. Some sort of S-shaped seat sat in the middle of it all, carrying pink squiggles on purple, and that mounded with pillows in every color, with dizzying designs. And fringe.

A chair angled toward it — pink again, with big green dots, and — were those feathers? *Feathers* rising up from the back in a bright rainbow fan.

Under the window — framed in more feathers — a bright green glossy table stood flanked by two pink chairs — purple dots. The table held a huge purple vase full of weird flowers.

Her heart started up again with a sputter as she spotted a U-shaped workstation, candy pink with a purple border.

"This can't be real."

"Charmaine put it together as a joke." Roarke shifted so he could cup Eve's face in his hands. "Which we'd both have enjoyed more if you didn't have murder on your brain."

"A joke."

"Designing what we'll call the polar opposite of what you want and need in the remodel here."

"Opposite."

"Completely opposite. I'll add when she sent this, and the three actual designs, she said she thought the shock of this would smooth the way to the others." He smiled now, traced a finger down the shallow dent in her chin. "Let's take a moment, just scan the others, and see if she's right. Just a quick glance. Then you won't worry I've nudged you into doing something you'll hate."

"You couldn't nudge me into that with a stunner on full. But I don't know if — "

"Computer, Design One, on screen. As I said when we talked about updating your space, nothing you don't want."

She started to argue, then saw the image. One of quiet colors, simple lines — and what had turned her tide in the first place — a big, kick-ass command center.

"Not a trace of pink — not a single feather or flounce," Roarke said. "Design Two, on screen."

29

Stronger colors, but rich rather than bright. Maybe a few more curves, maybe a little plush on the seating, but not embarrassing.

"And Design Three, on screen."

She thought this one hit between. The colors muted, a little more streamlined on the furnishings.

"Better?"

"Anything would be."

"You'll look at them later, when you've not so much on your mind."

"Okay. Take it down, will you? I hear somebody coming. It must be Lowenbaum."

His cop, Roarke knew, would be mortified if another cop discovered her considering interior design. He ordered the images off as she went to the door to greet.

"Lieutenant Lowenbaum," Summerset said, then backed away.

He came in grinning. She'd still term him frosty, but she got Peabody's Cute-O-Meter scale.

"Let me say wow, some place." He glanced around, quiet gray eyes taking in every detail. "You ever get lost?"

"Sometimes."

"I bet. Hey, Roarke."

"Lowenbaum."

"I just got here myself," Eve said. "I haven't set things up."

"No rush. Who's this?" He crouched down to scratch the cat who'd prowled over to check him out.

"Galahad."

"Oh, yeah, yeah, I heard the story. The cat tripped the asshole, saved your bacon. You took a hit."

"You heard the story?"

"You take down a sitting U.S. senator, Dallas, the story goes around. Two different eye colors. Frosty."

"He's a pretty good cat," Eve told him as Galahad preened under Lowenbaum's stroking hand.

"More a dog man myself, but yeah, he's a pretty good cat." He straightened. "So."

"Would you like a beer, a glass of wine?"

Eve frowned at Roarke's invitation. "We're working."

"Would a beer impair you, Lowenbaum?"

A quick grin that came with a flash of dimples. "Not hardly, and I could go for one."

"As it happens we have a special brew, just arrived. Deputy Banner's family brew," Roarke told Eve. "As promised."

"The cop from Arkansas," Eve explained. "Helped us bag those murdering lovebirds."

"Heard about that, too. Let's have a home brew and see what you've got."

"Give me a sec." Eve went to her desk as Roarke strolled into the adjoining kitchen. "Rink security disc. Peabody's rounding up security from the rest of the park, but this shows all three strikes."

She plugged in the disc, gestured to the wall screen. "Run disc where cued, on screen. See the girl in red?"

"Can't miss her. She's a beauty and she knows what she's doing."

"Was, did."

Lowenbaum nodded at the screen as Ellissa took her last flight. Then his eyes flattened out at the next strike. And the third.

"Run it again, cut the speed."

Roarke came back in, two brews hooked in one hand, a third in the other. He paused, watched the screen.

"Okay, enhance the last strike, start a few seconds before, slow it more."

Eve ordered the enhancement, slowed the speed. Narrowed her eyes when she thought she caught the faintest flash.

"Your shooter's nest is east of the rink, and that kind of accuracy? He's got serious training. That's not luck. East of the rink and above."

"Above."

"ME should confirm that, unless I'm full of shit. Thanks," he added to Roarke, took a beer. "I'm going to be surprised if general park security picks up anything. Even in New York, somebody's going to notice somebody else climbing up a tree with a weapon, and I'm thinking higher anyway. Run it back, watch again."

"I thought I saw a flash, a red . . . glimmer."

"The beam. Sorry," Roarke added.

"No, you're right." Lowenbaum nodded approval as he continued to watch the screen. "A laser strike emits a beam. Hard to catch it, and it's fast. You get this to the lab, they can clean it up more, bring it up more. But there."

Eve froze the image. "Yeah, I see it. And yeah, I can just make out an angle. East and above."

"My guess, even if this fucker climbed the park's tallest tree, is tactical laser rifle."

"What's the range on one of those?"

"That's going to depend on the weapon, and it's sure as hell going to depend on the shooter. But if he's good enough, equipped right? A mile and a half, two. Even more."

"A weapon like that? Has to be law enforcement or military. You can't just pick one up at the local 24/7. Black market, maybe, a weapons runner, but that's going to cost for one that's not a piece of shit."

"Twenty large, easy," Lowenbaum confirmed. "Even a licensed collector's going to find one hard to come by — through legal means."

"A complicated process," Roarke said, "but doable."

Eve turned to him. "You have one."

"Actually, three. A Stealth-LZR — "

"You got an LZR?" Lowenbaum's eyes shone like Christmas morning. "First man-portable laser rifle — pulse action. 2021 to '23. Heavy, clunky, but a trained operator could strike a dime credit in just inside a mile."

"They've improved considerably since then. I have the Tactical-XT, such as your team would use, and a Peregrine-XLR."

"Shut up." Lowenbaum pointed at Roarke. "You've got a Peregrine?"

"I do."

"Those suckers are accurate for five miles, more in the right hands. They just released for military use last year. How did you . . . " Lowenbaum paused, took a sip of beer. "Don't ask, don't tell?"

"All legal," Roarke assured him. "Considerable finagling, but I've all the proper paperwork."

"Man. I'd love to see it."

"Of course."

"Really?"

"What are the odds this shooter has something like that?" Eve began.

"If he does, he could've taken the shot from goddamn Queens. I'd really like a look."

"You just want to play with the toys, but fine."

"We'll take the elevator." Roarke gestured.

"You should have a look yourself," Lowenbaum told Eve. "Get a gauge."

"I've seen your weapon, Lowenbaum. I've used a laser rifle a time or two."

"It's more likely your shooter's using a tactical — something in that range." Lowenbaum stepped on the elevator with them. "Three strikes like that, in that time frame? You've got someone who's got possession and training of a long-range laser rifle."

"Law enforcement, military — or former in either. I'll get a list of collectors to add to that."

Eve stuck her hands in her pockets as the elevator opened outside the big secured doors of Roarke's weapons room.

Roarke laid his hand on the palm plate.

When the doors opened, Lowenbaum let out a sound a man might make when seeing a naked woman.

She supposed she couldn't blame him. Roarke's collection was a history of weaponry. Broadswords, stunners, thin silver foils, muskets, revolvers, maces, blasters, machine guns, combat knives.

The glass display cases held centuries of death.

She gave Lowenbaum a minute to wander and gawk.

"You and Roarke can play with all the shoot-it, stab-it, stun-it, and blow-the-crap-out-of-it toys later. Right now . . . "

She gestured toward the display of laser weapons.

Obliging her, Roarke deactivated the locks, opened the glass, took out the Peregrine.

She'd never seen it, or its like before. And admitted, to herself, she'd like to test it out. But she said nothing as Roarke took it from its place, offered it to Lowenbaum.

"Is it charged?"

"It's not, no. That would be . . . breaking the rules." And Roarke smiled.

With a half laugh, Lowenbaum lifted the weapon — black as death, sleek as a snake — to his shoulder. "Lightweight. Our tacticals weigh in at five-point-three pounds. Add another eight ounces if you're carrying the optimum scope. Spare batt's another three ounces. This is what, three pounds and change?"

"Three and two. It'll sync with a PPC, or you can use its infrared." Now Roarke opened the door, took out a palm-sized handheld. "This will read up to fifteen miles. Battery life is seventy-two hours, full use, though

I'm warned it will start to heat up at about forty-eight if not rested. Recharges in under two minutes."

Lowenbaum lowered it, turned it over it his hands. "You try it out?"

"I did. Packs a recoil, but I'm told they're working on that."

"Hit anything?"

"Simulation only. Rang the bell for me at a mile and a quarter."

With obvious regret, Lowenbaum handed it back to Roarke. "She's a beaut. But here's your more likely." He gestured at the bulkier weapon on display. "A military- or police-issue tactical. They haven't changed much in the last five or six years. I'm going to say, high probability, he owns his weapon. It's not something you take home after your tour like your service weapon. These are checked in and out, every incident. Most likely, again, for three strikes in that time frame, he had it on a bi- or tripod. Moving targets, and the first strike? She was moving at a good clip. Strike from one of these from a distance of — say a mile? It takes two and a half seconds to go from weapon to target. There's wind speed to consider, but that's about what you've got."

"You have to build that into the shot. Distance, wind speed, angle — speed of movement of the target." Eve nodded. It told her the shooter had watched his targets for a while, judged their relative speed on the ice.

"I never used a bipod — or not since weapons training. How much weight there, how big?"

"A couple pounds, and you can scope them down to under a foot."

"The rifle breaks down, right?"

"Sure." He glanced at Roarke. "I can show you."

Roarke took it down, offered it to him.

Lowenbaum checked the charge gauge, noted it was empty, but flicked the down switch anyway. "Safety first," he said. Then he turned a small lever, separated the barrel, the charger, the scope, and had the weapon in four compact pieces in about ten seconds.

"You could fit it into a standard briefcase broken down," Eve observed.

"Correct, but if you have any respect for your weapon, you have a case with molded slots for the parts."

"It wouldn't get through security in a government building, a museum, that kind of public building."

"Not a chance," Lowenbaum said.

"Okay, so most likely an apartment building, a hotel, a retail or rental space of some kind."

She wandered, thinking, as Lowenbaum competently reassembled the weapon.

"Who's best at this sort of reconstruction at the lab?" she asked.

"It's going to be Dickhead," Lowenbaum said.

"Come on, does it have to be?" They called the chief lab tech Dickhead for a reason.

"It does. You give him the push, I'll work with him when I can."

"I won't turn that down. Thanks."

"No thanks needed, because unless I'm way off, Dallas, you've got yourself an LDSK."

"An LDSK?"

Eve turned to Roarke. "Long-distance serial killer."

"Cops," he murmured. "Who else would have the acronym at hand?"

"Wouldn't need one if people weren't so fucked-up. Who do you know who could make those three strikes?"

Lowenbaum puffed out a breath. "I could. I've got a couple guys on my team who could. And yeah, I get you need to run them, but there's no way. I know a few other guys, and I'll make you a damn list. I'm going to say I know a few who could make the strikes. I don't know anybody who would."

"Names would help anyway."

"And it could be a pro, Dallas. You can pull up a list there as easy as I can."

"I will. But who'd hire a pro to kill a part-time student/part-time barista — female vic. An OB/GYN — vic two. A high school history teacher?"

"People are fucked-up," Lowenbaum reminded her.

"Yeah, they are."

"You're the murder cop. You do what you do there, and I'll do what I can on the tactical end. Three strikes like that?" The way he shook his head transmitted both admiration and concern. "The shooter's feeling pretty fine right now."

"And feeling pretty fine, he'll want to feel pretty fine again."

After Lowenbaum left, Eve set up her murder board, then sat to put together her notes and observations.

"You'll eat," Roarke said — firmly.

"Yeah, whatever."

"It's the stew you like." He solved the issue by pulling her out of her desk chair. "You can eat and think, and tell me what you know or what you think."

It helped when she did — and the stew thing smelled really good.

"You know, before I caught this, I was in my office thinking, Hey, quiet evening at home. A little wine, a little dinner, maybe a vid, a little sex."

Because he knew how much coffee she'd drink in the next few hours, he pushed her water glass toward her. "We'll fit some of that in, won't we?"

"The girl, Ellissa Wyman. I already had the gut feeling, but as soon as I reviewed the security feed, I knew. The way she flew. Had to be high impact, and nobody on the rink or around saw anything. You don't get off three streams without somebody seeing something. You sure as hell don't get them off when a cop reviews the tape, byte by byte, and sees nothing. The odds of me finding where those strikes initiated? I wouldn't bet on me."

He reached over, covered her hand with his. "I would."

"Yeah, but you're rich, and soft on me. I'm hoping Lowenbaum can help narrow down the area, but even then . . . "

She shook her head, ate. The stew tasted every bit as good as it smelled. "The girl? Nineteen, lived at home. Solid middle class. No current boyfriend. Ex is in college in Florida. No animosity between them. In fact, they tried the long-distance thing for almost a year before they drifted apart. Still friendly. She dates a little, but nothing serious. Skates for the joy of it, hoping to join a troupe — started when she was about eight, and fell in love. She's a regular at the rink, so I have to consider her as a specific target."

"She stood out," Roarke said. "Her grace, the look of her."

"Yeah, she did. Can't say the same about the first male: Brent Michaelson. Ordinary-looking guy, nothing flashy. But he's another regular. Not as often as the girl, but regular, routine. Divorced, but years ago. Civil relationship with the ex-wife. Tight with the daughter, enough that they'd all get together for dinner at the ex-wife's for birthdays and holidays — no drama. He liked to take his grandkids skating now and then. He's skated for years, nothing fancy. Said it helped him keep in shape, helped reduce stress."

"And the last?" Roarke said. "The one who was killed while holding his wife's hand."

"Yeah. You pay attention. Today's their anniversary. Five years. They were re-creating their first date. Some people knew they were going to the rink, but from what I can gather not many — it was more a personal thing. And what time they'd be there wasn't laid out."

"You see him as random. They all may be, but you're more certain he was. If one of the others was specific, then potentially two of them were no more than cover, so all would appear random."

"I think all or two out of three. I have to hope for two out of three, because then it's done. Or probably done. Like Lowenbaum said, the shooter's feeling pretty fine.

More, if one is target specific, I'll damn well find out who and why. But if all three were pulled out of a damn hat . . . "

"If it was all random, why the rink?"

He thought like a cop, but since he was being so helpful, she wouldn't insult him by mentioning it. "Public, big impact. Media frenzy. That would be a high motive for an LDSK. Maybe he has a problem with the rink itself. Maybe his wife, girlfriend, boyfriend, whatever, dumped him there. Maybe he used to skate but sustained an injury so he's pissed at skaters."

She brooded over it — so many maybes. "She's pregnant. The wife of the third vic. She just found out, hadn't even told him yet. Was going to tell him over the first-date lunch re-creation."

Roarke let out a sigh. "The ripples go on and on, don't they? It's never just the victim, just the dead, you stand over. It's also those they leave behind."

"Her father's Irish — a little more of an accent than you, but just a little. I think he and the ex have the civil, but I doubt they have holiday meals together, you know? But they were a unit around the daughter. And he — the father — stayed back with me for a minute, talked about his son-in-law. You could see he loved him."

"It matters," she said, reaching for her water, "because I think he's going to be the least of it. If one of the others was target specific, he'll be the least. An afterthought."

"Not for you, Eve."

"She was first. The girl in red. Couldn't miss her, like Lowenbaum said. Wouldn't you take out the target first, make sure you did the job? Part of me leans there. But then, I think, how cocky are you, you bastard? And it seems to me somebody who can do this, who does this, that's plenty cocky."

"So you bookend the target — one before, one after."

"Just another maybe."

"How can I help?"

She looked over at him. "You were working when I got home."

"No, actually, I'd just finished what I was doing when those designs came through. I was looking at them a second time when you came home. I've nothing I need to do."

He took her hand again. "I'm sorry for the wife, the parents, and all the other ripples. But it's the girl, that girl in red, who'll haunt me for a while. She had such joy on her face, such freedom in her movements. He ended that. I'd like to help you find who ended that."

Home, she thought again. Him. Where she could lean and not lose who and what she was.

"Collectors. Of the tactical, since Lowenbaum figures most likely there, but of anything that could make those strikes from outside the park."

"That's easy enough. Give me something a bit more challenging."

"Okay. Buildings, east of the park, let's say between Fifty-Seventh and Sixty-First. All the way back to the river. We'll eliminate any with solid screening. It's going to be a long enough list. And Lowenbaum said above, so buildings over four floors. We can jog that up or down if they can pinpoint angles more closely."

She ate more stew, cocked her head. "How many of them do you figure you own?"

He picked up his wine, smiled. "Won't it be interesting to find out?"

With Roarke in his adjoining office, Eve settled down to the routine that was never really routine. Running backgrounds on the victims and witnesses, on staff, running probabilities. She wrote up a comprehensive report, read it over, added more.

Then she sat back, fresh coffee in her mug, boots on her desk, and studied her board.

Why only three? That stuck in her gut. The speed and accuracy said this shooter could have taken a dozen, or more, within minutes. If the motive, as the general rule applied to LDSKs, was panic and fear: Why only three?

And why these three?

The girl in red made a bright target. The color, her youth, her skill, her speed and grace. Maybe a specific target, but all those attributes leaned Eve toward of the moment.

The third victim, part of a couple — and not regulars. Their plans to be on the ice on that day, at that time, not widely known outside a tight circle.

Of the moment again.

But the second victim. The obstetrician, the regular. That rink, that time, that day of the week habitual.

If there had been a specific target, her personal probability index rated Brent Michaelson high.

But it was a big *if*.

All random?

She rose with her coffee and circled her board, studied the positions of the bodies.

Then why only three?

"Computer, run crime scene security video, back one minute from cue-up."

Acknowledged . . .

Leaning back on the desk, she watched the skaters, studied the three victims as they moved on the ice. Then the first hit, the second, the last.

Some continued to skate for several more seconds, providing more targets. Others started to panic, rush, and stumble toward the exit, even over the wall. More targets. The two Good Samaritan medicals moved in, providing more targets, easier ones, she considered, than the three victims had been.

But only three, only those specific three.

The shit would hit, of course. The media would ring that gong and the killings would be top of the reports and stories for at least a few days. But take a dozen — kill or injure — that's top story for weeks.

That goes global.

Three dead meant a good chunk of people would avoid the rink, so possibly a motive against the rink itself. If she'd been holding that laser rifle and had a hard-on against the rink, she might have taken the girl in red, another target, but then she'd have taken out one of the security staff and at least one of the medicals.

"Three taken out," she murmured, still watching the screen. "Organized, skilled, had to plan this out in advance. So three was the goal. No more, no less."

She stopped the screen, went back to her desk to read the background on the victims yet again.

When Roarke sent her the list of collectors — in New York, all boroughs, and in New Jersey — with registered weapons that could have been used, she started backgrounds on all twenty-eight of them, searched for connections to the three victims, or the rink itself.

With more coffee, she got halfway through the list before Roarke came out.

"A collector's license for a laser rifle — any make, model, or year — is twenty-five large."

"I'm aware."

"Most of the licenses I've been through are to rich dudes. A couple so far grandfathered from a relative. The screening's pretty thorough, but that doesn't mean your average violent offender doesn't slip through."

"A problem in all areas of life." Bypassing the coffee, Roarke opted for two fingers of whiskey. "I've got your buildings."

"Already?"

"The longest part of the process was designing a program that met the criteria. After that?" He shrugged, sipped.

"You designed a program?" About half the time, she thought, she could barely operate a program without getting pissed off.

"I did. An interesting experiment."

"E-geeks are handy. You have the list of potential buildings?"

"I am, and I do. But I thought you'd like a visual. When your office is redone, we'll be able to do this via hologram, but for now . . . " He set down his whiskey and gestured for her to stand, took her place, tapped some keys.

A slice of Manhattan flashed on screen.

"These are the boundaries you gave me, from the crime scene back to the river, with the north and south streets. And here . . . " He tapped another set of keys, and buildings began to fade away.

"Okay, okay, I get it. High-security buildings eliminated. Excellent."

"And buildings under four stories."

"Right. So these buildings remaining are potential nests. I need — "

"There's more." Because he was quick, and she was focused on the screen, he had her pulled into his lap before she could object.

"Working, ace."

"So am I. What you see are buildings with a reasonably clear sight line to the targets. But — " Keeping an arm around her waist, he keyed in some more. Several other buildings faded off. "I eliminated those with mid- to high-level security. You might need to factor those in at some point, as there are always

46

ways around security, but for now, those remaining are zero to low-level. Apartments, mid-range hotels, SROs, and flops, your occasional studio for dance or art classes or what have you, a couple of office spaces."

"With low-level available, why risk high? But yeah, better to have them on tap if nothing else pans out. If I could — "

"Still more."

With another tap, thin blue and red lines flashed on.

"The blue is your possible — windows or rooftop of these buildings. Red is high probability, again factoring in your theory with Lowenbaum, from the east, low-security building."

She started to rise to her feet to get a closer look, but got pulled back down. And considering all, relaxed into it.

"The program contains an algorithm, utilizes your crime scene footage, with calculations built in for the wind speed, temperature, probable velocity and angle, and . . . more math and calculations than you want to hear about."

"You built a program that factors the variables with the known, and gives visual probabilities."

"In simple terms, more or less."

"You're not just handy. This is e-genius level."

"Modesty doesn't prevent me from agreeing. Actually, it was an interesting bit of work."

A lot of buildings — a hell of a lot, she considered. But also a hell of a lot less than she'd had to consider a couple hours before.

So she hooked an arm around his neck, shifted enough to look at him. "I bet it's not free."

"Darling, your appreciation is all the payment I need."

"And sex."

"I thought they were one in the same." Smiling, he kissed her.

"This probably rates appreciation sex." But for now, she shifted again, studied the screen. "How about the buildings with high probability that also have privacy screens — standard."

"Ah, clever girl. You'd hardly want some passerby or gawking tourist with a camera catching you poised with a weapon in a window."

"And working windows. Why shoot through glass? Why have to cut through glass — unless the LDSK used his own office or home window. That leaves a trail to follow."

"Give me a minute. No, I can work around you very well," he said when she started to get up again. "Though your new command center will simplify this as well."

He programmed the new parameters manually, and quickly, in a way she'd never comprehend, then ordered the new results on screen.

"That took out five more — or six maybe. How many do — "

"Wait for it. Computer, split screen with identifying data on current display."

Acknowledged. Working . . .

"So I'll be able to do this holographically?"

"You will, or I will until you get the hang of it."

"I know how to holo." More or less. "Even with this setup."

"Simpler and advanced from what you can do now from here or, from my standpoint, at Central. And there you are."

She had addresses and the types of buildings. And with each building address were the floors that fit the criteria. The tally was twenty-three buildings.

"I can work with twenty-three. And if this leads me to the nest, you can count on extreme appreciation sex."

"Would that include costumes and props?"

She rolled her eyes. "It hasn't led me anywhere yet."

"Perhaps a small advance." He nipped lightly at the back of her neck.

"Get your brain off sex."

"That would be beyond my programming capabilities. But until I collect my fee, you'll want to cross-search the licenses, and the victims, with the twenty-three buildings."

"Just exactly right. Before I do that, let me ask you this: You're an LDSK — organized, skilled, controlled."

"You assume controlled?"

"Three vics only. Literally dozens who could have been killed or injured — making a bigger impact, giving a bigger thrill. If impact and thrill are motives. So yeah, I assume controlled. Whether or not these three, or any of these three, are target specific: Would you use your own home — your apartment, even your office — as your nest?"

"Interesting question." He picked up his whiskey again to mull it over. "The advantage there would be time. You'd have all the time in the world to observe the target area from that nest. Complete privacy, and the opportunity to take any number of dummy test strikes from the position."

"Huh. Hadn't thought of the last one yet, but it applies. Practice, and practice from the exact spot. It weighs. Disadvantages?"

"Clever cops, such as my own, diligently working through the potentials. Risking that clever cop making a connection. And an office? Unless it's merely a front, most would have others working there, at least an assistant, building cleaning crew, and so on. Residence? Does your killer live alone, does whoever he might live with join in his desire to kill?

"I'd be more inclined to rent a space under an assumed name — which takes a bit of work," he added, "but would be worth it. That office space, small apartment, hotel room. Then after this was done, abandon it."

"So would I." She nodded, as her thought process had run along the same lines. "Can't rule out the other, but so would I. I'd trade the convenience of operating out of my own space for the lesser risk of using a temporary space. Hotels, work or living spaces leased within the last six months. He's controlled, but I can't see him using a rented space for longer. Okay."

50

Roarke held her in place another moment, then released her. "Why don't you do that cross-search. I'll do the other."

She rose, as did he, but she turned to him. "When this office thing happens, you could work in here on this kind of thing, if you wanted. Take the cop stuff out of your own space."

"I don't mind the cop stuff in my space."

"I know. We'll add that into the appreciation sex. I'll look at the designs again when I finish this, pick one."

"If one suits."

"Yeah, if that."

She manned her desk again, solo, began the cross-search. While it ran, she managed to figure out how to send Peabody the complicated program Roarke had written and implemented in under two hours.

She imagined fellow e-geek McNab would do a happy dance.

After adding an update, she went into the kitchen to program more coffee, reminding herself that space would change, too.

No need to hold on to the old, she told herself. And in reality, even the old had changed, since Mavis and Leonardo had her old apartment.

Nothing about it looked like the Spartan and basic cop place she'd lived in, not with all the color, the clutter, the kid.

The kid.

When Bella blipped into her mind, she remembered the party. She had to go to a baby birthday party, where surely there would be more babies. Crawling or walking in that drunk way they did, making those weird noises.

Staring like dolls.

Why did they do that?

She shook the thought away, got her coffee, went back to murder.

The incoming from Roarke signaled moments before he came back.

"Hotels, including an SRO flagged for you, and several rentals in the last six months. I've put those rented to families with children and multiple-use office spaces or with staff over three on low."

"You ran occupants?"

"That would've been next, wouldn't it?"

"Yeah. I've got a couple matches, but they don't ring. A guy from the license list who has an aunt in one of the buildings — but she's on a lower floor than works here. Plus, he's got no military or police training, doesn't actually appear to have any weapons training. We'll check him out, but this isn't our guy."

Leaning back in her chair, she picked up her coffee, propped up her boots in her think-it-through mode.

"The other's got a big residential on Park, does some designer hunting. It doesn't strike — not much skill from my background check, but he could have downplayed that. But added to it, he lives with wife number three, has a live-in nanny for the kid with wife number three, and a teenage son from wife number two lives with him half the time. Full-time housekeeper — not a droid. Still, I bet he has a private space in his digs, so we'll check."

She dropped her feet, pushed back. "No criminal to speak of on either. And no connection I could find to the rink or the victims."

Rising, she approached her board. "If this wasn't his mission, just this, he'll hit again and soon. Three strikes, three down. It's too successful not to hit again. Not the rink, that's done — unless it *is* the rink."

"You think, and I agree, if it were the rink, there would be more than three on your board."

"Yeah, that's what I think. Another public place, another multiple strike. If that's the plan, he's already got it selected, scoped, and has his nest. Anyone, anywhere, anytime. He's holding the cards now."

"You've plenty of your own."

"But I can't add more to them tonight, not with what's here. Morris, Berenski, they might add more tomorrow. Peabody and McNab are working their end. I'll get a profile from Mira, see if that refines things. It's not a pro."

She narrowed those cop's eyes at the board again. "A pro doesn't take out three unrelated targets, and they're not connected. Correction, a working pro doesn't. We could have a pro who's gone loony, but this wasn't murder for hire — or unlikely. Client could have paid to have three hits, with two as cover. Can't disregard even that."

"Lieutenant, you're circling."

"Yeah, yeah, yeah." She took one long last look at the girl in red. As Roarke said, she haunted. "Okay. Let's have another look at the design stuff."

"You don't have to do that tonight."

"It'll bug me until I clear it. How hard can it be to just pick something?"

"You're a rare woman, darling, as you not only actually believe that, but make it true."

He called the first design on screen.

"I don't much like this one. The colors are kind of girlie, and the stuff's sort of . . . I don't know, sharp and . . . slick. So plain it's fancy. I don't know the word, but that's how it hits. I mean, the setup's okay — where she's got things — but the things are going to make me feel like I'm in somebody else's place."

"Then we move on. Number two."

She shifted her feet as she studied it. Felt stupid and ungrateful. "The stuff here's okay. It doesn't have that I'm-new-and-cutting-edge-and-really-important deal going on. I could work here without feeling like somebody whose name begins with Summerset would give me the fish eye if I messed it up or spilled something."

"But?"

"Well, the colors are strong. Strong colors are good, I guess, but it's a little in-your-face. Distracting, I guess."

"How about these?" He brought up the third option.

She didn't know what fancy name the colors went by in some designer speak. Bullshit names like Contented Fawn and Zen Retreat and Chocolate Drizzle.

To her it was browns and sort of greens and whites that weren't bright and shiny.

"Yeah, see, the colors are good, and they're quiet but not girlie. They're not saying, Hey look at me. It's more like they've been there awhile. And the command center looks, well, commanding. No bullshit. But, I

54

guess, most of the other stuff doesn't look like anybody lives with it."

"Try this." He stepped over to her computer, keyed in a code. The second design slid on — with the color scheme from the third.

"Huh. You can just . . . Okay, yeah, this is . . . "

"If you're not sure, not pleased, we wait. I'll give her your input and she'll incorporate what you like and take away what you don't."

"It's just that . . . I like it. I really like it, and I didn't expect to. The stuff doesn't look as, I don't know, fussy in these colors like it does in the in-your-face ones. It looks more . . . real, I guess. I like it. I figured I'd live with the one I could live with, and that would be okay. But I like it. It's efficient, it's not fussy or weird." Sincerely baffled, she turned to him. "I like it. Jesus, the appreciation sex is going to get out of hand."

"My fondest wish." Hip-to-hip with her, he studied her choice, and found himself pleased he liked it, very much, as well. Still.

"Do you want to take a few days, think it over, make any changes that might occur to you?"

"No. Really no. It would make me crazy. Let's just go for it. But I can't have this place torn up or people running around in there when I'm working an investigation."

"Leave that to me." He turned to her, took her shoulders, dropped a kiss on her forehead. "This will be good for both of us."

"I know that, too. I won't miss it. I remember how I felt when you first brought me in here, when I saw what you'd made for me. That doesn't change."

"The reason I made it for you doesn't change, either." He slid an arm around her waist, led her out. "Hopefully you remember how you felt the first time I took you into the bedroom."

"That's imprinted."

"Good, as she'll have designs for the bedroom for us to go over in a day or two."

"You were serious about that?"

"Absolutely."

"But the bedroom — "

"Is ours, but was designed for me. Now it will reflect both of us, our needs, wants, tastes."

"We don't have the same tastes, exactly. I don't even know if I have tastes."

"You know what you like, what you don't. And won't it be interesting to see how it all melds? And as with your office, it has to suit you. It has to suit me as well, so may it take a bit more work than the two minutes you spent picking your office design."

It wouldn't take two minutes, no, not with Roarke weighing in on it. "Are we going to fight over, like, fabric?"

"I sincerely doubt it, but if we do, I'm sure we'll make up, on whatever bed we choose together."

Frowning, she stepped into the bedroom, looked at the enormous bed on its platform under the sky window. And couldn't imagine anything that could suit her more.

"I like that bed."

"And we may end up designing around it, but if not, we should bid it farewell as we did your desk. In anticipation."

"The way you are, we'll have nailed each other another five dozen times on this one before it's gone."

"Think of it as an undress rehearsal," he said, and scooped her up.

Since it was hard to laugh and protest at the same time, she just went with it, so when she hit the bed, she wrapped her legs, boots and all, around him.

"We're still dressed."

"I can fix that. In a minute," he added, and took her mouth.

Here was the payoff for a long and difficult day. His body pressed down on hers, that magic mouth sparking heat, spreading thrills. No dark thoughts pressing like bloody fingers against glass, pushing, pushing to come in. Here, she could have, she could take, love.

She heard the *click* as his fingers — as magical as his mouth — released her weapon harness. She shifted so he could tug it off, shove it aside.

"You're disarmed, Lieutenant."

"That's not my only weapon."

"I'm aware. But I've a few of my own."

When his teeth scraped lightly down the side of her neck, she thought: Yeah, you do. In response, she pressed up, center to center.

"And yours is, as usual, already cocked."

Against her skin, his lips curved. "Someone has her punny pants on."

"I'm thinking about trading them in for naked."

She managed to toe off her boots, the rise and fall of her hips with the effort pleasing them both. Rather than pull her sweater off, he slid his hands under it, skimmed them over the tank she wore beneath. When her nipples hardened against the snug material, he roamed down to unhook her belt, then up again to mold her breasts, to tease.

Down to unclasp a button, to slowly, slowly ease the zipper open.

He could spend years on her with just his hands. The firm breasts and long, lean torso under the thin, simple tank, the taut belly, the narrow hips.

He tugged her trousers down, just another inch, traced a fingertip under the waistband of the panties — as simple as the tank. His cop wasn't one for frills and lace. Yet those simple, unadorned underpinnings never failed to entice him.

He knew what lived beneath.

Just as he knew she'd relaxed, she'd put all else aside — the blood and the dead — for this. For him. For them. So he'd give her everything he had in this time away from the cold and the dark.

Now he peeled her sweater up and away, and the tank with it. When he cupped her breasts in his hands, she cupped his face in hers. Smiled.

"It's nice."

"Nice, is it?"

"Yeah." Lowering her hands, she began unbuttoning his shirt. "It's nice."

"I can do better than nice."

"I'm aware," she said, making him laugh as his lips brushed over hers.

She could do better than nice, too, but didn't mind that pace. For now. Like sliding into comfort. Under his shirt, that tough, disciplined body was hers to touch, to take — all that warm, warm skin, those tight muscles.

Hers to take, she thought again as he deepened the kiss. Fire kindled under her skin. With her legs again hooked around him, she levered over, reversed their positions. Now straddling him, she curved down, using her teeth to nip at his lips, his tongue while she rocked them both to quivering.

Even as she tugged off his belt, he flipped her over again. Dragging off her trousers, his hand brushed over the clutch piece strapped above her ankle. It added a quick, dangerous thrill. Leaving it, he used his mouth, his hands to destroy her.

She cried out, tossed up as his tongue swept over her, into her. Her fingers dug into the sheets, then into his back as he drove her relentlessly higher.

The orgasm ripped through her, a fast, hard jolt of staggering pleasure. Then the aftershocks, shuddering, shuddering, even as he urged her up again.

Breathless, blind, she dragged him up to her, rolling together now over the blue lake of the bed while she fought to strip away the rest of his clothes.

When he plunged into her, the world quaked.

His mouth — God, she loved his mouth — took hers again, ravishing like a man starving. Then he drove her, they drove each other, hands gripped together, bodies joined. On the edge, fused to the edge as the pleasure swelled to bursting.

When she came again, all she could see was the wild blue of his eyes.

After a long moment, after they both lay limp, like survivors of some brutal wreck, he turned his head enough to graze her throat with his lips.

"Nice, was it?"

"Worked for me. Appreciation?"

"Paid in full."

"Huh. And no costumes or props."

"You're still wearing your clutch piece."

Her eyes blinked open. "What?"

"That worked for me." On a half groan, he rolled off her, sat up. Letting his gaze wander over her as she sprawled, naked but for the fat diamond around her neck and the weapon at her ankle. "And would again."

"Men are just twisted."

He only smiled, then got up and fetched a bottle of water. After he drank, he held it out. "Hydrate."

She propped up on an elbow and did just that. But when she started to reach for her clutch piece, he took her hands.

"Not quite yet."

"I'm not going to sleep wearing it."

"Not sleep." Stretching out, he picked up her weapon harness. As he began to put it on her, she shoved out at him.

"What the hell?"

"Indulge my curiosity." Quick and efficient, he hooked it on her, then pushed off the bed again to take a good long look.

Propped on her elbows, a wonderfully baffled expression on her face, her eyes still glazed from sex, she stirred his heart.

And propped on her elbows, a weapon on her ankle, another hitched over the shoulders of that lean and naked warrior's body, she stirred something else entirely.

"Yes, I've imagined that."

"You've imagined me wearing my weapons without a shirt? Or pants?"

"I see now that even my exceptional imagination fell short. So, Lieutenant."

Her bafflement went to shock as he straddled her. "You've got to be kidding."

"Not even remotely." He gripped her hands again, pinned her.

"You can't possibly . . . " She glanced down, saw he absolutely could. "How did you do that?"

"It's something to do with being twisted, I suppose."

When he thrust into her, she cried out, came instantly. "Oh my God."

"I want to watch you, my well-armed cop." He thrust again, again. "Watch you while I take you, and take you, until we're both empty."

He took her slowly down into the dark, drenching her, saturating her with sensation. He made her helpless, took her past the point of caring that she had

61

no defenses. Into that dizzying desperate dark she slid, boneless, even as her body ached for more.

In the dark, he plundered until she was empty. Until he let himself go and emptied into her.

CHAPTER
THREE

Eve woke by sluggish degrees, like someone who'd been drugged. When her brain roused enough to work her eyes, she opened them. It had already revived enough — first degree — to smell coffee.

Roarke drank his on the sofa in the sitting area, a tablet in one hand, the morning stock reports scrolling on the wall screen.

He'd already dressed as the ruler of the business world. Dark gray suit today, a shirt a few shades lighter, a perfectly knotted tie that picked up the gray in thin stripes on a navy blue background.

Since his half boots were the exact shade of the suit, she imagined one had been made for him to match the other. His socks, she decided, probably matched, too.

And, though it was just shy of oh-six-hundred, she bet her ass he'd already wheeled deals or made decisions and given orders in any number of foreign countries and off-planet projects.

She, on the other hand, had to order herself to sit up, to get the hell out of bed, without groaning.

"Morning, darling."

She grunted — best she could do — stumbled to the AutoChef for life-giving coffee and, gulping it, stumbled into the bathroom and the shower.

"Full jets, one-oh-one degrees." She gulped more coffee while the glorious caffeine and the hot pump of water woke her the rest of the way.

If world order depended on it, maybe she could go back to all those years of fake coffee and piss-trickle showers.

Maybe.

And maybe it was a damn good thing she wasn't responsible for world order, just murder in New York.

And, she decided, if her thoughts could wind around all that, she was definitely awake.

Ten minutes later, feeling human again, she came out wrapped in a robe, noted Roarke had two covered plates and a pot of coffee on the table. The man, as he'd proven countless times in countless ways, worked fast.

He lowered the tablet, closed it in a way that had her cop senses quivering, just a little.

"What's on the tablet?" she asked as she walked over to join him.

"My tablet? Many things."

She just twirled a finger, poured more coffee. "Let's see it, pal."

"It might be a lewd photo from my lover, Angelique."

"Yeah, yeah. We'll frame it with the ones from my lovers, Julio and Raoul, the twins. Meanwhile."

Stalling, he lifted the covers from the plates, distracting her for a moment.

Oatmeal. She should have known. At least he'd surrounded the bowl with some bacon, a scoop of scrambled egg that looked cheesy, and there was a dish of berries, another of brown sugar — the real thing.

But still.

"This should start us both off well for the day."

"Your day started a couple hours ago, easy."

"Not my day with you."

"Uh-huh." She went for bacon first, saw Galahad's whiskers twitch and he strolled — as if just out for a little exercise — toward the table. "Tablet."

First Roarke gave the cat a look that had Galahad sitting down to vigorously wash. "Charmaine sent me the draft of a design for the bedroom, late last night, it seems. When we were otherwise occupied. She just wants to know if she's going in the right direction. I didn't think you'd want to see something this early on, or want to think about it."

Eve just twirled her finger again as she added heaps of brown sugar, heaps of berries to the oatmeal.

"I'll put it on the wall screen."

Roarke swiped the tablet. The strange scrolling symbols faded to the design.

Eve ate, frowned at it.

"First, those curtain things, they're too fussy. Too, I don't know, regal or something."

"I agree."

"I guess I mostly like the way she's got this area here laid out. The couch is roomier, but it's — "

"Too ornate. I've actually seen a piece in the Sotheby's catalog I like. I'll send it to both of you, and see. And the bed itself?"

Ornate was the word there, too — and massive with its four tall and burly posts and both the high headboard and the long footboard edged with a frame carved with Celtic symbols. All dark, rich, glossy wood that looked old and . . . important.

Still.

"I . . . "

"If you don't like it — "

"That's the thing. I do, a lot. I don't know why. It's not simple, and I figured I'd talk you into simple. But — I don't usually care about stuff like this, but, man, that's a hell of a bed. Where did she find it?"

"I found it, months ago. It's in storage as I bought it on impulse, then realized you'd more likely want the simple." As she continued to study it, he picked up his coffee. "There's a story with it, if you want to hear it."

"Let's hear it."

"Well then. There was an Irishman of some wealth and station who had this built as his marriage bed, though he had yet to find his bride."

"An optimist."

"You could say. When it was complete and moved into his manor, he was still a bachelor, so he had the room with the bed closed off. Years went by, and he was no longer young, no longer believed he would find the woman to share that bed with him, or his life, his home, to make a family with him."

66

"Sounds like an unlucky bed to me."

"Well, wait for the rest. One day, it seems, he walked through his forest as he often did, and came upon a woman sitting on the banks of his stream. Not the young beauty he'd once envisioned as his bride, but a handsome woman who engaged his mind. One who lived in a pretty cottage not far from the manor."

Considering, Eve scooped up some heavily doctored oatmeal. "He should've run into her before. I mean, how many people lived around there, and — "

"Well, he didn't run into her before, did he?"

"Maybe if he'd gotten out and about more, on his own land, he'd have found that bride."

With a shake of his head, Roarke sampled the eggs. "Maybe it was meant for that time and place. In any case," he continued, before she could interrupt with logic again, "they met, and conversed. And began to walk together now and then over that spring and into the summer. He learned she'd been widowed barely a month after she'd wed her young man, and had never wed again. They talked of her garden and his business, and the gossip and politics of the day."

"And fell in love and lived happily ever after."

Roarke shot her the look he often shot the cat. "It was a friendship they forged, a good strong one, and the man never thought of love over that year, for he believed that time for him had passed. But he valued her, her person, her mind, her manner, her humor. So he told her, and asked if she wanted to marry and they'd be companions for the rest of their days. When she agreed, he was content, but never thought to open the room or use the bed he'd once had made.

"But it was to that room she led him on their wedding night. And the bed gleamed in the moonlight, and spring, this new one, came through the windows. The linens, fresh and white, and flowers from her own cottage garden in vases, the candles lit. And in her he saw the bride he'd once imagined. Not the young beauty, but the woman, the substance, the constancy, the wit, and the kindness. And in this marriage bed, friendship, strong and true, became a strong and true love. Now it's said that those who share this bed will know the same."

A pretty story, obviously bullshit, but pretty. So Eve nodded. "We're definitely keeping the bed." And she realized she'd eaten the stupid oatmeal without thinking about it. "What color is that? The cover on it."

"It's bronze, a hint of copper."

She nodded again, polishing off her bacon. "It looks like the same color and fabric thing as my wedding dress."

"Because it is."

"Sap."

"That's twisted sap, I'll remind you."

"I like the color, and the bed, so that's a start."

"As do I, so I'll have Charmaine work from there."

"Good enough." She rose, went to her closet.

"It's to be colder today," he warned her. "Likely sleeting before afternoon."

"Peachy." She stuck her head back out. "Why isn't it *appley* or *melony*, or just *fruity*?"

He studied her, his cynical and often literal wife. Simply shrugged. "I've never given it a thought, and couldn't say."

"Exactly." She vanished inside again. "I'm hitting the morgue first, then the lab — I have to use Dickhead. Apparently he's the laser king." She grabbed a dark green sweater, warm brown trousers. As she reached for a jacket, it occurred to her if she picked wrong, Roarke would get up and get another one for her. So she took another minute, then two minutes studying her choices.

Why did she have so many? Why did it seem there were more choices every time she walked in here?

No one was more surprised than she was when she pulled out a jacket a few shades darker than the trousers that had that dark green subtly woven through.

She snagged boots, a belt, considered it done.

"I'll be in Midtown most of the day," he told her when she came out to dress. "I have a walk-through at An Didean this afternoon."

She thought of the youth shelter he'd built. "How's that going?"

"We'll see with this walk-through, but it's been going very well. We should be able to take residents in by April."

"Good." She hooked on her weapon harness, shrugged into the jacket, then sat to pull on the boots. Caught his glance. "What? *What's* wrong with these clothes?"

"Absolutely nothing. You look perfect, and completely a cop."

"I am completely a cop."

"Precisely. You're completely my cop, so have a care."

He sat, finishing his coffee, the cat sprawled beside him. And he smiled at her, in just that way. She went to him, caught his face in her hands, kissed him.

"I'll see you tonight."

"Catch the bad guys, Lieutenant, but stay safe doing it."

"That's the plan."

She found her coat, the snowflake hat she'd become weirdly attached to, a made-by-Peabody scarf, and fresh gloves on the newel post.

Her car, heater running, waited outside.

She glanced in the rearview mirror once at the warmth and comfort of home, then headed out to the morgue and the dead.

The sleet didn't wait for afternoon and started to fall, mixed with snapping little bits of ice, by the time she fought her way downtown.

That didn't stop the ad blimps blasting about cruise wear, white sales, inventory clearances, but it did cause the already lumbering maxibuses to slow to a crawl. And since even the thought of winter precipitation caused the majority of drivers to lose any shred of competency they might own, she spent most of her trip avoiding, leapfrogging over, and cursing every cab and commuter.

The long white tunnel leading to the dead came as a relief, even when she passed an open door and heard someone's cackling laugh.

To her mind no one should cackle in the dead house. The occasional chuckle, fine. But cackling was just creepy.

She pushed through the doors to the autopsy room, into the cool air and the quiet strains of classical music.

The three victims lay on slabs, almost side by side.

Morris had a protective cloak over his steel-gray suit. He wore a royal blue shirt that picked up the needle-thin lines in the suit jacket and had twined cord of the same color through the complex braid of his dark hair.

Microgoggles magnified his eyes as he glanced up from the body of Ellissa Wyman.

"A cold, dreary morning to start our day."

"It's probably going to get worse."

"It too often does. But for our guests, the worst is over. She made me think of Mozart." He ordered the music down to a murmur as he lifted the goggles. "So young."

He'd already opened her, and gestured with a sealed hand smeared with blood toward his screen.

"She was healthy, had exceptional muscle tone. I see no signs of illegals or alcohol abuse. She had a hot chocolate — soy milk, chocolate substitute — and a soft pretzel about an hour before death."

"A snack before she hit the ice. They have carts selling that kind of thing right outside the park. She'd been skating just under twenty-five minutes before she took the hit."

"Laser strike, mid-back, almost severing the spine between the T6 and T7 — thoracic vertebrae."

"Yeah, I got that. Severing?"

"Very nearly, so this was a high-powered strike. Had she survived it, she would have been a paraplegic without a long, expensive — and brilliant — treatment. But with the intensity of the strike, she would have been gone in seconds."

"The classic 'never knew what hit her.'"

"Exactly so, and a blessing as, though I've only begun on her internal organs, I see considerable damage."

She might not have been big on internal organs, but Eve had passed squeamish in autopsy long ago. So she accepted the goggles Morris offered, took a closer look.

"Am I looking at massive internal bleeding?"

"You are. With a burst spleen — as was her liver." He gestured to his scale, where that particular organ sat.

"Are internal injuries like this usual with a laser hit?"

"I've seen it before. But it's more common in combat injuries, where the enemy is intent on destroying as many opponents as quickly as possible."

"The beam pulses — like vibrates — once it hits the target, right?" Straightening, Eve took off the goggles. "I've heard of this. It's outlawed in police weaponry, in collections."

"I believe so, yes. This would be Berenski's area."

"Yeah, I heard that. He's my next stop."

After setting the goggles aside, Eve studied Wyman's body, turned to the two waiting for Morris.

"So somebody got their hands on a military weapon, or adapted another to military level. And somebody wanted to make sure these three people went all the way down."

"It's difficult to see why anyone would want to end this young woman's life. Of course, she may have been a stone bitch with a wait list of enemies."

"Doesn't look like it. Solid family, still lived at home, doing the work/college thing, with the ice-skating a big passion."

As she spoke, Eve circled the body — a young, slender girl who'd never known what hit her. "She was still friendly with her ex-boyfriend. I took a look through her room yesterday when I notified the parents. On the girlie side, but not crazy with it. No hidden stashes, no weird shit on her electronics — though EDD will take a harder look there."

"A normal sort of not-quite-adult who hadn't yet determined what to do with her life, and assumed she had all the time in the world to figure it out."

"That's how I see it," Eve agreed, "right now anyway. Her family's going to contact you about seeing her."

"I spoke with them last evening. They'll be in mid-morning. I'll take care of them."

"I know you will."

Turning away from Wyman, Eve studied the other victims. "If there was a specific target, I think it was the second victim."

"Michaelson."

"Yeah. But that's just theory, just gut. I've got nothing to hang it on."

"As your gut's generally reliable, and in much better shape than Michaelson's, I'll keep that in mind when I examine him."

"He knew what hit him. According to the wits who tried to help him, he was conscious, alive, at least for a minute or two."

"An agonizing minute or two," Morris added, nodding. "That would be part of the reason for your gut on him."

"Part of it."

"I noted in your report you're consulting with Lowenbaum. I'll copy him on all findings."

"Affirmative. How many LDSK investigations have you worked?"

"This would be my third — and first as chief ME." With his own goggles lowered, he gave her a friendly look out of long, dark eyes. "I've got, what, about ten years on you?"

"I don't know. Do you?"

He smiled at her, knowing that, especially for a cop, she took great care not to intrude in the personal business, or into the personal data, of colleagues.

"Roughly ten, which makes us both a bit young for any real memories of the Urbans, when such things were all too common. Technology that creates the weapons used on these three people increases what we'll call the science of the kill. And restrictions on those weapons decrease the accessibility, and the use of them for that purpose."

"But sooner or later."

"Yes, sooner or later. I don't know a great deal about this sort of weapon, but I'll learn." He looked down at Ellissa again. "So we can do our best for her, and the others."

"I'll go see if Dickhead knows as much about laser weapons as Lowenbaum says he does."

"Good luck. Oh, Garnet tells me you're having drinks."

"What? Who?"

"DeWinter."

"Oh, DeWinter." Dr. DeWinter, Eve thought, forensic anthropologist. Smart, a little annoying.

"We're friends, Dallas — without any added benefits."

Uneasy, Eve stuck her hands in her pockets. "Not my business."

"You were there for me when I lost Amaryllis, and being there helped me through the darkest days of my life. So while it might not be your business, I understand it's your concern. We like each other's company, particularly without the tension of 'Will there be sex?' In fact, she and Chale and I had dinner last night."

"The priest, the dead doctor, and the bone doctor."

Now he laughed, and Eve felt herself relax. "Quite the trio when you look at it that way. In any case, she mentioned she'd talked you into having a drink."

"Maybe. Sometime." At his arched eyebrows, she hissed. "Yeah, okay, I owe her for cutting through a lot of red tape. Did she put you up to poking me on it?"

He only smiled. "You'll see her at Bella's party."

"She's — How'd she get into Mavis's kid's deal?"

"When it comes to poking, Mavis is a charming expert. She gives me one every few weeks, just to be sure I'm not wallowing. The four of us went to the Blue Squirrel a couple weeks ago."

"You went to the Blue Squirrel . . . on purpose?"

"It's an experience. In any case, she and Leonardo invited Garnet, and her daughter, to the party. It promises to be quite the event."

"You say that like it's a good thing. I worry about you, Morris."

Fairly serious about that, she left him with the dead. She was nearly at the exit when Peabody came in, pink-cheeked from the cold and wearing her fussy-topped pink winter boots.

"I'm not late, you're early."

"I wanted a jump on it."

As Eve walked straight out, Peabody did a quick turnaround and followed. "Did Morris have anything?"

"He was working on the first victim. We need to corroborate with Berenski, but it looks like a military-grade weapon."

"McNab started researching those last night." Peabody hustled to the car, let out an audible "*Ahhh*" when she settled into the seat. "He was totally all about it. What is it with men and weapons?"

"I'm not a man. I like weapons."

"Right. Anyway. He was researching the weapon, or possible weapon, and started doing the math. The math I get, because geek, then you sent over that program Roarke wrote up. It was like Christmas and hot sex and chocolate pudding for him all together. Like having hot sex covered with chocolate pudding on Christmas. Hmm."

"Don't go there."

"Already did, but saving it for later. So he's playing with that, and I started on the wit list. Like I said in my report, the poor little guy with the broken leg and his parents didn't see a thing until they hit the ice. Then all they really saw was the kid, and the girl. It happened so fast. They were about to exit the rink when it happened, were looking the other way, and *bam!*"

"We'll finish the list, but it's not going to come down to wits at the rink on this. The strike came from too far away. I haven't found any connection between the victims, and I don't think there's going to be any."

"If this was completely random . . . " Peabody glanced out at the people on the street, at the buildings and all the windows rising up.

"I didn't say I'm convinced it was random. I want Morris's full results, and we're going to start checking the buildings on the short list Roarke worked out. The first victim, middle of the back, high-powered strike with echoes."

"I know what that means! McNab ran it for me last night. *Echoes* means the strike's designed to spread once it hits the target."

"She wouldn't have survived it — at least low odds — anyway. Nearly severed her spine. So that tells me the kill was imperative, not just the strike. And maybe that's why he stopped at three. Panic's starting, people heading for cover, or bunching up, ducking down.

You're going to get some solid strikes, but maybe not solid enough for a kill. This way, he's three for three."

"Don't take chances, lower your percentage." Peabody blew out a breath as Eve turned toward the lab. "How many buildings on the short list?"

"Enough that I'm pulling in whoever's not working a hot to help check them out."

Inside, in the warren of the lab, Eve headed straight for Dickhead.

While most of the techs wore white lab coats, the slick of dark hair on his egg-shaped head made him easy to spot as he huddled over his long work counter.

She imagined his spidery fingers working over a keyboard or on a screen. The man was a creepy pain in the ass, but he had skills. And she needed them.

He glanced up as she approached, and nearly knocked her off her stride. The poor excuse for facial hair he'd been trying to grow now resembled an anemic caterpillar over his mouth, and a tattered spiderweb on his chin.

If he'd developed the new look to lure women — and luring women was his greatest wish — Eve predicted brutal disappointment.

"LDSK," he said, with what might have been pleasure.

"That's right."

"We don't get those every day. Long-range laser rifle — Lowenbaum's right on the model, I figure."

"It has to be military grade. Morris said the first vic — as far as he'd gotten this morning — had damage to internal organs."

"Yeah, yeah, echoes. I figured it." He zipped down the counter on his stool, tapped a screen.

"See here? CGI sim of a strike with a Tactical-XT, military grade. Laser beam in red, range here is a thousand yards. Trigger to strike? One-point-three seconds. See the red hit the body, how the strike pinpoints, then spreads? That's your echo. See, it hits, then it blooms." He lifted his hands, upturned palms cupped, then drew them apart. "You ain't walking away from that."

"I have three people in the morgue who didn't walk away from that."

"You're on the dead. I'm on the weapon. ME says military grade, echoes, that caps that for me, as that's what I'm seeing on the security feed. Talked with Lowenbaum, and we're agreed on it."

"I'm not arguing it."

He just waved that away. "You gotta figure the range of a military-grade Tact-XT is — known record — three-point-six miles."

"I got that, Berenski, I need — "

"In the right hands, these strikes could've been made from a barge in the fricking East River. You gotta get *that*. But I want to meet the son of a bitch who could make that strike, that strike in New York, considering sight lines, wind variance, temperature, not to mention the movement of the targets."

"When I nail the son of a bitch, I'll introduce you."

"I'll hold you to it. But I don't figure we're talking full range, okay? I'm working on narrowing it. Working on a program to narrow it down, given the angles, speed, and so on."

"I've narrowed it down. I've got a program."

"The one we've used isn't — "

"I've got a new program."

He stopped waving her away, scowled at her instead. "What program?"

"Peabody."

"I've got it here on my PPC. And now," she said, after a few commands, "it's on your unit."

He ran it through once, hunched forward. Ran it through a second time. "Where'd you get this? NSA?"

"Roarke."

"Huh. How long's he had people working on this?"

"Just Roarke, last night."

He swung around on his stool. "You bullshitting me?"

"What for? I got three dead people, for God's sake."

"This is fricking genius." Running it yet again, Berenski rubbed the back of his neck. "I can see it could use a little fine-tuning."

"Don't mess with it."

"I ain't going to mess with it, I'm saying if he or his people fine-tuned it, he could sell it for . . . Guess he doesn't need to."

"It's not about need," she muttered.

"You show this to Lowenbaum?"

"I sent it to him, but it was late last night. He may not have seen it yet."

"When he does, he's going to say same as me. You got as close to accurate as you're going to. See here, he

80

calculated the wind variance at the time of the strikes, temperature, humidity, the angle of the strikes, the time between, the elevation, the sight line. It's all here. You're going to be humping for weeks clearing these buildings, but you've got a solid direction."

"Take out mid- to high-level security buildings." Eve glanced at Peabody again.

"Can I?" Without waiting, Peabody leaned over the counter, took the program to the next phase.

"Sweet. Yeah, yeah, hard to get that kind of weapon through security."

"For now, eliminate multi-person offices, residences with families."

He nodded as more buildings faded. "Okay. If he didn't use a suppressor, you're going to find somebody who heard three high-pitched discharges. Have you ever heard a laser rifle?"

"I've fired one."

"Then you know. If he did use one, that would cut the range a bit, but nobody heard anything. It's going to depend how he wanted to go, that's all. You're sure as hell after somebody who knew what they were doing. That's skill, Dallas. Serious skill. That last strike? That wasn't only skill. That was fucking cocky."

Though it pained her a little to agree with Dickhead, Eve had thought the same. "Cocky gets sloppy."

"Maybe."

"Work with the program, and if you can eliminate any more areas, I need to know."

Since he was already running the program again, she left him to it.

"You didn't have to threaten or bribe him."

"Because I gave him geek porn, and he's having too much fun." Eve had to admit, to herself, she kind of missed the bribe dance.

CHAPTER
FOUR

Eve drove straight to Cop Central. She needed to set up her board, snag whoever she could to start clearing buildings — and she hoped to slide in a quick consult with Mira.

It would mean battling Mira's hard-eyed admin, but a consult with NYPSD's top profiler and shrink was invaluable.

The minute she stepped into the bullpen, she scanned. No Baxter and Trueheart, which told her they were likely in the field. The way Carmichael sat on the edge of Santiago's desk indicated a consult rather than gossip.

Jenkinson scowled at his comp as he worked — and Reineke strolled out from the break room with a mug of cop coffee.

"Nothing hot?" she asked Jenkinson.

"Paperwork. I lost the flip."

"My office in five. Peabody, catch them up."

In her office, she opened Roarke's program, then set up her board, centering the three victims. To circumvent Mira's dragon, she sent a brief e-mail to Mira directly. A text might hit the admin first.

She stood, real coffee in hand, and studied the screen when Jenkinson and Reineke came in.

She'd have sworn the light changed in the glare of Jenkinson's tie. From his standpoint, she supposed the gold-and-green dots on screaming red struck him as classic, even subtle.

"You're going to start in this sector, work east from Madison. Peabody's going to give you the target buildings based on this program. It's a crapshoot."

"Sniper type," Reineke said. "You figure working alone."

"Most likely. I'm working on a consult with Mira, but going with percentages and probabilities, a single male, military or police training. A loner. You don't make these strikes without training and practice, so you hit wits on that. At hotels, flops, you're looking for somebody who came in light. He'd need the carry case for the weapon, but I don't see him hauling around much more. He'd need a window that opened — or he damaged it to make the strike. He'd want privacy screening. Unsuppressed, a weapon like this emits a whine — three strikes, three whines, rapid succession."

"Odds of somebody hearing that — "

"Next to zilch," Eve said with a nod to Jenkinson. "Maybe in a flop, or a low-rent apartment, someplace with no soundproofing."

"And of finding somebody who gives a crap when a cop asks."

"And that," Eve agreed.

"Could've used his own place," Reineke speculated. "Starts obsessing on the rink for whatever fucked-up reason, decides to do some duck hunting."

"Let's find out. Peabody and I will start at the sector farthest east, work in toward you. We'll probably be an hour behind you. We need to hit the second vic's office, and — "

She broke off as her incoming signaled, turned to her desk. "Okay, Mira's just coming into Central, and she'll stop by here. If she adds anything we can use, you'll hear it. Get going.

"Peabody, refine our list geographically, and contact Michaelson's office, tell them we're coming in to interview." She checked her wrist unit. "I want a quick one with Feeney before we head out. I can go to him."

"I'm on it."

Alone, she stepped to her window, looked out. She'd judge herself a decent marksman with a laser rifle. Better, a lot better, with a hand weapon, but okay with the long one.

And calculating, figured she could kill, maim, or injure an easy dozen from her skinny office window inside a minute.

How the hell did you protect anyone?

She turned back as she heard Mira coming. Those quick clicks that indicated some sort of classy heels.

The classy heels were on classy red booties in some sort of textured pattern that matched a skinny and useless belt on a suit in what — for some reason — they called winter-white.

Mira's soft sable hair curved in a smooth bob today that showed off little earrings where a tiny pearl dripped from a red stone.

How did anybody think clearly enough in the morning to coordinate that exactly — and not look like a fashion droid, but accessibly human?

"Thanks for stopping," Eve began.

"The price is some of that coffee. I was going to tap you for tea, but then I smelled your coffee."

Mira set aside her coat, her purse — white with a surprisingly bold red center stripe — and stepped to Eve's board.

"I saw the media reports, and read your report. Still no discernible connection among the victims except being on the skating rink?"

"None, and only a few people knew the third victim would be there, and even that's vague on timing."

"Killers of this type often choose randomly. The who doesn't matter. It's the kill itself, the panic it causes. A public place, from a distance — Thank you," Mira added as Eve passed her the coffee. "The three are diverse. Two men, one girl. The two men straddle two generations in age. One was alone, one part of a couple. It isn't a particular type of target, which again leans random."

"The first and third would have been dead instantly, or close enough. First, in the spine, nearly severing it. Third head shot. But the second, mid-body, and he was conscious for at least a minute or two, bleeding out. One and three didn't know what hit them. Two did."

"I see. And that leads you to suspect the second victim was target specific."

"That, and the fact the shooter had to be set up for this in advance — and the third victim's presence wasn't set in stone. The first victim . . . it's just long odds seeing her as target specific. Unless we go back to pure random. The red outfit, the skill on the ice."

"All right." Mira leaned a hip against Eve's desk. "You already know he's organized, skilled, a planner, which means controlled, at least situationally. To add to that, the purely random LDSK has a grudge against society or a political agenda, an anger at a kind of place — a military base, a school, a church. The goal would be to kill or injure as many as possible, to cause panic and alarm, and often to die as a martyr for the cause that drives him."

"'As many as possible.' These strikes took serious skill, and he only takes three? I keep coming back to that," Eve said. "So I'm low on the anger or grudge against the place when he stopped at three. In about twelve seconds — that's all it took. And yeah, suicide by cop or self-termination after the damage is done. But not this guy, at least not yet."

"He may not be finished with that agenda or grudge."

"Yeah." Eve blew out a breath. "Yeah, I keep coming back to that, too."

"I agree with your leanings toward a more specific target, or targets, due to the low body count." Studying death as Eve did, Mira sipped her coffee. "And now with the strike on the second victim not being instantly fatal as were the others? If he meant the second victim to suffer, that adds more weight."

"It could just be the nature of the strike, given the distance, the movement, but it sticks out for me."

"If the victim was specific, the killer chose this public arena, killed others to cover the specificity, and chose a difficult kill. We both know there are much more direct and simple ways to end a life, but the method is part of the purpose and pathology. He's not just skilled but the skill is part of his self-worth, his ego."

"There you go," Eve murmured, adding that to the picture she needed to build in her head.

"I would say causing panic, causing the media fury was certainly part of the motive. Also, the distance — not just the skill involved, but the actual distance — adds dispassion. A target, not a human being. As a military sniper must think, or a professional assassin."

"I haven't eliminated a pro, but it's low on my list. And if it's a pro: Who hired him and why? It goes right back to: Why these three? And for my gut: Why Michaelson?"

"He was a doctor?"

"Yeah, a, you know, woman doctor deal. Checking the works, delivering babies, and like that."

"All right. You might check on mortality. A patient who didn't survive treatment, or a woman who died in childbirth, a baby who didn't survive. It's extremely rare, but it happens, particularly in emergency situations. Or if the patient went against medical advice."

"Cross that with someone connected to her — spouse, lover, brother, father." Eve nodded, adding to the picture. "Or, rare but not impossible, we're dealing with a female shooter. If we draw those lines, this could be it. Why kill again — except . . . "

"It went so very well, didn't it?"

Eve looked back at her board. "Yeah, really good day. We're heading to Michaelson's office now. Maybe we'll hit something. Otherwise."

"You expect another strike."

"If there's an agenda, he's already chosen the next location, and scouted out his nest. You want panic, media fury? Hit again, and fast. Keep the momentum going."

"I have to agree."

"If he sticks with three, that's going to tell me three means something to him. Otherwise, he'll take out more next time. It's ego, right?"

"Yes, ego plays a part."

"When it plays too big a part, it leads to mistakes. Maybe he's already made one. I just have to find it. I should get started. I appreciate the time."

"And I the coffee." Mira handed the empty cup back to Eve, smiled. "I love that jacket."

"This?" Since she'd already forgotten what she was wearing, Eve looked down.

"I love those earthy tones. I can't wear them, but they're so perfect for you. I don't want to keep you," Mira said as she gathered up her things. "I'm available when you need me on this — and I want to add we're looking forward to Bella's party. It'll be so good for Dennis. That kind of color and joy."

Eve shuffled the actual party out of her mind. "How's he doing?"

"He'll grieve for the cousin he loved, even though that man ceased to exist, if he ever did, long before his death. But he's doing well. I was going to nudge him into taking a trip, a little time for us away, but realized he needs home and routine right now. So the party adds to it. What's happier than a first birthday party?"

"I could make a list."

On a laugh, Mira shook her head. "Good luck today."

With Peabody, Eve drove back toward Midtown and Michaelson's practice right off Fifth Avenue at East Sixty-Fourth.

A healthy walk to the rink, she thought, and an easy walk to his residence only a couple blocks away on Sixty-First.

She accepted the challenge of finding a parking slot, vertical lifted into a tight second level on the street. Peabody didn't breathe until the car clunked into place.

Then she cleared her throat. "Office manager is Marta Beck. In addition, he has a receptionist, a billing clerk, a physician assistant, a mid-wife, two nurses, and a pair of part-time rotating nurse's assistants."

"Good-sized staff for one doctor."

"He's been in this location for twenty-two years, and does a stint at the local free clinic twice a month."

Together they walked down, clanging on the metal steps, to street level while sleet slickened every surface.

"Basic background shows a good rep, professionally, and nothing that pops out personally."

On the main door of the trim townhouse was a simple plaque that read DR. BRENT MICHAELSON, and beneath his was one that read FAITH O'RILEY.

"O'Riley's the midwife," Peabody said as Eve stepped inside the quiet, surprisingly homey reception area.

The area was occupied by three pregnant women — one with a toddler perched on what was left of her lap, a thin woman in her mid-twenties, who looked bored as she scrolled through her PPC, and a couple who huddled together, hands clasped.

Eve went straight to the reception counter and, considering all the hormones in the room, kept her voice low.

"Lieutenant Dallas, Officer Peabody to see Marta Beck."

The receptionist, a pretty woman with skin the color of melted gold, bit her lip. Her eyes filled. "If you'd come through the door on the right, please." She swiveled in her chair to speak to a man in a blue lab coat. "George, would you tell Marta the . . . her appointment is here?"

The man had eyes the same color as his coat. He didn't bite his lip as his eyes filled, but pressed them together and slipped away.

The door led to a corridor with exam rooms — the sort of rooms that always tightened the muscles of Eve's stomach. The receptionist stepped into the corridor.

"I'll show you back. We — all of us, we're . . . It's a hard day."

"You didn't close."

"No, we have Dr. Spicker taking Dr. Michaelson's patients, and Ms. O'Riley seeing hers and others. We're going to try to see everyone who's booked. Dr. Michaelson and Dr. Spicker were talking about Dr. Spicker joining the practice, so Marta felt . . . "

They passed an offshoot with a couple of chairs, counters with clipboards and tubes and cups, and a scale where someone else in a lab coat — with flowers all over it — weighed another pregnant woman.

"How long did Dr. Michaelson know Dr. Spicker?"

"Oh, since Dr. Spicker was a boy. They're family friends, and Dr. Spicker just finished his residency. Marta — Ms. Beck's office is . . . "

She trailed off as a tall, broad-shouldered woman in a black suit stepped out of a doorway.

"Thank you, Holly." She stuck out a hand. "Marta Beck."

"Lieutenant Dallas." Eve accepted the brief shake. "Detective Peabody."

"Please come in. Would you like some tea? I can't offer coffee. We don't have any in the offices."

"We're fine."

Marta quietly closed the door. "Please sit."

Eve took one of the straight-backed chairs in the ruthlessly organized room. Not unfriendly, she supposed, with a couple of thriving green plants, a row of fancy teacups, even a small sofa with fancy pillows.

But you knew business was king here.

Marta sat behind her desk, folded her hands. "Do you have any suspects?"

"The investigation is ongoing. Did Dr. Michaelson have any problems with anyone on staff, any patients, anyone you know of?"

"Brent was well liked. He was a good doctor, a caring one, and his patients loved him. We have some who've moved to Brooklyn, New Jersey, Long Island. They still come here because he forged relationships. The patient mattered, Lieutenant. The wall in our break room is covered with photos of the babies he helped bring into the world. Photos of them as they've grown up. I worked for him for twenty years. He was a good doctor and a kind man."

She took a breath. "I assumed, from the media reports, this was a random killing. Some lunatic."

"We're investigating all possibilities."

"I can think of no one, absolutely no one, who would have wished Brent dead. I'd tell you if I did. He was a friend, a good friend, as well as my employer."

"What will happen to his practice now?"

She sighed. "It will go to Andy — Dr. Spicker — if he wants it. Brent discussed this with me while Andy was still a resident. Andy's parents are — were — Brent's oldest friends. He's Andy's godfather, and has been his mentor. They're all very close. Brent felt he himself could begin to cut back if and when Andy wanted to join the practice, and he felt he'd leave the practice in good hands with Andy. And with Faith — our midwife — when he decided to retire, or to simply travel more."

"Any doctor, however good, who's practiced for a couple decades has losses."

"Of course."

"Losses can cause loved ones to behave irrationally."

"Of course," she said again. "Several years ago Brent had a patient who lost her child, miscarried in her seventh month after her partner beat her severely. He left her unconscious on the floor, and by the time she came to, was able to contact nine-one-one, it was too late. The man who caused this threatened Brent when he was tried, when Brent testified. But that man was himself killed in prison two years ago. I assume that's the sort of thing you mean."

"I do. What about the woman who had the miscarriage?"

"She came back to Brent two years later when she'd conceived again with a very nice young man she married shortly after. They have a lovely daughter. Her photo's on the wall, and the mother remains a patient. There are a few others, and like any medical practice we've dealt with malpractice suits. But as far as an actual threat, that's the only one I know of."

"Any recent firings, issues with employees?"

"None. It can be a challenging practice to manage, as Brent tended to spend more time with patients than the industry norm. I learned years ago to factor in more time between appointments. Adding a PA — eight years ago now — has helped cut back on the wait time. And plans to bring Andy on would have helped even more. But that's a moot point, isn't it?"

She looked away for a moment. "I have to hold the line here. We can't fall apart. I've never experienced this kind of thing before. Loss, yes, everyone's lost someone, but not like this. I can't wrap my head around it. I know you need answers, but I don't have them. I just can't think of anyone, anyone at all, who'd want to do this to Brent."

Despite the officer manager's sensibilities, Eve took the time to speak with everyone on staff. When she felt she'd wrung that area dry, she walked out into sleet.

"Maybe I'm off," she said to Peabody. "I'm off, and Michaelson was as random as the other two. Wrong place, wrong time."

"I get why you're tugging that line."

"But?" Eve prompted as they climbed up to the car.

"Well, the third vic almost had to be random. But if I wanted to zero in on one of the others, I'd go with the first."

"Why?"

"Jealousy factor. Young, really pretty, really talented. And, in her way, flashy. Some asshole she didn't pay enough attention to, or shut down. And she was first. If I were going to take that kind of shot, I'd want to be sure my primary target went down."

"Reasonable points. Take her."

"Take her?"

"Turn her inside out," Eve said. "Work, family, school, friends. Find her pattern. Where she ate, shopped, what route she usually took. Subway? Bus? Walking? Talk to her family again, talk to her friends —

work friends, college friends, neighborhood friends. You take her, I'll take Michaelson. And we both take the buildings. I'll drop you at the college, you can start there while I take a pass at Michaelson's residence. Then you take the York and First Avenue locations. I'll take Second and Third. Reineke and Jenkinson started working east from Madison, so they should cover Madison, Park, and Lex. You start as far east as you can go without walking into the river."

"I can do that."

"If we're in the same vicinity, I'll pick you up. Otherwise, when you've covered the ground, head back to Central. We'll conference with Jenkinson and Reineke. If any of us catches a break, we move on that."

"Okay." With a little sigh, Peabody looked up at the ugly sky. "I'll take the subway from here. It's quicker than you driving me."

"Good."

As Peabody walked back to street level, Eve got in the car, lifted out as she'd dropped in, and headed to Sixty-First.

Dr. Brent Michaelson had lived well, Eve thought when she used her master to access his dignified white brick building. Solid security, discreetly done, including the spotlessly clean stairwell as she took that to the third floor rather than the elevator.

She'd already ordered the electronics taken in and reviewed by EDD, but wanted a sense of his living space.

A quiet hallway — only one neighbor sharing the floor. Again, good security on his apartment, which she bypassed with her master.

He had a spacious living area open to a small, neat kitchen, a dining area with a couple of never-lighted candles in a couple of chunky stands on the table.

The furnishings struck her as masculine and simple, comfortable, without fuss. One long table held a forest of photos. His daughter — various ages — his daughter's family. Photos of Andy Spicker and, Eve surmised, Spicker's parents. Others of his staff, a lot with babies.

Friendly, happy photos.

In the kitchen she checked his AutoChef, refrigerator, cupboards. Nothing like food to give you a sense of how people lived, in her opinion.

The man had a weakness for ice cream — the real deal. Preferred red wine, but otherwise ate healthy.

His home office was as simply decorated and as quietly organized as the living space. As in his professional office, this also boasted a wall of photos. She imagined Michaelson sitting at his desk, doing whatever doctors did at desks, and seeing that wall of life.

Many of the babies — the really fresh ones — struck her as creepy. They either looked like fish, or really pissed-off alien life-forms. But she imagined Michaelson had taken great pride in knowing he'd been a part of bringing them into the world.

He kept a small AutoChef and a mini-friggie — fizzy water, straight juice, and herbal teas in the friggie; fruit and veggie snacks in the AC.

Not a candy bar, a caffeine source, or a bag of chips in the place.

How did the man live?

"Not a problem now," she murmured, moving out to study his bedroom.

Tall, padded headboard on a bed with a simple white duvet and a stack of sleeping pillows cased in navy blue.

And books, she noted. Again the real deal. Novels, easily a hundred of them on built-in shelves or stacked on the nightstand.

No sex toys, not in the nightstand, and no indication in the closet of a woman who stayed over and left a robe or any clothes behind for convenience. Nor a man, as a quick survey lead her to think all the clothes were Michaelson's.

Suits, scrubs, casual clothes, gym clothes. And skates. He'd had two pairs other than the ones he'd worn on his last day.

She found male sex booster pills and condoms in his bathroom — so he'd had sex, or at least had prepared for the possibility. No illegals, nothing out of the ordinary.

She finished up in a well-appointed guest room and a shining-clean powder room.

When she left, her picture of Michaelson was of a solid, dedicated doctor who had a genuine love of babies, kids, women in general. One who took care of himself, lived quietly, liked to skate, liked to read, and valued his circle of friends.

Nowhere in that picture was a motive for murder.

Back in the car, she headed east, and considered Peabody's points.

Ellissa Wyman. Young, very attractive, graceful, apparently happy, well-adjusted. Not particularly interested in men or relationships — at least on the surface. But yeah, somebody might have been interested in her. Rebuffed or simply not noticed.

Or, they might find, digging deeper, there were relationships or a lifestyle her family, her friends didn't know about.

It had to be considered, just as Michaelson had to be considered.

The worst case had to be considered, too. Straight random. It hadn't mattered who. It wouldn't matter who the next time.

It might have been a crappy day to hike the streets, but Eve pulled into an annoyingly overpriced lot, dumped the car, and hoofed it to the first building on her list. Street-level French restaurant, men's boutique, and a fancy-looking shop with lots of fancy-looking dust catchers. Three floors of apartments above, all topped by a dance studio and a yoga studio, and those were capped by a rooftop that could be accessed by the residents and the studios.

Roarke's program gave the roof the highest probability, with the yoga studio next in line. So Eve started at the top.

The wind bit; the ice stung. But when Eve pulled field glasses out of her pocket, adjusted her position, she found an excellent view of the rink. A hell of a long way off, but a stronger scope? Yeah, she could see how it could be done.

No sleet and ice the day before, she remembered. Not so much wind. Maybe part of the reason for the timing.

Standing there she put herself into the mind of the shooter. Might have to wait awhile. A stool, some sort of lightweight, retractable seat. Rest the weapon on the ledge that way. Keep everything steady.

She crouched down, mimed sitting on a stool, her hands on an imaginary weapon, her eye on the scope. From that position she took stock of neighboring buildings.

No cover, she considered, and too many windows, too much risk of someone looking out. Lunatic or not, why take that kind of chance?

Still, she took out microgoggles, went carefully over the wall, the concrete, looking for marks. Finding nothing, she went back inside, tried the yoga studio.

She found a group in session with people — mostly female — in colorful skin suits twisting into weird positions on colorful mats. All while facing a slim and stunning woman with a perfect body, impossibly perfect form, and a wall of mirrors.

She had to give the group props just for showing up.

Soft, tinkling music played under the instructors soft, tinkling voice. Eve decided she'd probably want to wrap the woman's legs around her neck, tie her ankles in a knot, before the end of a single session.

But that was just her.

Eve stepped back, tried the adjoining dance studio.

Another wall of mirrors, more music played low. But this time, the music had a fierce, hard beat, and the lone woman in the room covered the floor to it — feet flying, legs flashing, hips rocking.

She executed three whipping spins, bounced into a one-handed handspring. And ended, right on that beat, with her arms thrown up, head back.

She said, panting but enthusiastically: "Shit!"

"Looked good to me."

The woman, black skin wet with sweat, grabbed a towel, swiped off as she studied Eve.

"Missed the count twice, forgot the damn head roll. Sorry, are you looking for a class?"

"No." Eve pulled out her badge.

This time the woman said: "Uh-oh."

"Just a couple questions. Let's start with who are you?"

"Donnie Shaddery. It's my studio — I mean I rent the space."

"Did you have classes yesterday?"

"Every day, seven days a week."

"My background indicates no classes yesterday between three and five P.M."

"That's right. Morning classes. Seven to eight, eight-thirty to nine-thirty. Ten to eleven, eleven to twelve — break twelve to one. One to one-thirty's sort of freestyle, then afternoon class from one-thirty to two-thirty. Then except for Fridays, I break until five."

"You're the instructor?"

"There are two of us. I had morning and afternoon yesterday, my partner had evening. Why?"

Not the place, Eve thought, with the schedule that tight. But.

"I need to know if anyone was here, or in the studio next door, between three and four P.M."

"I was here. I've got a call-back — for a new musical — today. I've been working on the damn routine every chance I get. I was here from about six-thirty yesterday morning until five."

"What about the yoga studio?"

"I know Sensa was here before seven. And she did her afternoon meditation about three — at least she always does, I didn't actually look in. She's got two other instructors, and one of them — that's Paula — came in around three, after the afternoon class, because she's a dancer, too, and she came over and watched me practice for a while."

"So, basically, someone was in the space all afternoon."

"Yeah."

"Did anyone else come in during that time frame?"

"Not that I saw. Or heard. Should we be worried about something?"

"I don't think so." Eve walked over to the windows. "Seven days a week," she repeated. "And someone's generally here — on the floor — in the afternoons."

"That's right. If we leave, we lock up. We have a sign — Sensa and I split the rent for the floor, and we share an excuse for an office, and keep some stuff in here. Extra mats, some costumes — we co-teach a belly-dancing class on this side twice a week. It's not much to steal, but we lock up. Was there a break-in?"

Eve scanned the space again. It just didn't fit. "No, I don't think so. One more question. Why 'break a leg'? How the hell can you dance if you break a leg?"

"Sorry, I — Oh, the saying. Theater suspicion. Saying 'good luck' is bad luck. So you say 'break a leg' when you mean 'good luck.'"

"That doesn't make any sense."

"Nope." Donnie gulped from a water bottle. "But that's showbiz."

CHAPTER
FIVE

Eve covered an office building, a residential building. She felt one apartment in the residential might warrant a trip back, and certainly a full run on the tenant. Single man in his mid-thirties, who'd served in the Army for five years.

The quick run she did, while hoofing it to the next building, showed he'd served as a supply officer — minimal weapons training — but she marked him down to be interviewed either when he was in residence or at his place of employment.

The ugly, incessant sleet began to thin, just a little, as she walked east from Third Avenue to Second.

She hit a flop, a struggling art studio, more offices.

Got no buzz at all.

The hotel, her next stop on Second, looked old but well kept. Low- to mid-range. "Family friendly," according to its billing, with some rooms boasting a kitchenette.

The lobby, quiet and small, held a skinny cafe, a closet-sized gift shop, and a single clerk at the desk. He smiled broadly.

"Good morning. Such a dreary day to be out and about. How can I help you?"

He had such a pleasant face, all round and cheerful with a voice to match, Eve almost felt bad about pulling out her badge. He blinked at it.

"Oh my, is there something wrong, Officer — no, excuse me, I see it's Lieutenant. Lieutenant!" he repeated before she could speak. "Of course, it's Lieutenant. Dallas. I loved *The Icove Agenda*, book and vid. I hope I can help one of the most dedicated public servants in the city."

"Me, too. I'm looking for someone who would have had a room yesterday, most likely on the ninth or tenth floor, facing west."

"A check-in yesterday. Let me — "

"Not necessarily a check-in yesterday. Could've been prior, but they'd have been in-house yesterday. We'll start with guests, but I may be looking for one of the staff, someone who could gain access to an empty room."

"I see, I see. No, of course I don't see at all, but let me check the rooms."

"It's likely a male, likely alone. But don't rule out female or a companion."

"Ninth floor, west . . . We have Mr. and Mrs. Ernest Hubble. They're here for four days, with a checkout tomorrow."

"You got a home address on them?"

"Oh, yes, Des Moines. They're return guests, this is their third visit. They come for the inventory sales and a show."

"Give me somebody who checked out this morning or late yesterday."

"All right. This is rather exciting." His pleasant face turned a little pink to prove it. "We have Mr. Reed Bennett, home address is Boulder, Colorado. I believe he's a salesman, and here for meetings. He checked in two days ago, checked out this morning. Just about a half hour ago, actually."

"Call off housekeeping. I'm going to want to see his room. Who else you got?"

"Ms. Emily Utts and Ms. Fry. Ladies of a certain age in from Pittsburgh. Here for a little reunion with some classmates — from college. Class of '19."

"Probably not. Any others?"

"Just one more. Mr. Philip Carson, from East Washington, accompanied by his teenage son, or daughter — I'm not sure, it's so hard to tell at that age, isn't it? Especially when they're wearing one of those hoods and all bundled up. I see here they requested that specific room."

A bell rang. "Specific room. Had they stayed here before?"

"I don't have that name in our database, but I did think Mr. Carson looked familiar."

"Do you remember their luggage?"

"I . . . " He closed his eyes, squeezed them, then popped them open. "I do! I do because I started to call for Gino to assist them, but Mr. Carson said they didn't need a bellman. They had two rollies, one each, and the child had a backpack. Mr. Carson had a case — a large metal briefcase."

"When did they check out?"

"Yesterday, though they were booked to stay through the night. They checked in about five the evening prior — I remember as I was about to go off my shift. I'm not sure I saw them at all until they checked out about three-thirty yesterday. Mr. Carson said they had a family emergency."

"I need to see the room."

"Oh my. Yes, yes, but I'm afraid it's been cleaned."

"I need to see it."

"Let me get Gino to cover the desk, and I'll take you up myself. Just one moment."

He bustled. At least that was the word that came to Eve's mind, moving quickly as a man in a bellman's navy uniform came out of a side room.

"I didn't get your name."

"Oh, I'm Henry. Henry Whipple."

He actually looked like a Henry Whipple, Eve decided as they stepped on the elevator together. One old enough that it required Henry to push a button for the tenth floor.

"Some guests enjoy the old-fashioned touches," he explained.

Old-fashioned, she thought. "Do your windows open? The guest rooms."

"They do, though not fully. Now we have privacy screens — guests expect that, but again some enjoy being able to open the window a few inches in pretty weather. Or because they want to hear New York."

"Soundproofing?"

"Some, yes, but not what you'd find in newer or more expensive hotels. We've been family owned for five generations, and have tried to keep our little home-away-from-home affordable for visitors, especially families."

"Got it."

When they stepped out on ten, Eve could hear the murmur of someone's entertainment screen — not offensive, just the mutter of it through the door of the room. Still, room security wasn't pitiful, and the corridor itself was as clean as the rest of the building.

She started to reach for her master, saw Whipple had his out, and let him unlock the room.

"Should I wait out here?"

"Just inside, shut the door."

The lights worked by switches — another old-fashioned touch. Two beds, well made with white duvets, crisply cased pillows, a good-sized dresser, a bathroom so clean she could smell the lemon scent from the cleanser. And a small but efficient kitchen area with a glass-fronted cabinet holding various drinks, another holding snack food.

But the windows were what drew her across the room.

She unlocked one, lifted it. Four, maybe five inches, she judged.

Room enough.

She pulled over one of the two chairs, sat, took out her field glasses.

"Fucking bingo. I just know it."

She looked down at the carpet — on the thin side, but clean. Took out microgoggles, studied the windowsill, shook her head.

"I'd like to speak with whoever cleaned the room."

"That would be Tasha. Excuse me, Lieutenant, you're looking toward Central Park, aren't you? With binoculars. The media reports . . . This is about what happened yesterday. About those poor people. On the skating rink."

"Keep it under your hat, Henry."

"Yes, yes, of course. But I believe I need to sit down, for just a moment. My legs." Pale, he dropped into the second chair.

"Don't go fainting on me." Pulling out her PPC, she did a run on Philip Carson, East Washington.

"No, no, I just need a moment. I've worked in hotels for twenty-three years. I've seen and heard and dealt with a great deal, as you might expect. But to think I may have . . . the person who did . . . But, he had a child!"

"Maybe. Is this the guy?"

Patting his chest, Henry studied the image on screen. "Oh, no, he was younger than this."

"How about this guy?"

"No, not that young. I'm sorry."

"Elimination's good." And that eliminated the two Philip Carsons in East Washington who were under eighty and over twenty. "Housekeeping, Henry."

He let out a long breath before pulling out a 'link, tapping a code. "Tasha, I need you in 1004, right away."

"If this room was used, I got really lucky, but luck can happen. Or I could be wrong. Do you have security feed from yesterday?"

"We — I'm sorry — We don't have it at all."

Another good reason to pick this location, she thought. "Can you describe the man and the kid?"

"Yes, yes." Some of his color came back. "I absolutely can do that. I'd be happy to do that."

"Okay, you're going to give me the basics in a minute, then I'm going to have you work with a police artist. Can you come to Central?"

"I — I just need to have someone come in to take my shift."

"How about I send the artist to you?"

"Thank you. It would be helpful."

"You're helpful, Henry. I've got it," she said at the knock on the door. She opened it to a tiny blond woman with enormous blue eyes.

"Tasha, this is Lieutenant Dallas. She needs to ask you about the guests who were in this room."

"And the room after they left it."

"Okay, but I didn't actually see the guests. They had their privacy light on, so I didn't see them."

"What can you tell me about the room, after they checked out?"

"They were really neat. I could tell they'd used the kitchen, but they'd washed up after themselves. Most people don't. I still washed everything, Mr. Henry. And they used the honor bar, so I replaced everything."

"The rug, over here by the window. Did you notice anything?"

"Now, it's funny you should ask. I could see they must've brought over the chairs and sat there by the window. You could see the, you know, dents in the rug.

110

And there were a couple other dents. I think maybe they had like a little telescope, and sat there looking at the city. People do that."

"Oh my," Henry murmured. "Oh my."

"I vacuumed up really good, Mr. Henry."

"I know you did, dear. The room is spotless, as always when you turn one."

"What did you do with the trash? They must've left some trash."

"Oh, that goes straight into the recycler."

"Sheets, towels?"

"Right to Laundry."

"I bet you scrubbed down the bathroom, every surface."

"Oh, yes, ma'am. We sanitize."

"Lieutenant," Eve corrected absently. "You wiped down the dresser, the counters, nightstand?"

"Oh, sure. Clean and comfortable. It's hotel policy."

"Light switches?"

"Sanitized."

"Henry, I'm going to want sweepers — the crime scene unit — to go over the room. Just in case. Thanks," she said to Tasha, opening the door to nudge her out. "Okay, Henry." Eve pulled over the chair so she could sit across from him. "What did these two look like? Every detail you can remember, including what they wore."

Satisfied she'd squeezed everything she could out of him, Eve sent Henry on his way, pulled out her 'link.

"Hey." Peabody's face — pink-cheeked — filled the screen. "Finished at the college. I'll write that up, but there's nothing so far. I'm on my way to the first building on First. Nothing on York I could find."

"That's because I found it on Second. Manhattan East Hotel, room 1004. Let Jenkinson and Reineke know."

"You found the nest? Are you sure?"

"Would I be calling you off otherwise? Head to Second, meet me here. Save the questions," Eve added before Peabody could ask another. She ended transmission, ordered the sweepers, contacted Detective Yancy, the police artist, then tagged Lowenbaum.

"That's some luck you got, Dallas. You oughta be playing the horses."

"You're going to want to see this, Lowenbaum, and I'm going to want you to verify I'm not talking out of my ass when I say the right shooter could've made the strikes from here."

"I'm on my way."

"Bring the laser rifle you figure with you, and a bipod."

"Already on the list."

After shoving the 'link back in her pocket, Eve wandered the room.

On the small side, she thought, but more than adequate.

Had to scout the room at least once before, alone most likely. Not with the partner. Had to be sure it could be done, and this was the place to do it.

Quiet hotel, no cams, but solid security on the guest room doors. Nobody's going to stroll in unexpectedly. Just a guy and his teenage kid traveling to New York — who pays attention?

Henry Whipple, she thought — and yeah, that was some luck.

Book the room — bogus ID, but the card used to register has to pass hotel scan, so it's good bogus. Carry your own bags, come up, lock the door, put on the privacy light, then —

She kept walking through it as she moved to the door to answer the knock, let in a slightly out-of-breath Peabody.

"How did you — "

"Front desk clerk who pays attention. Suspect was traveling with what Henry — front desk — believed was his minor child — teenage type. Not sure on gender. ID's bogus, but we'll push on it deeper. Philip Carson, East Washington. Requested this room specifically."

Eve pulled out her field glasses. "Have a look."

Peabody moved to the window, looked out. "Wow, it's a really long way, but yeah, it's a good view of the rink."

"Housekeeper's sanitized the works, but she noticed little dents in the carpet by the window, like a chair and a bipod would make."

"If this is it, they had to have been here before, had to know they'd have the shot."

"Henry thought the adult male looked familiar. And we've got a description — Yancy's heading in to work with him. Caucasian male, late forties, early fifties,

113

about six feet, on the thin side at about one-sixty, square jaw, short medium-brown hair. Not sure on eye color, but Henry thinks light — blue, green, gray. And maybe he had a cold, or was getting over something. He looked *drawn*, was the word. And his eyes looked tired. Wearing a black parka, black ski cap, jeans. Carrying a large metal briefcase and a midsized black rolly."

"That's a lot. If Henry's accurate, that's a lot."

"There's more. The younger suspect, mixed race, medium complexion — Henry claims beautiful skin there — green eyes, black hair in short dreads, about five-five, about a hundred and twenty. Dark green, knee-length coat, green-and-black-striped cap. He said no older than sixteen, but that may be the height, the build, and the assumption this was the adult suspect's offspring."

"And if it is." Peabody handed the field glasses back to Eve. "Well, Jesus."

"We can't verify that yet. They booked this room, checked in early evening, carried their own bags up, locked the door, engaged the privacy light. They took some drinks and snacks. One of them might have gone out for food — no cams in this place — or they may have brought in what they wanted. Housekeeper says they were neat — cleaned up after themselves."

"Wiped the place down, you can bet."

"You can bet," Eve agreed. "But efficient housekeeping took care of that anyway. I have sweepers on the way in case, but I don't expect to find anything. They

114

left about ten minutes after the strikes, claiming family emergency, as they were booked through last night."

"In case they missed the target, and to give them into the afternoon."

"They also booked the room over a week ago, so that takes the third vic out of target specific. Add this: They come in, set up. The rink was open, but they waited, spent the night, spent the morning before making the strikes."

"Okay, yeah, why not finish it? The rink's a popular spot at night, and well lit. People panic more at night, right? If that's the only motive, hit at night. But they spent hours in this room. It leans more toward one of the victims being a target."

"Eat some snacks, maybe watch some screen. Sit there, looking through the scope, thinking about all the people you could end from your perch. The ones walking home, going out to dinner, riding in the back of a cab? They owe their lives to you. That makes you feel powerful."

Walking back to the window, Eve looked out, hands in her pockets. "They're alive because you allowed them to live. And they're all as clueless as ants on a hill. They don't know all you have to do is step on them. You spent a long time in the night sitting here, thinking about that. Imagining. Anticipating."

"Which one?"

"The younger. Or if not the younger, it will be."

"Why?"

"What's the point otherwise? Henry? He's solid, and he's got a sharp eye. I can buy the second suspect may be into the twenties, but no more than that. Henry wouldn't be that far off — and we'll see what Yancy has to say when they work together. So why have the young one along? It's not for the fucking company. There's a purpose. Here's how it's done, kid, and next time it's yours to do. Or it's your time. Take your shot."

Hadn't that been the way between her and Feeney? Here's how it's done, kid. Now do it.

"Henry felt that father/child connection. Maybe that was because that's what they wanted to project. But that's often how it plays out with a trainer and a trainee, especially with that sort of age gap."

"It could go back to pros," Peabody suggested. "The older pro training the younger, related or not."

"Yeah, it could. Except when you look at the vics. Just not enough to gain. Michaelson was well-set, but not swimming in it. His practice will go to his godson — and the godson was already coming into the practice. So far I'm not finding any patients who'd want him dead. His ex is re-married and they appear to have maintained civility. He had a good relationship with his daughter — who'd benefit financially, but doesn't have any outstanding debt or anything that shows. It doesn't feel like money."

"Sex is always a good one."

"Nothing to indicate he had any serious partners there. All that holds, as far as we know, for Wyman. So, we keep looking."

"Yeah, I'm hitting the same, on Wyman. Just no gain to killing her. Nobody disliked her, knew of anyone who did, or hit on her hard enough to have a thing."

116

"Well, somebody had something on her or Michaelson."

Once again Eve went to the door to answer the knock, and let in Lowenbaum.

He walked in, black coat wet with sleet, pulled off his ski cap.

"I meant it about the horses." Contemplatively chewing his gum, he scanned the room. He carted in a large, locked case. "The guy at the desk went white as a sheet when he saw this." Setting the case on one of the beds, Lowenbaum tapped it. "After I badged him, he told me the man who was in this room had one just like it."

Fucking bingo, Eve thought again. "I don't know the horses, but maybe I'll lay some on tonight's Knicks game."

"Your man bought the Celtics, didn't he?"

"Yeah."

"Chill." Still scanning, Lowenbaum unlocked the case. "Decent room, decent place. He could've gotten a flop a lot cheaper, done the job. Longer odds us nailing that location."

"He wasn't alone."

Now Lowenbaum looked up. "Is that so?"

"Younger — undetermined gender. Desk guy thought teenager, but we can't narrow it there yet."

"Changes things."

Eve stepped closer as Lowenbaum opened the case and began, with quick, practiced efficiency, to assemble the weapon.

"How much would that weigh? Case included."

"A solid fifteen, with the extra batteries." He took out the bipod, tapped a button, telescoped it out.

"First window right of the bed," Eve told him. "The housekeeper saw the depressions left in the carpet from the bipod, and from a chair."

"You're shitting me now."

"Truth. They're observant here at Manhattan East. And the window opens, about five inches from the bottom."

"Handy." After setting the bipod in front of the window, Lowenbaum retrieved the rifle, secured it. "Thanks," he said when Peabody brought over a chair.

He sat, looked through the scope, made some adjustments, walked the chair over a half inch. "Pick 'em off like flies," he murmured.

"You could make the strikes from here?"

"Yeah, I could. I've got another two on my squad I'd count on to make it, and another three who'd at least wing the targets from here."

"Moving targets," Eve reminded him.

"I could, the two on my squad could. Moving targets, let's give the other three a fifty-fifty at this range. Take a look." He got up from the chair; Eve took his place.

The scope made her field glasses feel like a toy. She studied the empty rink, the barricades, made her own adjustments to widen the field, and watched gawkers taking photos of the rink.

She put a woman with a blue pom-pom cap and scarf in the cross-hairs.

Powerful, she thought again.

118

"Makes me feel I could make the strike, but that's not factoring in wind, temps, and all that other crap. Could the younger guy have been here to do those calculations?"

"You have a weapon like this, and you have the skill, you do your own. It's almost innate. And it's . . . you've got to say *intimate*. You and the weapon, I mean. You and the target, that's not."

Nodding, Eve rose. "You'd verify this is the location?"

"I would, but why not use the toys we've got to lock it down."

He sat again, took out his PPC. "I can plug in this location — the exact position of the weapon, the exact position of the targets, and do a reverse calculation."

"You can?"

"I can now because on my way in I had a conversation with Roarke about doing that using this new program. I figured, why the hell not ask the guy who came up with the program — more advanced than we've been using — and give it a try?"

"I should've thought of that."

"Then you wouldn't need me. Give me a sec."

While she waited, Eve jerked a thumb at the door for Peabody to answer. "If that's the sweepers, tell them we'll be ready for them in a minute. Have them hold."

"Another sec," Lowenbaum told her. "It's a lot of tech for me. Your genius was heading into a meeting — maybe he'll buy the Mets — or I'd tag him again, see if he could do it by remote. But I think I can . . . Okay,

okay, there it goes. And we have a ninety-five-point-six probability on this location."

He handed Eve his PPC so she could see the results.

"That'll be handy in court when we bag the bastards." He took the PPC back, put it away. "My work is done here. I'd like to see these ass-holes. You're going to shoot me the security feed?"

"No cams in the place."

"And the lucky streak dies."

"But I've got a solid description, and Yancy's coming in to do sketches."

"And rides again. Give me the basics," he said as he began to disassemble the weapon as efficiently as he'd assembled it.

"Caucasian male," she began, filling him in while he secured the weapon and the stand.

"I'll take a good look when you have the sketches. I know some guys who could make these strikes, either by face or rep, and some personally. Maybe it'll pop — or I can show it to some I trust aren't asshole bastard lunatics."

"You'll have it when I do. Appreciate it, Lowenbaum."

"I'd say all in a day's, but . . . not this time. I'll be seeing you. Keep it loose, Peabody."

"That's how I roll." Peabody let him out, let the sweepers in.

Once Eve had given them the basics, she and Peabody left them to it.

"I'll keep digging on Ellissa Wyman. With it leaning this far target specific, the suspects could be in the wind, well into it."

120

"You think they're done?" Eve countered.

"If they hit their target — "

"Why the partner, Peabody? Why the younger? Partner or, if we're really talking at least twenty years age difference, maybe apprentice? What's the training for? Some connection between the suspects and one of the vics, there's got to be. But people have more than one connection, and people with this kind of grudge? They've got more than one of those, too."

Eve stepped into the elevator, stabbed the button for lobby.

"They're not done."

CHAPTER
SIX

Eve tried Mira from the car, hit her v-mail. "Suspect has a partner, younger, possibly a teen, gender unknown. Full report to follow, but think about it."

She clicked off, tried Feeney next. "Peabody, tag the commander's office. I need ten minutes — fifteen," she corrected, "asap. Feeney," she continued when his basset-hound face came on screen. "I'm on my way to Central, I need a meet."

"On the LDSK?"

"Got the nest, got a description. I want to bounce this off you."

"Come ahead and bounce. I'll work you in."

"Appreciate it. Later."

"The commander's on a 'link conference, but I stressed the urgency. He can see you in about forty."

"That works. You head back to the bullpen, brief Jenkinson and Reineke. I may need to pull them in again. I'll send you my record on the interviews at the hotel. Start writing the report. If I'm not back, go deeper on the ID the suspect used. There may be a reason he used that name. Dig under the credit card."

"I've got it. Why Feeney?"

"He was in the Urbans, and he's worked LDSKs before." And, Eve thought, he trained me.

When she hit a traffic snag — somebody had wiped out on the slippery street, and was now arguing heatedly with the cabdriver he'd slid into — she thought: Fuck it. Slapped on the sirens, and went in hot.

"Call that mess in before there's bloodshed."

"Already done."

As she turned toward Central, Eve glanced over. She'd trained Peabody. Something else to think about.

She squealed into her parking spot in Central's garage, quickstepped to the elevator.

"You think another strike's coming," Peabody said. "That's why the rush."

"I think another strike's coming. And if I'm wrong on that, they've had a day to poof. We need to catch up."

As the elevator filled with cops, she hopped off when Peabody did, took the glide the rest of the way up to EDD.

Entering the odd cop world of color and movement, she spotted McNab — hard to miss in a fluorescent red-and-yellow shirt flopping over neon green baggies as he stood, skinny hips tick-tocking to his own strange beat. His screen was exploding with color and weird symbols.

She dodged around a female practically skipping across the room wearing a fuzzy pink sweater with an animated poodle doing backflips over her chest.

Eve beelined for the relative sanity of Feeney's office.

He stood working a large swipe screen two handed. His hips didn't bop — thank Christ — and he wore one of his shit-brown suits, already wrinkled, a darker shit-brown tie askew over a saggy beige shirt.

His silver-threaded ginger hair sproinged up from his comfortably worn face as if he'd scrubbed it with a wire brush. The room smelled of his candied almonds and coffee.

When he grunted at her, she stepped in.

"Can I close this door? All that color makes me dizzy."

He signaled her to go ahead and, when the door shut, wagged a thumb toward his AutoChef. "Coffee's under kale-and-carrot smoothie."

"Good choice." Eve programmed two, waited until Feeney nodded at the screen and stepped back.

"What ya got, kid?"

"The nest, a description. He made those strikes from Second Avenue, Feeney."

Eyebrows lifted. He let out a whistle as he dropped behind his desk. "That's some juice."

"He's got a partner, except . . . The second suspect is young, undetermined gender. Possibly a teenager. I'll know more when Yancy finishes with the wit. Adult suspect, probably early fifties."

"Doesn't sound like a partner."

"Exactly. Sounds like a trainee. Maybe the wit's off, but he comes off rock solid. When he says sixteen tops, I lean toward a kid. Who takes a kid into something like this unless he's molding said kid?"

124

As he thought about it, Feeney snagged a few almonds out of a lop-sided bowl. "Any chance the kid's a hostage?"

"Doesn't feel like it. This wit? He'd have noticed if the kid came in under duress. They checked into the hotel together, had already requested that particular room. Stayed the night, stayed through the morning. That's planning and patience. And it's lying in wait. So I ask myself: Why this kid? You took me."

Sipping coffee, Feeney nodded. "You had juice."

"I was green."

"You never had much green on you. I saw potential, guts, a working brain — cop's brain. Maybe a little bit of me there, back in the day. And you wanted Homicide. You took Peabody," he reminded her.

"Yeah, and thinking on that. I can't say I saw any me in her, but I saw potential, and that working cop brain. I figured, give her a shot at Homicide — because she wanted it — and try her out as my aide. Then it fit, that's all. We fit."

"She's got you in her. A sunnier outlook, and that Free-Ager base, but she doesn't quit. And it's not just the job matters. It's the victim. You saw some of that, or you might've put her into a cube in Homicide. You wouldn't have set yourself up to train her."

"Yeah. I guess. Yeah. So there's maybe some of the adult in the kid. The potential to kill. You took me, I took Peabody — and I gave Baxter Trueheart — but there's more than the potential, all three trainees were already cops."

With a nod, Feeney gulped some coffee. "You're wondering if the kid's already a killer."

"You don't pick an apprentice out of the air. You don't take them on because they're handy. Where'd they find each other? The adult suspect has to have police or military training, almost has to have been in uniform. So, do you pick this kid off the street, out of some war zone?"

"There's another choice."

"I know it. They're related. Father and son, uncle, older brother, distant fricking cousins. I get the description I can run it through Missing Persons, see if anyone's looking for a teenager. Let's say they're connected, why train to kill? This doesn't come off as a pro — none of the three victims had anything worth the hire. And there are a lot less visible ways to do a training exercise if you're heading up a fricking assassin's school. This comes off personal."

"A lot easier ways to kill for personal reasons."

"Damn right."

"Unless this is what you do." Companionably, Feeney nudged the wobbly bowl toward her. "Not an assassin for hire, but a sniper — police or military. That's where you're leaning anyway."

On a long breath, Eve nodded. It helped to have him lean where she did. "Yeah, that's where. You take on the trainee because you want him to share what you do, you want to give him something maybe. You want to see something of you in him. The age difference . . . "

"More like you and me." Feeney nodded. "I never worked an LDSK with a partner, or with a trainee, but

I'd say the trainee has to show a — what's it — propensity for the work, and some skill, and the same cold blood. You can't teach the cold blood, Dallas. It's just got to be there."

And again, he helped to hear him say what muttered in her mind.

"How'd they pick and train snipers during the Urbans?"

"Same way they do now, I'd say. You've got to have the skill, the control. You have to be able to see a human being as a target. You don't take that target until you get the green, and when you do get the green, you don't hesitate."

"Whoever made those strikes didn't hesitate," Eve said. "And they won't hesitate when they get the green again."

Working out the oral report in her head, Eve headed to Commander Whitney's office. Whitney's admin gave her a nod, held up one finger to signal for her to wait. Then tapped her ear-link.

"Lieutenant Dallas, Commander. Yes, sir. Go right in, Lieutenant."

He sat behind his desk, a big man with broad shoulders that carried the weight of command. His wide dark face was set in sober lines as he watched Eve come in.

"I've kept you out of this morning's media conference, as you were in the field. Tell me you have something."

"I have the nest, I have a description of two suspects, and Detective Yancy is working with the witness."

Whitney sat back. "That's more than something. Details."

She gave them all, quickly, to the point, and on her feet.

"A teenage apprentice," Whitney murmured. "It wouldn't be the first time. The D.C. snipers," he told her. "Early twenty-first century. The Ozarks snipers, 2030 to '31. Brothers, the younger barely thirteen when they began."

Eve made a mental note to research both cases.

"When we have the sketches, we'll release them, and this time you'll need to participate in the media conference. Stand by while I contact Kyung. We want to set this up carefully."

She wanted to work, wanted her board, wanted to think it through, but she stood, as ordered, and waited.

While Eve waited, so did the apprentice. Mixed with the cold blood was a hot thread of anticipation. This time it would be different. This time the knowledge of how it felt, how that power pumped from finger to target colored all.

The flop smelled of piss and roaches. But it didn't matter. The sight line straight up Broadway to Times Square was unobstructed. The thinning sleet, even the occasional sky tram winging by didn't distract.

"I have the target."

The trainer nodded, picking out the target himself through a scope. "You have the green. Take your time. Take the target out."

"I want more than three this time. I can do six. I want six."

"Speed and accuracy, remember. Three is enough."

"It sets a pattern, and I can take six."

After a moment, the trainer lowered the glasses. "Four. Don't argue. Do the job. Argue, we abort."

Pleased, the apprentice watched the people thronging the streets of Times Square, watched them walk and gawk, snap their pictures, run their videos, haul their bags of worthless souvenirs.

And began to do the job.

Officer Kevin Russo patrolled with his friend and fellow cop, Sheridon Jacobs. They'd just grabbed a couple of loaded dogs off a cart on their break, and his sat warm in his belly.

He liked his beat — always something happening, always something to see. Of course, he'd only been assigned to Times Square the last four months, but he didn't see it getting old anytime soon.

"There's Grabby Larry," he said to Jacobs as he watched the aging street thief casing the tourists. "Guess we'd better run him off."

"He's showing the miles." Jacobs shook her head. "There ought to be a retirement home for old street thieves. Guy has to be pushing the century mark."

"I think he passed it a few years ago. Jesus, he doesn't even see us coming."

They didn't hurry. Grabby Larry wasn't as nimble as he'd been in his prime; and the week before, his mark had beat him to the ground with her purse — the one he'd hoped to steal.

Russo started to grin at the memory, then today's mark — a woman of about seventy, with a bright red purse dangling from her arm — dropped like a stone.

"Ah, shit, call the MTs, Sherry." As Russo darted forward, a kid on an airboard in a small pack of kids on airboards went flying, took out a trio of pedestrians like bowling pins.

Russo saw blood bloom on the back of the kid's bright blue jacket.

"Get down! Down! Take cover."

Before the first scream, the first realization of those around him, Russo pulled his weapon. He leaped toward the kid in hopes of shielding him from another strike. But the third hit Russo in the center of his forehead, a scant inch below the brim of his cap. Russo was gone before he hit the ground, before the fourth body fell, and a fifth.

While chaos erupted blocks away, while screams ripped the air and tires squealed, the apprentice sat back, smiled up at the trainer.

"Five was a compromise."

The trainer lowered the scope, aimed stern disapproval. But pride shone through it. "Pack it up. We're done here."

In Whitney's office, Dallas's communicator buzzed almost simultaneously with Whitney's 'link signaling a breakthrough communication.

"I'll get back to you," he told the media liaison. His eyes met Eve's as they both answered.

"Dallas."

"Dispatch, Dallas, Lieutenant Eve. Officer down, Broadway and Forty-Four. Multiple victims. Four confirmed dead. Wounded unverified."

"Acknowledged. On my way. Sir."

"We have a dead cop. I'm coming with you. Let's move."

She tagged Peabody on the way. "Garage. Now. We have another strike, Times Square. He got a cop."

Automatically, Eve turned toward the glides. "They're faster, sir."

If anyone thought it odd the commander rushed to keep pace with her, weaving through bodies on the glides, they were discreet enough to keep it to sidelong looks — and most just quickly made a hole.

Halfway down, Whitney grabbed Eve's arm. "Elevator. I'll bypass from here."

When Whitney muscled onto the jammed elevator, cops, not so discreetly, came to attention. And no one bitched — out loud — when he swiped his ID card and called for the garage.

"What level?" he snapped at Eve.

"Level One."

After ordering it, he glanced at her. "Your rank rates higher."

"I like Level One."

"The way you like an office the size of a broom closet."

"I guess. Yes, sir. Commander, it's going to be mayhem."

He pulled a black scarf out of the pocket of the coat he'd yanked on as they'd rushed out of his office. "I've dealt with mayhem."

Eve decided to be discreet, and said nothing.

They shoved off the elevator into the echoing garage. One glance told Eve they'd beaten Peabody, and that gave Whitney time to survey her ride.

"What kind of vehicle is this, and why in hell don't you have better?"

"It's my personal vehicle, and better than it looks." Quickly, she opened the locks, glancing back as she heard the elevator clump. "Take shotgun, sir."

As he climbed in, she sent a warning stare toward Peabody. "Take the back. The commander's riding with us."

Eve slid behind the wheel. "Speed's key. We're going hot."

As Eve turned on the engine, screamed into reverse, Peabody leaned forward and murmured toward Whitney's ear, "Lock down your safety, sir. Trust me."

Sirens blaring, Eve burst out of the garage, barely hesitating to make sure traffic had cleared, and zipped around knotted cars, hit vertical to take the turn north.

"What *is* this thing?" Whitney demanded.

"It's a DLE, Commander," Peabody told him, strapped in, gripping the seat with both hands. "It's not even on the market yet."

"When it is, I want one."

So saying, he yanked out his 'link, made his first contact with Chief Tibble.

Eve blocked him out, zigging, zagging, leaping, and shoving her way through knots of traffic.

Multiple strikes on one of the busiest sectors of the city, the eternal party that was Times Square.

132

And a dead cop.

Mayhem would be putting it mildly.

She needed the scene secured, needed any potential wits quarantined and interviewed. She needed the dead protected, and the wounded, if any, out of harm's way.

She'd expected another strike, but to have it hit under twenty-four hours from the first . . . A pattern, an agenda. Maybe a fricking mission.

Killers on a mission didn't stop until they'd completed it.

"Peabody, tag Yancy, put a fire under his ass. I need those sketches. Get out of the fucking way! Do you *hear* the sirens?"

She went up, fast, skimmed over a couple of Rapid Cabs that appeared to be playing Chicken on Eighth.

As she'd suspected, when she nipped across Seventh, bulled onto Broadway, mayhem reigned.

A small platoon of uniforms fought to control hundreds. Panicked pedestrians, crazed vehicles, people with cameras and 'links trying to shove in for a better look, shopkeepers, waiters, street thieves — those seeing a bounty of profit in a small window of time.

The noise was amazing.

She stopped the car, flipped up her On Duty light, more to stop some overenthusiastic uniform from having it towed, and pushed clear.

"Commander . . . Sorry."

She shoved into the melee, leaving Whitney to Peabody, grabbed a megaphone from some hapless uniform. Bellowed into it.

"Get these people *back*. Now! I want the barricades up. Three uniforms to each DB, *now!* You." She grabbed another uniform by the coat sleeve. "Get this area blocked of any vehicular traffic other than official or emergency vehicles."

"But, Lieutenant — "

"Screw the buts. Do it. And you — " She grabbed another screen, all but heaved it at another uniform. "Privacy screens for the DBs. Why the hell are they still out in the open? Contain this crowd, do your goddamn job, and do it now. Peabody!"

"Sir!"

"I want fifty uniforms, asap. I need some fucking crowd control. Tag Morris. I want him on scene."

She snagged a thief by the collar of his oversized overcoat, shook him hard enough to have wallets and bags raining onto the ground. "You motherfucker. Show some respect. Get your ass out of here, or I'll personally see you rotting in a cage for the next twenty."

Maybe it was panic, or maybe he was pissed his payday got cut short, but he took a swing at her. The move surprised her enough — for God's sake, the place was swarming with cops — he actually glanced his fist off the side of her jaw.

More in fury than pain, she kneed him hard enough in the balls to flatten him, resisted — barely — kicking him for good measure. "Cuff him, haul his ass in. Now, fuck me, now! Are you cops or morons? Get me any and all security feeds on this area."

She shoved her way toward the body of Officer Kevin Russo, and the clutch of uniforms surrounding it.

"Give me room, move back. Give me his name."

"Officer Kevin Russo." Jacobs fought back tears. "I was with him. He's my partner. I — "

"Stay. The rest of you clear this crowd. Secure the goddamn scene. Backup's coming. Officer?"

"Jacobs. Sheridon Jacobs. We'd just come back from lunch break, sir. We were . . . " She took a hard breath, tried to steady herself. "We were moving toward a known street thief, and a woman went down — his mark went down. Hard and fast. I thought she'd fainted or had a medical issue. Then . . . it was a kid next. On an airboard. Kevin rushed toward him, shouting for people to take cover, to get down. And he went down, sir. I saw the strike take him, in the head. I — I moved to assist, and everything went crazy. I'm sorry, sir, it all went crazy, and I — we — couldn't control it. There weren't enough of us to control it."

"Which way was he facing?"

"Sir?"

"Pull it together, Jacobs. Which way was your partner facing when he was hit?"

"South, I think, south. It was so fast, Lieutenant, it all happened so fast. People dropping, people running, screaming, knocking each other over, trampling on them, on the bodies. I called for assistance, but it was a stampede."

"Okay. Stand by." Eve started to call for her field kit when Peabody pushed it into her hand.

"Dallas," Peabody said, gesturing.

Looking up, looking out, Eve saw that she was on every jumbo screen, coat flapping in the wind, face grim. The news ticker under her larger-than-life image, along with the dead cop at her feet, on the screen of One Times Square read:

LIEUTENANT EVE DALLAS, ON SCENE
AT TIMES SQUARE MASSACRE.

"For fuck's sake, kill that feed. Kill it!"

"I'm dealing with it." Whitney, his 'link at his ear, stared at the screens. "Do what you need to do. I'm dealing with it."

"He's ID'd by his partner," she told Peabody. "COD is pretty damn obvious. Get TOD. Make sure he gets a privacy curtain."

With her kit in hand, she crouched by the teenager Officer Kevin Russo had tried to shield.

She knew at a glance he was no more than seventeen, and would never see eighteen.

"Victim is mixed-race male, ID'd as Nathaniel Foster Jarvits, age seventeen. Today. Happy goddamn birthday. TOD, thirteen-twenty-one. ME will determine COD, but on-scene observation indicates laser strike, mid-back. Nearly the same hit as Ellissa Wyman." She paused. "Peabody, call the parents."

"Dallas, TOD on Officer Russo is thirteen-twenty-one as well."

Eve looked up, infuriated to see her own face still flashing on all the screens. No more respect than the

136

street thief, she thought, then rose and moved to the next.

She didn't look up at the screens again, didn't rail that she still had to raise her voice to get her findings on record. Quick glances showed her extra uniforms were swarming in, barricades were going up, and arrests were being made — loudly — as some refused to move back or to stop their attempts to record the horror.

She'd worked her way to what Jacobs reported was the first victim when Whitney crouched beside her.

"Feed's killed, but we can't stop the media from playing it on bulletins."

"I don't care."

"Your scene is now secured. This victim was with a friend who's been treated for shock, and can be interviewed. The minor was airboarding with five friends. They are all secured for interview. One other victim was unaccompanied at the time of the assault. And we have a survivor."

Her head whipped up. "A survivor?"

"Female. Office worker, but works downtown, doesn't usually come up around here. The strike hit her mid-body, left side. She'd been transported by medicals, is going into surgery. It's fifty-fifty, best."

"That's better odds than the other four. He won't like not making five for five. That'll piss him off. Sir, I need her under 24/7 protection — "

"Already done, Lieutenant. I'm a cop, not a moron."

"Apologies, Commander."

"No need. You pulled this together as quickly as anyone could." He looked back toward the curtained body of their fellow officer. "I don't think his partner's misremembering. Officer Russo gave his life protecting and serving."

"He may have been the target." She kept talking even when Whitney's eyes went hard. "Or the fourth vic, the advertising exec on his way to a lunch meeting. Not the kid — at least, it doesn't play right now. The first vic was a tourist. But Officer Russo? He was assigned this beat, he could be expected to be here at this time and place. The exec does work in the area, so maybe. None of the others, Commander. All the others were random hits. It's the cop, that's my lean. The cop who's connected. I'm going to find out why and how. They don't take one of ours and walk away. They don't take some harmless kid on his damn birthday and walk away."

She pushed to her feet. "Commander Whitney, I need to know everything there is to know about Officer Russo — personally and on the job. Everything. You could help with that. You could push that forward."

"Consider it pushed." His face stone, he looked toward the privacy curtain again, toward the uniforms ranged around it like an honor guard. "No, they don't take one of ours, not like this, and walk away." He, too, got to his feet. "Whatever you need, manpower, OT, it's yours."

"To start? I don't have time for a media conference."

"I'll cover you."

"I need Mira on tap."

"Done."

"I could use Nadine Furst — for media spin, for research."

He hesitated only a moment. "Tread carefully, but do what you feel needs doing. You'd be wise to coordinate with Kyung."

She nodded, and thought: Not an asshole. "Roarke. If he's available."

"Without question, and with appreciation from the department."

"Commander, if I'm on track, and Officer Russo or one of the other victims is connected to Michaelson — because it damn well has to be Michaelson, someway, somehow — this isn't over. It can't just be two. It's some sort of mission, and their connection will connect with someone else. Someone will know one of the shooters. Someone will recognize them. I need Yancy's sketches four-walled. You can push it out everywhere."

"Believe me, when we have those faces?" He once again glanced up at the jumbo screens, now unprecedentedly blank. "They'll be everywhere."

"They might dive into a hole once that happens. But the hole won't be deep enough." She looked around at the four bodies, curtained now from the gawkers. "I swear it won't be deep enough. Excuse me, sir, Morris is here. I need to speak with him."

As she walked away, Whitney stepped over to the fallen officer, pulled off the NYPSD lapel pin he wore, and laid it — reverently — on the shielded body.

CHAPTER
SEVEN

Morris's topcoat flapped as he stood over the body of the first victim. He pulled a can of Seal-It out of his own field kit, lifting his gaze to Eve as he coated his ungloved hands.

"I'll take them in order. Do you know if this is how and where she fell?"

"The bodies and the scene have been compromised." She stopped, shook her head. "Compromised, hell. They're FUBAR. I've called for any and all security feeds so we can reconstruct. The crowd panicked, and some, including at least some of the DBs, were trampled."

"An attack here?" He pulled gauges out of his kit. "We're lucky it isn't worse."

At the moment, Eve didn't want to think about worse. "ID'd as Fern Addison, age eighty-six. She was hit first, then the boy — Nathaniel Jarvits, age seventeen; then Officer Russo; then the male, David Chang, age thirty-nine. Another was hit, but survived — so far — she's in surgery.

"Four out of five then," Morris murmured, kneeling down by the body. "You've done your on-site on her?"

"Yes, all of them. We have TOD on all of them. You can verify."

"In this case, I will. It's best to be thorough." He arranged his gauges, engaged his recorder, and began. "Mid-body, deadly force. TOD thirteen-twenty-one. I can tell you more once I have her in my house. From this cursory examination, I'd say she was gone before she hit the ground."

He signaled to the morgue team. "They can be bagged, tagged, transported as we go."

Rising, he moved to the second victim. "Seventeen, you said."

"Yeah, seventeen. Today."

"Ah, Christ, life can be so cruel. Parents?"

"Yes, and a sibling. He was airboarding with friends, took the strike in the back, and — similar to Ellissa Wyman — the force and his own momentum propelled him forward into a group of pedestrians. Minor injuries, treated or being treated on scene."

"Mid-back, again from this on-site, similar to Ellissa Wyman."

Still he verified TOD.

"According to his partner, Officer Russo attempted to shield the boy, shouted for people to take cover. He was struck seconds later — at least according to my TOD results, he died seconds after the boy."

Once again Morris looked up, looked around. "You've contained this area quickly."

"Not quickly enough." She crouched beside him, decided she didn't give a rat's ass about the official record. "They had me and the victims on the goddamn jumbo screens. This kid's mother or father? They may see that replayed before we can notify them. I had to give that to Peabody."

Understanding, he touched her hand briefly, then rose to go to the fallen officer.

"He's young, too."

"Twenty-three."

"Head strike, mid-forehead. Do you suspect the shooter was showing off, as he was with the third victim at the rink?"

"I suspect the shooter knew Officer Russo would be wearing body armor as is procedure. He might have injured Russo with a body shot, but he wouldn't have taken him out. The goal was to take him out. You'll see the fourth victim was another body shot, and my information is the survivor was struck mid-body, but to the left. A few inches right, and she'd be lying here with the other four. She still may come to you."

"All victims are equal in my house, but . . . " Morris verified TOD.

"You kill a cop, it changes everything," Eve finished. "This shooter has to know that. There was a choice here, this was deliberate. He targeted a cop — and it may be he targeted this specific cop."

"Yet didn't stop there, but took another, and sent a fifth to surgery."

"I think — " She broke off as she heard the shouts, the hysteria. She saw a woman struggling with a pair of uniforms at the barricade, weeping, fighting, screaming a single name over and over.

Nate. Nathaniel Jarvits — the second victim.

"His mother," Morris said. "Would you like me to — "

"No, I've got it. Finish here, get the victims transported as soon as you can."

She rose, walked quickly.

Not even wearing a coat, Eve noted. The mother had run out of wherever she'd been in her street clothes.

"Mrs. Jarvits. Mrs. Jarvits! Look at me, look here. I'm Lieutenant Dallas."

"Nate. Nate. Where's my baby?"

"Mrs. Jarvits, I need you to come with me." Where the hell was she going to take her in this mess? As she considered her best options, Eve started to take off her coat, but Whitney moved more quickly.

"Mrs. Jarvits." He wrapped his own coat around her. "I'm Commander Whitney. Come with me now. Coffee shop." He gestured. "I've had it cleared. I'll take Mrs. Jarvits."

"Please, where's my son? Is he hurt? I need to see my son. He's Nathaniel Foster Jarvits. He's Nate."

Whitney wrapped an arm around her, steered her away as Peabody jogged up.

"I couldn't reach her. She must have seen a bulletin. I was able to contact the father, but I couldn't reach her. She works a few blocks away."

"She just ran," Eve concluded. "She saw the damn feed and she ran. All right." She took a breath to settle herself. "We'll take the witnesses in the coffee shop. We'll split them up. Jenkinson, Reineke."

"On the way. Traffic's insane. ETA ten minutes."

"Any word on the survivor?"

"Nothing new."

"Then let's do what we do." She looked over as Russo's bagged body was lifted onto a gurney for transport. At least a dozen uniforms stopped, stood. Saluted.

Eve did the same. "Whitney's giving a push on Russo. We'll have full data and we'll have it fast. He's priority — and not just because he's one of ours."

She scanned the faces of cops, then her eyes narrowed as Roarke moved around them, walking toward her. Inside the barricade.

She should've figured he'd beat her own detectives to the scene.

"You didn't need to drop everything and come here."

"I'm here. Whatever you need from me, you'll have. I'm sorry for your loss."

Nothing he could have said could have so completely closed her throat. He understood. She hadn't known Russo, but he'd been a cop, doing his best to serve and protect.

He'd died trying to protect.

Roarke shifted, shielding her from the sharpest bite of the wind. He didn't, as he wanted to, put his arms around her.

"The report said four dead, unknown injured."

"That's accurate. He went for five and one survived — so far. Others were injured in the panic."

"Whatever you need from me," he said again.

"If you could . . . " The sleet had turned to a thin, sad snow. As it fell, she took another moment to compose herself. "If you could work that program of yours on this incident. Coordinate with Feeney, or McNab, or both. Any data you can get is going to help. I nailed the first nest this morning using whatever the hell you put together."

"I'll start right away."

To her shock, he reached into the pocket of her coat. And he took out the gloves she'd forgotten she'd stuffed in there.

"Put these on. Your hands are cold. Once I have what I need out here," he continued, "is there a place you want me to work?"

Since he'd pointed it out, she realized her hands were cold. Pulling on the gloves, she huffed out a breath that formed a thin cloud, blew away in a snap of wind. "If you can get to my office, you can use that. Or if you need more room, Peabody can get you a conference room."

"Your office is fine. Otherwise, I'll use the lab in EDD. I know my way around."

"Yeah, you do. Looks like I owe you again."

"Not this time." He took her hand, squeezed it. "You have spare gloves in the dash box if you lose these. Take care of my cop."

It took more than two hours to clear the scene, to interview witnesses, to take contact information. She left Jenkinson and Reineke to deal with the dregs. Whitney had already left the scene, to personally notify the fallen officer's next of kin.

For a moment she just sat behind the wheel of her car, ordering her thoughts. Then, with no patience for knotted traffic, maxibuses, or anything else, hit the sirens.

"You'll head up to EDD," she told Peabody. "See if you can help in any way. The minute we have any target buildings, anything over seventy-five percent probability, I want detectives knocking on doors. Unless they're working hotter than this, they're all out there, working this. Can you coordinate that?"

"Yes, sir. I can take that."

"I'm going to sit on Yancy. We need those sketches. I need to talk to Nadine, work her into pushing angles we want pushed. I'll work with Morris, but I don't think he or the dead are going to tell us anything we don't know at this point. And with Mira, but same goes."

She drove fiercely, adding vicious blares of her horn to her sirens when people didn't get the hell out of her way fast enough.

"Here's a puzzle, Peabody. What do a respected OB-GYN and a cop still green under the edges have in common? Besides being dead."

"Why the cop, Dallas?"

"Because if you're killing for sport, no matter how cocky you are, most will lay off cops. This isn't sport. It's a mission. Because he was the only head shot. We need to find out what connects Michaelson and Russo, and we need to find out fast."

She pulled into the garage at Central, swung into her slot, braked hard. "Russo had just come back from his lunch break. Five minutes before, five minutes after, he's not in that spot. That's not a coincidence because — "

146

"Coincidences are bollocks," Peabody finished. "I got the memo."

"Fucking A, and according to his partner, they routinely took their break at that time, came back on duty at that time. A routine, Peabody, like Michaelson. None of the other victims had that routine. Only two out of the eight targeted had a routine, could be counted on to be where they were — that time, that place."

"Wyman," Peabody began.

"Was a regular at the rink, but she didn't go on specific days, at specific times, the way Michaelson did. She had a looser routine."

Eve strode toward the elevator. "They're trying to make it look random, but they can't. Because it's not. We'll find the link, we'll find the goddamn link, and we'll take them down."

"It's personal now. Don't say it's not," Peabody insisted. "It's always a little personal, but this is — "

She broke off when the elevator opened. Two uniforms and a couple of detectives stepped out. All four wore black armbands.

The older of the uniforms nodded to them. "Lieutenant, Detective. Anything you need."

Eve nodded in return, but said nothing as she stepped in, ordered their level.

Because Peabody was right. It was personal now.

Eve split off, headed straight to Yancy's division. More black armbands — it didn't take long for the word to spread. She nearly stopped short when she saw the pretty blond standing with Yancy at his desk. Laurel Esty, she remembered, a key witness in a recent investigation. One who'd worked well with Yancy.

Laurel brushed a hand down Yancy's arm, turned to go. When she saw Eve, she smiled in recognition, then her big eyes sobered.

"Lieutenant Dallas, I'm really sorry about what happened. I just stopped by to . . . Well, I'm just leaving."

"Okay."

"Ah, bye, Vince."

"I'll see you later." Yancy looked at Eve as Laurel wound her way out. He wasn't a blusher like Trueheart, but if he had been, his handsome face would have reddened all the way to his curly mop of hair.

"Um, she was just . . . "

"Leaving."

"Right. We were going to try to meet up for drinks, but . . ."

"Drinks?"

"Yeah, we're sort of seeing each other."

"Not my business."

"Well, no, but . . . Anyway."

"I'm a little more interested in the sketches. Your progress there."

"Right, which is why I canceled the drinks deal. It's taken me longer than I wanted, and Henry was a hell of a good wit — which is partially why. He gets details — and more of them when I asked if Mira would work with us. She does this cognitive memory thing and he struck me as a good candidate."

148

After a glance around, he dragged over a second chair from an unoccupied desk. "I wanted to let it sit an hour, go back and refine, but here's what I've got for you."

She sat, waited while he ordered the sketches on a split screen.

Eve's cop gut did a fast dance. "Jesus, Yancy, these are the next thing to photos."

"Credit Henry. Seriously."

She'd credit Henry later, but right now she studied the artist/comp concepts of a white male, early fifties, square-jawed, hard-eyed. Not what she'd call a gaunt face, but thin in a way that read illness or loss of appetite to her. Short, not quite military short, medium-brown hair worn in a brushback.

Clean-shaven, tight-lipped, fuller on the top. Eyebrows thick and nearly straight.

She switched to the second sketch.

No more than sixteen, still a little dewy, rounder in the cheeks, softer in the jaw. A mixed-race heritage in the deepness of the eye color, in the soft brown skin tone, in the texture of the hair — black hair in dreads under a ski cap.

But the shape of the eyebrows and jaw — that slightly fuller upper lip . . .

"I lean female," Yancy said, "but that's just impression. Could be a boy — Henry leaned boy by the end of our session. Boys can have a softness to them at that age. Male, I'd say no more than fourteen. Girl, maybe up to sixteen."

"They're related."

"I'm going with you there. Might be father and kid, or he could be an uncle, but there's a familial resemblance. Shape of the jaw, eyebrows, mouth. I've got more — full body on each."

"Have you run any face-recognition?"

"Not yet, I wanted to tweak a little."

"Run now, tweak later. Filter the run on the adult with military or police training. Let's see what pops."

"Hang on." Yancy swiveled to another screen, started the program, added the filters. "You should see the full-body. Even if we don't release these, it'll give you a clear sense of build, on both."

He brought up the next sketches, showing the adult male — broad-shouldered, long-legged. He struck her, again, as someone who'd lost weight, maybe some muscle tone. Not a weak sister, she mused, but due to illness or stress. A little hollow-eyed.

The minor suspect was definitely a more delicate build, but compact rather than gangly. Tough and . . .

"Kid's fit — there's a springy look there."

"Springy," Yancy repeated. "Yeah, yeah, that's a good word for it. I think — Wow, we got a hit already. I don't think it's going to . . . "

He trailed off as the ID image popped on screen. Then let out a deep breath, said, "Hot, holy fuck, Dallas."

Eyes on the ID shot, Eve gripped Yancy's arm. Hard. "Hold it down," she murmured.

"He's a cop," Yancy said under his breath. "He's a goddamn cop."

"Was," Eve corrected.

150

Reginald Mackie, age fifty-four, retired after twenty years on the NYPSD — the last eleven of them in Tactical. Prior to joining the force, he'd been U.S. Army — a weapons expert.

He'd been Lowenbaum's.

"Send me everything, now. And don't talk to anybody — anybody — Yancy, about this until I clear it."

She didn't sprint away, though she wanted to. Cops observed, and the primary in this investigation running through Central would lead many to the correct conclusion. She had a hot lead.

But she moved fast, yanking out her 'link as she went. "Lowenbaum. My office, asap."

"I've got a — "

"Drop it. Whatever it is, drop it, and move."

She cut him off without waiting for an assent, contacted Whitney next. "Sir, I need a conference room, and your presence, and Mira's, as quickly as possible."

"I'm on my way back from the notification." He studied her face, and she saw realization come into his eyes. "Twenty minutes. I'll take care of the room and Mira."

She risked the sprint on the glides — it wouldn't be the first time she'd bulled her way up or down them — and contacted Feeney next.

"I need you, Roarke, and McNab if you can spare him."

She didn't have to explain, not to Feeney. He only nodded. "Give us ten."

"My bullpen if you make it in under ten. Conference room — you'll need to check the log for which one — if it's longer."

She clicked off again, stepped into her own bullpen. "Whatever you're doing, stop. I want everyone who isn't about to close the case of the decade to prep for a full briefing and op."

"Yancy hit." Peabody pushed to her feet. "How sure are we?"

"I'm going with a hundred on that. Lowenbaum's on his way, the commander is booking a conference room. We roll there as soon as it's ready. And we keep this right here for now."

"Fuck me." Face grim, Baxter clenched his fists. "It's a cop."

"I'll have more data shortly. Close out whatever you've got — and if you can't, explain why, my office, in five. Peabody, with me."

Swinging off her coat, Eve strode to her office. "Computer, background data, in full, on Tactical Officer Reginald Mackie, on screen."

Acknowledged. Working . . .

"Close the door," she ordered Peabody, then began reading.

"Enlisted, U.S. Army, in 2029, pulled out in 2039, as a sergeant. Trained sniper, instructor. Started on the job six months later, moved to Tactical in '49. Retired last year, spring. Last CO — Lowenbaum."

She paced as she read. Without asking, Peabody programmed coffee, passed a mug to her.

"Married Zoe Younger, 2045, one offspring, female, Willow, age fifteen. Computer, ID photo and data on Willow Mackie."

When it came up, Eve studied it with cool, flat eyes. The hair, a bit longer than the sketch, but it was as in the bag as Reginald's.

"She's the one with him," Eve said. "That's confirmed. Divorced — Reginald Mackie, that is, 2052. Start running the ex-wife, Peabody. I want her current status, address. Who has custody of the kid."

"I'm on it."

"Married Susann Prinz, 2059. Widowed — and there it is, I'd bet my ass — 2059. November 2059. Married March, widowed November. Computer: How did Susann Prinz die?"

Accessing . . . Prinz, Susann, age thirty-two at time of death, was killed when struck by a vehicle as she crossed East Sixty-Fourth between Fifth and Madison Avenues. According to the accident report and witnesses, Prinz ran out between parked vehicles, and was struck when the oncoming vehicle was unable to stop. No charges were filed against the driver, Brian T. Fine, age sixty-two. Do you wish the full incident report and all follow-up data?

"Yeah, lock that in, but give me the name of the officer or officers who responded to the scene."

First-on-scene, and the officer of record, was Officer Kevin Russo, badge number —

"Hold that. That's enough. Was Prinz pregnant?"

Prinz was sixteen weeks pregnant at time of death.

"Her doctor? Her — what is it — obstetrician?"

One moment . . . accessing . . . Her obstetrician of record was Dr. Brent Michaelson.

"Pause run," she said at the knock on the door, and went to open it herself. "Lowenbaum. I need everything you can tell me on Reginald Mackie."

"What?" Shock, an instant denial registered on his face. "No. Come on, Dallas."

Deliberately, she shut the door behind him. "You knew he was off — you'd have seen it. Think back."

"Well, Christ." He took a moment, scrubbed his hands over his face. "Listen, Mac was wound tight, but a lot of Tacticals are. He was a good, solid cop. I worked with him for a dozen years. His wife died — an accident. They hadn't been married a year, and she was pregnant, and he . . . "

Eve waited until Lowenbaum added it up, fast. "Ah, fuck it. Fuck. This is about Susann. It has to be about Susann. He has another kid, a girl, about fourteen, fifteen."

"Willow, fifteen, ID'd as the second suspect. I'm going to fill you in, and you're going to fill us in. And

154

you're going to pick your best men — I want officers who can keep the lid shut — and prepare for a takedown."

"A lot of my best men worked with Mac. Susann's cousin's on the job, a friend of mine. That's how they met."

A former cop, Eve thought, with twenty in, would have a lot of friends and connections on the job.

"Pick carefully. And remember he's responsible for seven deaths, and one of them was a cop. A twenty-three-year-old uniform whose last act was trying to shield another victim. Mackie gets wind we've ID'd him, he'll either rabbit or he'll go the last-stand route."

"He won't rabbit." Pale, Lowenbaum scrubbed at his face again, pressed his fingers hard against his eyes. "Give me a few minutes to settle into this, order my thoughts. I know him as well as anybody, I'd say."

"And the kid? Do you know the kid?"

"Yeah, yeah, I know Will, a little anyway. She idolizes him. She's been in some trouble here and there — school shit — and her mother remarried, had another kid. It's split custody with Will. Let me organize this in my head. We have to stop him, and I'd like him to be alive after we do. Let me think."

"Think here. Peabody, find our conference room."

"It's A."

"Let's take what we've got, move this there. I need you in ten, Lowenbaum, organized or not."

"Ten's good."

Within five, Eve was putting her board together, putting her thoughts together, putting the outline of an op together.

When her detectives and uniforms began to file in, she glanced back at Uniform Carmichael.

"Uniform Carmichael, I need the following people brought in for protective custody. Brian T. Fine, Zoe Younger, Lincoln Stuben, Zach Younger Stuben, age seven, Marta Beck. Peabody will give you home and work addresses. If these individuals don't cooperate, arrest them for impeding a police investigation. Send out whatever people you need, and get those individuals into Central as soon as possible. You'll be fully briefed subsequently. Peabody, get him those addresses — home and employment. No chatter, Carmichael. Absolutely none."

"No chatter, LT. Absolutely none."

Eve went back to her board as Feeney came in with Roarke and McNab, as Lowenbaum — no longer pale — followed.

"Grab chairs, grab coffee if you need it. We start as soon as the commander and Mira are in the room."

Roarke moved to her, spoke quietly. "It's one of yours?" At her nod, he simply looked into her eyes, didn't touch her as he wanted. "I'm sorry."

"Yeah, so am I."

She heard Mira's heels — *brisk, brisk, brisk.* "Maybe you can see if there's any of that flower tea crap Mira drinks in this AutoChef. This is going to take a while. You didn't order in a bunch of food, did you?"

"No."

"Good. Don't. This is the sort of thing you're better off going into hungry."

She already had Mackie's ID photo — along with Yancy's sketch. Willow Mackie's beside it on the board. And the room full of cops muttered and mumbled around it.

Then Whitney stepped in — with Chief Tibble — and the room silenced.

"Lieutenant," Tibble said, and moved to a chair. "You have the room."

"Yes, sir. Everybody, take a seat, listen up."

CHAPTER
EIGHT

Eve turned to the board.

"Our suspects are Reginald Mackie, age fifty-four, former Tactical officer, NYPSD." She expected the mutters, rode over them. "And his daughter, Willow Mackie, age fifteen. We've identified these suspects through an eyewitness working with Detective Yancy. In addition to the physical identification, Mackie fits the profile. He was Army, weapons specialist and instructor, and for the last dozen years was part of our own Tactical unit."

She paused, focused on the image of an attractive woman. "While Willow Mackie was produced with his first wife, that relationship ended in divorce several years ago, and in joint custody of the minor child. Zoe Younger subsequently remarried and has a second offspring. Younger, her husband, and younger child are now being taken into protective custody. I believe the impetus for the recent strikes stems from the death of Mackie's second wife, Susann Prinz Mackie, shown here, and the fetus she carried. They died in a traffic accident in November of 2059. The full incident report is available, but to sum up: Mrs. Mackie ran out into the street into oncoming traffic and was struck and

158

killed. Accident reconstruction as well as eight eyewitnesses confirmed the driver, Brian T. Fine, was not at fault. Mr. Fine is also being brought into protective custody.

"Mrs. Mackie's doctor — whose offices are roughly a block from the accident scene — was Brent Michaelson, a victim in the strikes on Wollman Rink in Central Park yesterday. The first-on-scene at Susann Prinz Mackie's accident, and the officer in charge, was Kevin Russo, who was killed in the line of duty at Times Square this afternoon."

Eve stopped, looked at Mira. "Dr. Mira, would you concur Reginald Mackie is targeting individuals connected in some way to his wife's death?"

"I'll familiarize myself with all the data as soon as possible, but yes. The evidence clearly shows the suspect is targeting specific people through this connection. The others are a kind of cover. He has reached a point where these lives mean nothing. And to have involved his teenage daughter . . . I would say he believes this is not only revenge but justice.

"He is showing her, firsthand, his definition of justice."

"I think it's more than involving her, showing her. In each incident one of the victims was also a teenager. Serial killers most usually have a type. I believe Ellissa Wyman and Nathaniel Jarvits are Willow Mackie's type. Not just a cover for her. I don't believe Mackie himself would target a child or anyone near his daughter's age."

"You believe this teenage girl is the killer?" Whitney demanded.

"Sir, Mackie's time, due to divorce, with his first child is halved," Eve pointed out. "He lost the potential of a child. I don't see him targeting the young."

"Psychologically that may be sound enough." Whitney glanced toward Mira.

"Yes. It's possible."

"But the skill required here is more than considerable."

"Yes, sir. Lieutenant Lowenbaum, do you know if Mackie has trained or instructed his daughter in weaponry?"

"Yes. In fact, I've seen her on the range, dropped by one of her competitions."

"Competitions?"

"Target and combat simulation competitions. Nonlethal weaponry. Mac took her to the range regularly, and entered her in competitions. He was proud of how well she did."

"Willow Mackie has the training and the skill?" Eve prompted.

"I wouldn't have said she was good enough to . . . I haven't seen Willow in a couple of years, only saw her on the range with Mac a few times, and at the one competition. She was good," he admitted, blew out a breath. "She was better than good, and Mac was very proud of her abilities and interest.

"But these strikes? It takes better than good."

A couple years of practice, Eve thought, can hone a skill. "What can you tell us about their relationship?"

"They were always pretty tight. In fact, a couple years back she pushed to live with him full-time. He was considering it, especially after he married Susann, then after the accident, he wasn't in any shape to raise a teenage girl on his own."

"What was his state of mind?"

"Let me go back a little. I've known Mac for a long time. The last four years as his LT. He keeps his head — or did. He didn't like his ex's husband, but most of that came off as just the usual sort of resentment. He spent as much time with Willow as he could manage — the job can interfere, but he made her a priority. I know she started getting in some trouble at school, and his ex wanted her to go to a therapist. She didn't want to, and Mac backed the kid."

"Dr. Mira, could you find out if Willow Mackie did indeed see a therapist? You saw a change in him after the accident," Eve said to Lowenbaum.

"Yeah, no question there. It shattered him. I ordered him to take hardship leave because he wasn't steady. Who would be? I heard some talk about him seeing a lawyer, trying to go after the driver, but he wasn't talking to me much."

"Pissed at you?"

"Yeah, maybe. Some. We need to talk to Vince Patroni, from my unit. They were closest. Mac wasn't the same when he came back on the roll. He'd lost weight, was too often distracted. And angry under it. He never came in drunk, but I know he hit the bottle hard off duty for a while. But that stopped. Still, he wasn't solid. He was shaky and he was pissed. He was coming up on his twenty, so I talked to him about either turning in his papers or a reassignment."

"Did you push it?"

"Didn't have to. He said he'd already decided to take his twenty and be done. Have more time with his daughter, maybe travel some. I tagged him a couple of times after that, to see if he wanted to have a brew, grab a meal, but he put me off. I let it go."

"I need Patroni brought in."

"I'll get him."

"If they were close, he may feel some loyalty."

"I'll get him," Lowenbaum repeated, "I'll make certain he doesn't contact Mac."

Eve nodded. "It's highly possible the suspects have other connections to and communications with the NYPSD. It's imperative we keep this information inside this room. Any indication we have a suspect or are looking for Mackie may cause him to go under. Or it may force him into a confrontation. He's killed or encouraged his daughter to kill a police officer. He won't hesitate to do so again, even knowing the result may be his own termination."

"It's highly possible that's his end goal," Mira pointed out. "He has nothing to live for once this mission is completed or aborted. If he plans to protect his daughter, the best way to do so is his own death. The killings would be blamed solely on him, and as a minor, she could claim coercion, emotional instability."

"Which is why we need to take them quickly, smoothly, and soon. The suspect has an apartment on the sixth floor of a residential building on East Twenty-Fourth. Captain Feeney, I need an EDD team to determine if both suspects are in that apartment. A cop with that much experience would know what to look for."

"We can get around that. Don't happen to own that building, do you?" Feeney said to Roarke.

"No," Roarke responded, already checking on his PPC. "But I do own one across the street that might be helpful."

"Lowenbaum, I need a unit. Again, he'll know what to look for."

"And we know how to get around that."

"Reineke, Jenkinson, Santiago, Carmichael, you're on takedown. Baxter, Trueheart, you're on data and interviews. Trueheart will soften the mother up," Eve added before Baxter could object. "We're going to need her cooperation. Baxter, you're going to sit hard on Patroni, put the fear of God into him, if necessary. Fuck his loyalty, if any, to Reginald Mackie. I want three officers, soft clothes, to check out the minor suspect's school."

"School would be over for the day, Lieutenant," Peabody told her.

"There may be staff still there, after-school shit going on. We may be able to determine if she has any particular hangout. If we can take her outside the apartment, we take her. We're not just taking down serial killers, we're taking down a veteran police officer and his teenage daughter. We need it clean.

"We need a warrant to search the mother's residence, get into the kid's room there."

"Consider it done," Whitney told her.

"Peabody and I will handle that search before or after the takedown, depending on timing. The mother's residence is on First. Anyone not on takedown, get started now."

"One moment." Tibble rose, tall and lean and, under the control, Eve noted, furious. "I'd like to add to Lieutenant Dallas's statement. Reginald Mackie served the city and its people for twenty years. But he has broken his oath, his faith, his duty. He is responsible for the death of another police officer and six other citizens, one a minor. He has done this for his own purposes, and has disgraced himself, has made his own child an accessory at best, a killer at worst. Knock him down, take him out, bring him in. I would prefer he still be breathing at the end of this operation, but I want no other good cops killed today. Serve and protect, not just the citizenry, but each other. Lieutenant Dallas, good work. Commander, we have work of our own to do to support those who are going out into harm's way."

Eve let out a breath when Tibble walked out with Whitney. "He is pissed."

"So am I." Lowenbaum pushed to his feet. "I never saw it. You asked me, dead on, who I knew who could make these strikes. Mackie never blipped on my screen."

"Let me ask you now: Could he have executed these strikes?"

"Possibly. He wouldn't have been high on my list, but possibly. The thing is, he's been off my screen for close to a year. I never pushed to see how he was doing.

If I had, I might have had a better sense where his head was at."

"You said you tagged him."

"I didn't push."

"Were you pals?"

"No, not really. But we were comrades. I was his supervising officer when he broke."

"And you did what you could for him. Don't go there, Lowenbaum. If you have to go there, save it for later. Get me a SWAT team, one that knows how to take a suspect of this caliber alive, and can keep a lid on it."

On a brisk nod, he left the room.

"Feeney."

"Just hold it, your man's working on something."

"I've got something," Roarke corrected, "again that might be useful. Can I use the screen there?" Without waiting, he rose, walked over, and interfaced his PPC with the room comp.

"Your suspect's building," he began, when the image came on. "We'll draw in on his apartment. It's apartment 612, according to my data."

"Okay."

"And my building, just diagonal from the target. We have an unoccupied apartment — actually three altogether, but this one on the seventh floor provides a good location to set up. We could do a heat sensor search from there, and potentially set up ears at least, depending on the target's shielding."

"Do that," Eve said.

"How about we add this?" Feeney scratched his chin. "People move in, move out. We use a small moving van. We get McNab here, maybe another boy to cart in some boxes, or furniture, and our equipment moves in without sending up any flags."

"How soon can you have it set up?"

"Fifteen, maybe twenty."

"Roll it. Baxter, Trueheart, start compiling data, and check with Uniform Carmichael. Start the interview process as soon as we've got some of these people in the house. See if you can get the name of the lawyer Mackie talked to. We need to bring him in. He may be a target."

"Protecting a lawyer." Baxter shook his head. "What the hell. Come on, partner, let's get this started."

With only her takedown team in the room, Eve turned to the screen. "Okay, here's how I see it going."

Within thirty minutes, as data continued to stream in, Eve had her team in a police van, outfitted not only with body armor, but helmets. Which meant she had to do the same. While the coat took care of the body armor, the helmet bugged the crap out of her.

But a head shot would do worse.

Inside the van, on screen, she watched the feed Feeney sent her. She watched McNab and Callendar, looking every bit like a happy couple moving into a new place, haul boxes into Roarke's building.

"No heat source in suspect's apartment," Feeney told her. "We're running that from the van for now. They're not in there."

"When you're ready, McNab and Callendar can run that from inside, and you move off."

"Your man has a garage about a block away. We'll go in there, sit awhile. Lowenbaum's team is moving into position. One of them will use the apartment, two on the roof, and another two in another empty apartment in Roarke's building. See the window of the suspect's apartment?"

"Yeah, yeah. Privacy screened. I'm going to hit the mother's place now. Jenkinson, you're in charge here till I get back — sit tight. Peabody, I want constant reports. Roarke, you're with me. I'll be heading east, then south, on foot. I can be back here inside five minutes, so I need to know the first sighting on either suspect."

She stepped out of the van, moved fast. The suspects could be back any minute — or not for hours. Any data she could dig up might pinpoint their next target. Even now they might be holed up in some hotel room, some flop, some empty office space, preparing to strike again.

Nothing fell out of the sky now as the ugly day headed toward a bitter evening. Streetlights shimmered on, cutting the gloom with chilly white pools of light. As she walked, she studied faces. Pedestrians hurrying home, or to meet up for drinks, to get in more shopping. Others huddled at a cart that smelled of soy dogs and really terrible coffee.

They could walk here, she thought, father and daughter, back to the apartment, out to grab a slice. They *would* have walked here at some point, from the townhouse to the apartment.

Had they plotted along the way? Who to kill and when?

A block and a half from Zoe Younger's townhouse, Roarke stepped up beside her. "Lieutenant."

"I want to hit the kid's room. Whitney got the warrant for the whole place, but we're going to focus on the girl's room. It's unlikely the rest of this family are involved, or she'd leave handy clues in the living area."

"Understood."

When he took her hand, she linked her fingers with his. On duty, yeah, but no cops around to see.

"We will take a pass at any and all electronics — and flag them for EDD."

"I expect I'll be entirely more useful there than tossing a teenage girl's room."

She frowned up at him as they swam across the crosswalk with the tide of people. "You were a teenage boy — there can't be that much difference between male and female at that age."

"Oh, only worlds, I imagine." With her, he made the turn, walked up the five steps to the front right door of the pretty duplex. As he spoke, he took out his tools — quicker than her master, she thought, eyeing the security.

"You were a teenage girl."

"Not so much, or only sort of."

"As I was not so much, or only sort of a teenage boy, how well we suit. They have excellent security," he added, sliding through it like a knife through warmed butter.

168

"We clear it first." Eve drew her weapon. "Just in case."

After his nod, they went through the door together.

"NYPSD," she called out, sweeping left. "We've entered the premises duly warranted."

"No one's here — you can feel an empty house," Roarke said. "Ah, there was a day when a B and E into an empty house was my favorite thing."

"Now you get to do it legally."

"Not nearly the same."

While she agreed with the empty, she cleared the first level — living area, kitchen, dining, a home office, and a kind of family entertainment area.

The house smelled of the spicy rust-and-pumpkin-colored flowers on the dining room table. Some sort of board on the kitchen wall held kid art — weird stick figures, trees with blobs of green representing leaves. A kind of chart that listed duties — chores, she corrected — like clearing the table, setting it, making beds.

Beside the chart someone had pinned a Christmas photo. Zoe Younger, Lincoln Stuben, Zach Stuben, and Willow Mackie in a group in front of a festive tree, presents stacked beneath.

All smiled but Willow, who stared into the camera with hard green eyes and the faintest hint of a smirk.

"Arms folded." Eve tapped the picture. "There's defiance there. The boy? He looks happy enough to do handsprings for a few hours, and the parents look happy, content. Her? That's a fuck-you stare."

"Indeed it is, and I suspect Mira would add she's separated herself — the folded arms, the bit of distance while the other three are all touching. Then again, fifteen? It's an age, isn't it, to consider your parents the enemy."

"Hard for us to say. The ones we had *were* the enemy. But, on the surface anyway, it looks like these two worked to give happy and stable. The house is clean, but it's not sterile or perfect. Kid-type cereal box on the counter, a couple dishes in the sink, the boy's skids under a chair in the living area, somebody's sweater on the back of a chair over there."

He glanced over — hadn't noticed. "You're a wonder."

"I'm a cop," she corrected. "You've got this task chart — everybody does their share, and that's probably a good thing. Kid's weird drawings displayed. The family Christmas picture."

She took one more look around. "Reads normal, except it isn't. Under the surface, it isn't."

They went upstairs to the second floor, cleared that: the master suite, the attached office, the boy's room — a minor disaster area with strewn toys, vid games, clothes. A guest room identified as such by its pristine, unlived-in feel, then the girl's.

And there was a third floor, a kind of casual family area for watching screen, hanging out — which the scatter of games proved they did — with a small kitchenette and a half bath.

Eve headed straight back down to Willow's room.

Bed, sloppily made, and with none of the fussy pillows or weird stuffed animals Eve had encountered in other teenagers' rooms. A desk and comp under the window, a lounge chair, some shelves.

Posters on the walls. Some music group all in black with snarling faces and lots of tats. The rest were weapons, or someone holding weapons. Knives, banned guns, blasters.

"Clear where her interests are," Eve commented, moving to the closet.

A few girlie dresses — some with the tags still on them. Most of the clothes ran to black or dark colors, rougher styles.

"There's an order in here," she observed. "She knows where she puts her things, wants everything in its place. And if her mother or her brother poke around in here, she knows it."

Roarke had already started on the computer. "She has this passcoded, and fail-safed. A very intricate job for someone her age." He pulled out the desk chair and sat to work.

Eve started on the dresser. Plain underwear, winter socks, sweaters, sweats, all organized without looking overly so.

Purposely, she thought. Yes, she'd know if her mother shifted a pair of socks in the drawer.

"Keep going on that, but she wouldn't leave anything in here she didn't want her mother to find."

"You're sure of that?"

"She put a slide lock on the inside of the door — they took it off." Eve nodded toward the door and the telltale marks. "Everything in here is arranged in a kind of system. I always did the same — in foster care, in state. You want to know where your things are so, if necessary, you can grab what matters most, is needed most, and run. Or so you know when they've done the look-through. I'm betting her mother does the regular look-through. Mother swallows the posters," Eve continued as she kept searching. "Making the girl take them down only entrenches the interest, drives it deeper under. So she swallows that. But she's had the room painted in this pale, pretty blue, buys dresses that aren't worn — unless she forces that issue. She comes in, looking for something, anything, to give her more insight into her daughter. Or — more *and* — because she's worried she'll find illegals or weapons or a journal full of ugly thoughts."

"Did you have one? A journal."

"No, I kept my ugly thoughts to myself because they always . . . The brother's room!"

When Eve walked out, Roarke arched his eyebrows. He finished bypassing the fail-safe, then rose to see what his cop was up to.

She sat at the boy's comp in the middle of his boy mess.

"I didn't always keep my thoughts — ugly or otherwise — to myself. That's learned behavior, that's experience. Sometimes you're just writing a paper for school, and they get into your comp, and you get punished for writing how you like riding an airboard. So you start doing those papers in school, mostly. Or you're bored and unhappy and you write down some stupid wish list, and they find that, and you get your ass kicked over it."

Roarke brushed a kiss over the top of her head, said nothing — which said everything.

"It's not about me, it's just about . . . A couple of times when I needed to write something down — when you just need that tangible act — I figured out how to sort of hide it on another comp. One they didn't bother with. You've got a real kid — I mean the foster's real kid — in the house, and he's gold in their eyes, you can use that. The thing is, if she used that method, she's probably a hell of a lot better at it than I was — than I am."

"Let me."

When she rose, he took her by her shoulders, looked into her eyes. "What did you need to write down?"

"I kept a calendar — almost always, wherever I was — marking time till I could get out. For good. How many years, months, weeks, days, hours sometimes, before I could. How I was going to get out, go to New York. New York seemed so big and full, so I focused on New York pretty early. And the Academy. How I was going to be a cop because cops took care of themselves, and everyone else. Good cops, anyway, and I was going to be a good cop, and no one was ever going to tell me what and when to eat, what to wear — "

"And now I do."

She shook her head. "Not the same. Not close to the same. No one loved me, and maybe along the way that became my fault as much as the system's, but no one loved me. No one said eat something because I love you, because you matter. I was just another number

173

until I earned the badge. I was just a badge, mostly just a badge, until I earned you."

She took a breath. "I could have been this girl, Roarke."

"No."

"Yes, or at least something like her. If Feeney had been a different kind of cop, a different kind of man. If he'd been like Mackie, broken and twisted like Mackie. He *saw* me. Really saw me, and he pulled me out of the rest, paid attention, gave me time, gave me him. No one had, ever, offered me what he did. No one, ever, saw me like he did. I wanted to make him proud of me, wanted to be the kind of cop he'd be proud of. It drove me.

"And doesn't it look like she wants to be what her father wants? That is part, a big part, of what drives her."

"If the last part of that's true, it means she's turned her back on everything else she has. A mother, a brother. A good home from the looks of it."

"Maybe, but looks don't always mean dick. We'll see about that. But perception's truth, right? If nothing else, she perceived no one sees her, gets her, cares about her — not like her father. And she's killing for him. Killing because he's trained her, taught her to see that as her right, or at least as an answer."

She shook it off, had to shake it off. "It only matters why right now if the why helps us find them, stop them. So yeah, you take a look. Given his age, they probably have parental controls on this unit, but she could have hidden her own files in there."

174

"Easily enough."

"If so, you'll find them. I'm going to go back to her room."

Eve checked in with Peabody — no movement — then stood in the center of Willow Mackie's bedroom. A good space, fully triple the size she'd been able to claim at the same age. Nicely, comfortably furnished. The clothes all good quality.

No photographs, not of herself, her family and friends. Not even of her father. Maybe some on her computer, Eve thought, and she'd look there.

She searched through the three drawers in the desk, found a few school-type supplies. No junk. None of the weird junk teenage girls — and boys, for that matter — collected.

No discs, she realized. Data or music. No other electronics. No PC, no tablet.

Because she carted them with her, one week here, one week there?

Her gaze passed over the posters. Weaponry, violence. Would a teenager so focused on weapons live every other week without access to any?

She stepped back into the closet. A smallish space with that same sense of organization. The fussy clothes — obviously the mother's pick — in the back. And there, still in their boxes, a pair of heels, a pair a boots — both clearly, even to her eye, meant to go with the dresses or more stylish pants.

And both, she determined, studying the soles, never worn.

In the toe of a well-worn boot she found a little stash of cash. Just a couple hundred, which made Eve feel as if it had been put there deliberately, something her mother could find.

In the pocket of a hoodie she found a notebook and, engaging it, heard a girl's voice — a shock how young — complaining about her brother, her mother, her stepfather. How they didn't understand her. And on and on.

Also so her mother could find it, Eve thought, bagging it for evidence. They'd listen to all the whines and complaints, but the last entry at least had been clearly designed to make her mother feel guilty if she searched and found it.

So she wouldn't hide anything important in the closet, Eve determined.

Though she didn't believe she'd find anything in usual places, she checked them anyway.

She went over the closet floor, the walls, even the ceiling, looked under the bed, between mattresses, checked the cushions of the desk and lounge chairs, under and behind the desk.

She judged the dresser too heavy to be moved out without showing scuffs on the floor, but tried it anyway, looked under it, pulled the drawers out, looked under them.

As she slid the bottom drawer back into place, the design beneath it caught her eye. A kind of braiding, about two inches high, ran along the base. And when she'd slid that drawer in, pulled it out, there'd been the slightest need to tug, and the faintest little *click*.

Nothing that out of the ordinary, but . . .

She took the bottom drawer out again. It was a well-made piece of furniture, sturdy, nicely crafted of engineered wood.

The bottom drawer rested on a slab of that wood.

Curious, she ran her fingers over the twisted braid of decoration along the base, pushing, prying. Felt one twist give, just the tiniest bit.

She tugged. Nothing.

She kept working along the braid, found another twist give, then a third.

She didn't have to tug. The narrow hidden drawer slid out toward her.

Empty, she noted. Empty but for the cushioning foam with cutouts for two knives and two hand weapons. Blasters by her eye. Another cutout, a rectangle, would easily hold several IDs, maybe more cash, Eve thought.

"She's not coming back here," she murmured.

"I agree," Roarke said from the doorway. "You'll want to see this. You were right about using the younger brother's unit. The file I found was cleverly hidden. And even then," he continued as they walked back to the brother's room, "she was careful. This isn't a rash or impulsive young girl."

"Not even close." Eve studied the first document on screen. "It's their hit list. Just initials, not full names, but there's BM, KR — Michaelson, Russo — there's MB — and I'm betting on Marta Beck, Michaelson's office manager, there's BF, that's going to be Fine, the driver who hit the second wife. One of these others —

AE, JR, and MJ — is likely the lawyer we haven't identified. And two others. Two down, five to go."

"There's a second page to this document." Roarke ordered it on screen.

"Zach Stuben — that's her brother. Lincoln Stuben, her stepfather. Christ, her mother's on here. Rene Hutchins, Thomas Greenburg, Lynda Track — we need to identify them. And this one with initials. HCHS."

"It's her high school — I'm sure of it, as I found this document as well." Roarke called up a blueprint of Hillary Clinton High School. "Certain classrooms, certain areas were highlighted, egresses marked."

"Jesus, Jesus. She plans to hit her school."

"And already has her nest chosen. Closer this time than the other two attacks, but still an appreciable distance."

Eve looked at the next image. "The roof of her father's apartment building. She has these hidden here because this isn't her father's agenda. It's hers. When they finish his mission, she can begin her own. How hard did you have to look to find this?"

"A bit of work, but more to the point, I likely wouldn't have found it if I hadn't been specifically looking for it. It was shielded under a perfectly harmless school report on George Washington."

Eve paced. "Okay, let's get back. We need to access Mackie's apartment. It's likely he's got cams set up, is monitoring anyone going in or out of the building, certainly his own space."

"I can take care of that."

178

"Counting on it. We need to get in, see who's next. When and where. They may have moved straight to the next nest, and there are three people on his agenda we haven't ID'd. And we have to ID the unknowns on her list."

"There's more on hers. She's listed her kills. Animals," he said quickly. "The type, the place, the distance, the weapon, the date, the time. It appears her father's taken her hunting — illegally very often — into Montana, Wyoming, Alaska, the Dakotas, even into Mexico, Canada. She's listed over two dozen kills in the last seven months."

"Copy the file to my units. I'll have EDD pick this up, and hers. Hell, all of them, and now. She'll have a unit at her father's place. We need to get into that. She wouldn't have needed to be so careful on his agenda there, so maybe we'll have names."

Eve shoved a hand through her hair. "I wonder if Mackie knows what kind of monster he's created. And if he knows, does he care?"

CHAPTER
NINE

Eve tagged Peabody, reeled off the names from Willow's list. "These people are connected to the suspects, most likely the female. Nail them down, get contact information."

She clicked off, turned to Roarke. "If Mackie's monitoring the security cams in the apartment remotely, jamming them will tip him."

As they walked, Roarke simply patted her shoulder and contacted Feeney. Though they launched into e-speak that made her head bang, Eve understood enough to interpret.

"You — or Feeney — can override the cam and replay a loop."

"Exactly so. If Mackie's monitoring closely, it won't fool him for long, so we'll want to time it well."

"He could've rigged the door, right? He's a cop, he'd think of details. Rig the door to let him know when anyone goes in, so — "

"Darling Eve, this is hardly my first B and E. In fact, how happy am I it's not even my first of the day. Have a little faith."

The snapping wind had keened to a sharp edge. She caught the scent of soy dogs and chestnuts from a cart

180

— a puff of winter-fragrant smoke. Someone's vehicle alarm went off in annoying, rapid beeps as a couple of teenage girls ran by giggling like lunatics.

Roarke spoke easily to Feeney.

"Override in ten," Feeney announced.

"Copy that. Take the door," Eve told Roarke. "Unlikely he's got a way to monitor my master, but why take the chance?"

"And go," Feeney said.

They went to the entrance and, with Roarke's clever hands, were smoothly inside in under six seconds.

"No lobby cams, but the standard in the elevator."

"We take the stairs." Eve started up.

A decent enough place, she thought. Nothing close to the ex-wife's duplex, but decent. She noticed sporadic soundproofing, catching snippets of sound from apartments as they moved up.

But on Mackie's floor all held quiet.

"He bumped up his security."

Roarke nodded as they stood out of range of the camera over his apartment door. "I've got this one."

He took a device from his pocket, keyed in something, studied the readout, added more code. "Feed's looped. Let's see what other tricks he has for us."

When they approached the door, Roarke used the same device to scan the locks, the security swipe. "Clever," he murmured. "I'm reading a monitoring system, so you were right to be cautious here. No explosives, so that's a bonus, isn't it? Let me just . . .

Aye, that's it. Each in its time. Yes, clever enough. But . . . There you are. Hang on to this, will you?"

He handed Eve the device that hummed quietly in her hand while he took out his tools.

She watched him slip around a trio of police locks like they were thumb bolts.

Eve handed the device back to him, drew her weapon. "No explosives, good. But remember that old vid we watched a couple weeks ago? The guy booby-trapped his place. Had a big-ass shotgun rigged to go off if the door opened?"

"*Classic* vid," he corrected, "but I do remember, yes. So why don't we . . . "

They stepped to either side of the door. Eve turned the knob, dropped low, shoved the door open from the bottom.

No booby trap, no trip wires, no internal cameras.

And very little else.

She stepped into a living area that held one aging and sagging sofa.

"You reading this, Feeney?" She turned a circle to give him the three-sixty with her lapel recorder.

"Yeah, shit."

"We'll clear it anyway."

He'd left his bed, stripped to the mattress. A second bedroom held nothing but accumulated dust and some empty clothes hangers.

"They left this place weeks ago. Lowenbaum, stand down. They're not coming back here. Peabody, call in the sweepers. They can go over the place, for form's sake."

To release a bubble of frustration, she kicked the sofa.

"Copy that, sir," Peabody said. "I can give you those names."

"Give."

"Rene Hutchins, the school psychologist at the female suspect's high school. Thomas Greenburg, principal at the same school. Lynda Track works with Zoe Younger — and is Lincoln Stuben's sister."

"Have them contacted, interviewed. Assign protective details."

"On it."

"You don't believe they're in immediate danger," Roarke said.

"No. One mission at a time." Eve hissed out a breath. "Rounds out her hit list with two authority figures from her school and her stepfather's sister — who's likely friends with her mother."

She took a turn, put the second hit list aside for now, dealt with what was more immediate — the three unknown people on the first list.

"He figured we'd get here sooner or later. He prepared for that. Left the furniture that was too big and too old to bother with. Carmichael, Santiago, start knocking on doors here. Let's see if anyone can tell us when he booked."

She resisted, barely, kicking the sofa again. "Okay, all right. No more pussyfooting around. Feeney, will you contact the commander, give him the status? We're going full release on the IDs. I'm available for a media conference in an hour."

"Better you than me, kid."

"Lowenbaum, be available for same." She yanked out her 'link, started that ball rolling. "Nadine."

"Dallas. I've been trying to reach you all damn day. Everything's pushed to — "

"Where are you?"

"What? I just got home, but — "

"I'm coming to you. Which home?"

"My new place. My only place now. What — "

"No cameras. I'm on my way."

Roarke studied her cold, angry eyes. "Yanking the cork out of the bottle, are we?"

"That's right."

"What do you need from me?"

"Right now? I could use a ride."

In a fraction of the time she could have commandeered a police vehicle, she was sliding behind the wheel of a husky all-terrain. Peabody dropped in beside her.

"It's big and warm."

"It's temporary. Plug in Nadine's address. I don't know where the hell it is."

"Oh, it's great. She's still decorating it, but I heard it's already looking mag, and — "

"I don't care what it looks like."

"Right." Peabody sat back as the comp cued Eve on direction. "You want Nadine to break the story before you talk to the general media."

"I want her to fucking explode it. That'll cut down on the time I have to stand there giving statements, answering stupid questions. More, she'll dig in. There'll be stories and data about the suspects, about the victims. We have targets as yet unidentified, as yet unprotected. A good chance they'll come to us after this. We need more background on the dead wife."

"I did more digging while we were waiting. Birth family, education, employment. Nothing stands out. Pretty stable family, grew up in Westchester, no trouble in school, two years of college, general studies. Worked in retail. Moved to Brooklyn, roomed with a couple of girlfriends, switched jobs — still retail. Married Mackie, moved again, changed jobs again. Last employment Boomer's, clothing store on East Fifty-Seventh."

"She went to the doctor's, must've been heading back to work after the appointment. I want to talk to Marta Beck, find out what went on that day at the appointment. Let's find out the name of her supervisor at work. Mackie blamed the doctor, and Beck's initials are on the hit list, so he sees her as part of it."

"Beck isn't a medical. She's administration."

"Exactly. Beck said they often ran behind with appointment times."

"Ever been to a doctor that doesn't?"

"I try to avoid them. So maybe her appointment ran late, and she's rushing — why else does a sane person run out into the street? If she was rushing back to work, he might target her supervisor, or someone at her job. Get me names."

"Got that. Oh, you can park in the underground here, there's a visitors level."

"We're not visitors."

The building was sharp and sleek and silver. Not shiny and bright, but aged in a way to lend it character and dignity. She pulled straight up to the lavish front entrance, nosing in behind a limo disgorging a woman inside a massive fur coat carrying a tiny dog — also wearing a fur coat over his skinny dog body.

The doorman hustled to the lady with the dog, took a safari's worth of shopping bags from the driver. The doorman glanced toward Eve as she pushed out of the A-T, started to speak.

He stopped, gave a brisk nod as he juggled bags and hustled back to the door. "Lieutenant Dallas, I'll be right with you."

"I don't need you," she said, beating the lady and dog to the door, striding straight through.

"Charlie," the woman said, "will you just have everything sent up? Mimi is exhausted."

"Absolutely, Ms. Mannery. Lieutenant."

"Nadine Furst, expecting me. Leave my vehicle where it is."

Eve walked away from him, then realized she didn't have a clue.

Ground level soared toward vaulted ceilings where vines twined around white beams. Light sparkled on white marble floors from huge chandeliers fashioned from twists of that aged silver and balls of rich blue glass.

At a scan she spotted a bank, three boutiques, restaurants, a bakery and a gourmet food mart, a business center.

"Security will clear you right up." Charlie the doorman, still buried in shopping bags, hurried up to her. "Ms. Furst's penthouse can be accessed from elevator bank C — any car."

Eve headed to C, past a translucent wall of falling water that fell musically into a narrow pool banked with lush red flowers.

Eve stepped into the elevator, scowled when a disembodied voice proclaimed: **Two occupants cleared for Penthouse A. Please enjoy your visit and the rest of your day.**

"Yeah, because it's been a fucking day at the beach so far."

"We know where they're not, so that's something," Peabody muttered as she worked on her PPC. "Okay, got the assistant manager at Boomer's, one Alyce Ellison."

"Have her brought in," Eve snapped as the elevator doors open. "I want her in protective custody now."

"Who?" Nadine demanded, standing in a wide foyer flanked by matching pedestal tables holding blue orchids.

Eve had said no cameras, but as usual, Nadine Furst stood camera ready in a sharp suit of bold red, her streaky blond hair swept back from her foxy face. Eyes of clever green held Eve's gaze.

"Now, Peabody."

Behind Nadine the living area spread — sparcely furnished as yet, with glossy floors the color of the roasted chestnuts that had scented the street. A wall of windows opened the living space to a wide terrace, and a spectacular view of the city.

"I don't have much time," Eve began.

"Nice to see you, too."

"Nadine."

"Not much time, understood, but since you've been dodging me all day, I'd like a little room."

"Not dodging you. Dodging media period, and for a reason. I'm here now because I'm going to be part of a media conference in about an hour. I don't have much room to give."

"Got room for coffee while we do this?"

"God, yes."

"Follow me."

Nadine moved briskly — Eve noticed she wore house skids with the suit — across the living space, through a dining area with a long, slick black table centered with a big glass basket in orchid blue and surrounded by black chairs with blue seat cushions. Into a silver-and-white kitchen, complete with breakfast nook in a window alcove and a massive center island.

"You don't even cook."

"I can if I have to, and why not have a fabulous space for catering? It so happens I have Dallas blend stocked."

"What blend?"

"Don't you even know what you drink?" Nadine asked as she slid open a black panel to an AutoChef.

"Roarke's coffee."

"Which has several blends. Yours is Dallas."

"Huh. Peabody, can you use that wall screen?"

"Can do."

"Put up the ID photos while we get this coffee."

Nadine's fingers paused on the controls of the AutoChef. "You've ID'd the shooters?"

"Coffee, program coffee," Eve ordered, now fairly desperate for a hit. "Former Tactical Officer Reginald Mackie and his daughter, Willow Mackie, age fifteen."

"Holy shit." Nadine yanked open a drawer for a notebook, a recorder.

"No recorder, not yet. Suspects are still at large."

Not one to stand on ceremony where coffee was concerned, Eve opened the AC herself when it signaled, took out a white mug of black coffee.

"They've vacated Mackie's known residence. The minor suspect's mother, stepfather, and half brother are in protective custody."

"How did you ID the suspects?"

"Good police work. Look, you'll get what I can give you now; you'll get what I can give generally at the media conference."

Eve gulped down coffee, felt her system revive. And paced. "Pictures on screen, Peabody." Nadine passed Peabody a coffee regular. "You can take notes, Nadine, but no recordings until the official conference."

Quickly, succinctly, Eve outlined what she could, still pacing, still gulping coffee.

"You believe Willow Mackie is a willing participant in the killings."

"Here's some off-the-record until I clear it." Eve waited for Nadine's nod. "I think she's the shooter, and I believe — bullshit," she corrected. "I *know* she has a secondary hit list of her own. For whatever reason, his own physical or emotional state, or the fact he's a twisted, vengeful lunatic, I think Mackie's given his daughter the green."

"Why the unconnected strikes — two people at the ice rink, four at Times Square? Cover?"

"It looks that way." But Eve thought it was more, even more callous than that. "We believe the suspects have additional targets, and will move on them quickly. If they follow pattern, they'll choose a public area, somewhere the target routinely goes or lives or works. And they will take more lives."

"You want me to get their faces out there. When am I cleared for it?"

"Now. Their names and faces, as soon as you can. The other details, I need twenty minutes. The off-the-record stays that way until I clear it. That gives you a leg up on the rest of the media. That leg up comes with a price."

"Name it."

"Put up Susann Mackie, Peabody. I want this face, too. I want Mackie to see it every time he turns to the screen. I want him to hear her name, to revisit her life and death."

"You want to break him."

Eyes flat, Eve set the empty mug down. "I *will* break him. One more. The lawyer Mackie hired — he's a potential target, but I've got no name. You could dig there, too."

"I'll put some people on it."

"You hit anyone with these initials — JR or MJ — you let me know right away. Right away, Nadine."

"Done. How are you going to break her?"

"I'm working on it. We have to move."

"So do I."

"Swank digs, Nadine," Eve commented.

Nadine smiled. "Thanks. I wanted swank, and they're going to be swankier when I'm done."

As Eve turned to go, Nadine snatched up her 'link. Eve heard her say: "Put me through to Lloyd now. I don't give a hot fuck what he's doing. I said *now!*"

When they stepped into the elevator again, Eve took a breath. "Peabody, have the witnesses to Susann Mackie's accident brought in. None of their initials were on the list, but we won't risk it. And I want Zoe Younger in Interview. We'll see what Baxter and Trueheart got from her, but I need this round."

She checked the time. And she wondered where Mackie and his murderous offspring would be when they saw their own faces on screen.

They were in the converted loft Mackie had rented shortly before Thanksgiving, where he'd begun moving during the kickoff of the holiday season.

He'd bought some furniture — cheap, serviceable — and though it stung to pay rent on two apartments, he felt it worth the expense. Just as it stung to leave some money in his old bank account, under a name he no longer used.

He hoped to be able to clear out that account, but if not, again, it was worth the expense.

If things went well — Plan A — he and Will would be on their way to Alaska within the week, where they could live off the land quietly and remotely.

Where they could hunt, where they could build a home, a life.

Zoe would sic the dogs on them, of course. He wouldn't blame her for it. But they'd leave no scent, no trail, and for a few months, Will would be William Black, age sixteen, the son of John Black, a retired insurance adjuster from New Mexico. A widower who was home-schooling his only son.

They'd move again, inside Alaska, and become father and daughter again. And, as they did here in the loft, they would keep to themselves. He'd find peace in Alaska. He believed it, *had* to believe it. No more night terrors, night sweats. He'd ease himself off the funk, off the booze. His hands would stop shaking, his mind and eyesight would clear.

Susann and the son he'd longed for would be avenged. Justice well served by the daughter who gave him pride and purpose. And one day, when Will was old enough, he could leave her, secure in the knowledge that his only child could make her own way.

He could leave her to join Susann and the son they'd named Gabriel.

Thinking of them he began to drift away, into the comfort of imagining Susann in a white dress, sitting under a big, arching tree on a gentle green hill, with the baby in her arms.

There was a little farmhouse nearby, yellow with blue shutters, a white fence, a garden in bloom.

192

Their dream house, one they'd built in their dreams and conversations, the house in the country they'd dreamed of having one day.

She waited for him there, with the baby in her arms, and a brown puppy sleeping by her side.

He needed to see her there, her and his son. Under the big tree, in sunlight. At night she screamed for him in the dark, screamed his name, and the baby screamed with her.

But now she smiled, content to wait until he climbed the hill and sat beside her.

"Dad! Dad!"

He shot awake, reaching for the weapon at his hip.

In the gloomy light of the loft he saw Will standing in front of the short sofa, staring at the wall screen. She'd been cleaning her weapon, he noted, pleased to see the rifle on the table in front of her.

Still, the snap in her tone brought him to his feet, brought back the former soldier inside him. "Do we have a breach?"

"They've got our names, our faces."

He stepped over to stand with her, to listen to the breaking story.

His last official ID photo, and Willow's, filled the screen while the reporter's voice sounded over them.

"To repeat, police have identified two suspects in the Wollman Rink and Times Square attacks in which seven people, including a police officer, were killed and more than fifty people were injured. Police are looking for Reginald Mackie, a former Tactical officer with the

NYPSD, and his fifteen-year-old daughter, Willow Mackie."

The ID shots shrunk, swiped to the side of the screen while Nadine Furst in her bold red came into view.

"Police officials have scheduled a media conference to provide additional details. At this time, they ask if anyone has information regarding the whereabouts of these suspects, please do not engage, as they are believed to be armed and dangerous.

"Reginald Mackie, fifty-four, an Army veteran and decorated police officer, was widowed in November of 2059 when his wife, Susann Prinz Mackie, was killed in a vehicular accident. Mrs. Mackie," Nadine continued when Susann's picture came on screen, "was sixteen weeks pregnant at the time of the accident."

Susann's picture hung on screen, lips curved, eyes smiling. Then his came on, and Willow's while Nadine continued the report.

"How'd they make us? How'd they make us this fast?"

"Solid police work." He said it quietly as he saw his dream of a life in Alaska, a life of peace, fading.

Gone, he thought. No peace to come. No home. No life to build.

"But we've been so careful. They have Mom by now, don't they? And Lincoln and the brat."

"Your brother," Mackie reminded her. "He's your brother, Will. Your blood."

Something feral gleamed in her eyes, but her father didn't see it. "Yeah, they have them. You cleared out everything from your room? Anything that connects to the agenda?"

"I told you I did." Insult sliced through her tone. As if she'd leave anything. Her eyes, hard green against that soft, smooth skin, flashed toward him. "There's nothing in my room back there. I'm not stupid."

He nodded, moved over into the tiny kitchen area, programmed coffee for himself, got her a tube of the Coke she preferred. "This is why we worked out a Plan B."

"But, Dad — "

"Will, the mission comes first. You understood that. You trained for that. We go to the alternate plan, and regroup." He gave her a sad smile. "You need to cut your hair, honey, and get moving. I'll get to you when I can, but . . . In the event I'm captured or taken out, you know what to do."

He laid a hand on her shoulder. "I depend on you."

When she nodded, he stepped back. "Pack it up, clear it out, wipe it down. We both move tonight."

"The media conference. We need to watch. We need to know what they're releasing to the public."

Pride rose again. "That's right. Leave the screen on."

Eve might have hated media conferences, but she knew how to use them when it worked to her advantage. If the Mackies weren't watching live, they'd see the constant replays, the sound bites, the endless talking-head commentary.

So she made certain the killers got an earful.

"I'm not at liberty to divulge what investigative steps led us to identify the suspects other than to say the NYPSD has focused its manpower, its experience, and its man hours into doing so since the first strike in Central Park."

One of the reporters leaped to his feet. "Isn't it true that additional focus and manpower was put into the investigation after an NYPSD officer was killed?"

Eve said nothing for fully five seconds. "Ellissa Wyman, Brent Michaelson, Alan Markum," she began, and named every victim, in order of their deaths. "Those are the lives taken, the human beings killed. I wonder if the suspects know their names, looked into their faces, thought of their families. We did. So save your idiot remarks for somebody who hasn't stood in the blood of the seven dead. Nathaniel Jarvits was only seventeen. He died on his seventeenth birthday. Officer Kevin Russo, age twenty-three, was struck down while going to Nathaniel Jarvits's aid, trying to shield him from further injury. While doing his job as a police officer. Do you want me to give you a thumbnail on each victim? Because I can if you don't have the balls to do your job and report on who they were."

"Do you have a motive?"

"We believe the Mackies are targeting individuals connected in some way with Susann Mackie's accident. We're actively pursuing this line of investigation."

"Willow Mackie is only fifteen. Do you believe she was taken as a hostage by her father?"

"Evidence does not lead us to believe Willow Mackie is being held against her will or is being coerced. And don't bother because I'm not at liberty to share that evidence with you at this time. Both suspects are expert and experienced marksmen. Reginald Mackie trained his daughter in weaponry, in marksmanship. Seven people have been killed, more than fifty have been injured by what we term long-distance serial killers. The LDSK is, at the core, a coward. Skilled, cold-blooded, but a coward who kills at a distance, who sees the victim as nothing more than a target or a mark."

"Reginald Mackie used that skill as an NYPSD officer," someone called out.

"The skill, yes. Tactical officers aren't killers. Nor do they mark innocents. It's their job to use that skill to protect the innocent and other officers. And to take down a threat by forceful stun. Terminating that threat is only ordered when the risk to other lives is too great."

"Why didn't Mackie's predilection show on his evaluations?"

Before Eve could answer, Lowenbaum stepped forward. "That's on me," he stated. "Lieutenant Lowenbaum. I was Reginald Mackie's supervising officer."

Eve stayed back. Lowenbaum was clear, precise, accurate. He fielded follow-ups with more patience than she might have.

But when she'd heard enough, just enough, she moved forward again.

"If you want to angle a story that blames the department for the actions of a retired officer, go do that. But right now there are two suspects at large. You have their names, you have their faces. Maybe you should push forward with your trumpet call of the public's right to know and get this information out there. It might save a life. We're ending this session so we can go to work and make certain we save lives."

CHAPTER
TEN

Lowenbaum caught up with her — Eve moved fast — took her arm. "They may have a point."

"The reporters? Most of them only have a point on the top of their heads."

"I didn't see a killer, Dallas. He was one of mine, and I didn't see what he was."

"Because he wasn't." She had to keep moving, but she also needed Lowenbaum, and needed him steady. "If that was in him all along, the Army missed it, the NYPSD missed it, his former LT missed it. Testing missed it. What makes you so damn special?

"And where's that gum you always have?"

Perplexed, Lowenbaum pulled it out of his pocket as they worked their way through the maze of glides toward Homicide. "You want?"

"No. It smells purple. How do you chew something that smells purple?"

Since it was in his hand, Lowenbaum unwrapped a piece, popped it in. "I used to smoke."

"And Mackie used to be a pretty solid cop. Things change. Our job's to stop him, and after that it's Mira territory." She paused outside her bullpen, took a good look at him, and saw what she felt in herself. Anger, frustration, and adrenaline warring with bone-deep exhaustion.

"Tactical has scenarios, right, for containing attacks throughout the city? Your basic plays?"

"Yeah, and we've been running them holographically since the first strike. I've got the tech guys running probabilities — feeding them data as we get it — trying to project when and where he'll strike next. It's a crapshoot."

"What's your sense? Once he sees we've ID'd him and his daughter? Pause and reflect or up the schedule?"

"He's had months to pause and reflect. He'll want to take down as many targets as possible."

"Agreed. We've got all but three where he can't get to them. Talk to your men. Maybe, just maybe, he mentioned names."

"Been doing that, but I'll try a different angle."

"Do that. Good talk. I've got people to interrogate."

She left him looking bemused, and strode into the bullpen.

"Reports." She snapped everyone to attention. "Younger first. Go." She pointed at Baxter.

"Right call to have Trueheart soften her. She came in with a chip on the shoulder, bitching for a lawyer, demanding blah-blah. And where was her daughter? Trueheart suggested she contact the daughter, and the chip started wobbling some when she was unable to reach same, when she contacted the school and was told Willow Mackie was no longer a student at that facility. She started to ream the school office a new one,

200

but they had the paperwork — with her signature along with Mackie's."

"Her reaction to that?"

"Pissed off and scared. Trueheart played both. Over to you," he told his partner.

Trueheart shifted in his shiny black shoes. "She said she never signed anything, and that rang true. She believes Mackie abducted their daughter, so I worked that. We put out an Amber Alert, and she was more cooperative in providing information."

"Such as?"

"She last saw her daughter three days ago, when she left to switch off to Mackie. They haven't communicated, which Younger stated wasn't unusual. Her relationship with her daughter has been somewhat strained for the last several months."

Trueheart hesitated, then lifted his shoulder. "I think longer than that, but it got bigger, harder over the last several months. Ms. Younger stated Willow idolizes her father, resents the stepfather, often picks fights with her younger brother and/or her mother. Ms. Younger feels it's a stage, but has tried to persuade the daughter and Mackie toward family counseling."

Trueheart shifted his feet again. "She cried a lot, Lieutenant, claimed she hated her daughter's obsession — her word — with weapons, but as it was Willow's only real interest and outlet, and a connection to her father, she didn't want to forbid it. Couldn't have, as the shared custody put Willow out of her supervision half the time."

"Round it up for me."

"She's scared and she's holding on to the belief Mackie has the girl against her will, or at least is deceiving the girl. But . . . "

"Finish it."

"I think, I feel, she's as scared of her daughter as she is scared for her."

"Good. I can use that. Interview A?"

"We just had her brought up. She's pissed again," Baxter added. "Wants to go home, doesn't like being brought up and separated from her husband and son."

"I'll use that, too. Who took Marta Beck?"

"We had her." Santiago looked toward Carmichael.

"I'm just writing it up," Carmichael said. "She remembers Susann Mackie, and remembers hearing about the accident, and accompanying Dr. Michaelson to the memorial."

"They went to the memorial?"

"Not unusual for Michaelson, according to Beck. When they offered condolences to Mackie, he made no response, seemed cold and angry, which Beck considered understandable. We questioned her about Mrs. Mackie's appointment on the day of the accident, and Beck looked up the records. It was a standard exam — the mother in good health, the fetus progressing normally. There had been an emergency in the office earlier, with one of the patients going into labor. While that patient was seeing the midwife, Michaelson assisted, and appointments were backed up. The records show Mrs. Mackie's appointment ran forty-three minutes behind schedule. She was offered the option of seeing the PA or rescheduling, but opted to wait."

"What time was her appointment?"

"Scheduled for twelve-fifteen. She didn't get in for the exam until nearly one."

"That eats up a lunch break, doesn't it? You'd probably be in a hurry to get back to work. Who's got her supervisor — Mackie's supervisor at work?"

"She's on her way in," Jenkinson told her. "Reineke and I took Lincoln Stuben, the stepfather. He paints a darker picture of Willow Mackie than her mother. Sneaky, disruptive, disrespectful. Says she's a liar, stated she once threatened him with a knife and said if he told her mother, she'd claim he'd tried to rape her. Said she knew ways to make that stick. And when it stuck, her father would kill him."

"Did he tell the mother?"

"Did better. He hid a cam in the kitchen, goaded the girl into saying it again, and showed the mother the recording. When confronted, the girl responded with belligerence, locked herself in her room. She subsequently apologized — but Stuben didn't buy it like the mother did. Marriage is on shaky ground at this point, and he refuses to leave his son alone with the girl. Might be resentment, but he says Willow Mackie wouldn't need to be coerced or manipulated into being party to murder."

"They got a puppy for the boy his last birthday," Reineke continued. "Kid was crazy for it, slept with it, took it for walks himself. Couple months later, the kid comes home from school, and sees the puppy come flying out of the window on the third floor, goes splat at his feet. Broken neck. Kid's hysterical, people stop to help — somebody even calls the cops. A few minutes later, Willow shows up."

"Nobody can figure why the window was open, or why the dog went up there, why he'd jump out, but that's the way it looked. Except Stuben's dead sure Willow broke the dog's neck, tossed him out when she saw the boy coming. Then went out the back, circled the block."

"Nothing like practicing on puppies and kittens."

"I've got a little more on Mrs. Mackie, if it helps," Peabody put in. "I've talked to some family, some teachers, some employers and coworkers. The gist is, Mrs. Mackie was a nice woman — a polite, well-mannered, personable individual. A dreamer more than a doer. No particular ambitions, no career path. More a romantic who saw herself as waiting for her prince to come. Kind, soft, pretty, sweet, and a little on the ditzy side. Those are the terms that came up most often from various sources."

"All right. Trueheart, take the kid — the half brother. Reineke, take the father in with him. Let Trueheart lead on the boy. Willow Mackie strikes as the type who may have threatened the kid, and kept him afraid to tell anyone. She may have said more to him, bragged some. Peabody, with me. We're on Zoe Younger."

"Younger's what you'd say is the opposite of the second wife," Peabody said as they walked to Interview. "Has a career, is solid there. From the data anyway, a

204

more practical type of person. She may not be realistic about her daughter, but she's not a dreamer."

"Younger than Younger — ha — and softer, and someone who looked at him as her prince. Clearly, the accident was a result of her running late, not paying attention, but he can't have that. She was his ideal, and there has to be blame."

She stopped outside Interview A. "Trueheart softened her up, played to the maternal. I'm going to kick her ass."

Eve stepped in. "Record on. Dallas, Lieutenant Eve, and Peabody, Detective Delia, entering Interview with Younger, Zoe, in regards to case files H-29073 and H-29089. Ms. Younger, have you been read your rights?"

"My rights? I don't understand. We — I was brought in for protection."

"Correct. You're also here to answer questions regarding your daughter, Willow Mackie, and your ex-husband, Reginald Mackie, the primary suspects in seven homicides. Maybe you've heard about the Wollman Rink attack and the Times Square massacre."

"My daughter is only fifteen. Her father — "

"Have you been read your rights?"

"No."

"Peabody."

"It's just procedure, Ms. Younger. You have the right to remain silent."

As Peabody recited the Revised Miranda, Eve circled the room.

"Do you understand these rights and obligations, Ms. Younger?" Peabody asked.

"Yes, I understand them. I understand I'm entitled to legal counsel. I want to contact my attorney."

"Fine. Arrange that, Detective. We're done here."

"I want to know what you're doing to find my daughter!"

Eve glanced back, cold as winter. "You don't answer my questions, I don't answer yours."

"She's only fifteen. Her father — "

"Tell it to your lawyer."

"I want to be taken back to my husband, my little boy."

"I don't care what you want. You'll sit right here, wait for your lawyer. Your husband and son will, after interview, be taken to a safe location. You'll stay here."

"Why are you doing this?"

"Why am I doing this? I'll answer that one." Eve grabbed the file Peabody had brought it, tossed it open, spread out morgue shots of the seven victims. "They're why."

"Oh God. Oh my God."

"There's an eighth in the hospital. It'll be a while before she can walk again. Over fifty more who suffered injuries, including a boy younger than your own, with a broken leg. Peabody, arrange for that lawyer, then report to me."

"Yes, sir."

"You can't believe I had anything to do with this." Dark eyes shone with tears, with shock. "You can't believe a child of fifteen could take part in this."

206

"Ms. Younger, I'm not here to answer your questions, and as you've invoked your right to counsel, we have nothing to say at this time."

"Forget the damn lawyer then."

"Are you waiving your right to counsel?"

"Yes, yes. For now, yes." Younger pressed her fingers to her eyes, eyes the same deep green as her daughter's. "You have to understand. My daughter has been kidnapped by her father."

Eve sat, waited a beat while she stared at Younger. Smooth brown skin, deep green eyes, black hair in a mane of mad curls.

And lips that trembled.

"You don't believe that. You want to believe that, you're trying to convince yourself of that. But you don't believe it. Was her father there when she threatened your husband at knifepoint?"

"I — She was acting out."

"With a deadly weapon. Was her father there when she killed your son's puppy and threw him out the window?"

Younger's body jerked. "She didn't."

"You know she did. You've seen the signs. You've lain awake at night afraid of what she might do. Tell me, look at me and tell me when you last left her alone with your son?"

"It's because she's irresponsible."

"She's hurt him before, hasn't she? Just little things. He'd tell you he fell or he bumped his arm or make an excuse, but you knew. You couldn't control her, so you tried to control everything else. You had to deny what she is so you could live with it."

"I'm her *mother*. Don't you tell me what she is."

"Then I'll show you." Out of the file, Eve took copies of the hit lists, the blueprints.

"This one — that's the one your ex and your daughter put together. But this one? That's all hers. Look at the names. Your son's tops the list. Your son, your husband, you, then the school psychologist, the principal. Your husband's sister."

"Lynda. Lynda? No."

"And this? Recognize this? It's her school. Tactical uses plans like this, marked like this. She's learned very well. How many sons and daughters could she take down, how many teachers, parents, innocents?"

Younger's fingers shook as she drew them away, as she gripped her hands together. "This — this is Mac's, not hers. I go through her room, her computer every week. I would have found this."

"Like you found the secret weapon drawer in her dresser?"

"What? What are you talking about."

"Where'd she get her bedroom dresser."

"It — Mac. He — for her thirteenth birthday."

"It has a secret drawer designed to hold weapons. She had blasters in your home."

"No, no. I don't — we don't allow . . . "

"You went through her room regularly. Because you're afraid of her, because you know, under the denial, you *know* what she's capable of. We didn't find this list on her computer, in her room. Or in the

208

apartment where Mackie lived and she lived half the time. We found it hidden on your son's computer, a place you wouldn't think to look."

"Zach? On Zach's computer?"

"Where he did his schoolwork, played his games. She marked him for death. How old is he?"

"He's seven. He's seven years old. She hates him." Younger covered her face with her hands. Tears slid through her fingers. "She hates him. I can see it in her eyes. He's so sweet, so sweet and funny and easy, but she looks at him with hate behind her eyes.

"She grew inside me." Lowering her hands, Younger pressed them to her belly as tears ran down her cheeks. "I didn't have so much as a sip of wine while she did. I ate so healthy, I did everything the doctor said to do. I took such good care, and when she was born, when I held her, I promised I would always take such good care. I loved her, so much. I fed her from my body, I bathed her, and sang to her. Mac, I knew he'd wanted a boy, but he was good with her — really good with her. He loved her, do you understand? He was a good father, and then . . . he wasn't such a good husband anymore. Closed off, cold, disinterested in anything I was interested in, other than Willow. He said we should have another child, try for a boy, and I wanted another child."

"But not with him."

"He resented my work, my time away from Willow. I took two years as a professional mother, to give her that time, to take that time, but I wanted my work, too. Still, I took another six months, and another six working

209

only part-time. You're cops. You don't know what it's like to be married to one."

"We're cops. We have a pretty good idea. It's not easy."

"I tried. But he wouldn't *talk* to me unless it involved Willow, and even then . . . I loved my baby, but I needed to be a person as well as a mother, a wife. But I tried. I stayed in the marriage longer than I wanted, because we had a child. And when it finally ended, she was angry, too. With me. She adored him, and I broke our family. But for a while, it was better. She had her time with him, without me in the way. Then . . . she was barely seven when I found out he was teaching her how to use weapons. I found a stunner in her room, and we fought over that. I should've fought harder. I should've done something more. But all I could do was forbid her to bring weapons into our house, and after a while, for a while, I told myself it was good she had an interest — one I didn't share. She entered competitions and won trophies, so I told myself it was a sport. She didn't want to play ball or run track or join school groups, so this was her outlet. And if I didn't try to get in the way, she'd be happy."

She swiped at her face with her hands. "Lynda, I work with her. She's my closest friend. I knew Lincoln long before we . . . We didn't start seeing each other until after Mac and I separated. I swear to you we never — "

She broke off, closed her eyes. "That doesn't matter at all now. It's true, but it doesn't matter at all. Willow never liked Lincoln, though he was kind to her, tried to

210

connect with her. I told myself she'd come around, because I swear to you, he's a good man. Then we conceived Zach. She was so angry when we told her. I can still see her standing there, barely eight, just a bit older than Zach is now, with her hands in tight fists, her eyes so full of this cold, cold fury. She said: 'I've never been enough for you.' She said, God, she said: 'I hope you both die, then I can live with Dad.'

"Can I . . . I'm sorry, can I have some water?"

"I'll get you some." Peabody rose, stepped out.

"Detective Peabody, exiting Interview. Ms. Younger, did you consider counseling or therapy for Willow?"

"Yes, yes. I have a friend, but because Willow and Mac were so angry and opposed to the idea, I had her talk to Willow unofficially, you could say. Grace Woodward — she's a psychologist. Anger issues, obviously, displacement issues. We kept it to talk therapy, very casual, and it did seem Willow settled in. She wasn't interested in Zach when he was born, spent more time with Mac — I allowed it."

Younger shuddered, let out a couple of shaky breaths.

"It was easier. She never wanted real mother/daughter time. She made it seem like punishment if I took her out shopping or to a salon or a show. So I stopped, told myself it was all right that she didn't share my interests or I hers. But I'd go to some of her competitions, until she told me she could feel me disapprove and it messed her up. She asked me not to go."

She paused when Peabody brought her a cup of water, drank it slowly. "I was happy when Mac found Susann. He was so obviously enchanted with her, and she was so sweet, so kind. I worried Willow would resent her, too, but she didn't seem to. I think . . . Honestly, I think it was because Susann was — I don't want to say weak, that sounds critical. But she was soft, and undemanding. Willow didn't seem to be angry when Susann got pregnant, but that's when she got into trouble at school. She refused to do assignments, back-talked teachers, threatened one of the other girls with bodily harm. We agreed to in-school counseling — "

"With Rene Hutchins."

"Yes. Oh God, yes, with Ms. Hutchins. And Willow seemed to settle in again. Mac took her on a hunting trip out west, just the two of them, and we all felt that time with him showed her she wasn't being replaced.

"Then Susann was killed. It was a horrible time for everyone, for all of us. For Mac to lose Susann and the son they wanted so much. They'd already named him Gabriel, and then they were gone. I liked her very much, I really liked her. And I admit I'd hoped Mac's marriage to her, having another child — the son he'd always wanted — would help ease some of the resentment he still had toward me. Toward Lincoln. He was always so warm and lovely to Zach, but the cold would come back whenever he dealt with me or Lincoln."

"Did he ever threaten you or your husband?"

"Oh, no, no, nothing like that. It was resentment, and contempt. I could feel the contempt for both of us, and wanted that family therapy, as I felt Willow took her lead from him there."

"Yet you say she hated her brother, and Mackie was good with him."

"Yes." She closed her eyes again. "Yes, that's true."

"How did things change after Susann's death?"

"He fell apart, Mac did. No one could blame him. Willow wanted to spend more time with her father, and I allowed that. I felt he needed her, and she needed him. But he started drinking too much, even coming by to get her when he was drunk. And I had to tell them both she couldn't stay with him under those conditions. When I made her come home, when I drew that line, that's when the puppy . . . That's when it happened."

"You knew she'd done it," Peabody said gently.

Tears leaked through her lashes when Younger shut her eyes. "I believed she had. I couldn't prove it, but yes, I knew she had. And she knew I knew. I was comforting Zach. He was crying, and I was holding him, comforting him, and I looked over. She stood there, watching us. And smiling. She looked into my eyes, smiled, and I was afraid."

She drank more water. "That's when I started going through her room. I never found anything, and I hated myself for it, but I went through her things routinely. I spoke with Grace — she'd moved to Chicago, and she advised me to do what I knew I should do. Get Willow into structured therapy. I couldn't."

Now Younger used her hands to wipe away tears, made an effort to straighten her shoulders. "You can say I'm her mother, and she had to do what I told her to do, but her father refused to back me, and she warned me if I forced it, she'd accuse Lincoln of abuse, she'd go to court — she was old enough for that — and petition to live with her father. She'd go to the police, with her father, and get a restraining order on Lincoln. She'd ruin him. I tried to reason with her — we'd all go to counseling — but she wouldn't budge. These last months, she's spent more time with Mac, and I didn't interfere. Her grades went back up, the trouble at school never reoccurred. If things were strained at home, at least she wasn't disruptive or angry. But once in a while, I'd look up or over, and she'd be standing there. Just standing there, smiling at me. And I was afraid."

Younger dissolved into tears again. "I'm sorry, I'm sorry. I don't know what I did or didn't do. What I should or can do now. She's my child."

"Ms. Younger, you have another child to protect."

"I know. I know."

"Your daughter is a psychopath, trained by an expert in the science of killing."

As Younger's sobs increased, as Peabody opened her mouth to speak, Eve shook her head.

"The signs are all there, the evidence is all there. The dead are all there. We need to stop your daughter and her father. We need to prevent them from killing again. We need to find her, stop her, and get her the help she needs. Where would they go?"

"Alaska."

"What?"

"Mac actually talked about going there after Susann died. He was drunk or — or maybe high. I think he's been using, too. But there was enough detail for me to know he'd looked into it. He and Will — he never calls her Willow — would take off for Alaska when she got out of school. They'd live off the land. It sounds like drunk talk, but once I did find some information on Alaska on her computer — like a school report, but it wasn't. And the next time I looked, she'd deleted it all."

"They're not in Alaska. They're in the city."

"I don't know where they are, I swear to you." Like a plea, Younger held out her hands. "I swear it. I was married to a cop, and a cop has been killed. I know what that could mean for my daughter. Mac has lost his mind, Lieutenant. Losing Susann and their baby broke him. Maybe, I don't know, maybe some of this was always there in him, but contained. The way Willow seems contained so much of the time. But he broke, and he'll die trying to finish what he started. Willow's fifteen. Do you remember fifteen, how you feel at fifteen? You feel immortal, and you feel like dying for a cause is romantic, whatever the cause might be. I don't want my baby to die. I'll do anything I can, tell you anything I know."

She took a deep breath.

"His hands shake."

"Mackie's hands shake?"

"Yes, not always, but it comes and goes. I haven't seen him for nearly a month, but the last time I did, he looked . . . off. On the frail side, shaky. I haven't been a cop's wife for a long time, but I don't think he could execute these strikes. I think, God help her, I think he's trained Willow to make them."

She stared down at the table. "I want to believe it's against her will, but I know it isn't. But he's used her love for him, her admiration. He's made her think what she's doing is heroic, is right, is what her father wants and needs. She's only a child. She isn't responsible."

Yes, Eve thought, she is, but let it go. "Do they have a favorite restaurant, pizza joint? Somewhere they went habitually?"

"I don't know."

"You said she competed, won trophies. Anywhere he'd take her to celebrate when she won?"

"I don't know. She didn't want me there, didn't want to share that with — Wait. Divine's."

"Ice cream." Peabody put in. "They've got frozen desserts and yogurt, but they also have the real deal."

"Yes. Willow loved that place, loved their caramel sundaes. They're pricey, and you often have to wait up to an hour to get seated, but Mac and I started taking her when she was a toddler, and . . . I guess it got to be their place. He'd take her there on special occasions."

"Peabody, send Uniform Carmichael and Officer Shelby to Divine's, with the ID shots, and the sketches."

"Yes, sir! Peabody exiting Interview."

"Is there anywhere else that strikes you, any other routine they had?"

216

"The target range — the indoor one in Brooklyn, I don't know the name. And there's some other place for target shooting, indoors and out; it's in New Jersey."

Eve shook her head. "Anywhere less structured?"

"I know he took her out west — Montana. And I think they went out west without clearing it with me. I stopped asking because they'd lie, and Willow would lie in a way that made it clear she lied. Do you have any children, Lieutenant?"

"No."

"Then you don't know what it's like to fail as a mother." Younger looked away, her eyes shattered. "I don't know how to save her now."

"Ms. Younger, we're going to do everything we can to find her, to bring her in without harming her, to stop her before she causes more harm. What you've told me may help us do that. I'm going to have you taken back to your family. We're going to take all of you somewhere safe until we find Willow."

"Will I be able to see her, to talk to her when you do?"

"Yes."

But she may not talk to you, Eve thought.

CHAPTER
ELEVEN

Eve didn't have time for hysteria, and ten seconds after walking in to interview Alyce Ellison she wished, bitterly, she'd left the woman to Jenkinson and Reineke.

"Why is he trying to kill me?" Ellison's shriek cut a dull, jagged groove through Eve's skull. "I didn't do anything. I didn't hurt anybody! Somebody's trying to kill me."

"Ms. Ellison — "

"The police came to my *apartment!* I didn't even finish my *dinner!* People are going to think I've been *arrested!* I didn't do *anything!* I could be killed any *second!*"

As she raved, Ellison whirled around the room, her arms alternately waving like flags, then coiling around her stick-figure body as if to hold what there was of it together. Her eyes, heavily lined in glittery blue, bugged out of her narrow face. Her mouth, heavily dyed in shiny red, never stopped moving.

"Sit down and knock it off."

"What? What? Would you sit down if your life was in danger?"

"Lady, I'm a cop. My life's in danger daily and I know how to sit down. Watch this."

To demonstrate, Eve sat at the Interview table.

"Being in danger's what you get paid for! Someone's trying to kill me."

"Not at the moment, so sit the hell down. *Sit!*" Eve snapped.

"You can't talk to me like that." Now tears swam, an ocean between glittery shores. "I'm a citizen."

"Right now you're wasting the time of the investigators on a series of homicides. Sit, shut it, or get out."

"I'm not going *anywhere*. You have to protect me. I'll — I'll *sue!*"

"You have to be alive to sue." Eve got up, walked to the door, opened it. "Sit or get out. Now."

Ellison sat, dissolving into wild sobs. "You're mean. You're just mean."

"I can be meaner because blubbering's wasting my time, too. Suck it up. You're alive and well and in protective custody. We plan on keeping you alive and well. Want that? Pull yourself together and answer some questions."

"I don't know *anything*."

"You knew Susann Mackie."

"I didn't hurt her!" Ellison lifted her blubbering-splotched face. "I could have fired her, but I didn't. I gave her another warning, that's *all*."

"What kind of warning?"

"About being late, and about forgetting to check the stock, and about how long she talked to customers. It's not my fault she got hit by a car!"

"When did you give her the warning?"

"Which time?" Ellison sniffled now, blinked fat tears from her sparkly eyes. "I had to talk to her every month, explain again how uneven her evaluations were because she was never on time to work or from her breaks, and she'd end up talking to a customer for like ten minutes instead of selling anything."

"Why didn't you fire her?"

Ellison sighed. "Because when she did sell, she did really well, and a lot of customers came back and went to her, especially. And she was nice, you just had to like her. She had a really good eye for fashion, for what looked good. She always looked good, and she could — when she wasn't off daydreaming — steer a customer to just the right outfit or accessory. I liked her. We all went to her memorial. I cried and cried."

I bet, Eve thought.

"Did you warn her the day she went to the doctor on her lunch break?"

Those glossy red lips trembled. "I had to. It was evaluation day, and I had to. I told her she had to be on time, just had to show improvement in that area. She said she was sorry and she would. She always said that, and she'd usually be on time for a few days, even a week after eval, and then . . . But that day, she never came back from lunch."

Ellison started to cry again. "I was so mad. We were really slammed — we had a major sale going, and I was really mad. I tagged her 'link, and got v-mail, and I was harsh. I said how if she didn't respect me or the position enough to be back from her lunch break on time, she just shouldn't come back at all. I didn't know she was *dead*."

"Okay." Since she was actually getting information now, Eve softened her tone. "You were doing your job."

"I *was!* If she'd told me she had a doctor's thing, or if she'd tagged me up, let me know she was running late because of one, I wouldn't have been harsh. I swear. I don't want to *die!* I'm only twenty-nine."

Official ID data said thirty-three, but Eve let that pass.

"You're not going to die. Did you speak to Reginald Mackie after the accident?"

"We — we sent flowers and a sympathy note. And we went — a whole group of us — to the memorial."

"Right. Did you speak to him personally?"

"I just couldn't. I couldn't stop crying."

"Did he speak to you, at any time?"

"No. His — his daughter . . ."

"Willow Mackie."

"Yes. She came into the store. I recognized her because she'd come in before, so Susann could help her find clothes. And she came up to me, right up to my *face*, and said how I had to be sorry Susann got killed because I didn't get to be a big shot and fire her. How Susann and the baby were *dead* because I wouldn't give her enough time to go to the doctor's. And she said: 'Enjoy your crappy job and your crappy life while you have them.'"

"When did this happen?"

"I guess about a month after the memorial. She didn't even look mad or upset. She was sort of smiling the whole time. I was really upset, and I tried to say I was sorry, but she just walked away. She knocked over a display of T-shirts on her way out. On purpose!"

"Did she ever come back?"

"Not while I was working. I never saw her again, until I saw her picture on the bulletin. All I could think was I wasn't surprised."

"Why is that?"

"Well, I said how she didn't look mad or upset when she came in and said those mean things to me? But she looked a little bit crazy. Darla said so, too. Darla's one of our top salespeople, and she was right there. She saw the whole thing, and she said how that girl's just crazy in the eyes."

Eve headed back toward her office, and Peabody walked briskly out. "Dallas!" Peabody moved into a jog. "We just confirmed the Mackies in Divine on the afternoons of both attacks. They're on the feed today, at the counter ordering, at fourteen-twenty-five.

"Both?"

"Yeah. The security feed's a twenty-four-hour loop, so we've missed catching them after the first incident, but while Uniform Carmichael reviewed the feed, Officer Shelby talked to some of the staff. Two of them remembered the Mackies, and the day because of the attack. Both agree they came in around quarter to four. Just after the peak of the after-school swarm."

"Were they carrying anything?"

"I — "

"Find out, find out now! Did he have any kind of case, did she? Backpacks, bags, rollies. Now, Peabody."

"Yes, sir."

Eve went straight to her office, snagged the results from EDD the minute she saw them.

"On screen."

Hands on her hips, she studied the buildings highlighted in order of probability. They'd gotten lucky with the first nest, she thought. Maybe that luck would hold.

"She had a backpack." Peabody came to the door. "That's it. No briefcase or luggage or bags of any kind on the feed. Just a backpack. The wits don't remember any bags either from yesterday."

"So they went to their hole after the strike, had time to stow their weapons, then get fucking ice cream. Get me a conference room."

"We've got A. Whitney has it reserved for us for the duration."

"Briefing, everybody, five minutes."

"Do you want EDD?"

"I said everybody."

Eve grabbed what she needed, went straight to the conference room. She updated the board, brought up the EDD map on screen, split it, and began assigning sectors to various officers and detectives.

She glanced over, frowned when Roarke came in.

"I didn't know you were still here."

"I wasn't, now I am. As they didn't need me, particularly, in EDD, I did some remote work. Now I'm back. How can I help you?"

"I don't — Actually, you could bring up a map on the other screen, focus on a place called Divine on the East Side."

"I know it. So do you — at least their products."

"I've never been there."

"Because we stock it at home. One of the perks of owning it."

"Your place?"

"Actually, it's in your name."

Even with her mind full of cop details, she stopped cold, blinked at him. "I own an ice cream joint?"

"You own what many consider to be the premier ice cream parlor in the city," he told her as he worked.

"No one can ever know."

"Sorry?" Distracted, he glanced over and saw her eyebrows drawn together. "What?"

"Especially Peabody. No one can ever know my name's on some big-deal ice cream joint."

"I see we'll be canceling our plans for the Lieutenant Dallas Frosted, but as you like."

"You — That's a joke. Ha-ha. Why is my name on — No, later. I'm losing my focus."

"Then tell me: How does Divine play into this?"

"They go there — the Mackies. It's their celebration place. They went there after each strike."

The amusement, the slight curve of his lips faded away. "Kill people, enjoy a banana split?"

"Something like that."

"You've dealt with some monsters in our time together, but these . . . They're a separate breed. Father

224

and daughter, celebrating death over ice cream while families mourn."

"He rewards her. He trained her, helped make her, so he rewards her for a job well done. I'm looking for their hole. If they went to Divine — having stowed the weapons first — I lean toward them holing up in a place within reasonable walking distance of the ice cream joint. According to my information, Divine has been their place since she was a kid."

Others began to file in as she spoke. "I'm going to ask you to take a deep dive into Mackie's finances, but even considering pension, death benefits from the wife, he's paying rent on two places. He's had to acquire all the weapons, the false IDs. That's got to stretch his income. So the hole's likely low rent, maybe a month-to-month. It's doubtful he's had it more than six months."

"Dallas, Uniform Carmichael and Officer Shelby are on their way in," Peabody told her. "They won't be here for at least fifteen."

"Loop them in remotely. They don't need to come in."

"Loop Chief Tibbie," Whitney ordered as he stepped in.

"I've got them." Feeney moved to the comp.

"Everybody else, give your attention to screen one. Note the buildings highlighted. These are potential nests for today's attack on Times Square. Note your sectors," Eve added.

"In the first strike, the suspects used a hotel room, a conventional check-in. They may have done the same here. You'll search your sectors — hotels, flops, office buildings, studios. The program used to determine these probabilities also, as you see, lists probable angle and direction of strike. You have the most likely floors and angles.

"Hit all, hit thoroughly. Talk to clerks, supers, beat cops, LCs, merchants, dog walkers, residents, cleaning crews. They didn't pick the nest at random, so at least one of them cased it previously. Find it."

She turned to the other screen.

"Divine," she began.

"Best Rocky Road in the city," Jenkinson commented, then shrugged. "Just saying."

"Your endorsement's so noted. Apparently the suspects agree — although she prefers the caramel sundae. We've learned the suspects indulged themselves after both strikes."

"Fucking cold," Feeney muttered. "And I ain't talking ice cream."

"Zoe Younger, Willow Mackie's mother, states Mackie has taken his daughter to Divine regularly, as a reward. That pattern remains here. The Wollman strike took place at fifteen-fifteen. Times Square at thirteen-twenty-one. The Mackies were caught on Divine security feed today at fourteen-twenty-five. And witnesses state they came in at approximately fifteen-forty-five after the Wollman attack. In both cases, Mackie carried nothing, and the daughter only had a backpack."

"So they left the nest, went to wherever they're holed up, stowed the weapons. Then went out for dessert," Baxter concluded.

"And consider the timing. On the afternoon of the Central Park attack. They packed up the weapons, left the East Side hotel, and were ordering ice cream about thirty minutes after the first TOD. Today, the time between the attack and the wits' statement of their arrival at Divine is more than an hour. It's a full thirty minutes longer for them to travel from where we project they used a downtown nest for the strike on Times Square, to the East Side location of Divine for their celebration."

"Takes longer to get there from downtown," Santiago began, "that's a factor. But both times they ditched the weapons, the bags. Could they have their own transportation?"

"He didn't," Lowenbaum said. "Never knew Mackie to have his own vehicle."

"East Side Hotel has garage parking for guests," Eve added. "The Mackies didn't check a vehicle there."

"And unless he's bought one that's as secure as our Tactical units," Lowenbaum added, "there's no way he'd leave weapons inside a vehicle, garaged or on the street. If he has transpo, he'd still stow his weapons in a secured location."

"He may have recently acquired a vehicle, as he plans to settle with his daughter in Alaska when he's finished here, but I agree a trained officer isn't going to leave a laser rifle in a parking lot while he gets ice cream."

Once more, Eve gestured to the screen. "It takes longer to travel from any of the highlighted locations downtown to the parlor — add that thirty minutes. But

227

after the first strike, they arrive at the counter, according to the wits, thirty minutes after the first vic's TOD."

"Their hole's on the East Side," Jenkinson said. "Probably within walking distance of the parlor. You said it's their place, a father/daughter deal?"

"That's right, and that's right. So we focus on this area. First Avenue to Lex, Fifty-Fifth to Fifteenth. That puts the parlor in the center of that quadrant. They could easily have walked from their nest on Second Avenue to any location in that area."

"That's a lot of doors to knock on," Carmichael calculated.

"Which is why the e-geeks will eliminate the unlikelies while the rest of you find the nest.

"We have potential targets in protective custody. You should all familiarize yourselves with the interview recordings conducted today. To summarize, it became clear during the interview with Zoe Younger, Willow Mackie displays psychopathic tendencies, which include offing her brother's puppy, threatening her stepfather with a knife."

"The brother, too, sir." Trueheart flushed as she stopped, turned to him. "I'm sorry to interrupt."

"Forget that. Go."

"The kid broke down during Interview."

"I call it opening up," Baxter corrected. "He felt safe, and he hasn't. He felt like he could talk to Trueheart, and Trueheart would believe him."

"That, and I think he felt like she — his half sister — couldn't get to him." Trueheart glanced at the board.

"The kid's been terrorized, Lieutenant. He said sometimes he'd wake up in the middle of the night and she'd be in his room, just sitting there, staring at him. Once she held a knife to his throat, dared him to call for help."

"He never told his parents?"

"He was afraid to." After a moment, Trueheart hissed out a breath. "I could see how scared he was, Lieutenant. She said maybe he'd end up going out the window, going splat on the sidewalk like his puppy. Or maybe his father would end up with his throat slit some night if he didn't keep his mouth shut. Or how his mother might fall down the stairs one day, and when the cops came, one of his toy trucks would be there. They'd put him in jail for that. She'd make sure of it. He's just a kid, sir. He believed her."

"He was right to. She planned to kill all of them once she completed the assignment for her father. Anybody here thinking of her as a child, stop. Until she's in a cage, she's deadly. Anyone thinking of Mackie as a fellow cop, stop. He and his daughter are cold-blooded killers. Find the nest, compile all data and evidence when you do. Anyone assigned to the field, dismissed.

"Feeney, do whatever you can to lower the number of locations for the hole."

"You got that. You wanna play?" he asked Roarke.

"I do, yes."

"Come up when you're ready." Rising, Feeney stuck his hands in his baggy pockets. "Any sense there's anything weird going on with these two?"

"I think being LDSKs — Oh." Eve's hands slithered into her own pockets. "No, nothing like that."

"Okay then, he's going to want a place with two bedrooms. She's nearly sixteen, so they maybe share a nest, short term, but for longer term, probably two bedrooms. Guy wants to go to Alaska, he's probably trying to save money where he can, so like you said, nothing upscale. Yeah, we can knock the number down some. McNab, let's get started."

"I was just thinking."

"He does that."

With a half grin, McNab rubbed his earlobe and part of the forest of silver hoops riding on it. "You gotta eat, right? Single dad right off, and you add they're huddled in to work out how to kill a whole bunch of people. Probably not a lot of cooking, even stocking an AutoChef with much more than your basic grab-and-gos."

"Takeouts, deliveries," Eve said with a nod. "Pizza, Chinese, subs, those would rank high. And 24/7s, carts."

"Even thinking with his stomach, that's not bad." Feeney gave McNab a light punch. "We'll add it in."

"Lowenbaum, do you have Officer Patroni on tap?"

"I brought him back with me. Do me a solid, Dallas, don't talk to him in Interview."

In his place, Eve thought, she'd have asked for the same for any of her men. "We'll talk in the lounge. The three of us. Why don't you go get us a table?"

"I appreciate it."

"Peabody, I want you to check that all the civilians we brought in are now secure. And it's that needle-in-the-hay-pile thing — "

"Stack."

"Whatever. Run the initials of the yet to be identified against every fricking lawyer in the city. Start with ones who advertise, who specialize in personal injury and wrongful-death suits."

"That's a teeny little needle in a lot of haystacks, but I'm on it."

With only Eve and Roarke left in the room, Whitney rose. "Lieutenant, HSO is inquiring about your investigation."

She actually felt her spine turn to a rod of steel at the mention of the Homeland Security Organization. "Inquiring, sir, or looking to take it over?"

"Inquiring with the concept, we'll say, of taking it over."

"It's a murder investigation, Commander."

"That could be considered domestic terrorism. And, in fact, is being labeled that by much of the media."

Part of her brain might have been raging *Politics, fucking politics*, but her tone held cool and even. "That may be, sir, but the evidence clearly indicates the motive here is murder, and targeted murder. The rest is, or was, nothing but an attempt to cover the specific target."

"It may be possible to tap some HSO resources without them taking the lead."

"Respectfully, sir, I feel we don't have time to jump through those hoops. If I come to believe those resources are more valuable than that time, or that we are unable to move the investigation forward, I would welcome the assistance."

"Agreed. It's your case, Lieutenant. And you're clear for as much overtime as you deem necessary. The proper paperwork on same will have to be submitted in a timely manner."

"Yes, sir."

"Shut them down, Dallas. Shut them down."

When he walked out, Eve pressed her fingers to her eyes. "Fucking HSO. Fucking paperwork. Fucking fuck."

"Have you eaten anything since this morning?"

"For Christ's sake."

He pulled a nutribar out of his pocket. "Eat this and I won't add *fucking nagging* to your list."

"Fine, fine." She ripped off the wrapper, took an annoyed bite. Maybe the fact that something that bland tasted delicious meant she needed the damn *nutri* part of it.

"And since you won't actually want cop coffee, you could drink a bottle of water during this next meeting. I'm with Feeney, but I'd like to know if you go into the field."

He caught her face in his hands, kissed her, firm and hard, then left her.

On a sigh, she polished off the nutribar — half wished she had another — as she gave the board one more study.

In the lounge, she saw Lowenbaum at one of the tables with another cop.

Vince Patroni — mid-forties, dark hair cut high and tight over a sharp-boned face — brooded into a cup of cop coffee. Since Roarke had it right, she went for water, and was almost disappointed when Vending burped out the bottle without a hitch.

"Lieutenant Dallas," Lowenbaum began as Eve and Patroni eyed each other. "Tactical Officer Patroni."

"The lieutenant says you're sure, a hundred percent, on Mac."

"That's right."

"And his kid, his girl."

"Right again. Do you need me to run it down for you?"

"No." Patroni lifted a hand, rubbed his fingers over his eyes. "We were both Army, me and Mac, both weapons specialists, trained at the one-nine-seven. We didn't train at the same time, but we knew some of the same people from back then."

"You connected."

"Yeah. I got a boy, ten, from a busted relationship, and he had Will. We'd have a brew a couple times a week, catch a game, hit the range. He'd bring Will whenever he had her — to the range, I mean. Girl's got some serious skill, I mean she's a killer on the . . ."

Obviously he heard his own words. "Jesus."

"Let it go," Eve told him. "You went with them to the practice range regularly."

"Yeah, not for the last year or so, but before. I brought my own kid a few times, but he's not interested much. Wants to be a scientist. And anyway, our kids didn't much hit it off."

"Age difference?"

"Not really. Owen, he gets on with everybody, old, young, whatever, but he didn't like her. He told me after the couple of times I took him along that he didn't want to hang with Mac when she was around. He didn't like the way she looked. I was surprised, because like I said he gets along with people. I said how he couldn't judge people by how they look. But he said it wasn't the way she looks. It was *how* she looked. At him, at people," Patroni explained. "She had too much mean in her eyes. He said when she shot at a target, she saw people, and liked imagining them dead."

"That's pretty perceptive for a kid."

"Yeah, well, he's got that, you know, extra. We think. We haven't had him tested yet, both his mother and I think he's too young for it. But he's got that extra, so when he said he didn't want to hang with her, I stopped taking him. Mostly, I put it down to Will not liking anybody pulling her dad's attention off her, and Mac really likes Owen. Mac's crazy about Will, don't get me wrong, but he wanted a son. I guess he sort of thinks of Will that way. Not much girlie about her, you know?"

"He got married again."

"Yeah, Susann was the love of his life, no question. He said Will loved her, too."

"He said?" Eve prompted.

"Yeah, well . . . " After shifting in his seat, Patroni frowned into his coffee. "My perspective, Will was okay with Susann. From what I could see Susann never got between Mac and Will, encouraged them to have time together. And he was looser, happier, with Susann.

234

Over the moon when she got pregnant. When she died . . . Broke him to pieces, took him down into the dark, man, deep down. Drinking till he blacked out, every night. I couldn't talk to him. He shut out everything and everybody but Will. I hauled him out of bars a few times, but then he started just drinking at home, locked in."

"You didn't report that behavior to me, Patroni."

Patroni looked up, met Lowenbaum's eyes. "It got bad after you had him take the hardship leave, LT. I didn't see what good it would do to report he was drinking himself sick on leave. And I honestly didn't think he'd come back on the job. He wasn't ready to come back on the roll, LT, you knew it. He'd pulled it together some. He was careful there, but we all knew it. You gave him desk work because you knew it, and nobody was surprised when he took his twenty and stepped out. But after that, after he put in his papers, I think he did more than drink himself blind."

His ex-wife thought the same, Eve remembered. "What more?"

"I went over a few times. He'd lost a lot of weight, looked sick. He had hand tremors, and his eyes . . . Even in the early stages, even when it's just a little use, you can start to see it in the eyes."

"You think he went on the funk," Eve said.

"Goddamn it, Patroni, why didn't you tell me?"

"He was retired," Patroni said to Lowenbaum. "You weren't his lieutenant anymore. And I couldn't prove it. I knew it in my gut, but I couldn't prove it. When I tried to talk to him about it, he denied it. I went back a couple times after that, but Will was there, said he was sleeping, said he was doing better, was pulling out, how she'd talked him into taking some time away with her, out west."

"She talked him into it."

"Camping, she said, fresh air, change of scene. She had it all worked out. The fact is, he'd taken her out to Montana, maybe up to Canada a couple of times before, and Alaska maybe more than a couple."

"When's the last time you saw him?"

"A while now, maybe three or four months. He made it pretty damn clear he didn't like me dropping by, and I couldn't say, 'Hey, let's go have a brew.' I tagged him a couple times about catching a game, or hitting the range, but he put me off, always had something going with Will. Or she'd answer his 'link, tell me he was busy, he'd get back to me, but he wouldn't."

"Did he ever talk about payback, for Susann?"

"Not in the I'm-going-to-kill-a-bunch-of-people sort of way. He's my friend, Lieutenant Dallas, but I'm a police officer, and I know my duty. If he'd made serious threats or if I'd suspected — "

"I get that, Patroni."

"Right." He scrubbed a hand over his hair. "When he was still talking to me, drinking heavy, he'd talk about how somebody had to pay. I think he hired a lawyer."

"What lawyer?"

"He never said. But he talked about hiring one. He'd say stuff like his wife and baby had been murdered, and where was the justice? How he'd served his country, served this city, but nobody gave a shit about his wife

236

and baby being murdered. I could talk him down. Hell, I combed over the accident report, the reconstruction. I even talked to Russo and the wits myself. It was an accident — a goddamn tragedy, but an accident. When he was sober, I talked to him straight about it. He didn't much want to talk to me after that."

"Do you know when he moved?"

"I didn't know he had, but I thought, the way he put me off, the way Will blocked me, he'd just moved on. He didn't want the contact with me, with things or people who reminded him of what he'd lost."

"Did he ever talk about moving?"

"Sure, he did. He had this thing about Alaska, talked about heading there when Will was eighteen — this was before Susann. After Susann, it was a farm somewhere. Always some dream about getting out of the city, living off the land."

"But nothing about moving within the city? He had a wife and a baby on the way."

"Right, right." Patroni closed his eyes as he thought back. "Yeah, yeah, they were saving up. Yeah, yeah, I remember about this. Susann was going the professional mother's route. In fact, she really wanted to quit her job and start nesting or whatever. But he said they needed her income over the next few months so they could get a bigger place. They'd looked at some townhouses, low-end, places that needed work. East Side — I remember that because it would keep Will in the same school, keep them sort of in the same neighborhood. And Mac was making noises about pushing for full custody of her. Around on Third, maybe. Or Lex. I think that's the area, in the Twenties or south of there — one of those old post-Urban places that got tossed up. Crap mostly, but you can get them pretty cheap. Ah, they wanted something where they could walk the baby to a park or playground. That was where they were looking."

"Buy or rent?"

"They wanted to buy, or try one of those rent with option deals. You can do that with those post-Urbans, or he said you could. I figured yeah, because they're prefab boxes, mostly falling apart unless somebody's gone in and put a lot of money and time into it. I lived in one myself — Lower West — when I was in my twenties. I swear the place swayed in a strong wind. But yeah, that's what they wanted. An investment until they fixed it up, until he could put in his papers, and they moved to that farm. Pipe dreams, I figured, but a guy's got to have them."

"Anything else, something he said, someone else he blamed? These initials JR and MJ, do they mean anything to you? JR, MJ," she repeated. "These two names are on his list, and as yet unidentified."

"He stopped talking to me about the accident after I looked into it and talked to him, he didn't want to talk to me about it. There's nobody I can — wait, 'MJ'? I don't see how it could, he could . . . "

"Who?"

"Maybe Marian. Marian Jacoby. She has a son who goes to Will's school. Divorced. Susann fixed us up once, we dated a couple times, just didn't click that

238

way. She works at the lab. She's an evidence tech at the lab."

"Hold on." She yanked out her 'link. "Peabody, Marian Jacoby, evidence tech. Find her, get her covered and brought in. She's a potential."

"I don't know why he'd go after her," Patroni began.

"Maybe he went to her, maybe she tried to do him a favor, ran a reconstruction on her own time, studied the evidence, the reports, and told him what he didn't want to hear."

CHAPTER
TWELVE

Eve rushed up to EDD, tagging Berenski as she pushed her way on the glides.

"Marian Jacoby. Where is she?"

"Hey, I'm putting in extra hours on your deal. How the hell do — "

"Is she in the lab?"

"Repeat, how the hell do — "

"Find out. Now."

"Jesus, she's on swing this month, so she oughta be here. If she's in the field — "

"No, right the fuck now."

His face, one large scowl, filled her screen as he ran his counter length on his rolling stool. "Yeah, yeah, she's around. What the fuck?"

"Get off your ass, go get her, take her to a secured location. I've got cops coming in for her."

"You think you're going to come in here and arrest one of my — "

"She may be a target, Berenski. She knows Mackie, and she may be one of his targets. Get her safe and secured until my cops get there."

"Done." The scowl turned to a snarl, and his face blurred as he shoved to his feet. "Nobody screws with one of my people."

He cut her off, and with her 'link still in hand, Eve bypassed the noise and color of EDD central and shot toward its glass-walled lab.

"Marian Jacoby — potential target. Being secured now. That leaves one. Apartments, condos, townhouses, East Side, likely in the Twenties or below — the post-Urban toss-ups. Probably Third, possibly Lex."

She caught her breath as Feeney immediately started a search and scan. "Finances," she said to Roarke. "They were saving to buy."

"I can tell you he all but emptied his account September eighteenth, and took the lump sum on his pension only last week. He had a two-hundred-fifty-thousand-dollar life insurance policy on his wife, doubled with accidental death, and prior savings of two hundred thousand and change. With the lump sum, he has more than enough for a downpayment, but wouldn't that be foolish?"

"He may not be thinking straight, but I agree and lean toward rental. Even if he's not thinking straight, it's becoming clear the daughter is, in her own twisted way. Other accounts, he must have put the money somewhere."

"Working on that."

"We've already eliminated some buildings and locations." As he worked, Feeney gestured to a screen where Eve saw numerous buildings blacked out. "We zero in on the post-Urban prefabs, we eliminate more."

241

Nodding, she answered her 'link, looked at Dickhead.

"I've got her, in my office. She's scared shitless."

"Put her on. Jacoby."

"Lieu — Lieu — Lieutenant, I — "

"Pull it together. You're safe, you're going to stay safe. You know Reginald Mackie."

"Lieutenant, please, my son. My boy's home alone, just the house droid. My boy."

"We'll take care of it. MacNab, dispatch protection detail to Jacoby's residence. Jacoby, the minute we're done, contact your kid, tell him to expect officers. Tell him to ask to see identification before admitting them."

"He knows that, he knows that already. He wouldn't — "

"Good. You know Reginald Mackie."

"Yes, my son and his daughter have some classes together. I knew his wife, Susann. I — "

"Did he come to you, ask you to investigate her accident?"

"He was desperate, grieving. He — "

Before Eve could shut down the excuses, she heard Berenski's voice. "Yes or no, Jacoby. Nobody's going to burn you over it. Truth and brief. Now."

"Yes, he came to me, asked me. I did the reconstruction on my own time, and I ran the evidence, analyzed the reports, everything. I had to tell him it just wasn't anyone's fault. I didn't tell him it was Susann's, but that's the truth. He was angry, accused me of covering up. Then he apologized. He didn't mean it, but he apologized. I haven't seen or spoken to him since."

242

"Okay. You're safe, your boy's safe. McNab, officers' names?"

"Task and Newman dispatched. ETA two minutes."

"Task and Newman — make sure he verifies those officers. They'll be at your door in two minutes."

"Thank you. Thank you."

"Use your own 'link," Berenski said, snatching back his own. "So your kid recognizes it. Bag this crazy son of a bitch, Dallas, before he targets somebody else in my house. Shit, before he targets me."

"We're closing in."

She clicked off, dragged a hand through her hair.

Swing shift, she thought. Dickhead was putting in overtime, too. She made a mental note to cut him at least a sliver of a break the next time he exhibited Dickheaded behavior.

"Working on possibles on Second," Feeney announced.

"Still eliminating on Lex," McNab bounced back.

"Feed me the data." Roarke worked a keyboard with one hand, a swipe screen with another. "I'll fold it into financials and ID."

When her 'link signaled again, Eve stepped back from their chatter.

"Jacoby's secured, and being transported to a safe house. Officers are with her son now," Peabody announced. "Nobody's hit on the nest, as yet."

"Get me a consult with Mira."

"If you mean now, Dallas, it's nearly twenty-hundred hours. She's not in her office. Do you want me to contact her at home?"

"It can wait." She already had a good picture of the Mackie dynamics. "Anybody who hasn't had a dinner break takes one — thirty minutes. We pull the search for the nest at twenty-two-hundred. All officers and detectives report for full briefing at oh-seven-thirty. Until that time, everyone's on standby."

"I'll make the contacts. You're in EDD? Can you use me up there?"

"I can always use the She-Body," McNab said.

"Awww."

"Knock it off." Eve paced the lab. "We have a target outstanding."

"I'm running the initials — actually eliminated some lawyers with them. There are so damn many lawyers," Peabody added. "And paralegals, and ambulance chasers, and disbarred lawyers, and just passed the bar — "

"Keep at it. Take a damn dinner break, but keep at it."

She paced some more.

"Five strong possibles. Three ranging Twenty-First and Fifteenth, between Second and Third. Two on Third at Eighteenth."

She turned to Feeney, began to scan the data.

"Two on Lex, between Nineteeth and Fourteenth," McNab added. "Another two between Lex and Third, one on Twentieth, one on Sixteenth."

"Two apartments, two townhouses, one loft above retail space."

"I've got two apartments, two townhouses," McNab said.

Eve scanned the data. "Let's see the houses first. More privacy, and you're in control of security. ID on tenants."

"On screen." Eve frowned at the first ID shot when Feeney put it up, then at McNab's. "Not Mackie. Let's see the others."

"Zip." McNab grabbed his fizzy, slurped some. "We'll move farther south, and east to Second."

"Wait a minute. The townhouse on Third. Pull that back up, Feeney. Gabe Willowby," Eve murmured. "Willow, Willowby. Younger said he and the second wife picked Gabriel as a boy's name."

Feeney's droopy eyes lit. "Too fucking tidy."

"Way too. It's not Mackie in the ID shot, but look at the data. His height. His age bracket, his eye color."

"Easy enough to create a dupe ID, one that pops on a search," Roarke began. "And have another using the same name, that matches your face." He smiled. "Or so I've heard."

"Yeah, I bet. McNab, full level-three run on Willowby." She pulled out her 'link again. "Cancel dinner breaks. Everyone report back to Central for full briefing. We just caught a break. Send me everything you get," she said as she turned toward the door. "Conference Room A, as soon as you can."

Wishing she had Whitney's elevator bypass, Eve took the glides. And as the wish made her think of Whitney, she tagged her commander — at home — then Lowenbaum, still in Central.

Peabody ran to catch up when Eve hopped off the glide and arrowed toward the conference room.

"What break?"

"McNab's running a level three on a Gabe Willowby, Third Avenue address. Not Mackie's face, but same general description."

"Willowby. That name — I think that name popped on one of my travel runs." Peabody pulled out her PPC to check as they entered the conference room. "I just need to — Yeah, yeah, Willowby, Gabriel, and minor son, Colt, on the manifest for a shuttle flight to New Mexico in November."

"Colt? That's the name of a gun manufacturer. She's passing as a boy. Get Colt Willowby on screen."

"That's not her," Peabody said when the task was done, "but — "

"Hair and eye color, an easy change. But this kid could be her cousin. Her cousin of the same age, the same height and weight. Run a level three on that ID, use your PPC. I need the comp."

"What are you doing?"

"Running a face recognition on the kid's ID — let's see if anything pops." As it worked, Eve studied the board, paced in front of it. "He'll have multiple IDs for both of them. Cashed in his pension, and got an insurance payout for the wife's accidental death. He could afford them — or a twenty-year vet? He might know how to generate them."

"More likely the kid could." Peabody shrugged. "Kids are just quicker with tech, evolving tech, and a teenager's always interested in fake IDs, ones that'll pass a level one anyway. Like this one did."

246

"Either way, he'd have more than one. Rent the place, do some travel using this one. Other travel using another. If he has an account for his finances, that's in another. Credit cards, 'link account. Mix it up."

She spun back when the comp signaled. "There's the face, and Colt Willowby is actually Silas Jackson, age sixteen, from Louisville, Kentucky. Forget that search, we've got them. No, let it run — the more evidence the better — but use the comp now to get me everything you can on the Third Avenue property."

"I have that for you," Roarke said as he walked in. "Already sent."

"Handy. Peabody, put it up."

"I also ran a facial recognition on Willowby — who is actually Dwayne Mathias, fifty-three, from Bangor, Maine."

"That's cop thinking."

"And you insult me," he said, flicking a finger down the dent in her chin, "when I have a dozen pizzas on the way."

"Pizza!"

Eve gave Peabody and her happy dance a sidelong look.

"Nobody got that dinner break," Peabody pointed out. "I grabbed a yogurt bar, but that's it."

"And hungry cops may be more likely to make mistakes," Roarke concluded.

"I thought hungry kept you lean and mean. I'm feeling mean." Eve stared at the blueprints on screen. "But pizza sounds okay."

Cop thinking, she mused, and he'd done the work faster than she had. Plus pizza. Hard to complain.

"Tri-level duplex," she observed. "Johns on the first and second only, so I'd say: Keep first level clean — they're going to get deliveries, don't want weapons or plans in view — sleep second, use third for strategy sessions, storage. Fire escapes, rear, and potential roof access. Third bedroom on the second floor could be used for work, too. Subway's an easy walk, or run if you need to run. Bus stop's convenient. It's a good location, a good HQ."

"One that's showing its age," Roarke added, "and the effects of poor construction. Willowby rented with an option, and as the asking price is easily fifty thousand dollars over what it's worth, I'd conclude he didn't bother to negotiate."

"He doesn't plan to buy it."

"I agree with that. The rent's low in any case."

Lowenbaum stepped in, looked at the screens. "You got him."

"We will."

"Then let's get to work."

Cops came in from the field minutes before pizza. Eve allowed the wolf attack — Roarke was right, cops had to eat — and brought them up to date while they ate.

"McNab, your level-three results."

He swallowed a hefty bite of pizza, loaded. "The ID cruised through a standard level one, and would have passed a sloppy, even a down-and-dirty level two, but it cracked like an egg on three. Totally bogus ID, Dallas,

248

but a decent one. Nobody but law enforcement runs a three — and then generally only when there's a major crime involved."

"Same on the second suspect," Peabody put in. "Just like the one the suspect used for check-in at the hotel."

"That keeps it clean, establishes pattern. Peabody, push the warrant through now. We go with the same op as before. Lowenbaum's got his team in their ready room. EDD will roll out, using sensors to let us know if the suspects are inside. There's an art studio on the west side of Third. McNab and Callendar will set up there.

"Lowenbaum."

He rose, used a laser pointer to highlight the projected positions of his men. "Patroni will access the studio with McNab and Callendar. He requested the assignment," Lowenbaum told Dallas. "He's one of my best. He'll stick."

"All right then, saddle it up. Peabody, we roll with EDD."

This time they rolled in the dark, after a long day of hunting. As they drove across town, Eve went over every step, tried to calculate every possibility.

"He'll want to protect his daughter," Roarke said, but she shook her head.

"He's not running this show, he only thinks he is. She may play the student, the apprentice, but she's driving the ball now. Maybe she's been driving it for a while."

"Do you see them as willing to die for this?"

"She doesn't want to die, she wants to kill. He has a mission, fucked-up as it is, and would probably die for it. But she wouldn't have stopped there. She wants to kill. We've taken all but one of the targets off the board. We take them down here, or she'll find that last target. Then? She can wait. She's young, she has resources, she has IDs, and likely she can get more. How long can we keep everyone she's after protected? She's got time on her side of this. We take them down here and now."

When they reached the drop-off point, McNab gave Peabody a finger wiggle and slipped out with Callendar.

Didn't look like cops, Eve thought, in the bright coats, patterned airboots. They walked briskly, as anyone would on a windy night in January.

Eve ran through check-ins from her men, from Lowenbaum and his as Roarke and Feeney got to work.

"He's got it barricaded," Feeney told her.

"What do you mean, barricaded?"

"Shields on the doors, on the windows. Stun deflectors. He's put some work in here, and some serious moola."

"Can you get through them?"

"Not with a stun or a laser on anything under five. He's got some jammers set up, too, but give us a minute here."

"Last stand," she murmured. "He figured he had more time, time enough to finish the mission, hoped to get out with his daughter. But if and when it came down to it, he'd take his last stand here. Are they in there?"

250

"Working on it," Roarke muttered while Feeney coordinated with McNab and Callendar. "The place may be a pile of shite, but he invested well in his bloody moat. There now, nearly there now. Feeney?"

"Yeah, I got you. McNab, you following?"

"Right behind you, Captain. It's wobbling, it's sputtering, and . . . we got it. Several heat sources popping, but . . . "

"I don't think so," Roarke said quietly. "Another minute here."

"He's set them up. Counterfeits — it's false imaging," Feeney explained. "We can survey and eliminate."

"First floor's generated. No warm bodies there," Roarke said.

"Surveying second level." Feeney nodded at the small screen. "And it's clear."

"We're on three," McNab announced. "Knocking down the bullshit."

"And that's one." Callendar's satisfied voice came through. "Single heat source third floor, north corner facing west, behind shielded window."

"That's not the girl." Eve hunkered down for a better look. "Too tall."

"She could have gone out for food," Peabody suggested, "supplies."

"I don't think so. He's on duty. He's waiting for us. We'll give it thirty, in case. If she went out for food, that's enough time. Baxter, Trueheart, split off, take a walk, check takeout joints, 24/7s, delis, any market still open within a three-block radius. If you spot her, don't let her make you."

"Peeling off now."

"If she's outside, bringing home some egg rolls, we take her down — fast, hard, done. We may be able to bargain Mackie into surrendering if we have her as weight."

"But you don't think so." Feeney turned to her. "He sent her out, stay covered, stay safe so you can finish the mission. He's the distraction."

"Yeah. Yeah, that's my gut on it, but we have to see it through. She could be anywhere. Lowenbaum, we need him alive. He can be hurting, but we need him breathing. Have you got a shot?"

"He knows how to keep covered, Dallas, and that's what he's doing. We can punch some holes in the barricades, but right now, we can't take him out."

"Battering ram would take down the door," she considered, "but give him time for whatever he has in mind by the time we get to the third floor. Taking out as many of us as he can, taking himself out. Worse, targeting civilians."

She closed her eyes a moment, held up a hand so nobody spoke and interrupted her thoughts. "Lowenbaum, does Tactical have anything handy that'll cut through those crappy walls — the common wall?"

After a beat of silence he answered. "Yeah. Yeah, we've got something."

"Stay where you are. I'm coming to you. Can you spare Roarke?" she asked Feeney.

"I think the kids and I can handle things."

"You're with me. You don't look like a cop."

"Why, thank you."

"Peabody, give me that stupid coat."

"My coat!"

"Pink coat, snowflake hat." She pulled it out of her pocket. "I don't look like a cop."

"Beg to differ," Roarke murmured.

"I know how to not look like a cop. I need like a . . . " She gestured.

"Purse?"

"Yeah, yeah, a bag thing. Tool or tools can go in that. What've we got in here?"

Feeney pulled open a drawer. "McNab's old satchel."

The old satchel was a wild green just short of fluorescent, with a jagged lightning bolt pattern done in Peabody pink.

"Christ, it's nearly as bad as one of Jenkinson's ties."

"I heard that," Jenkinson said in her ear.

"It's not a secret. Okay, give me your coat." Eve took off her much-loved coat, put on Peabody's girlie pink coat, and dragged her own cap onto her head. "The scarf, too."

Eve wound Peabody's bold, brightly colored scarf around her neck.

"It actually looks really good with the bag."

"Don't ever say that again." She hitched the bag on cross-body like a sensible New Yorker, and slipped out of the van.

"We need to circle the block, come around from the south, hook up with Lowenbaum. Then we're going to walk fast, hold hands, laugh and talk, straight to the connecting duplex."

"So I assumed." And, though there was no need to do so at this point, he took her hand as they walked west. "There are heat sources in the attached house — three of them. One would be a small dog, possibly a large cat."

"We'll deal with that."

"I don't doubt it."

As they walked they passed Baxter, who kept going as he spoke in her earbud. "No sign of her yet. Trueheart?"

"I've hit two places with previous sightings — pizza joint, deli. Nobody's seen her today or tonight."

"Finish the sweep, then retake your positions. Without her as a bargaining chip, odds are slim to nada on talking him out."

As they rounded the next corner, Lowenbaum hopped out of the big armored van. "Got battering rams, sledgehammers, torches, but I figured you didn't want to make that much noise."

"Not if you've got something else.

"Laser cutter. She'll go through those interior walls like shit through a goose. Not as noisy as the other options, but she hums. If he hears it, he'll know what it is."

"We'll make sure he doesn't hear it."

"I can go in, create an entry."

"I need you out here, Lowenbaum. The chances of me taking out a trained sniper most likely in body armor with my sidearm? Low. We're the distraction, and believe me, we're going to duck and cover when necessary. I need you to take him down — that's on you. We'll get him to move — you tell me when and where — and we'll make it happen so you can take him down."

"You can count on that. Do either of you know how to work a laser cutter?"

"I do, yes." Roarke took it, studied it. "And a fine one it is," he added as he put it inside the satchel.

"I'm going to call Trueheart and Baxter in. Make sure everyone's aware there are civilians in the attached house. We'll get them to a secured area, but stay aware."

She started to walk again. "Baxter, Trueheart, back to post. Roarke and I are heading for the corner of Third and Eighteenth, about to move into suspect's eyeline."

"In that case." Roarke wrapped an arm around her, glued her to his side. "Could we look less concerned about murderers?"

When they stopped at the corner, she tugged him down to her for a kiss, studied the target location, and murmured against his mouth, "He's scanning the street, so he's seen us. But he hasn't moved to cover the back. Might have some sort of early warning system set up for that."

She snuggled in against him as they crossed at the light. "We're going straight to the neighbors, like we're expected."

"Jan Maguire, Philippe Constant. I looked them up while you were changing coats."

"Jan and Phil, got it. Do you want to tell me how come you know how to work a laser cutter?"

He grinned down at her. "Not at this time."

She grinned back, let out a laugh she hoped carried. "Thank God we're here. I'm freezing! We're springing for a cab on the way home."

"Let's see how it goes."

They walked up the steps and, with their backs to the target, pressed the buzzer.

CHAPTER
THIRTEEN

Roarke shifted his body to block any possible view from the adjoining duplex when Eve palmed her badge.

"First trick is to get them to open the door, fast. After that, just move in. We'll deal with the rest inside."

She didn't need a trick, as the door opened.

The man, mid-thirties, wearing a gray Mets sweatshirt and jeans with holes in the knees, frowned at the badge.

"What?"

"Hey, Philippe!" With a blast of a smile, Eve moved forward. Roarke closed the door at their backs.

"Wait just a — "

"There's trouble next door. I'm Lieutenant Dallas, NYPSD, and this is my consultant. I need you to call Jan — just call her from wherever she is."

"But I want to know — "

"Philippe," Roarke said in a smooth, easy tone. "The quicker you follow the lieutenant's instructions, the quicker we'll explain. How's your soundproofing?"

"Our — well, we're working on it. Why — "

"I see you're doing some renovations," Roarke continued in that same conversational tone, then glanced at Eve. "Handy."

"Yeah, should be. Call her, get her down here." As she spoke, Eve stripped off the pink coat because it made her feel like an idiot, tossed it on a seriously old-fashioned hall rack someone had painted bright blue.

"Let me see that badge again."

Eve held it closer, waited while he studied it, and her. And, still watching her, he shouted out, "Jan! Come on down here."

"Phil, I'm in the middle of — "

"Come on, Jan."

Moments later a tall woman in paint-splattered overalls, blond hair bundled up under a Yankees cap appeared. A mop head of white scurried down after her, yipping all the way. "I was just putting another coat of — Oh, sorry. I didn't know there was anyone here."

"They're the cops."

"The — "

Jan stopped when Eve put a finger to her lips, then scooped up what had to be a dog, continued down the stairs.

"Let's take this back there." Eve gestured. "Have you got a music system? How about you put on some music, like you would when friends come over. There's trouble next door," she repeated. "You share a wall, and your soundproofing's iffy. Put on some music, we'll go in the back, and I'll tell you what's going on."

As the dog wiggled to get down, Jan groped for Philippe's hand. "Behave, Lucy! I told you something was off with the new people, Phil. What did they — Okay." She shook her head, sucked in some air. "Let's

258

go back to the lounge. You won't believe how great it looks now."

Eve gave her a nod of approval. "Can't wait to see it."

"Put on some tunes, Phil, and let's crack that wine. I don't know how much they can hear over there," Jan said quietly as they headed back, past dingy walls, spaces where dingy walls had obviously been torn down. "We can sort of hear them — their screen noises, and on the third floor some thumping around. That's where our workshop is, so we spend a lot of time up there."

When they reached what Jan called the lounge, Eve noted it was pretty great. They'd transformed the space into a cozy, retro-style kitchen with warm gray counters and a lot of plants thriving under dull silver gro-lights. It spread into a lounge space with big cushy furniture, floor pillows, funky lamps on one side, and a long table with eight mismatched chairs under a trio of wire balls that served as pendant lights.

In the corner sat another pillow with three short sides, and a bone-shaped toy in fluorescent blue.

"Isn't this charming."

"Thanks." Jan offered Roarke an uncertain smile as she set the dog down. It scurried — Did it have feet under that hair? Eve wondered — grabbed the bone, and scurried back with it clamped in its teeth like a bright blue cigar. "We've been working hard on it. Month fourteen now."

Roarke tapped a finger on the kitchen island. "You're doing the work yourselves?"

"With some friends as slave labor. We wanted this area done first, and the powder room down there. We're nearly finished with the master suite now."

"Great." While she understood Roarke's line of conversation served to calm the civilians, time mattered. She tapped her earbud. "Feeney, where is he?"

"Still third level."

"Let me know if he moves. This is an NYPSD operation," she began as the dog stared up at her — she could just see its eyes. "The individuals next door are suspects in an ongoing investigation. We know the adult male is currently stationed on the third floor of the adjoining building. Have you seen the second individual?"

"The boy?" Philippe frowned, looked at Jan. "I don't remember seeing him today, but I was at work, didn't get back until around six."

"I worked here today, third floor. I was painting. I saw him head out, maybe about four, four-thirty? I'm not sure of the time, it could've been a little later. He had his backpack and some sort of big case. I don't know if he came back. They're dangerous, aren't they?"

"Yes, they are. We need your cooperation," Eve continued as Jan scooped up the dog again, held it like a baby in her arms. "Let me assure you, there are police stationed outside, and our first priority is your safety."

"Oh man." Philippe pulled Jan against his side. "What did they do? We've got a right to know."

"They're the prime suspects in the strikes on Wollman Rink and Times Square."

"I'm going to sit down." Jan's color drained away as she pulled out a counter stool. "I'm just going to sit down a minute."

Scared, Eve noted, but not surprised.

"Have they approached you?"

"The opposite," Jan said. "Both made it clear they didn't want any neighborly interaction. The boy's only here half the time."

"Actually, it's a girl."

"Really? The man calls him — her — Will. I heard that a few times. He — damn it, she goes off every other week. I figured it's a custody deal, and would've felt a little sorry about it, but *she* gave me the creeps. Something about her just had the hairs on the back of my neck sticking up."

"She's just a kid," Philippe murmured.

"Who, along with her father, is responsible for the deaths of seven people. We could wait him out, but other lives are on the line. In the case she carried away with her is, we believe, a long-range laser rifle. We need to capture her father and learn her location and the name and location of her next target. The quickest, cleanest way, we feel, is to do that from inside."

"Inside what?"

"Phil." Jan shook her head at him. "Inside here to inside there. Common wall."

"Go through our place to his? He's armed, isn't he?"

"He is. So are we. There are twenty cops, armed, ready to move in. If we take the building by force, there will be injuries, possibly fatalities. This way lessens."

"You have to get Jan out, get her to safety first."

"We can work with that."

"No." Jan pushed to her feet again. "No, because first I'm not going without you, and if we both go and he sees us, the whole thing falls apart."

"We could walk Lucy."

"Phil, you walked Lucy right after you got home. It wouldn't look right if we went out again with her, and we've got . . . well, company."

"We can keep you safe inside," Eve told them. "My word on it. Do you do any renovations in the evenings like this?"

"Sure. We knock off anything that's annoyingly noisy around ten, but most of this is done in the evenings and on weekends."

"We need to see the second floor. You're just taking your friends upstairs, showing them the work. Okay?"

"Jan?"

"We're going to be okay, Phil."

"I'm not letting anything happen to you, so yeah, we're going to be okay. So let's get married."

"You said — what?"

"I love you, you love me. We adopted a dog together. We're building a home together, and I'm taking this as a sign. Let's get married."

"I . . . yeah." On a half laugh, Jan threw her arm around Philippe's neck, pressed with the little dog held between them. "Let's get married."

"Congratulations, but maybe we could hold off on the wine and applause until *after* we've taken the killer next door into police custody."

262

"Sorry. This is the strangest, scariest night of my life." Philippe dropped his brow to Jan's. "And it made me realize I want to spend all the rest of them with you."

"Sweet. Kudos. Let's move."

As Eve strode out, Roarke dropped a hand on Philippe's shoulder. "Love changes everything. I proposed to my wife after we limped away from a physical altercation with another serial killer. Good times."

"Feels surreal, but I guess not so much when you're a cop."

"She is. I'm not."

Eyes widened, Philippe pointed at Eve, then at Roarke, got a nod.

"And trust me, you and your fiancée couldn't be in better hands."

Eve walked straight back — rooms without doors, rooms full of building supplies — to the master suite in progress.

"This is directly under him," she said quietly. "Anything that's not inane chatter about decor and marriage, keep it down."

"This room's soundproofed," Jan told her.

"All the better." Eve looked up, imagined Mackie, then studied the communal wall.

It didn't matter to her it was smooth, clean, and the color of Irish moss. It mattered that the wall led to Reginald Mackie.

"I just finished the second coat — or nearly finished." Jan sighed. "Does it really have to be this wall?"

"Quickest, safest. The department will have it fully repaired, and in a timely fashion. I'll make sure of it. Feeney?"

"Got you. He's maintaining position. I read four people in your location, and the dog, directly under his."

"We're going in from here. The two civilians and the dog will return to the main level, rear — get your outdoor gear," she told them. "And be ready to be removed to safety if necessary."

"Copy that," Feeney responded. "Two civilians and, ah, a dog, to be taken out when needed. How about a little distraction on the street — draw his attention while you're cutting through."

"Couldn't hurt."

"Tell me when you're ready."

Eve pulled the laser cutter out of the satchel. "We're ready."

"Jenkinson, Reineke, you're on," Feeney announced.

"That's top-of-the-line." Drawn to the tool, Philippe moved closer. "We invested in a good one, but that's top-of-the-line."

"It's yours," Eve said on impulse. "When we're done here."

"No shit?"

"None whatsoever." She handed the cutter to Roarke. "Get your gear, go downstairs, back to that lounge area. If we need you out, cops will get you clear. Otherwise, hold tight, keep quiet."

Eve gave the dog — still clamping the blue bone — a steady stare. "And keep the dog quiet, too, if you can."

Jan took one more look at the wall. "It's just paint. And new wiring. And soundproofing."

Philippe put his arm around her to lead her out. "And every time we look at it, we'll remember the night we got engaged."

Eve waited until they were clear, then pulled out her weapon. "Just big enough for us to get through."

Roarke hunkered down, switched on the tool.

It hummed, but to Eve's ears Galahad's sleeping purr pitched louder.

"Curtain's up," Feeney said in her ear.

Eve sidestepped to the window, spotted her detectives — hanging on to each other as drunks do. Soundproofing and what she took to be new windows aside, she could hear them singing.

Top of the lungs, she imagined, in some sort of actual harmony.

Stumbling, falling-down drunks, carrying each other home.

Not bad.

She moved back to Roarke, who'd cut a thin line from the baseboard up about two feet, and began to cut another two feet away.

"Can't you cut faster?"

"Do you want it quiet or fast?"

"Both."

"Just hold your water, Lieutenant."

"What does that even mean?"

"Don't piss yourself," Feeney informed her.

"Then it oughta be 'don't piss yourself.' He's nearly through." She angled her recorder.

"Copy that. He shifted some, but they don't have a clear shot. Your boys have his attention. Jeez, some street LC's trying to work them. You see that?"

"I can live without seeing two of my detectives getting propped by an LC. We've got a hole. Going through."

Even as she bellied down, Roarke slid in front of her. She tugged, jerked her thumb behind her, but he just shook his head, and wormed his way through.

"Roarke's in," she whispered. "I'm behind him." She blocked out annoyance — who was the cop here — and slithered through into a room dark as pitch.

Roarke touched her arm, then switched on a penlight.

She followed it, scanning a room about the size of the one they'd left. She made out an air mattress, a sleeping bag, a batt-powered lamp, and a nearly empty bottle of liquor — maybe gin, maybe vodka. Folding table and chair, she noted, with a tablet and a small printer.

The door stood open to more dark.

"He's got it blacked out in here," she murmured to Feeney. "Probably has night-vision goggles. We're moving. Stay low," she told Roarke, and combat crawled toward the door.

He stayed ahead of her again — he was longer, and he had the light. She'd have something to say to him about that later.

"Through the door, moving toward the stairs. Going silent."

She moved into a crouch, slowly started up toward the third floor. Halfway up, she started to tap Roarke, have him turn off even that thin beam. But he tapped her first, kept his hand on her arm, cut the light.

When they reached the top, the mini motion detector aimed at the stairs set off a wild beep.

"He dropped! He's moving toward you."

"Take cover!" Eve shouted to Roarke, and rolled. She saw the streak from the strike whiz by, laid down a stream of suppressing fire. "Stay clear, you stay clear! Punch those holes, get me some light." She rolled again, sprang up. "Move in, move in."

A high whine had her dropping, a series of tiny holes punched through the barricades on the window. She felt more than saw Mackie hit the stairs.

"He's going down to two. Roarke, are you clear?"

"Clear. You're not wearing any armor. Stay behind me."

"His aim's crap," she said, and bolted down. She heard Roarke cursing viciously behind her, heard the battering ram crashing, crashing against the door down below.

Felt her way along the wall until her hand came to a doorway.

"At your six!" Feeney shouted.

She dropped and rolled, heard the thud of something striking the wall, fired toward it.

"He's moving past you, made a left."

"Roarke, move left — hit the wall, stay down." She did the same. "Mackie! It's done, it's finished. Throw out your weapons and surrender."

He answered with a volley of strikes that whined and speared through the opposing wall.

She put her lips to Roarke's ear. "Get the penlight. Stay out of range. Aim in at the doorway."

"I can widen the beam."

"Do that. Feeney, exact position?"

"Back wall, between the windows. Five feet east, ten feet north of your position. They don't have a shot."

"Copy that." She squeezed Roarke's hand. "In three, two."

She moved on one, hurtling down the narrow hall, calculating distance as the light flashed.

She got a glimpse — hand lasers, full body armor, night-vision goggles.

With her stunner two clicks down from full power, she aimed for his eyes.

She felt the burn streak down her arm, heard him cry out, rolled clear. Laid down another stream as Roarke rushed to flank the doorway. His stream hit Mackie low, biting into his boots, hers went back for the goggles.

This time, he dropped.

"Suspect down, he's down." She rushed in, kicked away the weapon that dropped out of his shaking hand. "Get me more light, get me some damn light." But she yanked Mackie's arms back, snapped on restraints before she tested the pulse in his throat.

"He's alive." She felt the wet on her fingers, smelled the blood. "He's bleeding. We need the MTs. We need a bus."

She heard breaking glass, the booming crash of the door and barricade giving out, then the rush of boots.

"He's down," she repeated. "Hold your fire. Get the damn lights on."

"He cut the power." Lowenbaum dropped down, pulled a flashlight out of his belt. "They're working on it." He trailed the light over Mackie. "Goggles shattered. Looks like he got shards in his eyes. Let's get a medic!" he shouted.

"He can wait. The lieutenant's hit."

At Roarke's terse statement, Eve glanced at her arm, saw the blood seeping down her sleeve. "Grazed me is all."

"Bollocks to that." So saying, Roarke hauled her up, dragged the jacket off.

"Look, simmer. I know when I'm really hurt."

"More bollocks. If you knew so bloody much, you'd be wearing your armor."

"I had it — the coat." She hissed when he ripped off her sleeve, used it to staunch the blood.

"You aren't wearing the shagging coat, are you?"

"I — "

"And I didn't think of it until it was too late." He bound up the wound, then caught her face in his hands. When her eyes fired out a warning — Don't even *think* about kissing me — he nearly smiled. "You'll have that tended to properly."

"Yeah, yeah. Nice field dressing, thanks for that. Now I'm going to make sure my suspect stays alive."

She turned as Peabody hurried in. "Civilians?"

"Secure — still in their own residence. Magly cute dog. MTs on the way — ETA one minute. The house is being cleared, and Feeney's working with McNab and Callendar to get the power up again. You got hit!"

"Grazed."

"But — but — you had my magic coat."

"I took it off. Don't," Eve said before Peabody could harass her as Roarke had. "When the power's up, get EDD to check out any and all electronics. Then — "

"Dallas, you want to take a look here."

She looked back as Lowenbaum played his light around the room.

Or, more accurately, the armory. A battered worktable held more than two dozen weapons — long and short range, knives, boomers. More body armor hung on pegs, along with other goggles, field glasses.

"He must've been stockpiling for a while, maybe even before his wife died."

"There's another knife stuck in the wall out there," Peabody said.

"So that's what that was." Eve looked down at Mackie. "You're going to find that funk, too. I could see the tremor in his hands."

She stepped back as the MTs came in. "Patch him up, bring him around. I need him in Interview."

To keep Roarke off her back, she let the MTs treat her arm while she, Lowenbaum, and Feeney had their roundup.

"He had a two-level barricade on the doors and windows," Lowenbaum told her. "If we'd tried storming, he'd have picked some of us off."

"Maybe — didn't want to risk it — but he's not the marksman he was. My team found two kegs of funk hidden in the closet of his room. Probably hiding it from the daughter, but she'd have been blind and deaf not to see the effects."

"Prided himself on his exceptional vision and steady hands." Lowenbaum shook his head. "But he goes on the funk, goes on what takes those away."

"Ever known a funky-junkie who didn't think they'd beat the effects until they didn't? I'm going to the hospital — I've got four cops on him. Unless he's fricking dying, he'll be in a cage tonight."

"Heard the MTs say he'd need surgery on his right eye — maybe the left, too." Feeney shrugged. "Even then he ain't getting it all back — some of that's the funk. Got some burns on his lower calves where the boot leather seared into him. I'm not going to cry about it."

"He was a good man once. I'm not going to cry about it, either," Lowenbaum added. "But I'm goddamn sorry he lost the man he was."

"The daughter's still out there." Eve pushed to her feet, ignored the low-level burn down her arm. "And there's no evidence suggesting she has any trouble with steady hands or eyesight. We get him patched up, get him in a cage, break him."

"It's his daughter, Dallas. I don't see how you can break him down enough to flip on her."

"He's a junkie," she said flatly. "I'll break him."

But not that night. Eve argued with nurses, with doctors, and ultimately with the surgeon. Reginald

Mackie would not and could not be released from the hospital for at least twelve hours.

"We removed sixteen shards of infrared lens out of his right eye and seven out of his left."

"He killed seven people in two days."

The surgeon huffed out a breath. Maybe his own eyes looked exhausted, but Eve didn't give a shit.

"You do your job, Lieutenant, I do mine. I'm giving you the facts. His addiction has already compromised his vision, his retina, and his optic nerves. This trauma has left his corneas and his retinas damaged further. Once cured of his addiction, he would be a viable candidate for organ replacement, or at least additional surgery, but at this point we've done what can be done. He and his eyes need rest. We need to keep him under observation, as we're concerned about more deterioration or infection."

"Is he awake?"

"Yes, he should be. And he's restrained and guarded. We have our own security backing up your officers. We're fully aware of who he is, and what he's done."

"I want to talk to him."

"I have no medical objection to that. His head is in a stabilizer. We don't want him to move his head, jar his eyes in any way, for the next twelve hours. After that, I'll examine him, and hopefully clear him for release to your custody."

Accepting it was the best she'd get, Eve made her way to Mackie's room. She moved through the two uniforms on the door, inside where she had two more keeping watch.

Mackie lay still, his head slightly inclined inside the cage-like stabilizer, his eyes covered with bandages. Tubes ran from him into machines, and the machines clicked and hummed busily.

God, she hated hospitals, had hated them since she woke up in one at the age of eight. Broken, battered, with no idea where she was, who she was.

But Mackie knew who and where.

She signaled to the uniforms to give her the room, then approached the bed.

"Record on," she said clearly, and saw Mackie's fingers flex in reaction. "Dallas, Lieutenant Eve, questioning Mackie, Reginald. Mackie, in case you missed it, you've been placed under arrest for multiple counts of murder, conspiracy to murder, possession of illegal weapons, armed assault on police officers, and a whole bunch of lesser charges. It's what we could call a freaking cornucopia of charges. Also, in case you missed it, I'm going to reread you your rights."

As she did, slowly, she watched him, watched his jaw tighten, his mouth firm, and those fingers tap, tap, tap on the sheets.

"Do you understand your rights and obligations in these matters? I know you're awake and aware, Mackie," she said after a beat. "And you know that you'll be out of here and in a cage very soon. Stonewalling me gets you nowhere. We'll find her."

This time his thinned lips curved, just a little.

"Don't think so? Think again. We'll find her, and when we do, she'll spend a lot more years in a cage than you have left. Fifteen years old? She could spend a hard century in a cage, off-planet. Never see the sun again. If you think her age will play in her favor, think again there, too. I put away one younger than she is. If I have to hunt her, I'll make it my mission to see she spends every day of the rest of her life locked up like an animal."

His hands shook, but he managed to lift the middle finger of his right hand.

"Gee, that stings. I guess you're feeling pretty smug, lying there getting pain meds and something to cut down on the funk withdrawal. But that won't last. I wonder if you're thinking Willow's on her way to Alaska. Yeah, that's right," she added when his hands fisted. "We know all about Alaska. We'd bag her, bag, tag, and toss her in that cage. But she's not heading to Alaska, you idiot. She had a hit list of her own. Headed by her mother, her stepfather, her little brother."

"Liar." He croaked it out.

"She has blueprints of her school."

"Get out."

"The names of specific school employees and students she plans to take out."

His breathing sped up, quick, short breaths. The trembling increased. He said, "Lawyer."

Eve deliberately misunderstood him. "We know you had the lawyer on your list. I'm talking about hers."

"Lawyer," he repeated. "I want a lawyer."

"So you understand your rights and obligations?"

"I understand, and I want a lawyer."

274

"Your choice, a bad one, but that's not a surprise considering your track record. Give me a name, a contact, and we'll get your lawyer."

"Provided. Appointed."

"You want a court-appointed representative. Okay. Seriously bad choice, but I'll start that ball rolling. The doc says you'll be ready to move in under twelve hours now. Enjoy your plush accommodations while you can. They're going to go seriously downhill. End of questioning."

Eve stepped to the door, switched off her recorder. "A lot of blood on your hands, Mackie. Your daughter's may be on them before this is over. You think about that while you wait for your lawyer."

She stepped out, jerked a thumb at the two uniforms to send them back into the room.

"He said lawyer," she told the other uniforms on the door. "I'll be arranging that. No one but the lawyer, if and when he arrives here, and authorized medical personnel are to enter his room. Check every ID, and scan anyone going in for weapons."

"Yes, sir."

"Drag over a couple of chairs," she advised. "It's going to be a long night."

She walked away, hunted up the head nurse. Badged her. "I'm to be informed the minute Reginald Mackie is medically cleared for transport."

"Of course."

"He's requested a lawyer, and I'll arrange one. No one but the lawyer, when appointed, medicals required for his care, and authorized police officials are to be given access to him."

"Understood."

"If anyone attempts to gain information about his status, you are to log the contact, and tell them nothing."

"Lieutenant, it's not my first roundup. I know the drill."

"Good. Make sure everyone else does, too."

Stepping away, she used her 'link to begin the process of granting Mackie his right to a court-appointed lawyer.

Roarke walked over, held out a tube of Pepsi. "The coffee here is marginally better than at Central, but it's close."

"Thanks. I need another couple minutes. I want to update the commander, Peabody, make sure Mira's on tap, with all her hats, when I finally get Mackie into Interview tomorrow. And I want to talk to Nadine, have her blast the daughter's picture on screen. Other media will follow that lead."

"Take your time."

It took another thirty, but when she felt she'd done all she could do, she two-pointed the empty tube into a recycler.

"He may delude himself that she's off to Alaska, but she's still here. Still in New York, and prepping for the next strike."

"I agree with you, but there's nothing you can do here and now. You need to go home, get some sleep."

"Yeah, maybe." She glanced back as Roarke steered her toward the elevator. "I hope he sleeps right and tight tonight, because it's the last night he'll spend outside of a goddamn cage."

CHAPTER
FOURTEEN

She fell asleep in the car, her PPC falling out of her limp hand onto her lap. Reaching over, Roarke slid it into her pocket, then lowered her seat back.

She worried him. No matter how completely he understood she did what she had to, pushed herself and others because she had no choice, she worried him.

He knew how thin her defenses were when she worked herself into exhaustion.

At least she'd get a few hours' sleep in her own bed, he thought as he drove them through the gates. And he'd see she ate a decent breakfast in the morning.

He, too, did what he must, and the most important must for him was Eve.

He would have carried her in, and straight up to bed, but she stirred.

"I'm okay," she mumbled as she pushed herself up to sitting. "I've got it."

"Sleep," he said as he slid an arm around her on the way to the door.

"Yeah, I'm mostly already there. I need to be up at six. No, five-thirty's better. I want to clear some things, go into Central, and be ready when they transport Mackie."

"Five-thirty it is then."

"I can count on you for that." She leaned her head toward his shoulder, realized she could have slept standing up. "Does it have to be oatmeal? You're already thinking about what you're going to feed me in the morning."

"Pancakes." Swamped in love, he brushed a kiss over her hair. "And bacon and berries."

"And lots and lots of coffee."

He ended up carrying her the rest of the way, pulling off her boots as she dragged off her coat. Together they got her undressed. She managed a "Thanks" as she burrowed under, and was dead asleep before he slipped in beside her, wrapped an arm around her.

And let himself join her.

Eve stood on the circle of white ice with its spreading pools of blood. The wind cut like razors. In the deep, dark night, the blood read black against the white, and the bodies it flowed from were a pale and sickly gray.

She faced the girl, the girl with smooth skin and black dreads and bold green eyes.

And what she felt in that moment, looking into those bold green eyes, was a kind of pity. One she had to shove away, even in dreams.

"I'm better than you," Willow said with a glinting smile.

"At killing unarmed civilians? Sure, I'll give you that."

"Better than you all the way. I know what I am. I *like* what I am. And I'm the best at what I am. But you? You pretend to be what you're not."

"I'm a cop. I don't have to pretend."

"You're a killer, same as me."

"We're not even close to the same." Yet something shuddered through her at the words — Willow's, her own. "You kill for sport, for jollies. You kill the defenseless and the innocent. Because you can — until I stop you."

"It's the kill that counts, and I already have more racked up than you. Reasons don't matter."

"Yeah, they do. Who's running and hiding? Not me."

"I'm right here." As the wind whipped, Willow opened her arms. "And you hide every day, run and hide every day from who you are, deep down."

In the dark night, the red light began to pulse, washing over the white ice. "You did that to your own father."

Eve looked down at Richard Troy's body, at the blood seeping from more than a dozen wounds.

"I did that, and I'd do it again."

"Because you're a killer."

"Because he was a monster."

"Who says you get to choose and I don't? People hurt my father, now they're dead."

"Your father's a selfish, twisted son of a bitch."

Willow smiled again. "Yours, too, but my father loves me. He taught me, helped make me what I am. So did yours."

"I made me what I am, despite him. How did she hurt your father?" Eve pointed at the dead girl in red.

"I didn't like her. Show-off. The kind who thinks they're better than me. Like you do. When I'm done, I'll come back for you."

"When I'm done, you little freak, you'll live in a concrete cage. You and your old man."

Willow threw back her head and laughed. "You'd kill me if you could, because that's who you are. But you won't find me. I listened to my father, bitch. I learned, I worked, and I'm not finished. Before I'm done, I'll check off every name on my list, then I'll kill everyone you care about. I'll save you for last."

Willow raised her assault rifle. Eve drew her weapon.

"And then," Willow said.

They fired together.

Eve woke with a jolt, Roarke's arms around her.

"Shh, baby, it's all right. Just a dream."

"She said we're the same, but we're not. We're not the same."

"All right now. You're cold. Let me light the fire."

But she wrapped around him. "We're not the same. Sick bastard fathers don't make us the same. But she won't stop and neither will I. What does that mean?"

"It means she's as sick as her father. It means you'll do your job. You'll do whatever you can to protect others, even while you stand for the dead, for those she's killed. Not the same, darling Eve. Opposites."

"We could have been the same. We could have." She pressed her face into his shoulder, a shoulder that was always there when she needed it most. "How much is you?" She drew back, framed his face with her hands. Even in the dark she could see the wild, wonderful blue of his eyes. "I love you."

"*A ghrá*." He kissed her softly. "My only."

"I love you," she said again, pouring herself into the kiss. "You saved me."

"Each other." He laid her back, covered her with his body. "We saved each other."

She needed him, the tangible act of loving. Mouth on mouth, hands on flesh, heart beating to heart.

Not the cold, the dark, not the ugly pulse of red light and blood black against white. But warmth and beauty and passion, and all the brilliance he'd brought to her life simply by loving her.

Whatever she'd been, whatever she'd become, she was more because he loved her.

So strong, he thought, and so vulnerable. The two aspects of her in constant conflict. But that pull and tug made her what she was. And what she was, here and now, was his. Only his.

So he soothed her with long, gentle strokes. And aroused her with depthless kisses. And took the gift of her for himself, saturated himself in the feel of those long limbs, those tough muscles under soft skin.

The pulse in her throat, in her wrists, the beat, beat, beat of her heart, all that life twined with his.

She needed this, just this, more than sleep, more than food, more even than breath at that moment. Needed his body joined with hers. A testament to what she was, what he was. What they were.

282

Away from death, away from brutality, away from the cold.

She opened for him, took him in, gave herself utterly to that joining. Rising and falling together, pleasure building on pleasure until nothing else existed.

And reaching, reaching for that moment, that exquisite moment when they emptied all they were into the other.

Filled with him, she wept.

"What's this, what's this?" Undone, he gathered her close again, tried to kiss away the tears.

"I don't know." Trembling, she held tight.

So he shifted, cradled her, rocked her, and still felt helpless.

"It's stupid. Who am I crying for?"

"You're worn out, that's all. Just worn out, worn down."

It was more, she knew it, but couldn't pinpoint it. The tears, so hot, so strong, came from something, fell for something.

"I'm okay. Sorry. I'm okay."

"I'm going to get you a soother."

"No, no, I have to be up in a couple hours, right? What time is it?"

Even as she asked, her communicator signaled.

She bolted up, cheeks still wet, scrambled for the device still in the pocket of the pants she'd worn the day before.

"Lights on ten percent," Roarke ordered.

"Block video." Eve sucked in a breath. "Dallas."

"*Dispatch, Dallas, Lieutenant Eve. Report to Madison Square Garden, Thirty-First and Seventh. Multiple victims.*"

"Acknowledged. Contact Peabody, Detective Delia, Lowenbaum, Lieutenant, ah, Mitchell. I'm on my way."

Roarke tossed her clothes, grabbed his own.

"It has to be the lawyer," Eve said as she dressed. "Unless she's gone off script, it's the lawyer we couldn't find. It's after two in the goddamn morning. How did she find him?"

"Concert at Madison Square," Roarke told her. "Newly rebuilt. I expect it let out near to two. Christ Jesus, the place would have been packed. Eve, Mavis was one of the headliners."

Her hand jerked as she hooked on her weapon harness, then she forced herself to move, to just keep moving. Mavis wouldn't have exited with the crowd. It wouldn't be Mavis among the fallen.

I'll kill everyone you care about.

"We had tickets."

She pulled herself back as she dragged on boots. "What? Tickets, to this thing?"

"I gave them to Summerset."

He moved so fast, so efficiently, tossing Eve her coat, grabbing his own. But his eyes, she saw now that his eyes were stricken.

"You drive," she said as they both bolted out of the room. "I'll try to contact both of them."

Everyone you care about, she thought again, snapping Mavis's name into her 'link while they rushed down the stairs.

*Yo! Can't chat 'cause I'm doing something mag!
But I'll catch you later. Fill me in on what's the
what. Cha!*

"Mavis, tag me back. It's urgent. If you're still at
Madison Square, stay inside. Stay inside."

Even as she jumped into the car, she tried
Summerset.

*I'm unavailable at the moment, please leave your
name, a contact number, and a brief message. I'll
return your call as soon as possible.*

"Fuck, fuck, fuck. They're all right. They're both
fine." She wanted to try Leonardo, but realized if he'd
stayed home with the baby, she'd just terrify him.

No point, no point, she told herself as Roarke
bulleted through the gates.

Instead she set the dash 'link on a loop, tagging them
each in turn while she punched in Baxter, and hit the
sirens.

He didn't block video, looked wild-eyed and
exhausted at the same time, showed a shadow of beard
and hair in messy sleep tuffs.

"Baxter."

"She hit Madison Square — big concert. I'm on my
way. I need you to contact the squad. I want Jenkinson
and Reineke on scene. The rest report to Central unless
I tell you different."

"Done."

She cut him off, tagged Feeney.

"I'm on my way," he said the minute he came on. "McNab filled me in. ETA, maybe fifteen. Do you know how many?"

"No, we're five minutes out. I need a location for Mavis's and Summerset's 'links. They were both at this concert."

"Christ. I'll work it. Goddamn it."

He cut her off. Eve did the only thing she could think of. She touched Roarke's hand, squeezed briefly. Then prepared to deal with what came next.

"As soon as we find them, I need you, Feeney, McNab working that program. We want the nest. She won't be there, but we want the nest."

"I think he was taking Ivanna — Ivanna Liski. He said something about having dinner with her and broadening his musical horizons with this bloody concert. And I . . . I told him he should take Ivanna backstage to meet Mavis. He should see about arranging that."

Delicate blonde, Eve thought, former ballerina — and former spy. And maybe former flame of Summerset. "So it's likely they were both inside when this hit. We'll find them."

Seventh Avenue was chaos. Roarke cut across Thirty-Fifth, snaking through other vehicles and barricades while lights glared and sirens screamed.

She'd been in this chaos before, when the Cassandra group had blown up the arena in its crazed quest to destroy New York landmarks. And now, rebuilt, renewed, reopened, that resilience had been used as a target by another killer.

Should she have realized it? Anticipated it?

She shoved those thoughts aside as she and Roarke leaped out of opposite doors.

"Wait. They won't let you through, and I need my field kit."

She grabbed it, yanked out her badge to clip it to her coat, before the two of them bulled their way through the clamoring crowds pressed to the police line.

"Lieutenant. Jesus, Lieutenant, we got a hell of a mess here."

"Hold the line, Officer, and start moving it back. I want this area cleared back to Sixth on the east, and Eighth to the west — two blocks north and south. How many victims?"

"I can't tell you, sir. We came in on crowd control. I heard up to twenty, but I can't say for sure."

She kept moving through an area alive with cops, with MTs, with weeping civilians. And, she saw as they neared the arena, with the dead and the injured.

Copters circled overhead — police and media — and on the street, on the sidewalk, cops and medics fought to help the injured, to shield the dead.

To hold order when another strike could come from anywhere.

The world flashed blue and red from the police car lights, roared full of the terrible sound of screaming, and stank with the copper smell of blood.

"Ah, Christ." Because they were shoulder to shoulder she felt the shudder move through Roarke. "He's there. Over there, helping the medics."

She saw him, too, the bony frame, the shock of gray hair, those thin hands smeared with blood as he knelt by a woman bleeding from the side, from a gash along her temple.

Her own chest shook as they veered toward him.

"Are you hurt?" Roarke dropped down beside Summerset, gripped his arm. "Tell me if you're hurt."

"No, we were inside. Just coming out. Just . . . I heard the screams. I saw — I need to stop this bleeding." His voice was clipped, cold, but when he looked up, Eve saw both horror and grief. "Mavis and Leonardo are fine. Inside, still inside. I sent Ivanna back in to them."

The back of Eve's eyes burned, the inside of her throat, too. She could only nod. Then on a deep breath, she crouched, looked Summerset in the eye. "Turn on your 'link."

"What?"

"You need to turn your 'link back on, in case I need to contact you. I'm going to need to talk to you later, in depth, but right now, just turn on your 'link, and keep doing what you're doing. You're in good hands," she told the bleeding woman, who stared at her with eyes glassy from shock. "Good hands," she repeated and pushed to her feet.

She turned, sucked in a good, steady breath. "You — you," she snapped, snagged two uniforms at random. "I want a detail escorting ambulances and medivans to this location. I want a clear path for the medicals, in and out. Nothing, repeat, nothing and no one gets beyond Sixth, beyond Eighth, beyond Thirty-Sixth, beyond Thirty-Second who is not NYPSD or medical. Move it, do it. Now. And you."

She whirled on two more. "You think gawking's helping these people? Get inside, establish some order. No one comes out until I clear it. Move your asses."

"The sergeant said to hold," one began, and Eve sliced him with one sharp look, tapped her badge.

"What does this say?"

"'Lieutenant.' Sir."

"The lieutenant just gave you an order." She moved quickly toward an MT she recognized. "Can we move some of the minor injuries inside?"

"We could," the MT said as she treated what appeared to be a broken leg. "But they've blocked it off."

"I'm unblocking it. If you can spare a couple medics, they can handle the minor injuries inside. We're working on clearing a path for transport."

"Say hallelujah."

"Do you know how many?"

The MT shook her head. "I counted a dozen dead, twice that injured. Could be more."

"Dallas."

She glanced over, shocked to see Berenski limping toward her, one eye swollen and bruised.

"How bad are you?"

"Just got banged up some in the panic. Came with a couple buddies from the lab. We're all okay, but . . . People running, screaming, trampling each other trying to get out. They thought it was going to blow again."

His breath short, his eyes a little glazed as he looked around. "Christ, Dallas, fucking Christ."

"Do you need a medic?"

"No. No. I got some basic medical training, but I don't know if I've got enough to do anything here."

"There's Feeney coming through. You're with him and EDD. Work the program."

"Yeah, I can do that. I can do that," he repeated, limping toward Feeney.

No way to preserve the scene, she thought, and she'd done what she could to secure the area for now. So she took another breath, cleared everything else out of her head, and looked.

Wait for the concert to end — probably being streamed, probably a way to watch it on screen or at least get updates.

Was a target here? A name from the list? Or was this just a way to show how much you could do?

Doors open, people start streaming out. Did you wait? How long did you wait until you gave yourself the green?

She walked back to Summerset, noted he'd stopped the bleeding and was carefully tending the more superficial head wound.

"You're drafted as an expert consultant, medical."

"I — "

"You see that MT over there?" She gestured. "She's solid. You're going to work with her to arrange for the minor injuries to be taken inside. I want them comfortable but contained. One of my people will talk to them, and they'll be released when cleared. More severely injured will be triaged where they are, and transported asap to a medical facility. I need to tend to the dead, you get that? You can help tend to the living."

"Yes, all right."

"I need a running list of names of anyone you treat or move. Understand?"

"Of course."

"I'll tap you when I need you otherwise."

She saw Roarke and Feeney going inside, with Berenski limping behind them.

"See that guy, the one with a head like an egg, limping?"

"Yes."

"When you have time, look him over. He got banged up. He'll be with Roarke and Feeney."

"I'll do what I can."

"If you see Mavis, tell her . . . "

"That is also understood."

"Okay." Shifting her field kit, she walked away to begin tending to the dead.

She'd identified two, had begun her work on a third when Peabody rushed to her.

"I'm sorry. Jesus, Dallas, we couldn't get through. It's damn near a riot behind the barricades. Whitney called out every cop in the city, or it seems like it, to get people off the streets. Do you want me to start on IDs?"

"We've got the target here. Rothstein, Jonah, age thirty-eight, attorney. This is going to be the lawyer we couldn't nail down. This gut shot wound? He'd have bled out before anyone could do anything for him, but he'd have had a few minutes of agony first. He tried to crawl — see the blood smears. And see his legs. Gut shot, then she put two more strikes into him, one in each leg. It's the first I've seen where she hit more than once. This is the target."

Eve sat back on her heels. "He comes out, moving with the crowd, probably juiced from the concert. Maybe he's with somebody — he's divorced — and she's watching for him. This time, yeah, I say this time, she puts him down first. Wouldn't want to lose him in the crowd when the panic starts. Then she just picks at random. That's not for cover now, no need for cover now. That's for fun.

"Contact Morris."

"I already did. He's on his way. He might have beaten us here."

"I haven't seen him. We need this victim transported first. Have Rothstein bagged and tagged, tagged priority."

"I'll coordinate with Morris. Dallas, do you know how many dead?"

Eve got to her feet. Medicals continued to triage the wounded, but many had been taken inside, the uninjured were cleared and released.

It looked, she thought, like a battlefield after combat, bodies strewn over the cold and bloody pavement. She could count fourteen down, beyond help. There could be more.

"Let's take it one at a time."

In the end it would be sixteen dead on scene, two others who died of their wounds within hours. Another eighty-four injured.

They would weigh on her, every one, as in the cold, cold hour before dawn she left the dead to go inside. To do what came next.

She looked around the huge sweep of the lobby, the marble floors under the brilliance of the lights. Crossed to Jenkinson.

"Fill me in," she said.

"Conflicting reports. Most people don't know what the hell. The bulk of them never got outside, got banged up, knocked down, trampled in here. Somebody started yelling about a bomb and that lit the fricking fuse."

Face grim and tired, he, too, looked around the lobby area, cleared of wounded now, but with smears of blood still on the floor, and scattered belongings dropped and forgotten in the panic.

"Same deal outside, from what we're getting. Conflictings on the first strike, but I got a security guard who kept his head, and he's firm the first couple went down around one-fifty, one-fifty-five. Say ten minutes after people began crowding out.

After rubbing the back of his neck, Jenkinson checked his notes. "A male, black topcoat, blond medium-length hair — that's who the guard says took the first hit. Then a female, black or gray coat, red hair, but he says the first victim took a second hit, and maybe three hits. He's not sure if it was after the

293

second vic went down or the third. Things started to get crazy."

"Was this guy ever on the job?"

"Funny you should ask. Put in twenty-five, most of it in Queens."

"He's still got it. First vic, male, black coat, blond hair, was the lawyer. Rothstein, Jonah. Three hits. Keep the guard on tap in case he remembers more details. DBs are in the morgue or on the way. Still some injured being treated outside, but it's under control. I need this sector blocked off until we clear it all. You and Reineke can switch off with Carmichael and Santiago, get some crib time."

"I hear that. You need more of us down here, Loo, we're good for it. Took a booster." He scrubbed his face. "Hate those bastards."

"I hear that. A little crib time, because you won't get much more today. Where's EDD set up?"

It took her a full five minutes at a brisk stride to make it to the impressive security area where her geek team was working. She glanced at the screens, tried to block out the e-chatter, and saw the beams striking the Seventh Avenue area of Madison Square from Lexington and from Third. The Murray Hill area, she noted.

"We're narrowing it," Feeney told her, "or Lowenbaum and Berenski are."

Dickhead, she thought, watching him hunched over a monitor with Lowenbaum.

"If she's using the same weapon as her asshole father had, we think we got it pegged down to a couple blocks." Berenski rolled his shoulders, swiveled on his stool. "You add the weapon factors in, range, velocity, calculate full power because why the hell not, and — "

"You can save the formula for now, and just give me the most likelies. Maybe later I'll have you give me a lesson on the rest."

He blinked, rubbed his excuse for a moustache. "Yeah, sure. Could do that."

"We're leaning here." Roarke highlighted three buildings. "Two on Lex, one on Third."

"She likes the East Side," Eve noted. "Knows that area best."

"Apparently. Having our weapons experts add to the program has narrowed it considerably. These three are all low security, rental units or flops."

"We'll start there. Can you apply the same to the Times Square hit?"

"Doing that," McNab said. "We'll be able to give you most likelies, with these factors."

"Peabody, send the results to Baxter and Trueheart, get them and Uniform Carmichael and his picks working them." She checked the time. "Be ready to leave for Central when I tag you."

She had one more stop to make, wound her way back down, asked directions, and made her way backstage. It was unlikely she'd gather any information that would add to the manhunt. But she couldn't leave, just couldn't leave, without seeing the people she cared about.

The people the dream Willow had threatened to kill.

She heard Nadine before she saw her, the voice thick with fatigue. She sat on the floor, back to the wall, outside one of the dressing rooms. Face and hair unsurprisingly still camera ready, a bold blue leather jacket over a sleek black skin suit.

She sat hip-to-hip with a man with purple-streaked black hair that curled madly past the collar of a black T-shirt and a studded, sleeveless black vest. He wore black jeans, scuffed boots that laced up his calves. He rivaled McNab for ear hoops.

He met her eyes — his a heavy-lidded, sharp crystal blue. His mouth curved a little, deepening the creases in his cheeks.

"Here's your cop pal, Lois."

"What? Oh, Dallas." Nadine shoved to her feet. "What do you know? What can you tell me? I'm cued in to the station, and we need more details."

Best, probably best, Eve thought, that she hadn't known Nadine was here. Hadn't had one more person to worry about.

"What do you know?" she countered. "What did you see? What did you hear? My job's priority."

"I didn't see or hear a damn thing. I was down here, in Mavis's dressing room, when security rushed in, said there was an incident. They won't let us leave the area. Summerset's friend was brought down. She's in there with Mavis and Leonardo. Trina's in there, too."

Nadine gestured to the facing room with Mavis's name emblazoned on it. "Come on, Dallas, spill. I'm having to feed things in crumbs to my producer."

Eve just looked at Nadine's companion. "Who are you?"

Nadine let out a quick laugh. "Told you."

"Refreshing," he said. "I'm Jake Kincade."

"That won't click, either. Dallas, Jake's a rock star, literally. Avenue A? His band's been rocking the charts for about fifteen years."

"Give or take. Doesn't really apply right now, does it? Anyway." He rose on long legs, stood about six-five in his boots, offered a hand. "I'd say nice to meet you, but well, hell."

"How many dead?" Nadine insisted. "Will you confirm that? It matters, Dallas."

"Yeah, it matters. Sixteen at this time. A couple more aren't likely to make it, but sixteen confirmed dead on scene."

"Jesus." Jake stared down the corridor. "My band's piled up in dressing rooms, and we've got roadies flopped out like puppies. They're all safe. All of them are safe, but . . . I've got names of some people we got tickets for, about a dozen people. Can you check to see . . . "

Eve pulled out her notebook. "Give me the names."

She checked as he reeled them off from memory.

"None of them are on the dead or seriously injured list. I don't have all the names, yet, of minor injuries."

"That's good enough. More than. Thanks. They, hell, they won this contest, got to hang with us at rehearsal, come backstage before the performance."

"It's been eating at him that any of them got hurt," Nadine said. "Or worse."

"I'm going to clear it so you can go home, all of you. It may take about thirty to have someone come down, escort you out."

"I'm not going anywhere without a one-on-one," Nadine insisted. "They can do it by remote."

"Go get 'em, Lois," Jake murmured, and had Nadine shooting him a sparkling look.

"The city's going to be waking up," Nadine continued, checked her glittering wrist unit. "In fact is. People need to know, Dallas. It's their city, and last night was important. Someone smeared that with a lot of blood. It's your job to stop them. It's mine to let people know, not only what happened here, but that you're doing whatever it takes to stop them."

"She's good." Jake hooked his thumbs in his front pockets. "She says you're good, too."

"I'll give you five — it's all I can spare," Eve said before Nadine could protest. "But I need to . . . " She glanced toward Mavis's dressing room door.

"I'll get it set up."

"I'm going to get the band up and moving."

When Jake moved down the corridor, Eve turned to Nadine. " 'Lois'?"

"As in Lane, ace reporter for the *Daily Planet*. Superman, Dallas, you've probably heard of him."

"Yeah, where is he now?" She opened the door quietly.

Inside, Leonardo slept in a chair, Mavis curled like a fanciful cat in his lap. Trina — likely there for hair and makeup — stretched out on the floor, a colorful rug.

Eve recognized Summerset's old friend Ivanna Liski, asleep on a sofa.

But her eyes returned to Mavis, hair a tumbled rainbow, pretty fairy face relaxed in sleep, with Leonardo's big arms wrapped around her.

Because her eyes stung, her stomach jittered, Eve rested her head on the doorjamb, just let herself breathe.

In comfort, Nadine rubbed a hand on her back. "Whenever you're ready."

With a nod, Eve straightened, shut the door to give them a few more minutes. "Let's get this done."

CHAPTER
FIFTEEN

While he worked, once again aligning himself with cops, worry sat heavy in the back of Roarke's mind. Though he was a man who'd trained himself to remain cool and clearheaded in crises — else the hothead who lived inside him would have spent most of his years in a cage of one sort or another — that worry stiffened and tightened his shoulders to dull aches.

His wife — the center of his world — was running straight into exhaustion, had barely recovered from an ugly dream inside the scant two hours of sleep she'd managed.

He'd read it on her face when she'd come to check their progress, that pale and shadowed look, the one of nearly translucent skin and bruised eyes.

He could feel much the same from the good cops who worked with him, that drawn-tight-as-a-spring fatigue under their gut-deep determination to push on. And push on.

And there was little he could do to fix it. Not the time, the place, to order in gallons of good coffee or platters of food. Neither the money nor the power he'd worked all his life to attain could help.

So he applied his skill, his creativity with tech, and felt it wasn't nearly enough.

How did one catch a killer by knowing where they'd been, and where they surely weren't any longer?

She would say, his cop, every detail mattered. So he applied himself to finding those details.

Worry for Eve mixed and melded with worry for Summerset.

What help was he there?

The look on Summerset's face, the grief and horror, the blood on his hands, and more, the slight quaver in his voice haunted.

It jolted, always jolted, those rare glimpses of frailty in the man who had essentially raised him, who had saved him from the alleys, the beatings, the hunger, and the miseries. Who had helped him develop that clearheaded control and bank the furies that raged under it.

Where would he be, who would he be, without these two complicated and opposing forces? He couldn't say, would never know, but surely not where and who he was now, working alongside cops he'd once reviled.

Eve tracked a killer, prepared to face down the one who'd trained his own child to kill. Summerset tended the wounded.

And he . . . Well, he'd done all he could do here to narrow down locations, positions, possibilities.

He rose, looked toward Feeney. A father figure for Eve. It was all father figures, wasn't it? Feeney, Summerset, Mackie. Those who trained and schooled, for good or for ill.

"I need to find Summerset, make certain he's all right."

"Go," Feeney told him. "We're good here. Better than I figured we'd be. You gonna license this program to the NYPSD?"

"We'll consider it a gift. I'll arrange it."

That was something, at least, he thought as he left them.

He tried Summerset's 'link, but only got v-mail. Forgot to turn the shagging 'link on, he thought, or was too busy staunching blood or splinting bones to answer.

He started to try Eve, decided she'd not welcome an interruption to her work any more than he would have to his at a crisis point.

He wandered through, and cops on guard or at tasks merely nodded to him. Once, they would have chased him hard and fast, he thought. Those days were done, and however much he might entertain a bit of nostalgia for the thrill and adventure of them, he wouldn't trade a moment of this life he had, not even with the weight of worry.

He saw her first, coming through a door he realized with the blueprint in his head must have led backstage, house left. So pale, he thought, and because he knew those eyes so well, he knew there had been tears somewhere.

As she walked, she spoke into her 'link, giving more orders, he assumed, coordinating details, and taking reports.

As he started to go to her, Summerset came through the doors, house right.

Frail, Roarke thought again, the bones of his face too prominent against the drawn skin. Something more than fatigue in his eyes. Tears again, the sort that burn in the belly, scorch the heart, and aren't cooled by the shedding.

In that instant he felt caught between them, these two vital loves, opposing forces.

Then he saw Summerset sway, just slightly, and reach a hand down to the back of a seat to steady himself. There the choice was made for him, and he changed angles to go to the man who'd given him a life.

"You need to sit." Roarke spoke more brusquely than he meant to as that worry leaped hard into his throat. "I'll get you some water."

"I'm all right. So many aren't. There were so many."

"You'll sit," he said again just as Eve stepped up to them. "Both of you will bloody well sit down for five bloody minutes while I find some bloody water."

"We need to go to Central. I need you to come in," she said to Summerset, "give a statement."

"Well, fuck that," Roarke snapped. "He needs to go home, he needs to rest. Bugger it, have you no eyes to see?"

"It'll be easier, away from here. I can have you taken home after."

"He's going nowhere but home. I'll be taking him myself."

With sudden and bright fury, Eve rounded on Roarke. "This is a police investigation, this is a goddamn crime scene, and I say who goes where and when."

"Then arrest the pair of us since you've apparently nothing better to do. Is this how you treat him after he's fagged to the bone from mopping up blood?"

"Don't tempt me. I don't have time for drama."

"I'll show you drama right enough."

"Stop it, both of you." Summerset's tone, straw-thin with fatigue, still held an edge. "Behaving like cranky toddlers needing a nap."

"I told you to sit the hell down."

"And I believe I will, despite your rudeness. Because I need to."

Summerset lowered into an aisle seat, let out a sigh. "I'll go into Central, of course, but I need to know if Ivanna is all right before I leave."

"I just saw her. She's fine, and we're having her taken home. I told her you'd contact her as soon as you could."

"The others. Mavis, Leonardo, Nadine, Trina?"

"The same. They're all . . . " Eve's voice broke; she cleared it. "They're all good."

"That eases my mind." His eyes met Eve's a moment, and he sighed again. Then he looked at Roarke. "I could use some water, as it happens."

"I'll get it. You stay just where you are."

"I frightened him," Summerset told Eve when they were alone. "It's difficult to see weakness in the one who raised you."

"Understood, but — "

"And you worry him. You look, Lieutenant, as brutally tired and heavy as I feel. And what can he do for us, he asks himself, when one he loves above all else must use one he cares for as a child for a parent? Why, snarl at them both, of course."

He smiled a little.

She could feel herself teetering on some rocky edge, knowing that if she leaned too far one way she'd crumble. No choice then, she thought, no choice but to lean the other way, and hold on.

"I'm sorry, but time's so narrow. I can't wait to move to the next step."

"Understood." He echoed her. "I would like to go home. The boy has that right. I would very much like to go home. We could save each other time by doing this here and now. Is that possible?"

"Yeah, I just figured you'd want to get away."

"You never get away, do you?"

Roarke came back with two tubes of water.

"Hush, boy," Summerset muttered as Roarke started to speak. "I'm about to give the lieutenant my statement, as we've agreed to do so right here."

Eve sat across the aisle. "I have eyes, but I need to know what yours saw." She engaged her recorder, read in the salient data.

"Tell me what you remember."

"We were nearly to the doors, Ivanna and I, nearly outside. It was a diverse, celebratory evening. The crowd — I believe they must have sold out tonight, so we were hemmed in by the crowd at first. But . . . "

When Summerset rubbed at his temple, Roarke pulled out a small case, took out a blocker.

"Take it." At Summerset's cool stare, Roarke's jaw set, but he added, "Please."

"Thank you." Summerset cracked the tube, took the pill, sipped the water. "I think, yes, I think I was about to lead Ivanna through the doors when I saw someone fall to the ground — a belly wound, I could see that, too. There were screams as someone else fell — a head wound. Then panic. People running, shoving. I pulled Ivanna aside, worked back until I could get her clear. She argued, but she understood there wasn't time. She promised she'd go backstage, to Mavis. We'd visited before the concert, and I was confident she'd make her way. Everyone else was trying to get out."

"The one who went down first. Describe him."

"Middle thirties, I would think, blond hair. Caucasian. He had a black topcoat, open, and I'd seen the blood spread. By the time I was able to get outside to him, he was gone. Two more strikes — one in each leg. I heard the screams, and the cars — brakes squealing. Even as I moved to try to help a woman who'd been knocked to the ground, I saw another struck by a car as she ran into the street. And then I . . . "

"What next?"

"For a moment, longer, I fear, I was in another place, another time. In London, during another strike, during the Urbans. The same sounds, smells, the same terrible fear and rush. Bodies on the ground, bleeding, wounded calling for help, the weeping and the desperation to escape."

He stared at the tube of water for a moment, then drank from it. "I froze, you see, just froze between that time and this, and did nothing. I stood there, just stood there. Then someone shoved me, and I fell. I fell beside the body of a woman who was beyond help. Nothing to do for her, nothing at all, and I came back to myself, to the moment. There was a boy, barely twenty, if that, I'd say, knocked senseless. Someone trampled right over him, stepped on his hand. I heard the bones crack. I did what I could for him until the medicals began to arrive."

He paused, drank again. "People were still falling, but the medicals, the police rushed in. I called out that I was a medic, and one of them threw me a kit. So we did what we could do, just like on any battlefield. I don't know how long — minutes, hours — then you came, you and my boy here. The worst was over quickly then, you saw to that. I tended more outside, then inside. And here we are."

Eve waited a beat. "The woman you were working on when we came?"

"Stabilized, enough, I think. They took her once she was stable enough. They said at least a dozen dead. How many? Do you know?"

"Sixteen DOS, and two more who didn't make it. So, eighteen. There would have been more if you hadn't been here, if you hadn't helped."

"Eighteen." Summerset lowered his head, stared at the water in his hand. "We couldn't save the eighteen, so we look to you to make them matter, to find them justice."

"They matter. So do the wounded. I'll get you their names, the living and the dead."

He lifted his head, met her eyes. "Thank you."

"Roarke can take you home."

"No, I think he'll stay with you. There's nothing for me to do here, and everything for you. I'll take a soother and go to bed," he told Roarke, and seemed steadier when he rose.

"I'd rather you weren't alone."

"I'll have the cat." Summerset smiled a little, then did something Eve hadn't seen him do before. He leaned in, kissed Roarke's cheek.

Moved, embarrassed, Eve got to her feet. "I'm going to arrange transportation." She started out, stopped. "The medicals and cops who rushed in? Saying it's their job doesn't diminish the risk or the courage. It wasn't your job, but you took the same risk, showed the same courage. I won't forget it."

"I should go with you," Roarke said.

"No." Summerset shook his head. "I want quiet, and my bed, and I'll admit the cat will add some comfort. Wars never really end as long as there are those who feel entitled, even obliged, to take lives. It's not my war now, but it's hers, and because it's hers, it's yours. I'm proud of you both, and hope you'll bring me peaceful news when you come home."

He let out another sigh, a long one, then squeezed Roarke's shoulder. "I'm going to check in with Ivanna, settle myself there, and let our lieutenant have me taken home."

"We'll have you both taken home," Eve told him. "I'll take care of having all of you taken home."

"Thank you. I'm well, boy. Just tired."

"Then I'll take you back to Ivanna, walk you both out."

Later, Roarke walked Summerset out, to the police car waiting at the curb. When Eve joined him, he could feel the stiffness in her body, part anger, he mused, part sheer determination to stay on her feet.

"There's nothing you can do now," she began, and he found himself snapping toward her.

"I feel useless enough at the moment without you adding to it."

"Useless, my ass. We wouldn't have the nests without you, and we now have all three. Maybe they'll help track her next position, her next target. Fuck your 'useless.'"

"Then there's always something else I can do."

"You should've gone with him. You should go home, make sure he goes to bed, and get some sleep yourself."

"He wants what he wants, and I'll sleep when you do. Shall we waste time arguing about it?"

"Fine." She started off at a fast clip. "I sent Peabody ahead. I've got a consult with Mira, then I'm taking Mackie into Interview."

"I'll see what help I can be elsewhere." Stopping, he took Eve's arm — firmly. "He looked shaken and fragile. I couldn't stand the idea that you would push him. And yourself. I couldn't stand being caught between the pair of you when you both looked ready to drop, and neither would give way."

"He held up." She hissed out a breath. "I wasn't going to push him, but I needed to know what he saw.

He was right there, front lines, and he's been there before. It gives me insight. She's going to hit again, and likely quicker now. I needed him."

"I know it."

"What he did? I admire it more than I can say. He could've gone back in, stayed safe, but he went outside, he risked doing that to save lives."

"He saved mine, and so did you. It's a tricky dance for me."

She stopped at the car. "You were the making of him, that's what I see." The stunned look on Roarke's face had her shaking her head. "He wouldn't be with you still if that wasn't the way it is. You say you and I saved each other. Well, before I came along, the two of you did the same. Another way, another path, but just as true. You gave him purpose, and you gave him a son. So let's just table all this crap."

"Crap tabled." Then he pulled her into his arms, held tight. "No one's paying attention to the likes of us right now. So give me this, as I need it. I swear, I need it."

She gave what he needed, and took what she needed. Held on. "You know, you got more Irish in there, trying to bully us into doing what you thought we should do."

"A bloody lot of good it did me." He drew back. "I'm going to find you a booster. Not now, not the sort you hate, as they wire you up. I'll find something that suits you."

"If anybody can. You can drive. I've got people to talk to."

He got behind the wheel, glanced over at her. "Will this new sort of understanding, as it were, also table the daily sniping between you and Summerset?"

"Not a chance in hell."

"Well then, there's something to look forward to."

She moved fast through Central, didn't notice — as Roarke did — the other cops, support staff who recognized her, step aside to clear her way.

Even as she strode into Homicide, Peabody stood up behind her desk. "Mira's in your office. Sweepers are all over the nests. We're culling through wit reports. A few may be viable."

"Keep it going. Mackie?"

"En route, with counsel."

"In Interview, the minute he's in the house. Give me ten with Mira."

"I'll take myself off to EDD," Roarke told Eve. "And if I can't be of use there, I'll be elsewhere."

"You could catch an hour's sleep in the crib."

"Not in this lifetime, or the next."

"Snob."

"So be it." He'd have kissed her, actively longed to. But he understood there were Marriage Rules on either side. So he just flicked a finger down the dent in her chin and wandered away.

They'd both do what they could — and he'd access his home system, make certain Summerset was home, and in bed.

Then he'd find his cop a damn booster.

Mira stood in Eve's office facing the case board. She'd tossed her coat on the visitor's chair. Clothes might not have been high on Eve's list of priorities, but observation was. And she observed Mira wore leg-hugging black pants with knee-high black boots and a floaty blue sweater rather than her usual pretty suit and heels.

"I need to update that."

Mira didn't turn. "It gives a good sense, and I'm fully briefed on this morning's attack."

"I need coffee. You want that tea stuff?"

"Yes, thanks. She continued her father's agenda. Still seeking his approval."

"She likes to kill."

"Yes. Very much yes, but she's still a child, and the child seeks to please the father. This is their bond. It began with weaponry, honing her skill there, and devolved into revenge. As his skills lessened due to his addiction, hers have sharpened. The apprentice has exceeded the master. She became his weapon."

"She likes it," Eve insisted.

"Again, I agree." Mira took the tea, holding the cup as she studied the dead. "In the first attack, the other two victims were, essentially, cover. Or he convinced himself of that. But I wonder. Did he feel pride when she so skillfully struck three targets? I think he did. In the second, we had five struck, four dead, so he allowed her to test her skills. Or she increased on her own. And now the third."

"Eighteen dead."

"Yes. Now she has her head. She has no one to tell her to stop."

"Will he feel pride?"

"I believe he will. He may see, some part of him may see, she's reveling in the kill — not the agenda, not the mission, but the power of the kill. And still, she's his child, one he taught. One he loves."

"What kind of love is that?" Eve snapped it out. "What kind of love raises a kid to be a monster?"

"However twisted, for him it's genuine. He sacrificed himself to save her. He sent her away, not only in hopes she might eventually complete the mission, but certainly to protect her."

She turned now to face Eve. "He was a police officer. He certainly had to know, once you'd identified them, you'd also identified at least some of the targets. So those targets would be out of reach."

"Tell that to Jonah Rothstein." Eve took the ID shot out of her field kit, put it on the board.

"There's no point blaming yourself when you know who's responsible."

"I just couldn't . . . No." Eve sucked in a breath. "No point. So, the instructor — the master — wants the mission completed, and for it to be completed, the student needs to stay safe. Free. And the father protects the child, even as he helps twist her into a killer. Because I think to do what she's done, it was always in there. Inside there. He just had to recognize it and exploit it.

"But he doesn't know her agenda — she was smart to keep that to herself. Will he care? When I hit him with hers in the hospital, he wasn't ready to believe me. Her own mother, her own brother, teachers, kids in school? He slapped that off. When I make him believe it, will he give a fuck?"

"You need him to," Mira said with a nod. "You need him to, we could say, give a great many fucks in order to pressure him into giving you information on her whereabouts."

Another time it might have amused her to hear Mira's clinical use of the f-word. "That's exactly right."

"I believe children are important to him. With the divorce, a man in his position — a demanding career — could have opted for generous visitation rather than co-parenting. It was the loss of his wife and the potential of another child that broke the restraints on his control."

"The kid brother then, the school."

"Will most likely be your best levers."

"She's not going to Alaska to live wild and free, as in his plan for her." Eve nodded. "She's going to stay right here, shift over to her own mission. He taught her to kill, now she's going to take what he taught her and eliminate anyone who's annoyed her. Keeping herself in my cross-hairs. Not safe. Yeah, yeah, I'll play that."

"Do you want me in Interview?"

"No, I want him looking at me. The one who's hunting his offspring. A cop killer. I want him thinking about that, knowing she's still here. Knowing she's close, and I'm close. And remembering, as a cop, how we feel about those who target our own. It won't be hard to make him believe I'd take her out rather than

314

give her a chance to play the misled card and spend time in a cushy facility for minors."

When Mira said nothing, Eve shifted her gaze, met her eyes. "No. In fact, that's last resort. I want her looking at me, knowing I'm the one who stopped her. I want her to remember me every day of the rest of her very long life."

"She's not you."

"Could've been. Who knows what Richard Troy would've twisted me into if he'd had more time."

"No. Nature, nurture, both matter, both form us. But at some point, at so many points, the choices we make, the paths we take, they define us. You made yours. She's made hers."

"Yeah. Yeah. And we're going to come together, I swear to Christ we are. Then we'll see what each other is made of. So I need to break Mackie. I will break Mackie."

"I'll be in Observation. If you need me."

"Okay."

As Mira turned to go, Cher Reo stepped into Eve's doorway. "Mackie's in Interview A," the APA stated. "I'm here to tell you that my boss says no deals for him. Former cop, now a mass murderer, and a cop killer. Evidence is thick and heavy. A confession would be nice, of course, but the PA's office believes we have more than enough for a conviction."

"I hear that."

"However — "

"Bugger the howevers."

"However," Reo continued, "if Mackie gives us the location of his daughter *before* she takes another life or injures anyone else, and if she surrenders peaceably, the PA's office will agree to try Willow Mackie as a minor."

"Bullshit, Reo."

Reo held up a hand, skimmed the other through her windblown, curly hair. "We're giving you ammunition, Dallas. He needs incentive to lead us to her before she takes out another swath of people. Dr. Mira?"

"It could play on two levels. On his paternal instincts to protect, and on his need to have the mission complete — however long it might take."

"Which is just what she will do if we let her walk at eighteen."

Reo angled her head. "And what are the odds of that actually happening? The odds of a peaceful surrender and no further harm done?"

Eve started to speak, then waited for her initial outrage to fade, and for more caffeine to kick in. "Okay. Okay, I get it. No way she surrenders without a fight. That's in stone? That part's nonrefundable?"

Reo smiled. "She resists in any way, stomps her evil little foot and stubs your toe, the deal's void."

"Let me work him awhile first. If I can't break him down, we'll toss this in. That way it sounds and feels like a concession. I don't want to walk in with any deal."

"That's good, that works. He's got a court-appointed as his counsel. Guy named Kent Pratt. He's got a rep as the public defenders' patron saint of lost causes."

"All right. Let me get started."

"I'll be in Observation if you need to pull me in for the deal."

"If I do, we play it up. I'm going to be really pissed. I may call you rude names."

Reo smiled again, sunnily. "Wouldn't be the first."

CHAPTER
SIXTEEN

Eve tagged Peabody as she gathered what she needed.

"One of the injured who'd stabilized has taken a turn," Peabody told her. "I don't have all the details — it's medical and complicated — but she's back in surgery."

"Name?"

"Adele Ninsky."

The woman Summerset was treating when she'd arrived on scene, Eve thought, then set it aside.

"I want you to play up the father-daughter connection. Parental duty, poor young girl. You can be tough on him, but soften up with the girl."

"Got it. I guess it's not much of a stretch."

"It should be. Look at the board. It damn well should be."

Scooping up files, Eve strode out.

Peabody quickened her pace to catch up. "Baxter and Trueheart hit one wit they think saw her minutes after the Times Square attack. He didn't recognize her until they interviewed him, showed him Yancy's sketch. He says he was heading into the building as she was coming out. He held the door for her. She was carrying a large metal case, and a rolling duffle. Had a backpack.

He remembers because he said, like, 'Let me help you,' and held the door, and he claims she gave him this, quote — 'scary smile' — unquote, and said she didn't need anybody's help. He was a little steamed so he stared after her for a minute. He thinks she was headed for the bus stop. Half a block down. They're checking it out."

"Good." Eve paused at the door to the Interview room. "No mistakes," she said and then walked in.

"Record on," she began, reading the data into that record as she sized up the two men at the table.

Mackie, pale, defiant, his eyes shielded behind lightly tinted goggles. Through them she noted the eyes were bloodshot, bruised, and she felt nothing.

The lawyer wore a cheap suit and a skinny black tie. His face sported a night's worth of scruff, with his idealism shining bright under it.

Eve sat, stacked up her files, folded her hands over them. "Well, Mackie, here we are."

"My client is under medical care for severe injuries sustained under questionable circumstances. Therefore — "

"Bullshit. If you reviewed the record, Counselor, you know there are no questions. Your client fired on police officers."

"It's questionable if said officers clearly indentified themselves as same. We will be pursuing charges of illegal entry, police harassment, and excessive force."

"Yeah, good luck with that." She smiled at Mackie as she spoke. "You know that's lawyer bullshit, and it doesn't change a thing. Here we are."

"Due to my client's injuries, you're limited to one-hour intervals for Interview. My client will take his guaranteed thirty minutes after the hour. I request on my client's behalf that he be returned to the hospital for a full medical evaluation after said hour."

"Denied, which is within my authority, as his medical team has signed off. He can take his thirty in a cage, or if you insist, be evaluated here, medically, by a doctor. He's done with the hospital. You're done with the outside, Mackie. It's all cages all the time now. That's going to be fun for you in general population. You know how much they love ex-cops in GP. Don't waste my hour," Eve snapped at Pratt. "I have questions for your client. Here's the first: Where is she? Where is your daughter? Where is Willow Mackie?"

"How would I know? I've been in the hospital."

"Did you keep up with current events? Has your counsel informed you of what your daughter did last night? Eighteen dead this time around. Must swell your chest with pride."

"My client was held incommunicado during the time of that incident, and cannot be held responsible for — "

"And the bullshit keeps coming. You're responsible. You're responsible for turning your own flesh and blood into a stone-cold killer. Eighteen people. Fathers, mothers, sons, daughters. And all because you had some bad luck."

"Bad luck?" Mackie lunged forward in the chair.

"Yeah, bad luck. Your wife didn't look where she was going. Now she's dead."

"They ran her down in the street!"

"No, she ran out into the street, into traffic, because she was too stupid to pay attention. And you couldn't handle it so you went on the funk. Look at your hands shake. Pathetic. What they give you to keep you level just isn't enough, is it? It's never going to be enough. You destroyed yourself because your wife couldn't remember to walk down to the fucking crosswalk. And when that didn't fix it for you, you decided to destroy everyone else you could think of."

"Including his own daughter." Peabody said it just loud enough to be heard, and in a voice that rang with emotion. "That's what I can't get under, can't get through. She's just a kid, and he used her, he screwed her up. You destroyed her, Mr. Mackie. How is she ever going to live with what she's done? What you, her own father, told her to do?"

"You don't know anything about my Will."

"I know at fifteen she should be thinking about boys and music and schoolwork and meeting friends for pizza and vids. I know she should be angsting over what to wear."

"Not my Will."

"Not your Will," Peabody repeated, with disdain. "Because you wouldn't approve. You think all those things are frivolous, aren't important, but they are. They're building blocks, they're rites of passage. They're part of the childhood you stole from her. Now she's a murderer, a fugitive. Her life's over."

"Just beginning," he replied.

"He thinks she's going to Alaska," Eve tossed out with a deliberate smirk, "to live off the land, free as a . . . What the hell do they have in Alaska?"

"Bear. Moose. Wolves, too, I think. Deer. Lots of deer."

"There you go. Like a deer. But people hunt deer, don't they? Don't they do that up there? Isn't that part of living off the land?"

Eve leaned back. "I'm hunting her right now — like a deer. I've got some of my best trackers on her. She's left a trail, Mackie." Eve opened a file, read off the addresses of the three nests. And saw his trembling hands close into trembling fists. "Already got a wit at one of them who saw her exiting the building. Here's what I wonder. Did you tell her to get her ass to Alaska when you sent her off, or did you tell her to finish the job first?"

"My client denies any and all allegations pertaining to his daughter, Willow Mackie. She is missing due to her fear of the police, due to your department's false accusations against her."

"Right. I'll wade through the lawyer bullshit all day. A decent father would have told her to run, run far and fast."

"He's not a decent father," Peabody put in.

"I'm a good father!" Insult and rage flashed hard color into Mackie's cheeks. "I'm a hell of a lot better than that useless prick her mother married."

"That would be the useless prick with the good job, the nice house." Eve studied his ruined and furious eyes

322

through the goggles. "The one who's not a funky-junkie. Yeah, that's a burn on the butt all right."

"He's not her father."

"Nope, but she lived with him half the time. You were working to change that, to get full custody, then oops, dead wife. That got messed up."

The trembling of Mackie's hands increased. Red splotches came and went on his face.

"I figure you said run. 'Get to Alaska. Live a little.' Then you're the sacrifice, the distraction. She can come back in a couple years, finish the mission: Marta Beck, Marian Jacoby, Jonah Rothstein, Brian Fine, Alyce Ellison. But, hey, that's a teenager, isn't it? Defiant, rebellious. She disobeyed Daddy. Now eighteen more people are dead."

Eve opened a file, spread out the photos. "Eighteen people who did nothing but go to a concert."

She watched his gaze skim over the photos, back and forth.

"Their bad luck this time. Bad luck they were in the same place at the same time as Rothstein. He's a lawyer," she told Pratt. "Like you. Mackie hired him to try to sue the driver who hit his jaywalking wife, and the cop who gauged the scene correctly. Just a lawyer, like you, doing his job, like you. But he couldn't get Mackie what he wanted, so he was supposed to die."

"My client denies — "

"But she missed." Eve watched Mackie's shielded eyes jerk up. "That's her oops. Got so excited, I guess, and missed the target."

"Will never misses."

Eve leaned forward. "How would you know? Have you ever seen her aim at a human being?"

"I said she never misses. Where's his picture?" He shoved at the dead. "Where is it?"

"Who chose the collaterals? Did you let her pick? You picked the main target, so did you let her pick the rest?"

"Where is Rothstein's picture?"

"I said she missed."

"You're lying. Will can pick the left ear off a rabbit at a half mile."

"Mr. Mackie," Pratt began, laying a hand on his arm.

Mackie shook him off. "I want to see his picture on this table."

"It was crowded. Night, late, crowded."

"I *trained* her." Not just his hands shook now, but his arms, his shoulders. "She wouldn't take the shot unless she was sure."

"Maybe it's different when you're not there to give her the green. You were there, giving her the green for the ice rink, for Times Square."

"It's no different, not for her. She doesn't miss."

"But you were there before, giving her the green, to kill Dr. Michaelson, to kill Officer Russo. Yes or no."

"Don't answer that," Pratt insisted.

"Yes! Yes, but it doesn't matter." Insult, this time clearly for the stain on his daughter's skill, raged through his voice. "She's the best I've ever seen. Better than I ever was. She wouldn't have missed Rothstein."

"You're telling me a fifteen-year-old girl made the strikes that killed Michaelson and two others on Wollman Rink. Killed four people including Officer Kevin Russo in Times Square?"

"Do you think I could make those strikes with these hands? With these eyes?"

"She made them for you?"

"For us. Susann would've been more of a mother to her, a *real* mother to her. We were going to be a family. They destroyed that. They destroyed my *family!* They don't deserve to live."

"You and your daughter, Willow Mackie, conspired to kill the people on this list." Eve took a printout from the file. "And however many others you deemed necessary in your attempt to cover up your connection to these targets."

"This Interview is over." Pratt got to his feet.

"She's my eyes! She's my hands! It's not murder. It's justice. Justice for my wife, my son."

"All these people." Eve opened the other files, spread out more pictures. "All those who just happened to be in the same place at the same time?"

"Why do they matter more than Susann and my son? Why do they deserve a life, a family, when I have none?"

"Why do they matter less?" Eve countered.

"I said this Interview is over." Obviously shaken, Pratt struggled to keep his voice calm. "I need to consult with my client. We'll take our break now."

"You do that." Eve began to gather the photos.

"Where is Rothstein?"

"You can't get to him." Eve rose. "Or any of the others on your list. And she won't. Think about that. We'll resume in thirty. Interview end."

She walked out, kept walking straight to her office. While Peabody moved to the AutoChef for coffee, Eve sat, studied the go-cup in the center of her desk, with a label that read: DRINK ME!

She opened the lid, sniffed suspiciously. Frowned, as it smelled like a chocolate malted.

"What is that?"

"Something Roarke came up with." Cautiously, Eve took a sip. It tasted like a chocolate malted. A real one.

She looked at the coffee Peabody set on her desk, back at the go-cup. And thinking of Roarke, drank half of the booster.

She held the cup out to Peabody. "You look like crap. Drink the rest."

Peabody tried a testing sip. Her eyes widened. "Oh, it tastes like a zillion calories. But — " She downed it.

"That was genius — making him think she'd missed Rothstein."

"Just came to me. Either he'd be pissed at her for screwing up, or pissed at me for saying she did. His ego — for himself and his protege — locked him into confessing to multiple murders, and implicating her. It was enough for the first round."

"I'm kicking myself for not thinking of it," Mira said as she came in. "Pride. There's a lot of paternal pride mixed into his psychosis. She's his eyes, his hands, his weapon, his child. They're all conflated. He will go into a cage, Eve, and it's unlikely he'd be deemed legally insane, but he's a very disturbed man."

"He can be disturbed for the rest of his useless life, as long as he's in that cage. One down, one to go. He may not give a shit about his ex and her husband being targets. He may not give a shit about the seven-year-old kid being a target. But if she's his eyes, his hands, they aren't *his* targets. Let's see if he can rationalize her planning on taking them out. And the school, all those kids. If that doesn't work, and I can't trip him up otherwise, we go with the deal. The deal gives him room to believe she'll be safe inside for a couple years, then come out and finish. Her agenda, her hit list, that's weight she's not leaving the city, and he'll lose her, lose his eyes and hands."

"He believes he's a good father," Peabody commented. "He genuinely believes it, I could see it. It's like he took her innate talent and honored it, helped refine it."

"He's resentful of the stepfather. More stable and successful — and with a son," Mira added. "He still harbors anger toward his ex-wife. But the half brother may strike a nerve. I'd put pressure there."

"Peabody, see how many cute photos of the kid you can come up with. Birthdays, Christmas, like that. Baby shots. They had a puppy, right? Puppy shots."

"Got it."

"Make him look at them," Mira said when Peabody hurried out. "The innocence, the sweetness. Remind him that child shares blood with his. It will matter, I believe, that his child plots to kill her own blood. The mother, perhaps not. She's an adult who made choices Mackie disagrees with, choices he resents. But the child has no choice. Just as his son, if he'd come to be, would have none."

"And would have shared her blood. I got it."

"Your color's better," Mira noted.

"Yeah? Roarke boost."

"Is that a euphemism? When would you have had the time?"

"I just — no, jeez." Amused, appalled, Eve held up the go-cup. "Booster. Roarke-supplied booster. He probably arranged some for half the cops in here while he was at it."

Trying not to think of Mira thinking about her having sex, Eve shifted gears. "How come you're not wearing a suit and ankle breakers?"

"I was a bit rushed to get here this morning. And it's Saturday. I don't have formal office hours on Saturday."

"Saturday." When did it get to be Saturday? "Oh."

"Recharge." Mira patted Eve's shoulder. "I'll be back in Observation when you start again." Mira paused at the door. "There are cracks forming. And you've shaken his lawyer as well."

"If they didn't have the break coming, I could've widened the cracks. Now they have time to shore them up, steady up. But I'll get there."

She'd get there, Eve thought, and prepared for the next round.

She recharged. Maybe it was the break, maybe it was the booster, but her mind cleared, her energy lifted.

Before tackling Mackie again, she checked in with Baxter.

"Yo, Dallas. The bus driver remembered her — or remembered a 'youth' getting on loaded down with the bags the previous wit described. It's looking like she went straight to the flop she used to hit Madison Square. Me and my boy, we're following up with buses on that line. I got a little tingle going."

"Make it happen. I'm going back at Mackie. If he lets anything through the cracks, I'll point you."

"Make it happen."

Yeah, she thought as she pushed away from her desk. They'd make it happen. She had a little tingle of her own going.

When she walked into the bullpen, she saw Peabody talking to a civilian.

"Lieutenant, this is Aaron Taylor. He attended last night's concert with Jonah Rothstein."

"I was — we were — I heard that . . . Are you sure Jonah's . . . "

"I'm sorry, Mr. Taylor."

Eve's words had him covering his face with his hands. "I don't understand. I don't know how this could . . . "

Peabody popped up, dragged over a chair. "Sit down, Mr. Taylor."

"I don't know what to do. I went out the other way — it's closer to where I live. We had Orchestra seats, man. Jonah scored them back in November. We . . . "

"You and Mr. Rothstein were friends," Eve prompted.

"Since high school. We came to New York together, roomed together until I got married. He's my best friend. I just . . . "

"You went to the concert together," Eve prompted.

"Yeah. Yeah. He's been bragging about scoring those prime seats all over his social media. It's all he talked about for weeks now. We went together, and . . . I went out the other way after."

"He talked about his plans for last night on social media?"

"He had a countdown going." Aaron pressed his fingers to his eyes, pressing at the tears that swam in them. "We're big Avenue A fans. Jonah's the biggest there is, since we were in college. He worked his schedule around the concert — he had out-of-town meetings all week, but he worked it so he'd be back for last night. He was saying, kept saying: 'Dude, did you ever think back all those times we sat in the nosebleeds to see Avenue A, to see Jake Kincade, we'd be here. Orchestra seats, Madison Square.' I went out the other exit. He said, 'Let's go have a drink,' but I needed to get home. He was going to come over tonight. He's supposed to come over tonight, but he went out one way, and I went out the other."

"Mr. Taylor . . . Aaron," Eve amended, studying his devastated face. "There's no sense in it, no reason. I want to ask you if Jonah ever talked to you about his work."

"Yeah, sometimes. Like a sounding board. We went to law school together. I'm in tax law."

"Did he ever talk to you about Reginald Mackie?"

"The guy who's been all over the screen? With the kid? The guy who's doing this shit." The threat of tears dried up in shock. "You saying Jonah knew him?"

"He never mentioned Mackie to you?"

"He wouldn't have given me names. He might give me an anecdote, right? A funny story. Or blasted off some, but without naming the client. We're like brothers, you know what I'm saying, but he wouldn't have shared any privileged information."

"Okay, but did he talk to you about a client who wanted to sue others for the death of his wife? She'd run into the street, was hit by a vehicle. She was pregnant."

"I . . . I — I remember something about that. Is that why he's dead?" Leading with fury now, Aaron shoved up from the chair. "Is that the reason? He tried to *help* that asshole. He did it pro bono because he felt for him. His own time. Mostly did it because the poor bastard didn't have a case. She ran into the street, into traffic. People saw her. Jonah talked to all of them, even did background — on his own time. And when Jonah had to tell him there was nothing he could do, the fucker went off on him. And the kid . . . He tried to help them, his own time, his own dime. He's a good guy, do you get that? Jonah's one of the good ones."

"I get that. What about the kid?"

"The . . . Jonah told me how the guy — that's this Mackie, right? He said the guy was a wreck. Pushing for some sort of closure, somebody to blame — even the doctor because the appointment ran late, and yeah,

331

the wife's supervisor at work. Everybody was to blame but the person who ran into the street, you know?"

"Yes, I do. The kid, Aaron."

"He said she was scary — that's what he said. How she came up to him a couple weeks after he told Mackie he couldn't help him, after he tried to steer Mackie into rehab and counseling because he said the guy was on something for sure. The kid came up to him when Jonah was grabbing some takeout on the way home. She came right up to him, said she bet he figured everybody died, so what's the big. How he'd find out just how big. How it was too bad he didn't have a wife because somebody might give her a reason to run out into the street. How maybe somebody would give him one, showed him a stunner, what looked like a stunner she had in her pocket. Spooked him."

"He didn't report the threat? Or the weapon?"

"Jewel — my wife — she pushed him to do just that, but he said the kid was like thirteen or fourteen, whatever. Just mouthing off, and he figured the stunner was a toy, a fake. But it spooked him. I know all the lawyer jokes, right? But Jonah, he really believed in the best of people. He really believed they needed somebody to stand up for them. With this guy, there was nothing to stand on, but he tried. Now he's dead."

"Now we're standing for him. I promise you, I'm standing for him. You've helped us by coming in. You've helped him."

"Can I see him? Is there somewhere I can go to see him? His parents — we were sleeping in, me and Jewel. We didn't even know until his dad . . . They're coming

332

in from Florida. They do the winter in Florida thing, and they're coming, but . . . Can I see him?"

"Detective Peabody, would you arrange that, and for Aaron to be taken to see his friend, then taken home?"

"Yes, sir."

"He really believed in justice."

"So do I," Eve said, and moved off to where she'd seen Lowenbaum waiting.

"I caught some of that, didn't want to break in."

"Just one more reason to crack Mackie, and to hunt down his psycho daughter."

"I wanted to ask if I can get in on the next round, if I can help you interview Mac."

She'd expected this, and drew him out in the corridor to answer.

"I'd want the same in your place, and I may ask you. But he's going to see you as his lieutenant, and that muddies this. You made rank, and you had to nudge him out."

"I get it, but I just — "

"Lowenbaum, if he'd managed to complete this mission of his, I don't think he'd have headed off to Alaska. Or if he did, he wouldn't have stayed there. It wouldn't have given him what he needed, he wouldn't have felt finished. He'd still have all that inside him. And he'd make a new list. Your name would be on that list."

She waited a beat. "You've already concluded the same."

"Yeah." Lowenbaum looked down the corridor, looked at nothing. "Yeah, I concluded the same. My name, the ex's husband, Patroni, probably more. But he's not there yet."

"Sure of that?"

After a moment, Lowenbaum shook his head. "Nah, nowhere near sure of that. It's just . . . "

"Hard to sit back, but I've got to ask you to. Observe, and if you observe anything that can help me, give me a signal."

"You're right. I know you're right." Accepting that, Lowenbaum heaved out a breath. "Okay. Push the kid, the half brother. He was still pissed about the ex — a lot of people stay pissed about exes for the rest of their lives — but he liked the kid. I heard him say Will and Zach were the only things Zoe ever did to add to the world. Dragged Willow to a couple of the little guy's school deals — plays and concerts — because he thought it was important she participate in the kid's life."

"Good. Good to know. I'll use it." She waited while a couple of uniforms came out with Aaron, guided him to the elevator. "More ammo," she stated, then gestured to Peabody. "Sit tight, Lowenbaum. Stay close."

"You've got that."

She took a moment in Observation herself, just to gauge the ground. The lawyer spoke, tense and intense by her measure, while Mackie stared straight ahead, face set in stone.

Pissed, she thought. Good, good. Stay pissed.

And his hands shook. However tightly he gripped them together, she saw the tremors had increased. He'd need another medically approved hit very soon.

She nodded to Peabody. "Let's start the clock."

When she walked back in, Pratt sat back, stayed quiet.

"Record on. Dallas, Lieutenant Eve; Peabody, Detective Delia, resuming Interview with Mackie, Reginald, and counsel." She sat again, dropped files on the table. "So, where were we?"

"I restate my request for my client to be returned to the hospital for medical evaluation."

"And I restate my 'bullshit' for reasons already on record."

"Rothstein is dead." Mackie looked into Eve's eyes. "I had him check during the break. I knew she didn't miss."

"Correct. The man who tried to help you, pro bono, who spent his own time, without fee, to take your bullshit case is dead, by your daughter's hand, and through your conspiracy."

"He did nothing but toe the line, and cover up what really happened."

"My client can't be held responsible for your allegations against his minor child," the lawyer began.

"Did they neglect to explain the term *conspiracy* in your law school, Pratt? Your client — that's you, Mackie — has confessed, on record, to conspiring to murder, to being an accessory to the murder of twenty-five people to date."

"My client was hospitalized and in police custody during the incident at Madison Square, therefore — "

"Please, stop wasting time. Plotted and planned and on record. I don't give a rat's ass if he was in Argentina last night. He's as guilty as she is. Just like he's just as guilty if she attempts to complete the names on your client's list. And the names on her own list."

"She doesn't have her own list. You're lying. Just another lie."

"Like you don't know about it," Peabody said in disgust. "You're her father. You know what she's planning. You started it."

"There we disagree." Eve shrugged at Peabody. "I don't think he knew. Not about her hit list. Not that she had her own mission. Just like I don't think he knew she confronted some of the names on his list, like Rothstein for instance. Threatened them on her own, flashed a stunner. That's not good strategy, and he's got enough training, even with the funk, not to make a boneheaded move like that."

"You're lying again. Just like you lied about her missing Rothstein."

"Don't have to this time. I've got her list right here." Eve opened the file, but paused before taking out the document. "Oh, we know she travels on foot or by bus. We've got some bus drivers who remember her. The girl makes an impression."

Eve took out the list, pushed it across the table. "She didn't bother using initials. Full names for her, since she didn't figure anyone would bother to check the little brother's comp and find where she'd hidden it."

"You put this together." After barely a glance, Mackie shoved the hard copy aside. "This isn't hers."

"Oh, part of you, the part under the funk, knows it's hers. It's what she is. Part of you knew what she was, and needed it. Your eyes, your hands, and a mind and heart as black as midnight. Maybe seeing that in someone who came from you was another reason you hit the funk. It blurs the hard parts."

"Just more lies. You want me to believe Will would hurt her own mother, her little brother? Try again."

"I note you don't say anything about the stepfather, the school employees, but we'll slide there for now." She took out the photos of Zach Stuben that Peabody had dug up.

"Cute kid. Me, I'm not big on kids, but yeah, he's cute enough. And the puppy — he used to have a puppy, right? Looks like love there, the way he's hugging that stupid dog, the way the stupid dog's all cuddled in. I guess that's why she broke its neck and tossed it out the window at the kid's feet."

"She never did that."

"She absolutely did that — I bet you taught her how to break a neck, how to apply the pressure, how to work the angle. And she used it on a stupid little dog. Because she hates this kid right here, this cute, harmless kid. She hates him because he exists. Just as she'd have hated your son, if you'd had one. *She's* all that gets to exist."

"You don't know her!"

"I do." Eve slapped her palms on the table, stood up, leaned in. "And so do you. Under it, you know. She hurt him. He was afraid of her. Your ex told you, but you didn't want to see it. Funk helps with that, helps you not see what you don't want to see. But you knew, you always fucking knew."

"My client is addicted to a substance that — "

"Shut the fuck up!" Mackie exploded.

"Mr. Mackie, let me help you. Remember what we discussed, and let me do my job. I need to consult with — "

"I said shut the fuck up! What good are you? You're just like the rest of them, toeing the line, gaming the system. I don't need you."

"I represent you, Mr. Mackie. Let me do my job, and — "

"You represent *you*. That's how it is. Now shut the fuck up and get out. I don't need you. I don't want you. I don't need anyone." He lurched up, yanking on the restraints bolted to the floor.

Pratt jerked sharply, and the resulting fall from his chair saved him from Mackie's grasping hands.

"Sit down or be put down." Eve straightened, slowly.

"You're a *liar*. He's in on it, too."

"Sit down, or I'll put you down."

"Try it."

As Eve started around the table, Pratt scrambled up. He stayed out of reach, but Eve gave him props for not running for the door.

"My client is in withdrawal. He needs — "

"I'm not your client! Get the fuck out."

"If you want him gone, you need to fire him, on record." Eve spoke coolly. "You have to waive your right to counsel, on record. Otherwise, he stays."

"You're fucking fired. I fucking waive my right to bullshit counsel. Come on, bitch, try me."

"Love to."

She easily dodged his restraint-hampered punch, took him down with a sweep of her feet. "Stay down," she warned him. "You're in no shape or position to take me on. I'm going to give you the chance to reconsider firing your court-appointed counsel. Take a minute, Mackie. Pull yourself together, and consider."

The trembling ran up his arms, quivered over his chest. "Get him out. The weasel tried to talk me into making a deal. You think I'd take a deal? Get him out."

"That's pretty clear." Peabody got up, walked to the door. "The suspect has terminated his counsel, and waived his right to counsel. I'd get gone, Pratt, before he puts your name on a list."

Saying nothing, a bit green around the edges, Pratt retrieved his briefcase and left the room.

"Terminated counsel has exited Interview." Peabody closed the door.

"Are you going to sit, or do I have you taken back to a cage?"

From the floor Mackie eyed Eve. "Your turn will come."

"Yeah, sooner or later, but you won't be around to see it. In the chair, Mackie."

CHAPTER
SEVENTEEN

He sat. The red splotches stained his face again, and his eyes had reddened more.

Eve took a document from the file, the blueprint of the school, pushed it toward him. "This is part of her mission. You can see where she's marked egresses, weak spots. You'd have taught her how."

"No."

"Mother, stepfather, brother. They came first. The hate, the rage, it goes deeper there. Then she'd be free of them, and she'd target the principal, the counselor, and the students she felt had wronged her or insulted her or were against her. You taught her how to hone those slights into crimes, you gave her the excuse to kill."

"Lies."

"You know better, but hold on to that if it helps you get through. You're looking rough, Mackie. I can authorize another medically approved hit if you need it to continue."

"I don't need anything from you, you lying cunt."

"Okay then. Let's go back to this." She shoved a couple of Zach's photos closer. "She killed his puppy, and she means to kill him. He's in protective custody, for now. You know that can't last forever. And she'll wait, she'll wait as long as it takes unless we stop her, and she'll put a strike through his brain. He shares her blood, they share a mother. He could've been yours, and she'll wait as long as it takes."

"She's got no reason."

"She's got *every* reason." Eve slammed a fist on the table. "He *took* from her. Didn't you help her justify using the skills you taught her to put down anybody who took from her? Some guy's driving down the street on a rainy day, and a woman runs out in front of him. He tries to stop, tries to swerve, but it's too late. Did he aim for her, Mackie? Did he get up that morning planning on killing her? Did he spend days, weeks, months, like you, working on the details? Did he tell himself he could take innocent bystanders, too, because they didn't matter? The kill mattered."

"He killed her, and they did *nothing*."

"So you target him, this guy who tried to stop, and you target the doctor and his office manager because her appointment ran over, and you target her supervisor, who gave her grief because she kept coming in late, wasn't doing her job."

"She did her best!"

"Who says somebody's best is always good enough? What world do you live in? You target the lawyer *you* went to because he couldn't make it all better for you. And you use your daughter to make the kills because you're so fucked-up you can't make the strikes. Whose idea was it to take out more? Hers, I'm guessing. Hers because she wanted that power, that thrill. That practice. Practice so when she got to her own list, she could take out her mother and her little brother."

His abused eyes twitched now. "We're going to Alaska."

"She was never going to Alaska. What the hell does she want to go to Alaska for? She's a fifteen-year-old girl from New York, and the city has everything she wants and needs. Targets galore.

"She'll kill this little boy, this cute little kid because her mother had the nerve to have another offspring. She won't get to him today or tomorrow, not next week, but in six months or a year, when he thinks he's safe again? When he's out playing with some friends, she'll wipe them all out, all those kids. Because she can, because you gave her the excuse, and you taught her how."

"She won't."

But his ravaged eyes cut away.

"You know she will. Maybe he'll be twelve when she comes for him. He and a couple of pals heading down to the arcade or riding airboards, or hanging in the park. And done! She ends them all. Just like she ended him." She pulled Alan Markum's photo out of the file. "He and his wife, having a day together, their wedding anniversary. She was going to tell him they're having a baby. She never got the chance, like that baby will never have the chance to know its father. You did that, Mackie, you and Willow. You took that life on a fucking whim, and now another kid grows up without ever knowing its father. For what? So you can cover up killing a doctor who was busy bringing another life into this screwed-up world so his appointments ran late?

"You stole from them. From this pregnant woman, just like your wife was pregnant. By your rules we should execute you and Willow. You took the father from the child."

"They took from me."

"How did he take from you?" She shoved the picture closer yet. "How did Alan Markum take from you? He never met you, you didn't know him. What did he do to you to deserve death, to deserve never holding his son or daughter?"

"We . . . We had to protect the mission. Collateral damage."

"That's it? That's what you taught her. So this boy, this kid on his seventeenth birthday?" She tossed Nathaniel's photo on the table. "This boy whose mother loved him, who never did you any harm, he's just excess? His life means *nothing*?"

"We had to finish." The tremors rose up in his voice now, and his eyes watered. "We needed justice for Susann. For Gabriel."

"You needed blood, and Willow craved it. She craves the kill like you crave the funk. You gave it to her. You needed someone to blame so you made your list and fuck anybody who happened to be caught in her crosshairs. Now he is." She tapped Zach's photo. "That's what you created. It's what you've fucking wrought."

"She'll go to Alaska. Live free. You'll never find her."

"She's not going anywhere. Don't you fucking get it?" Eve demanded as she sprang up, swooped around the table. "She's not done, and she won't be. Tell me, fucking tell me, if you weren't already thinking about other names. Who else screwed things up for you in your fucked mind, Mackie? The stepfather? Oh, I'd bet my badge he was on your next mission."

She saw the flicker in his watery, ruined eyes. "He took your place. Lowenbaum. He pushed you out. Patroni. He didn't understand. Oh, yeah, you were already working all that out in your head. And she's like you. She's looking for blood, for blame. Your eyes and hands, Mackie. She's an addict, Mackie, just like you. Her addiction is death, and you gave her the first hit."

"She's avenging — "

"Nothing!" Eve interrupted. "You broken down piece of shit, this isn't about justice. It's not even about revenge. It's about murder. It's about you giving her the green to kill whoever she wanted. That's what she's doing now. And this boy here, he's top of her list. Don't make me take her out. Look at me, goddamn you. Don't make me take her out, and don't think, not for a second, I'll hesitate to do that if she gives me no choice. Her life's in your trembling hands, because with or without you, I'll find her. With or without you, I'll stop her. But without you, I may have to give someone else the green. Without you, she may never be sixteen."

"You won't find her."

"But I will. She can put me on her list if she hasn't already, but I'll find her first. She's a cop killer, Mackie, and every cop in this city is hunting her. Some of them may not wait for the green. You're not there to hold her back. You're not there to keep her level. She's already made mistakes, and she'll make more. She's fifteen, and she'll make mistakes without her father to help her. She's alone, and every target on your list and hers is out of range. She'll lose control, she'll hit another location, more collateral damage, and we'll end her. Then her blood's on you, Mackie. Your daughter's blood's on your hands."

"No."

"She disobeyed you already," Peabody said quietly. "You told her to get out of the city. You'd have had a route plotted out, but she didn't take it. She didn't leave, didn't go somewhere safe to wait. Because she can't."

"She can't," Eve agreed, "because the missions, yours and hers, come first. As long as he's breathing." Once again, Eve tapped Zach's photo. "She'll stay. And because she'll stay, I'll find her. Pray I find her before another cop does. I'll give her a chance to surrender. Pray she takes it."

"She'll . . ."

"Die," Eve said flatly. "Is there enough funk in the world to blur your vision on that one?"

"Get away from me."

"Sorry, Mackie, time to get used to not getting your way. I don't have to get away from you. You've been arrested for conspiracy to murder, multiple counts, and you have confessed on record to same. Your life as you knew it is over. You'll live the rest of it being told where to go, when to eat, when to sleep, and every second of that in an off-planet cage."

He looked at Eve now, with hate. "You want that for my girl."

"I want your girl to live. You can believe that. I want her to live, Mackie. Do you?"

"She's my flesh and blood."

"Does that matter to her? This little boy's her flesh and blood. Her brother. And if she could get him in her sights right now, he'd be in the morgue. Don't make me put her there, Mackie. Help me bring her in, don't make me take her out."

"To live in a cage for the rest of her life?"

Eve let out a long breath, straightened, paced the room. Gave the slightest nod to the two-way mirror.

"That tells me you'd rather she be dead than breathing, so I'm wasting my time with you. Peabody, take this worthless fuck back to — "

She broke off, cursed under her breath, stalked to the door at the brisk knock. "What? I'm in Interview."

"And I'm here to offer the subject of that Interview a deal." Reo sailed in, set her briefcase on the table.

"Screw that. Let's take this outside, Counselor."

"We're all here to protect and serve this city and its people. For the record, Reo, APA, Cher, now in Interview. The PA's office has a deal for Mr. Mackie."

"I didn't ask for a deal. I told that worthless PD no deals."

"He didn't ask for a deal," Eve snapped. "Get out."

"The deal involves Willow Mackie. Her future. Do you want a future for your daughter, sir?"

346

"I'm not helping you."

"Then help her. I'm authorized to offer you this. If you give us information leading to your daughter's arrest before — and I stress before — she kills or injures anyone else, if she surrenders peaceably, we will agree to try her as a minor on all charges brought."

"Bullshit, that's bullshit!" Raging, Eve gripped Reo's arm. "Outside, Reo."

Reo simply shook Eve off. "Dallas, this comes from the top, and has been agreed to by your boss, and mine."

"What kind of chickenshit, weaselly bullshit are you trying to serve here? She killed twenty-five people in cold blood. Dozens of others suffered injuries and trauma. She's no kid on a joyride, you gutless bitch."

Reo turned steely. "And if you'd apprehended her by now, I wouldn't have to make this deal. If you can't find and stop a teenager, that's not on me. Bitch. Go on, put your hands on me again," she warned when Eve took a step toward her. "You'll be off this investigation in a snap. Do your job, Lieutenant. I'll do mine."

"Oh, I'll do my job. Peabody, we're out. We're hunting." She wrenched the door open. "Better make that deal fast, because if I find her before the ink dries, she's mine. Dallas and Peabody, exiting the goddamn fucking Interview."

She slammed the door behind her, rolled her shoulders, then bulleted to Observation.

"Quite a performance," Roarke said. "I'm glad I got here just before curtain."

Eve just muttered, "Come on, come on," and stared through the glass.

"Explain 'tried as a minor,'" Mackie said.

"You know very well that due to the severity of the crimes she's accused of, Willow Mackie could and would be tried as an adult." All business now, Reo sat in the chair Eve had vacated. "She could and would be tried, convicted, and sentenced to life in prison, again multiple sentences. She would be transported to an off-planet penal colony, where she would spend, given current life expectancies, the next century."

"Maybe I forced her to do it."

"It won't fly, Mackie," Reo said calmly. "You couldn't force her to complete the expert strikes with such accuracy. You weren't there last night when eighteen people were murdered."

"I pressured her, influenced her. Brainwashed her."

"You can try that, of course, but I can promise I'd rip that to pieces in court. I'd tear that to pieces," she continued, "and have the evidence of her plans to kill others to help me do just that. She was not under duress. She was co-parented and has never indicated duress to her mother, to her teachers, to anyone. And, in fact, as Lieutenant Dallas learned through her investigation, she has her own list of targets."

Reo paused to let it sink in.

"Despite all this," she continued, "Willow Mackie is fifteen, and we will agree to these terms in order to save the lives of innocent people. It's a one-time offer, and the clock's ticking on it. As hotheaded as the lieutenant may be, she is absolutely correct. Willow Mackie will kill again. I suspect she'll do so very soon if not apprehended. If you help us prevent that, if she harms no one else and is apprehended peacefully, she will be tried as a minor and be eligible for release on her eighteenth birthday. She will, understand this, be evaluated physically and mentally. And she will have to agree to residence in a halfway house and counseling, with further evaluations, from her eighteenth birthday for a period of one year. Those are the terms. Do you wish to have a representative read the terms and discuss them with you?"

"I don't need anyone. Let me see it. Let me read it."

"He's going to sign it," Eve said, watching.

"You broke his confidence. And using the little boy," Mira added. "That shook his trust in her. He's afraid for her, but not only afraid she'll be caught and stopped, even hurt. He's afraid of what she'll do without him to hold her back."

"He knew what she was, what she had in her. He can pretend he didn't, but he did. And he used it when it served his sick purpose. Maybe she'd have killed without him at some point, but he gave her the skills, the weapons, and the reasons. They'll both have a long, long time to think about who led who."

"If he signs," Peabody said, "she'll be out in under three years."

"Let him sign. Then we'll see."

"It's a crap deal," Peabody said. "I know you were playing to him with Reo in there, but it's still a crap deal."

"If it helps us find her before she takes out another twenty-five civilians, not so crappy. And she'll go for more next time. She's keeping score. She'll be watching screen, too, see what we're saying about her, reading between the lines. Change her appearance a little bit. Go more for the boy look maybe. Or get herself a wig — go all girl. She's planned it. Her father's daughter."

"I want another guarantee," Mackie said to Reo. "I want a guarantee she'll be brought in alive and unharmed."

"Mr. Mackie, I'm an APA, not a police officer. I can't guarantee what may happen during the attempt to apprehend her. If she resists, if she fires on officers or civilians — "

"They bring her in, alive, or no deal."

"I can amend the deal this way. I can promise that every attempt will be made to bring your daughter in alive. That no officer will use excessive force or give a termination order. If I told you I could do more, you'd know I was lying to you. I'm giving you the best chance for her."

"Add that in. Add that in and I'll sign it."

"Let me clear it. Reo, APA, Cher, exiting Interview."

She stepped out, took a breath, whipped out her 'link. And as she spoke to her superior, held up a hand for Eve to wait.

"That's right. Yes, sir. I have the primary right here, and she understands the additional terms. Done." She clicked off, nodded at Dallas. "Done. They'll add it in, send the amended agreement. Can you enforce it?"

"I'll make it clear. I want her alive, Reo. I want her in the same box as he is. I want to look in her eyes and tell her she's finished."

"And when she's eighteen?"

Eve merely smiled, flat and cold. "Go pick up your paperwork, then we'll see what he has to say."

Eve turned away to answer her own 'link. "Dallas."

"Heating up, boss," Baxter told her. "We caught a whiff of her heading east on Fifty-Second this morning. We're heading back to her old neighborhood."

"Ask around that ice cream place. Divine. She's got a weakness."

"On it. Can always use a scoop of Chocolate Sin in a sugar cone. How's it going there?"

"Closing it up. I'll be in touch."

She waited for Reo.

"I've got your chickenshit right here," Reo said.

"Then let's make it work. We think she's got a hole back in the place her father had them before the first strike. Let's see if he can get us closer before she kills somebody else."

Eve stepped back in, restarted the record. Mackie's skin had gone transluscent under a sheen of sweat. He needed a fix, Eve thought, was hanging on by a thread.

"You can get her a free ride." Eve poured disgust over her tone. "Save her life, and maybe — though you don't give a cold shit — save innocent lives."

"Three years inside isn't a free ride," Reo said briskly and, sitting, offered the amended agreement to Mackie.

"Tell that to the twenty-five dead, and the ones left behind to mourn them." Eve slapped her palms on the table, leaned into Mackie's sweating face. "You think my hands are tied? Only for now. When she gets out, I'll be on her. I'll know when she sleeps, when she eats, when she farts. And I'll be right there when she makes a mistake. Remember that. Count on it."

"The priority here is to find Willow Mackie before she harms anyone else. It should be yours, Lieutenant." Reo offered Mackie a pen.

"You sign first," Mackie said.

With a nod, Reo signed in her pretty, perfect penmanship.

Mackie snatched the pen, managed a shaky, jittery scrawl.

Reo put the agreement and the pen in her briefcase, closed it. "Mr. Mackie, where is your daughter?"

"She should be on her way to Alaska. We worked out three routes. She was supposed to take a bus to Columbus, then choose one of three routes west."

"But she isn't on her way to Alaska, is she?" Reo kept her voice reasonable. "Where is she? This agreement is null and void unless you offer information that leads to her arrest."

"She's strong willed, determined. The girl's a winner."

Eve's sound of derision had Mackie's blurry eyes cutting up to her face. "You don't know her."

"If you do," Eve shot back, "where is she?"

"She wants to finish what we started. She's no quitter."

"She wants more than that. You know she wants more than that or you'd never have signed that agreement."

352

"The asshole her mother married's always on her case."

"So, naturally, he has to die. If you want to save her life, the life of that little boy, tell me where the fuck she is and stop making excuses for her."

"If we ever got separated, or she needed to regroup, couldn't get out of the city right off, she was to go back to the apartment — to the area we'd scoped out. Where she knows the lay of the land, where she's a familar face so nobody much notices."

"You want us to believe she went back to the place we've already nailed down?"

"It's got a basement, a storage room, an old laundry room. Machines are busted down there so nobody uses it. We laid in some supplies."

"You think we didn't go through that building, pull in those supplies, and seal it up?" Eve dropped down into a chair. "You're wasting my time."

"If she couldn't get into the building or if she felt it was being surveilled, there's a flop on Lex, between Thirty-Ninth and Fortieth. If she needed time to regroup, or wait for me, or let things cool, she'd go there, lay low. Wait it out."

"What's she carrying?" When he hesitated, Eve leaned forward again. "You want her taken alive? What's she carrying?"

"She's got a Tactical-XT, military, with long-range scope. Night-vision option. Two hand blasters, a police-issue stunner, pump laser, six flash grenades."

"Sharps?"

"Combat knife, flip sticker, telescope baton with bayonette."

"Body armor?"

"Full body. Plus helmet, of course."

"If you've left out so much as a penknife and she uses it on one of my people, that agreement isn't worth jack."

"She's got a multitool. It's got sharps. Tell her I said to stand down. Tell her that her father said to stand down and live. The basement of the apartment or the flop on Lex. Those are the planned retreats."

"Then you'd better hope we find her. Interview end."

She turned him over to uniforms, with instructions to put him on suicide watch. She let Reo deal with the legalities. Lowenbaum had already moved out of Observation, barking orders into his comm.

"You want to ride with us?" he asked her.

"No, I've got my own to set up. I've got two detectives in that area already. If she's there, I don't want her making them and popping off strikes. Get your op set up — odds are on the flop. She could get into the basement, but it's a wrong move when she knows we've been in that location. She wouldn't make that wrong a move."

"Agreed, but we'll sweep for heat source — if I can pull your EDD team with us."

"Take them." She pulled out her own comm as she strode toward her bullpen. "Baxter," she began, then filled him in.

"Reineke, Jenkinson, suit up. Uniform Carmichael, pick six and do the same. Santiago, Detective Carmichael, you're second unit, full suits. Suspect is Willow Mackie, age fifteen. She is armed and dangerous. Weaponry includes military-grade Tactical-XT with scope and night vision, two blasters, stunner, pump laser, flash grenades, various sharps. Do not, repeat, *do not* let her age deter you from stunning the living shit out of her. We want her alive. SWAT is moving in to surround and secure. Peabody, get a fricking map of the sector on this half-assed screen."

Eve worked it out as she went. "She won't go easy, and if she spots us or Lowenbaum's team, she will attempt to pick us off. She's not in the fricking basement," Eve muttered. "It's bad planning. She'd want higher ground, an eyeline. We'll clear it, but that's not where she is. The flop . . . "

"Would you like the building's details?" Roarke said from behind her.

"Helpful."

He stepped over to Peabody, interfaced his PPC with the comp. "Post-Urban construction," he told Eve. "Currently an SRO primarily used by low-level LCs, transients, addicts, and petty criminals. Eight stories, twelve rooms per story. A small lobby with droid service. Cash only. Rooms by the half hour, hour, night, and week. No soundproofing, no privacy screening."

"Got it. Heat sourcing will give us occupied rooms — and anyone who's alone. She won't have company. Ears may help."

She paced back and forth in front of the image. "We'll hit the droid, get verification. If she's in there, we'll get people out — if possible. Single room, single window, single door."

"She may have the door booby-trapped, LT," Reineke said.

"Yeah. I would. I don't like it." She paced again. "It's not a basement, but where the hell's her out? Fire escape? She'd know we'd have the exterior covered."

"She may believe she can fight her way out," Mira put in. "She's fifteen. Indestructible, and the star of her own personal drama."

"Maybe."

But it niggled at her, niggled as she refined the op, as she prepared to move out.

"I'm with you," Roarke told her.

"Okay." Distracted, she frowned at him. "Why?"

"Is that a personal or professional question?"

"You'd be more use with EDD."

"Not necessarily. Particularly as you don't think she's where they're going."

"I don't see why he'd lie. Why he'd go through the whole agreement deal just to lie. He wants her to live, and it was the right angle, pushing the brother, her plans to do the kid, the others. I could see him take it in, see he knew she'd go there. But he wants her to live, and he wants her to get out, to know she'll only spend a few years inside."

"She's his child."

"He wasn't lying, but . . . "

"Take a minute."

Shaking her head, she pulled a combat knife from her drawer, slid it from the sheath, back in. "Clock's ticking," she said as she hooked it to her belt.

"And Lowenbaum is even now putting men in position to pin her down. Take a moment, and let whatever's brewing in that head of yours out."

"It's more gut."

But she stopped, sat, put her boots on her desk, stared at the board.

When Peabody started in, Roarke held up a hand to silence her.

Head, gut, instinct, sixth sense, or cop logic — whatever it was, he knew it was working inside her.

They'd wait.

CHAPTER
EIGHTEEN

She should be on her way to Alaska — but she wasn't.

She was supposed to take a bus to Columbus — but she didn't.

They had a mission — but she had another of her own. Hidden from her father, her teacher, her mentor.

He wants her to live. She wants to kill.

He tells her to run, stay safe, wait it out.

Running? Safety? For losers. Waiting takes too long. She wants to kill.

"She's not going to listen to him," Eve murmured. "It's not because she's fifteen. Maybe that plays a part, but that's not the crux. It's just not. She knows she's better than he is. He's lost his physical edge, and hers is still sharp. He's weak, isn't he?"

She shoved up then, paced, her eyes on the board.

"Who accomplished that? She did. Not him. Stay safe? She doesn't want safe, she wants action. She wants the excitement, the points, the targets.

"Her targets."

"Where would she go?" Roarke asked her.

"Not to some mangy flop with whores and junkies. Not to some hole to curl up and wait until whenever. It's all now. It's all today. It's about her. She's the center. She wants the center. If she wanted safe, she'd be gone. She's not gone because it's now, and it's about what *she* wants. Her mission now. She'd go home."

"If she's at the apartment — " Peabody began.

"That's not home. That's HQ, her father's HQ, and that mission is done, at least for now. The townhouse. Her mother's house." She turned around, and Roarke saw it in her eyes. Instinct became knowledge.

"It's comfortable, it's hers. Clothes, food, entertainment. Again an area she knows — and right now, an empty house. And better, more important, fucking vital? They'll come back. A few days, a week, but they'll come back, the three people who top her list. That's something she'll wait for."

"We sealed it."

"She'll get in. Her father would've taught her how to get around and through a seal. She can have the place to herself — privacy screens down. She can watch the screen, judge when the media play eases off. Tuck up somewhere and wait. They come in, they feel safe, or safer. She just has to hole up, just wait until the house is locked up tight, until it's all quiet. Take the stepfather first, then the mother, then the kid. Then take what you want, whatever you want, and walk away. Find somewhere else to kill."

"Should I pull the op?" Peabody asked.

"No." As she weighed percentages against instinct, Eve dragged her fingers through her hair, pulled at it. "I could be wrong. I'm not, but I could be. Let it play."

"The three of us then."

359

Eve nodded at Roarke. "If you're up for it."

"Personally or professionally?"

"Funny. Peabody, bring that location on screen." She pulled out her comm. "Reineke, I'm peeling off."

It was a risk, Eve thought after she'd checked out her weapons, after they'd gone down to the garage. She loaded a laser rifle, a scope, the equipment Roarke would use in her deceptively ordinary DLE. The earbud kept her in constant communication with the others teams.

If the percentages proved true, she could be with the main team in minutes. If her instincts were on target, she could pull in the main team fast.

EDD reported no heat source in the basement, none in the apartment. They continued to identify sources in the flop.

Carmichael would pose as an LC, Santiago as her mark. They'd enter the building, and deal with the droid.

"I can send backup," Lowenbaum told her. "I can send you a couple of guys."

"We've got it for now. One of us is going to be in the right place. When we know, the other gets their ass there fast."

"I hear that."

"Try not to kill her, Lowenbaum."

"Same to you."

Eve handed Peabody a visored helmet. "She'll aim for your head."

"That's comforting." Peabody slid into the backseat.

"I'll drive," Eve told Roarke. "You work the portable. She can't keep watch out the windows 24/7, but she may have cams set up to give her a view of the street, the sidewalks." She glanced at Roarke as she pulled out. "How close do you want me?"

"The boys in the van snagged the best toys, but I can make do with this. Try for within fifty feet of the building."

Eve drove, considered. Contacted Nadine on her wrist unit. "Get ready to go on with a bulletin."

"What?" Nadine shoved a hand at her hair — tied back in a short tail and far from camera ready. "How hot? I got home an hour ago after doing spots on last night, on Mackie's arrest, on the manhunt for his daughter. Have you got her?"

"Just be ready when I tag you back." She cut Nadine off, whipped around a Rapid Cab. "She'll be ready."

"For what?" Peabody wondered.

"To go on with a bulletin that will pull our suspect's attention away from the street, the sidewalk."

"You're going to blow the other op," Roarke concluded.

"Not if she's there. Not if I'm wrong. And not while there's a cop unsecured. But . . . "

"If she's not there, you're not wrong, and the rest are secure, you'll feed Nadine the other op. As if it's going down." Roarke smiled as he fiddled with the sensor. "She'll be very annoyed with you, our Nadine."

"She'll get over it when I give her the exclusive on this op."

"This helmet's heavy. And it echoes."

Eve flicked a glance in the rearview mirror at Peabody with the black helmet and visor in place. "Take it off until you need it. You look ridiculous."

"Not at all." Roarke smiled back at her. "Sexy Stormtrooper."

"Really?"

"Stay on point," Eve warned. "I'm still figuring out how to get in without giving her time to kill us."

"I have every confidence," Roarke said, continuing his work on the portable, hoping to boost its range.

"I don't want to double park, drawing her attention when people start blasting horns and bitching. How much inside fifty feet?"

"I think I can get a read at sixty now. It's worth a try."

Eve considered the option of using a building, flashing the badge and getting Roarke set up in a neighboring house. But she spotted a curbside barely big enough for a mini. She could make it work.

Making it work meant using the DLE to nudge another vehicle up to the bumper of the one in front of it, and doing the same to the one behind. With that, and a lot of maneuvering, she squeezed in.

"This is more like sixty-five than sixty."

"If you can't do it from here, why didn't you say so before I got here?"

"I didn't say that. Just give me another minute."

She put a hand to her ear. "Yeah, go," she said to Jenkinson.

"Santiago and Carmichael are in. The check-in droid gives a negative on the suspect."

"How reliable a negative?"

"They say it's wonky, so Feeney's sending Callendar in to work on it. We got about a dozen single heat sources. Feeney's done some calculation and takes four of them out. You can't get accurate height and weight, but his calcs say those four are way too big for the suspect."

"Good enough. We're about sixty-five feet from the target location. Roarke's working on scanning for heat sources. We'll let you know."

She ended transmission, shifted to Roarke. "Well?"

"You understand this is meant to work at much closer range, which I'd already managed to increase before you added to that range, so bugger off a minute."

She buggered off by tapping her fingers on the steering wheel.

Better if they nailed her at the other location, Eve thought. Better if they had that flop surrounded, took her there.

But . . .

"All right then, let's see if I've performed a small miracle."

Roarke programmed the coordinates, tapped in codes, scanned the small screen.

"Geeks rule." With her chin on the back of his seat, Peabody studied the screen through her visor. "You've got a read."

"Now let's see if there's anyone home."

He began a slow scan, starting with the main floor.

"A narrow basement area beneath, in case you didn't know. Nothing there, nothing on the main floor. Starting scan of second floor."

Nothing flared as he scanned slowly foot by foot.

"Second floor clear. Starting scan on third level."

Here or there, there or here, Eve thought, waiting for one of her team to report back. Waiting for something to flare.

"Ah. Geeks and cops rule, it seems. There she is, Lieutenant."

"I see her," Eve noted, and watched the flare of the heat source on screen.

"Stretched out. I bet she's bored. Watching the screen, watching monitors. We're going to give her some excitement. Lowenbaum!"

"Got you back," he said. "Your EDD cutie's in there, working the droid, but word is his memory disc doesn't show the suspect in the last twenty-four. That's as far as he goes."

"Because she's here."

"Son of a bitch."

"I want you to leave some of your men on that building. Visible, Lowenbaum, but not too obvious about it. I'm going to use your location as a distraction. Throw her off. The rest of you come in fast and quiet. We're going to take her, Lowenbaum."

"Bet your superior ass."

"Reineke, you copy?"

"That's affirmative."

"Leave some of the uniforms. Make them visible. And get the rest of the team to this location. Barricades at the end of the block, both sides. Keep out of eyeline unless and until I say different. We're going to move in five."

"Watch your ass, LT, and the rest of you."

She tagged Nadine again. "NYPSD officers, including SWAT, are moving in on the remaining suspect in the recent LDSK murders. Lieutenant Eve Dallas is supervising a takedown of Willow Mackie, believed to be holed up in an SRO building on Lexington. Dallas reports an arrest is imminent."

"What kind of bullshit is this? You never report that — and you never feed the media during an op."

"You're not just the media, are you? Go with it, go now. I can promise you, it'll be worth it. Every level worth it. Go with it, Nadine."

"I'll go with it, damn it. You're going to owe me."

"I've already got the payment ready. Later."

Eve engaged her comp screen. "It shouldn't take her long."

In fact, it took just under two minutes before Channel Seventy-Five's feed went to their hot blue and jittery red Breaking News flash.

The on-air reporter announced an important development in the hunt for the suspect in the Madison Square attack, and threw it to Nadine, whose voice came over with a photo of her in the corner of the screen.

"This is Nadine Furst reporting by remote as even now police officers and SWAT units converge — "

Eve cut off the screen, shoved open her door the instant she saw the heat source move from recline to stand.

"We got her attention. Gear up." She tossed Roarke a helmet.

"Now, really, Eve."

"Wear it or stay here." She pulled out her own, shook her head at it. "Hate these. They're heavy and they echo."

"What I said!"

"I never said you were wrong. First, we get in — that's on you," she said to Roarke. "I take the front stairs. Peabody, you go through, go up the back stairs. If she's wearing body armor, aim for the head. Nobody sits around watching screen in one of these damn helmets. Make damn sure your stunner's on mid-range. We aren't giving her any love taps, but I don't want to risk paralysis. She doesn't go down, you amp it up. Roarke, I need you to hang back, second level, in case she gets by us. She gets by us, you take her out."

"Backup?" Peabody asked.

"By the time we're in position, by the time we get in, they'll be here. Where is she?" Eve asked Roarke.

"Sitting, very likely on the floor of the room — third floor, front of the house, far side."

"Watching the screen. Keep it going, Nadine. Sixty-five feet. Let's cover it."

They moved fast, eating up the ground on a cold, clear day, with Roarke keeping track on the portable.

Not a lot of tourists on this more residential street, Eve noted. And most natives barely spared a glance at three people half jogging down the sidewalk wearing visored helmets.

But even jaded New Yorkers would gather and point at a SWAT unit. The goal? Get in before the op drew any sort of attention. Before Willow Mackie realized her location was blown.

They reached the door, crouched down together.

"Peabody, take the portable. She moves, we know it. She'd need to be at the window, angled and looking down this way to spot us. Roarke, do your thing."

"Scanning security first."

"Reineke, status."

"Barricades going up. We'll come on foot from here."

"You and Jenkinson take the back of the building. Hold there until I tell you, then come in hard. Lowenbaum."

"Copy."

"Target is third floor, southeast window. She's on the floor, watching screen, so if you're going to move your men, do it now, do it fast."

"We've got her. Feeney's located her. We're moving. I'll have men on rooftops, facing buildings. Sending another team with yours to the rear. She's pinned, Dallas."

"Pinned isn't done. We're working on silent entry."

"She's a clever girl," Roarke said. "She's jury-rigged a secondary alarm. I expect it signals her 'link. It's clever, but relatively basic. Just another moment."

To give her time, to give her a heads-up, Eve thought, when the family came home.

She glanced around, scanned, caught a flash of movement on the roof of the building directly across the street.

"Peabody?"

"She hasn't budged."

"Roarke?"

"Alarms down. I'm on the locks. And they're popped."

"All teams, all teams, we're going in. Peabody, rear steps; Dallas, front; Roarke front to station on second level. We're on the move."

She reached for the door handle. "Leave the portable, Peabody. Straight back. Straight up."

As she eased open the door, she drew her weapon.

Technology aside, she swept the foyer, straightened slowly. "We're in," she murmured for the recorder, and signaled Peabody to go.

With Roarke, Eve started up the stairs, said nothing when he held a weapon very similar to her own.

"Feeney?"

"Got you, kid. Got Roarke, got Peabody. Target's in the same position."

"Heading up to her now."

She gestured to Roarke: *Stay here*. "Baxter, Trueheart, Santiago, Carmichael, move in the front, fan out inside."

She started up the next flight, ears cocked. Halfway up she heard the murmur of voices, identified Nadine's.

She made it up two more before she heard the distinctive creak from the back stairs. She didn't need Feeney's warning in her ear that Willow heard it, too. She caught the sound — the scramble of feet, started up in a run.

"Move, move, move! Police!" she shouted, leaping up the last stair. "This is the police!"

The flash grenade exploded on impact, two feet in front of her. Even with the visor, the blast of light burned against her eyes. Momentarily blinded, she laid down a stream along the floor, hoping to keep the target contained.

She felt return fire — heat and pressure against her shoulder, her hip, pivoted.

Willow hit her hard — a shoulder in the sternum, with momentum behind it. It took Eve down, stole her breath, but she rolled, threw out a hand, managed to snag the girl by the ankle.

Got a vicious kick in the head that had her helmet vibrating.

She heard shouting through the glare, the smoke, through her ear-bud. Pounding feet. More than seeing, she felt her quarry swing around, shove up from where she'd fallen, and fire toward the shouts. Because Eve rolled again, the next kick glanced off her ribs. She tossed up her legs, scissored them, connected hard enough to send Willow stumbling.

Seconds before the next flash exploded, she saw the blur of movement shoot to the left. She feinted right, heard the whine of the strike from the handheld shimmer the air where she'd been. From a crouch, she did a fast forward roll toward the doorway in the direction the blur had gone.

She dove left this time, so the strike shot through the opening.

Thinking of her team, thinking of blocking escape, Eve kicked the door closed.

She couldn't see, not clearly enough through the smoke, through the glare. Which meant she couldn't be seen. Any attempt to communicate with her team would give away her position.

She did what Master Wu taught her in those strange and fascinating lessons in the dojo. She breathed through her toes, became the fish — whatever the hell that meant. She risked lifting her visor — she couldn't breathe, couldn't hear through the echoes. She went absolutely still, and let her senses rule.

The faintest sound, like the movement of the smoke in the air. Following instinct, Eve fired toward it, aimed low. Heard the hiss of shock, rolled, fired again.

The door crashed open, and shouts rang through it. The volley of strikes zipping through the smoke, the opened door had her shouting to *Get back! Get back!* even as she sprang up to dive clear herself.

She caught a glimpse, barely a glimpse through the glaring billow of smoke. The girl wearing a riot vest, the laser in one hand, the grenade in the other. The grenade hand unsteady — it was unsteady — from a glancing stream.

Eve's weapon and the grenade went off simultaneously. Still tuned, Eve heard the rush of boots across the floor, leaped over, slammed the door. The resulting *thud* and fall brought only an instant of satisfaction.

Eve fell on the target, grappled with her in the choking smoke.

It was ugly. A hard knee to the crotch seared straight through Eve, an elbow shot had her eye burning, watering, but she managed to grip Willow's weapon hand with her left, began to twist. They rolled, with the girl getting in a couple of decent punches while Eve focused on disarming her.

The laser went off, shot a strike through the privacy screen, smashed the window.

"Give it up!" Eve ordered. "There's nowhere to go."

"Fuck you!"

When the door slapped open again, Eve rapped Willow's weapon hand hard on the floor. "Hold fire! Hold fire! I've got her — almost. Don't fucking stun me."

She shifted, using her weight to increase pressure. Later she'd think that slight change in angle had caused the point of the combat knife Willow jerked out of her belt to slice along her hand rather than her throat.

But the pain, the smell of her own blood, changed Eve's tactics.

"Fuck this." On that sentiment, she gave Willow a sharp head butt — the advantage was hers considering the helmet — then she short-jabbed her fist into Willow's larynx.

She heard the knife clatter, felt the laser hand convulse, then give. Still working half-blind, Eve shifted again, shoved Willow over, yanked her arms behind her back.

"I've got her," Eve called out as she snapped on restraints. "I've got her! Hold fire. And somebody get this smoke clear."

A little light-headed and queasy from it, Eve dragged off her helmet. It didn't make it better, and, in fact, brought it home that her head pounded like a bass drum.

Someone moved through the haze toward her. Of course it would be Roarke.

He crouched beside her, took her bleeding hand. "We need the MTs."

"Just need to mop it up."

"There are plenty to mop her up, so — " He guided her toward the door as her team flowed in to deal with the rest.

"Just a little fresh air," she managed. "How long was I in that crap? An hour?"

"Under five minutes from the first flash to the takedown."

"Under five." She gulped in clearer air on the second floor. "It felt like an hour."

"Every bit of it," he agreed as he took a handkerchief from his pocket to wrap around her bleeding hand. "Couldn't get to you," he told her, "and when I nearly did, you slammed the door in my face."

"Timed it so she ran right into it. I didn't want her getting out of the room. Didn't want to risk it. Or one of my team getting blasted, or blasting me by mistake. Magic coat or not, a lot of weapons on scene. Couldn't call out and give her a bead on me."

"So I concluded. Back to the kitchen, I'd say. Cleaner air, some water, a chair."

"I can go for all three. I breathed through my toes."

"What now?"

"Master Wu. Couldn't see in the smoke and flash, couldn't hear clearly with the helmet. Breathed through my toes. Became the fish. Or maybe it was the pebble." Man, her head thumped and banged. "Had to lift the visor to do it, but — "

"Which is why you'll have a black eye."

"Yeah?" She lifted her hand, poked with her finger. "Ow. Anyway, it worked. Best Christmas present ever."

"You're welcome," he said, taking a firmer grip when she stumbled, drunk on the smoke.

He steered her into the kitchen, where McNab was pushing water to a gray-faced Peabody.

"The stair creaked." Peabody croaked it.

"One of those things," Eve said.

"When the grenade hit, I couldn't see a damn thing, and I misjudged the stairs. I went down like a brick."

Eve angled her head as Roarke got more water. "Is that the chin bruise?"

"Hit the tread when I tripped." Obviously disgusted, Peabody tapped the flat of her hand under the raw bruising on her chin. "The helmet rapped up. Bit my tongue, saw stars. And I didn't have your back."

Eve held up a finger, guzzled the water until the burning in her throat went down to raspy aching. The head banging, eye throbbing, hand stinging probably required more than water.

But God, it tasted, just then, better than real coffee.

"So you just sat on the steps crying like a baby?"

"No! I — "

"She crawled." McNab rubbed Peabody's shoulders.

"I couldn't see. At first I could hear you. I could hear the banging around, and she was firing. You, too. But I didn't want to risk a stream hitting you."

"You called out." Eve went back over it all in her head. "Drew her fire. You, too," she said to Roarke. "Stupid risk, but . . . that's backup in my book."

"Then I couldn't hear you," Peabody continued. "Or see you. Feeney's shouting you're to my left, to my left, but it's a wall. And Roarke's there, pulling me up. I can hear the others coming. We finally found the door."

"Magic coat," McNab added, resting his cheek on Peabody's head.

"I'd have taken one mid-body without it. You, too," Peabody said to Roarke.

"Aren't we the lucky ones?"

"But you shut the door."

"And she ran right into it, knocked herself down. Then I had her."

"But you're bleeding."

Eve took another blissful swallow of water. "You, too. But we got her. So let's take a moment here." She closed eyes that felt as if they'd been scrubbed with sand. "Then we'll go clean it up."

CHAPTER
NINETEEN

Eve took her time, even let the MTs clean up and slap some NuSkin over the gash on her hand.

The bruises elsewhere, and she had plenty of them, could wait.

Because she wanted privacy, and air, she stepped outside with Roarke.

They'd moved the barricades in, closing off the area directly around the building. That didn't stop the gawkers and reporters — and really, what was the difference — from pressing against those barricades. But she could, and she did, ignore the questions spewed out, turned her back to cameras aimed in her general direction.

"You'd think people would have something better to do."

"For most of these? Murder doesn't come into their lives every day."

"Then they should be grateful." She actively wanted to kick something. And her own ass would have done the job. "I screwed up in there."

"What? When and how?" he demanded. "And remember I was there."

"You weren't in here." She tapped her temple. "Too much in here kept thinking of her as a kid. I told everybody, forget her age, it doesn't apply. But I didn't. She got off strikes, at you, at Peabody. Strikes that could have done serious damage, and the flash grenades on top of it, because I didn't move faster and harder."

"You're going to have to review your own recorder and see for yourself how completely bollocks that is."

"Faster and harder," she repeated. "Even when I had her one-on-one, I . . . I think maybe I held back just a little, just enough."

"If that's true — and, as I've had a look at both of you after that one-on-one, I tend to disagree — the only one that got hurt is yourself."

He wanted to take that wounded hand, kiss it, brush his lips over the darkening bruises on her face. But he judged, at that moment, she needed her dignity more than the distraction.

"She's not like you, Eve. She's never been like you, will never be like you."

"Got that." She blew out a breath that streamed white in the cold, vanished. "Maybe I didn't before, but I've got that solid now. And I won't be holding back when I take her in the box."

She looked at him then, those wild blue eyes. Had it really been that same day they'd — tired, sickened, stressed — swiped at each other with Summerset between them?

It felt like years had passed.

"You should go home," she told him, "and sleep."

376

Reaching into her pocket, he pulled out the snowflake cap, pulled it over her head. "Did you miss the memo, where I sleep when you do?"

"Then you should go home, buy a couple planets. Seriously, you must have work you've shuffled aside for this."

"I can work at Central."

She blew out a second breath, met those gorgeous blue eyes again. "We're going to have to get you a damn office at the shop."

"Tempting." He smiled. "But thanks all the same. That makes it just a bit too official for the likes of me."

"The likes of you helped bring her down. Don't forget it. Those people over there? The ones who don't have murder in their lives every day, and are really hoping to see some blood, maybe a DB? Any one of them, Roarke. Any one of them could have been next, and they don't get that. They'll talk over a brew later about being *this* close to a killer. They'll be able to talk about it because you helped bring her down."

"Yet I'm not the one with a six-inch gash on my hand, a black eye — and I suspect bruises elsewhere."

"Yeah." She shifted her aching shoulders. "We'll get to the elsewhere later."

"Ah, my personal bonus."

"Well." She flicked her good hand over the cap, nodded. "If you're going to work at Central, let's get moving. Peabody! How about you drive?" she said to Roarke. "I've got some things to set up."

She started setting them up as they circumvented the barricade, ignored the crowd, and headed back to the car.

Nadine came first.

"You fed me false information," Nadine said immediately, with some serious rancor.

"No, I didn't. I just didn't give you all the information. Why does your face look like that? What's wrong with your left eye?"

"Nothing! I'm trying to get camera ready between lightning bulletins." And she continued to expertly line her left eye as she ranted. "You weren't anywhere near Lexington Avenue."

"Not personally, but there was an op in place there, as I told you."

"But *you* and Willow Mackie weren't in that place, in that operation. Now I've got to get my ass into the station, go on air, and spin all my earlier bulletins so I don't look like an ass, while New York-One happened to have a damn reporter half a block from where you took that bitch down, and has already done live remotes right on scene."

"Well, you could do that," Eve said as Roarke drove. "Or you could get your half-camera-ready self down to Central and broadcast a one-on-one exclusive with the primary who led the op and took that bitch down. If you take option two, you'd better get there fast."

"Fifteen minutes," Nadine said and cut Eve off.

"Peabody, arrange for Willow Mackie to be brought into an Interview room as soon as she's medically cleared. And find out if she's asked for a lawyer. Reo," she said into her 'link. "Willow Mackie's been taken into custody."

"So I heard — New York-One's all over it. I'm on my way into Central."

"Good. We need to talk."

"Did you get your face banged up in the arrest?"

"Yeah, there was a little . . . scuffle."

"Isn't that a shame?" Reo smiled sweetly. "Put some ice on it. I'll see you there."

Eve spent the rest of the drive contacting Mira, then Whitney.

The minute Roarke pulled into her slot in Central's garage, Eve hopped out. "Peabody?"

"Interview A. She's been cleared medically, and will be brought up within the next ten. She hasn't said the L word yet."

"Good. I want you to forget her age."

"Done. Believe me."

"But work her like that's a factor for you."

"Sympathetic." Peabody sighed, and sighed long. "I'm always sympathetic."

"Because it comes off real. But over that, play the disappointed and somewhat angry teacher to the student who fucked up. Adult to child, and the adult's in charge."

"I can do that."

"There's more, and we need to work out the timing in a huddle with Reo. I'm going to square things with Nadine." Eve rocked on her heels in the elevator as she calculated. "All in all that should give her a solid twenty minutes to sit and wait in the box."

"She's used to waiting," Peabody pointed out.

"Not for this. If you want to observe," she began, glancing over at Roarke.

"I'll be in and out. And close enough when you're finished with this."

She got off the elevator, headed straight for her office.

"I'm going to tap your coffee," Roarke told her, "before I take myself off to a quiet spot for an hour or so."

"You can use my office."

"I may end up there, but you'll need it for a bit, won't you?"

Even as he said it, they stepped in to find Reo waiting.

"That was fast."

"I'd just gone to my office. If I'm working on Saturday, I might as well work. Hi, Roarke."

"I'll be out of your way in just a moment. Coffee?"

"Oh boy, yeah. What happened to your hand?" she asked Eve.

"She had a knife." Eve sat on the edge of her desk, took the coffee Roarke offered.

"I'll take mine to go." Unconcerned about Eve's dignity in front of Reo, Roarke caught Eve's chin in his hand, kissed her firmly. "Go finish it."

"I'll see you tomorrow." Reo smiled at him. "At a happier event."

"What's tomorrow?" Eve demanded as Roarke strolled out.

"Bella's birthday party."

380

"What? No, that's . . . tomorrow?"

"Sunday afternoon," Reo confirmed. "And really good timing as it turns out."

Eve stared into her coffee. "I just can't catch a break."

"Oh, what's your problem? It's happy! There'll be cake — and surely adult beverages. Now let's talk about our murderous teenager."

"Yeah, wait. I want Peabody in on this."

To make that happen, Eve merely stepped to the door, shouted, "Peabody!"

But she did program a coffee regular and shove it into her partner's hand when Peabody came in, double-time clomp.

"Close the door. Okay, here's how I want to play it. There's some timing involved."

Eve ran it through for them. Together they discussed strategy, tactics, legalities. As she finished off her coffee, she glanced over at the sharp knock on her door.

"That's going to be Nadine. Peabody, go on and check on our suspect — from Observation. I'm going to need about ten minutes."

Eve opened the door. Before Nadine could spew out the words that went with the hard gleam in her eyes, Reo stepped forward.

"Hey! How are you? I heard you were at Madison Square."

"Backstage and out of the action."

"Plenty of action around here, and more to come. If I don't get a chance to see you before you leave, we'll talk tomorrow."

"Same goes." And Peabody, recognizing that gleam, hustled out with Reo.

Now Nadine shut the door. "You lied to me."

"I did not. Would I, if it saved lives? Absolutely. But I didn't. I used you," Eve added. "And as a result you saved lives. One of them could have been mine. Thanks."

"What kind of bullshit — "

"It's not. You can spend the time I have to give you bitching at me, or you can let me lay it out for you then have your exclusive. Your choice."

The gleam stayed hard. "We're supposed to be friends, over and above the rest of it, Dallas. We're supposed to be friends."

"Yeah, that happened. That happened and because of it I never thought of or considered tagging anyone else. I know my friends. I may have more of them than I actually want, but I know them or they wouldn't be. And I knew I could count on you."

"You could have told me the truth, and still counted on me."

Since she'd figured they'd have to push through this first, Eve shrugged, programmed coffee for Nadine.

"I did tell you the truth. I left out the part of it that would have compromised your journalistic integrity." She passed Nadine the coffee. "Because, fuck it, Nadine, we're not supposed to be friends. We are."

"Just how did — " Obviously still riding on plenty of mad, Nadine stopped herself, held up a hand. "Fine. Lay it out."

382

"I was on my way to the op on Lex. And I peeled off on a hunch. It hit me, that's all. It just did, and when it did, I knew I needed a distraction if the hunch played out. I fed you the Lexington Avenue op when I verified the suspect was holed up — with a fucking armory — at her mother's house. She'd have spotted us coming in, and it's a pretty sure bet somebody, many more than a couple of somebodies would be in the hospital now, if not the morgue, if we hadn't been able to distract her. You coming on with the bulletin fixed her attention on her screen. It made her believe she was safe where she was, and I could call in the rest of the team while we moved in on her.

"She's in Interview now, Nadine, and with minimal damage to all parties, because you told her what I needed her to hear."

Nadine scanned Eve's face. "You call that minimal. You've got a black eye. And what's wrong with your hand?"

"Minimal," Eve said again. "You gave me the window. I used you to open the window. You went on the air with what I gave you, which wasn't a lie. I couldn't give you the rest, for obvious reasons. And I couldn't give you the rest and ask you to report half a story. I don't know all the Friendship Rules, but I'm going to say one of them's not asking and expecting a friend to compromise her professional integrity to open a window for you."

Nadine huffed, then pulled out Eve's desk chair and sat. She drank some coffee. "The Lexington Avenue op wasn't bullshit?"

"No, it wasn't. We were following a viable lead. Viable because the person giving us that lead believed it. That would be her father."

Nadine straightened in the chair. "Her father flipped on her?"

"Not exactly, and if you want to ask questions, why don't we do it? I've got a case to close."

Nadine sat another moment. "I *hated* getting scooped by that putz from New York-One."

Eve shrugged again. "Happens, right? He's probably going to hate you going on with details of the arrest — with a follow-up on the result of the interview with said suspect."

"Yeah, he is." Nadine pushed up. "I need to trust you."

"And you can. Nadine, both Roarke and Peabody took hits — body armor kept those hits from sending them to the morgue."

"You?"

"Yeah, and me. The thing is, without the distraction, she might've hunkered down and distracted us by picking off civilians a couple blocks away. But she didn't have time to go there because we got in. She focused on you, then she had to focus on us. Minimal damage," Eve repeated.

"All right. I'm going to think about all that. But right now, I'm going to tell my camera to come in. We'll get this on the air. I suppose offering you makeup for that face is a waste of time. You want those bruises to show."

"Hey. I earned them." Eve smiled.

384

Peabody stepped out of Observation, where she and Mira had been watching a bored, sulky-eyed Willow and talking about tomorrow's birthday party.

She walked to the Interview room door, opened it.

Willow glanced up. She'd shorn off the dreads so her dark hair hung shaggy and short. Like Eve, she sported some visible bruising.

"About fricking time."

"It's going to be another couple minutes," Peabody told her. "Do you want a drink?"

"Jesus. Yeah." Willow shrugged. "Orange fizzy."

On a nod, Peabody turned, then jolted when she came face-to-face with Eve. "Sorry. I didn't think you were ready. I offered to get the kid a drink."

"Fine. Just — here comes the APA. Just don't take all damn day."

"Rabbit quick." In her haste, Peabody left the door slightly ajar.

"Dallas."

"Reo. I told you we didn't need that damn deal."

"We made the deal with Mackie for good reasons, and you know it. And without his information you wouldn't have known what kind of firepower you were going in against."

"That's the least of it. Dealing with him for information on her? Making that agreement that ties into trying her as a minor? I'd've brought her down without it. I did bring her down, goddamn it. How about you explain to families of all the victims how the person who took their lives does a couple of years for it?"

"Would you have preferred notifying more families their loved ones were in the morgue?"

"With your deal, I can just wait until she's out at eighteen to start doing that again."

"Rehabilitation — "

"Oh, don't even start that crap with me. People like me risk everything to put people like her in a cage. Then you deal it down to nothing so they walk out and do it all again. She does under three years, and you call that a win."

"It's not about winning, it's about doing our jobs. We both did our jobs, and this is where we stand. If you convince her to confess, we can save the taxpayers' money, avoid a trial, and move on. Now do you want to tie this up so we can both go home, or do you want to stand here and bitch at me about how the system works?"

"The system sucks."

"Are we ready?" Peabody asked as she came back, fizzy in hand.

"We're ready. I don't need you in there, Reo."

"Not your call. We're on the same side, Dallas, so suck it up."

Peabody pushed open the door.

Face set, eyes still flashing with anger, Eve walked in. "Record on. Dallas, Lieutenant Eve; Peabody, Detective Delia; Reo, Assistant Prosecuting Attorney Cher, entering Interview with Mackie, Willow."

She reeled off the rest of the data as Peabody set the fizzy on the table. Willow picked it up, held it in her restrained hands, and sipped with a smirk on her face.

"Have you been read your rights, Miss Mackie?"

"Yeah. And sure, I understand them fine. Banged you up pretty good. Too bad your hand got in the way of my knife."

"Don't be disrespectful." Peabody sent her a disapproving scowl. "You're in deep enough."

"Could've taken you," Willow shot back. "And you'd be as dead as that idiot who played you in the vid."

"Back-talking adults isn't going to help you," Peabody warned. "You're in serious trouble, Willow."

"You busted into my house. I defended myself."

"We entered your mother's house duly warranted," Eve corrected. "And found you in possession of numerous illegal weapons. You utilized those weapons to attack police officers."

Willow smiled. She might have been an attractive young woman, despite the bruises and scrapes a few passes with the healing wand and some ice packs hadn't soothed away. But there was ugliness in that smile.

She lifted her middle finger, scratched her cheek with it as she looked at Eve. "Not my weapons. I used them to defend myself."

"You fired on police officers," Eve reminded her.

"How the fuck was I supposed to know you were cops?"

"Because we identified ourselves as same."

"Like that means dick."

"You saw the vid? *The Icove Agenda?*"

"Sure. Every time I watch it, I root for you to get blown up in the Icove lab." Smiling, Willow rolled her eyes toward the ceiling. "Maybe one day."

"But you didn't recognize me?"

"Only saw you for a second."

"That would be the second before you tossed a flash grenade in a bid to escape."

"Defense." Willow shrugged again. "Doesn't matter if I knew or not. I was defending myself and my home. I've got a right."

"Willow, you knew who we were." Peabody shook her head — the disapproving teacher. "This disrespect isn't helping. Maybe you were taken by surprise, maybe you acted on impulse, instinct, but — "

"Yeah, maybe."

"What were you doing with all those weapons?" Eve demanded.

"Keeping them secure."

"Where did you get them?"

"Not mine, remember? I'm too young to buy or own weapons. Fifteen." She grinned wide. "Remember?"

Teeth set, Eve shot a hard glance at Reo. "You were in possession of the weapons. You used several of the weapons."

"I know how to take care of myself."

"How did you learn to use the weapons, the laser rifles, the flash grenades, the handhelds?"

"My father taught me. He's twice the cop you ever thought about being."

"I guess that's why I put him in a cage, where he's going to stay for the rest of his life."

"You only have him because he let you."

"Is that so?"

"Fucking A, it's so."

"If you think I can't bring a funky-junkie down, you didn't pay attention to the vid."

"Vid's bullshit anyway. Just Hollywood crap."

"Your father's a junkie, and that's no bullshit."

"So he couldn't hack it." Lip curled, Willow jabbed out a finger. "See how you'd handle it if some fucker smeared your sugar daddy all over the pavement."

"And the way to handle it was the funk for him, and planning how to kill everyone he blamed. Or having you do it because he can't even hold a weapon steady these days."

"So you say."

"So I do. Do you want to deny it?"

Willow yawned, kicked back some to stare at the ceiling. "This is boring. You're boring. Dallas," she said, shifting her gaze to meet Eve's. "Dallas, Lieutenant Eve. One of these days you're not going to be wearing body armor. One of these days maybe you'll just be walking down the street, and out of nowhere — *Bang!* You're dead. Bet they won't make a vid out of that."

Eve kept her gaze steady, and she saw, clearly, what Zoe Younger had feared. She saw the killer inside. "You want me dead, Will?"

"I'd rather you were dead than me sitting here bored out of my mind."

"Bored? Then let's move it along. Stop wasting time. Let's go back to Central Park. Three dead there. How did you pick them?"

"Who says I did?"

"Your father. He's confessed. He called you his eyes, his hands. You made those strikes, Willow. He couldn't pull it off."

"I got my eyes and hands from him."

"He ruined his own by going on the funk."

Willow shrugged, then studied her fingernails. "That's his deal, not mine. The way I look at it, drugs, alcohol, all that shit is bogus. They don't keep it real."

"You like it real."

"What's the point if you're not feeling it? You're not knowing it? You're not doing it?"

Eve opened the file, took out photos of the first three victims. "How did you feel when you did this?"

Willow shifted forward, gave the photos a good, long study. What Eve saw in her eyes wasn't curiousity or interest. It certainly wasn't shock.

It was glee.

Not bored, Eve realized. Enthralled, excited, and stringing the process out. Because it kept her at the center.

"Those are primo strikes." Willow paused to take a swig of her fizzy. "Anyone who can make strikes like that? They're the elite."

"Are you the elite?"

"No such thing as second best." Smug, she tipped her fizzy side to side. "That's just a wuss term for *loser*. It's first, or it's nothing."

"So making strikes like this puts you in first, makes you elite."

"Could you do it?"

"Can't say." Now Eve shrugged. "Never tried. Then again, I'm not interested in killing somebody a mile away while they skate around on an ice rink."

"You *couldn't*, and that's bottom line. I'm guessing you can barely hit the mark at anything over ten yards with your sidearm, much less handle a long-range weapon with any accuracy. You'd've missed by that mile, zipped some asshole bopping down Fifty-Second Street."

"But then I wouldn't have, what is it, about ten years of training, instruction, practice. Wouldn't have a former Army sniper and SWAT officer indulging my hobby."

"Hobby, my ass!" Teeth bared, Willow shoved forward. "And it takes more than training, instruction, takes more than practice. All that's important, sure, but it takes talent, it takes innate skill."

"So you were born to kill."

Easing back, Willow smiled again. "I was born to hit what I aim at."

"Why aim at her?" Eve tapped Ellissa Wyman.

"Why not her?"

"Just random, just because?" Eve angled her head, shook it. "I don't think so. Come on, Willow, she was a type, just the type you can't stand. Out there showing off, day after day, like it mattered she could do a few spins and jumps on a pair of blades. Like being pretty made her *somebody*."

"Now she's just a body."

"How did it feel to make her just a body? To cut off her life with one pull of the trigger with her out there in her show-off red suit? I think it got you off. It got you juiced so your aim was off with the main target, with Michaelson."

"Bullshit." Insult, rage, a wash of disgust skimmed over Willow's face. "He went down the way I wanted him to go down. Gut shot, bleeding out on the ice. Feeling it, knowing it."

"You wanted him to suffer?"

"He did, didn't he? I don't miss, got that? Do you *got* that? I gave him time for pain, time to *know* he'd never get up again. If the old bastard had put us first, my father would still have his eyes and hands."

"Then he wouldn't need you to do his work. He wouldn't need you."

"I'm his. I'm his first. His only."

"You wouldn't have been his only if Susann hadn't run into traffic."

"She was an idiot."

Eve widened her eyes. "You killed all these people over an idiot?"

In her default gesture, Willow shrugged, looked up at the ceiling.

"I know you must have loved her." Peabody infused her voice with just enough pity. "To do all this, I know you must have loved her, thought the world of her."

"Oh please." Derision dripped through the two words. "She could barely remember how to put her own shoes on every morning. Totally loserville. Sooner or later my old man would've walked away from that. Winners walk away. But he didn't get the chance."

"These people are dead because your father couldn't walk away a winner." Eve considered it. "Maybe that's part of it. You killed Wyman fast, aimed so Michaelson could suffer, then — what about Alan Markum?"

"Don't know him."

"Your third." Eve nudged the photo closer.

"Right. Didn't like his face. Laughing and smiling while he stumbled around the ice with the bitch. I could've taken her out, too. Two for one, but I didn't want to push my father right off. We'd agreed on three."

"Lay it out for me." Eve gestured. "How the two of you planned it, picked the nest, stalked Michaelson."

"Seriously? What's the point?"

"The record. You've got nothing better to do."

"Anything's better."

But with a huge sigh, Willow laid it out.

She spoke of her father drinking, starting on illegals after Susann died. His anger, depression.

"Just sitting around the apartment most of the time, half-drunk, half-stoned, especially after that fuckhead lawyer told him no chance for a suit, for his day in court. I pulled him out." Fiercely, Willow jabbed her fingers at her own chest. "I got him out of that hole."

"How did you do that?"

"Crying's for losers. He needed to get *pissed*. Take action. They fucked with us? We fuck with them, and we fuck harder."

Eve leaned back. "You're trying to tell us it was your idea? This mission? Killing Michaelson, Officer Russo, Jonah Rothstein, and the others on the hit list —

including innocent bystanders of your choice — was your idea?"

"Is something wrong with your hearing? Do you need me to speak louder?"

"Watch your tone."

Willow merely flicked a sneer at Peabody's order. "Oh, fuck you and your tone. You want me to lay it out because you're all too stupid to see it. I'm laying it out."

"Why not start with Fine?" Eve demanded. "He's the one who killed Susann. He was driving the vehicle that struck her."

"What, are you brain dead? We hit Fine, even an asshole cop could make a connection to Dad. We *end* with Fine."

"He wanted to save Fine until last."

Once again Willow leaned forward, sneering. "Did you get the part where I said he was drunk and stoned most of the time? Crying into his brew the other half? I figured the who and where and when. You think he could come up with a mission? He couldn't get out of his own way until I pulled him out of it."

"You pulled him out by suggesting you kill the people you felt were culpable in Susann's death."

"You could say I laid it out for him — and put conditions on it." Picking up her fizzy again, she gestured with it. "He had to cut back on the booze and the funk, pull himself to-fucking-gether. He mostly stopped drinking altogether. Funk's harder, but he throttled back a little. And when my old man's himself, he knows how to plan ops.

394

"He came up with adding to the range, so we took a few more trips out west, and I worked on my skills. He's a damn good instructor when he's on."

"You stalked your targets, got their routines, and/or researched where they'd be at certain times. Like Jonah Rothstein. You knew he'd be at Madison Square for the concert."

"The guy was a raging fan-o-holic. Counting down the days, then the hours till he saw that old, totally over rocker. My dad, he did most of the research, but I helped when I could get away from Zoe — that's the bio-tube where I incubated. And I picked the nests. He wanted closer initially, but then he saw I could do it."

"How long did you work on the plan, on the details?"

"A good, solid year. He needed to clean up, at least some. We needed to stockpile weapons, the IDs, walk through the strategies and tactics."

"You moved out of his apartment."

"We needed a secure HQ, so yeah, bit by bit we moved what we needed to the new place. We knew we'd have to move fast when we started, hit targets daily, keep the chaos going. You got lucky, nailing down our ID."

"Is that what you call it when somebody's better than you, smarter than you? Luck?"

"Give me half a break. If you were so good, so smart, I wouldn't have to sit here spoon-feeding you every detail. You'd already know."

"Got me there," Eve said, because she did. She saw it all, in hideous detail. "Don't stop now. Educate me."

CHAPTER
TWENTY

Willow Mackie overflowed with details, smirks, and insults. Eve gave her the center spot she craved, and basking in the attention, she rolled.

For three hours Eve listened, probed, nudged, with the occasional question or comment from Reo or Peabody.

Pushing wasn't necessary, not as Willow warmed up to the idea of being important.

At one point she demanded another fizzy, and around hour three demanded a bathroom break.

"Peabody, have two uniformed officers, female, accompany Willow to the bathroom."

On a hard laugh, Willow sneered at Eve. "You've been listening to all I can do, and you think I can't take a couple of girl cops?"

You couldn't take me, Eve thought, but nodded. "Make it four, Peabody."

"That's more like it."

"Interview paused," Eve said, and strode out.

Reo caught up with her just outside the bullpen. "Jesus Christ, Eve."

"You were expecting a sulky teenager?"

"I was expecting a stone killer. I guess I wasn't expecting a raging, showboating psychopath inside a teenager. I need to update my boss, and I want to talk to Mira. I want to make dead certain this girl is legally sane."

"She's as legally sane as you and me. And she's a vicious little bug that needs squashing."

"I'm with you on part two. Let me make part one absolutely solid."

"Take fifteen." Rocking back on her heels, Eve tried to decide if she felt disgusted or satisfied. Realized she could feel both. "I want her sitting in there again, waiting, getting worked up about telling us the rest."

"We've got enough to put her away for countless lifetimes already. But yeah, I want the rest, too. Fifteen," Reo said, then hurried off.

Eve stepped into the bullpen, surprised how many of her team remained. "I'm not done, but I can promise you she is. She's confessed to all of it, and I'm wrapping her up. For God's sake, anybody not on the roll, go home."

"How's the eye, LT?" Jenkinson called out.

"It stings like a bitch, but that's from looking at that tie. Go home."

She walked into her office to see Roarke sitting at her desk, working his own PPC and her comp at the same time.

"Done?"

She shook her head. "What's that?" She pointed at her own screen and what looked like some sort of ancient castle surrounded by some kind of cage.

"Ah, that's progress on the projected hotel in Italy. I'll have it off your unit before I leave. Coffee?"

"No. No, I need something cold." She glanced back out. "I should've hit Vending — probably literally — for a Pepsi."

"They're stocked in your AC now."

"They are?"

"To save you the frustration of Vending."

She surprised herself by being absurdly touched. And needing to sit down. She dropped into the ass-biting visitor's chair.

"That bad, is it?" Roarke rose, ordered the tube himself.

"She's told us everything up to and including Madison Square. I didn't expect her to feel remorse, to feel anything for the victims. And I did expect her to feel pride. But ... It's the glee. The goddamn jubilation. I didn't expect the extent of that, how her ego rules all.

"It was all her idea. Part of me knew that, all of me wondered. You had to consider Mackie's state of mind. He'd never have been able to do all this, think of it all. But she did. He was paying too much attention to his grief, and not enough to her. She didn't say it, but it came across clear. She had no respect for her stepmother, called her an idiot. She used her father's grief, his weakness — it wasn't him using her, but her using him — to realize her greatest ambition. To take lives."

"Here now, use your own chair."

"No, no, I can't sit anyway." She rose, took the tube from him, then just paced without drinking. "She remembers everything, even remembers what some of the victims were wearing. Sometimes that's all it took for her to make them a target. Hate that hat — you get to die in it."

Saying nothing, Roarke eased a hip on the corner of the desk, let her spew.

"She believes the killings, the initial realization of their plan, the progess of their mission, made her father stronger. Gave him purpose. And he focused on her again."

As she paused, she cracked the tube, drank. Breathed.

"I guess Mira would say there's a part of her, the child, who craves that focus from her father. His eyes and hands, his partner, his equal, his only child. She brought him along so he could praise her."

"You considered her his apprentice — we all did. And for a time she was. But what you're saying is he became hers. She taught him the death of his so-called enemies by her hand — his hand through her — united them."

"Yeah. Plus, he was her audience, her witness, her goddamn cheerleader. Even when he wasn't there, as with Madison Square, she knew he'd hear, knew he'd be proud. Knew she'd remain his center."

"And he proved she was by sacrificing himself for her."

"Their Plan B — we got to that. She'd get gone, get away, and he'd draw us to him. He'd take the fall. Only that didn't work on any level. Roarke, she's in the box, and she's preening. 'Look at me, look how good I am. Yeah, I did it, did it all. Because I'm the best. Number one.' And it makes me more sick than pissed."

"You'll be pissed before it's done. I have every confidence there."

She nearly smiled. "You're not going home?"

He nearly smiled back. "Do you know the only color in your face is from the bruises?"

"The bruises look good on the record. And the booster you dug up for me helped. I'm tired, but I'm not shaky with it."

"This should help as well." He pulled a chocolate bar from his pocket.

"Is that mine?" She shot one furious glance toward the wall, and the framed sketch Nixie Swisher had done of her. "Is that from my stash? Did you compromise my stash?"

"I didn't, no, though that might've been entertaining. EDD has candy in Vending."

"They do? Why do they rate?" But she grabbed it, ripped the wrapper. "Thanks."

"I'm going to make it up to both of us by seeing you have a decent meal at the first opportunity."

"Whatever." She closed her eyes, let the first glorious bite of chocolate do its work. "Did you check on Summerset?"

"Often enough that he's now annoyed with me."

"Okay." She folded the wrapper over the half candy bar remaining, stuck it in her pocket. "This may take a couple more hours."

"When I finish here, I believe I'll wander over to Observation so I can watch you wrap her up as you did that candy bar."

She stepped to him, let her head rest on his shoulder, just a moment. "Mackie might've been a good man once — Lowenbaum thinks so anyway. But he made his choices, choices he can never come back from. She's one of them. But even without him, she'd have been in somebody's box one day. It was just his choices, just the timing of it all that made it mine."

She drew back. "And since it's mine, I'll go finish it."

When she left to do just that, Roarke wondered if she thought of how many more would be hers — victims and killers.

And knew, as he knew her, she did.

By the time Eve returned to Interview A, Peabody and Reo stood outside the door. Both of them, she noted, looked worn to the bone. Peabody held two fizzies, Reo a tube of Diet Pepsi.

"She's in there," Peabody said. "I got her another fizzy before she can snap her fingers at me for one. Hitting the sugar myself."

"Cold caffeine for me, as I can't stomach Vending coffee."

"Hell." Eve pulled out the half candy bar, broke that in half, held the pieces out to them.

"Chocolate? Really?" Pleasure put some energy in Peabody's voice. "Loose pants be damned. Thanks. Thanks, Dallas."

"Thank Roarke."

"Thank you, Roarke." Reo took a minute bite.

"Eat the damn thing, don't mouse-nibble it to death. We've got work."

"I like to savor the unexpected, but." Reo popped her share into her mouth.

"I'm going to keep her going, get her to tell us about this Alaska crap, then lead into her own agenda. I want the intent to kill on record. We're going to start challenging her. The more we do, the more she'll be compelled to brag."

Eve pulled open the door. "Record on, Interview resume. All parties present."

Peabody set the fizzy down in front of Willow.

"I wanted cherry this time."

"You got orange, take it or leave it." Peabody's eyes narrowed on Willow's face. "And if you throw that at me, I'll have you up on charges of assaulting a police officer."

"Assault with a fizzy."

Peabody didn't crack a smile as Willow hooted in disdain.

"I'll make it stick, you ungrateful little shit."

It seemed the challenging had begun, Eve noted, saying nothing until Peabody took her seat, sipped from her own drink.

"Tell me about Alaska."

"It's cold."

"Your father states that you and he planned to relocate there. That, according to your alternate plan, should something go wrong, happen to him, you were to make your way there."

"Alaska? About as lame as Susann. Sure I liked seeing it, doing some hunting the couple times we checked it out. No way would we live up there."

"He was very clear you would."

"If we needed a place to lay low for a few months, sure, that would do it. Mostly, I went along with him because he needed to hear it. It helped keep him focused on the mission."

"So you didn't intend to make your way there, as outlined, after his arrest?"

"I like the city. It's fine spending some time out west, even up there in Nanook country, but I wasn't going to drag my ass all the way to Alaska. Plus, I finish what I start."

"Which you proved by targeting Jonah Rothstein and seventeen other bystanders at Madison Square Garden. But after that, you'd have run into a problem. Were you aware we'd identified your other targets and had them in protective custody?"

"Yeah, yeah. BFD."

"Is that why you returned to your family home rather than the location you and your father had chosen should you need to remain in New York?"

"They're not my family, okay?" Those green eyes gleamed with disgust. "Bio-tube, her banging buddy, and the brat they spawned. That's it. It's a house, and it's as much mine as anybody's. I got my stuff there."

"Not all of it."

"So you took my electronics. BFD-squared. I had backups."

"Right. We've got them now, too. I wonder, will EDD find any backups to the documents you tried to hide on your brother's comp?"

Surprise sparked first, then anger. Quickly followed by a so-the-fuck-what smirk. "He's not my brother."

"Same mother — or 'bio-tube,' if you prefer. Were you going to snap his neck the way you did his little dog's?"

Though she sipped from her fizzy, Willow couldn't hide the quick grin. "Why would I waste my time with a stupid dog?"

"Because it was fun. Because your brother loved it. Because you could."

"He's *not* my brother. And so what if I did? Are you going to charge me with dog killing?"

"Animal cruelty," Peabody supplied. Willow yawned.

"Go ahead, add it on. Like I care. Like it means a damn thing."

"You killed the dog, then tossed its body out the window in front of your brother — "

"I *said* — open your fucking ears — he's not my brother."

"You admit to these acts?"

"I broke the little fleabag's neck, tossed him out. If that's what you want to talk about, I'm done here."

"Oh, we have more. Let's talk about your separate agenda or mission. Your separate list of targets, which you attempted to hide on — we'll just call him Zach — on Zach's computer."

"They monitor mine like prison guards. Zoe thinks I don't know she goes in my room, goes through my things? The bitch is on my case 24/7, and did jack shit when that perv she married went at me."

"He never went at you."

"My word against his."

"I'd like the details," Reo put in, and made notes on her pad. "When this incident, or incidents, happened. What he did."

"She's lying," Eve said.

"She has a right to tell her side of it. Did Lincoln Stuben sexually or physically assault you? If so, please detail the circumstances, the number of incidents, the times."

"Bored. Bored. Bored. He wanted to do me, but I can take care of myself."

"Did you have an altercation?"

"'Did you have an altercation?'" Willow mimicked. "Sure, plenty of them. He was always trying to tell me what to do, how to do it. Always bitching about showing respect. I don't have to respect some loser."

"Which is why he was on your list," Eve put in. "You had him, your mother, your brother, your school counselor, the principal. Oh, and you had a blueprint of your school."

"Not hard to come by. Marksmanship's not my only skill."

"So noted. You planned to attack the school? To kill students, teachers, others."

"It was a thought." Gazing at the ceiling again, Willow circled her finger in the air. "Can't charge me with thinking."

"You returned to the townhouse, used the room on the third floor, added another alarm to alert you if somone came in."

"So what?"

"You were lying in wait. They'd come home eventually, right? And there you'd be. How did you figure to do it? Just walk down, 'Hi, everybody,' and blast them where they stood?"

When Willow shrugged, Eve leaned in. "Not much skill required for that. An ambush, three unarmed civilians. And not much fun from where I'm sitting. Over and done so fast. Is that the best you could do?"

"I can do what I want!" Willow shoved the fizzy aside. "Maybe I was thinking — because I'm *allowed* to think — how it would be after they came back, after they all went to bed. Maybe I was thinking how it might feel to take out a target up close, with a knife. Like I almost did you."

Eve held up her bandaged hand. "Not even close."

"Close enough."

"Take out the kid first — he's the prime target."

"You don't know dick about tactics. You take out the biggest threat first, moron. I'd slit Stuben's throat. That's quick, that's quiet. And he's nothing. He's always been nothing."

"And then?"

"Then good tactics say I incapacitate Zoe, then restrain her. That gives me time to get the kid, wrap him up, haul him down."

Her eyes glowed as she spoke, as she, Eve was sure, saw it all so clearly. "Hurt him a little — just a little so when she comes around she sees he's hurt, sees he's bleeding. I let her beg — the bedroom's sound-proofed. Hell, she can scream if she wants. But if she screams, I'll just slit his throat. But she can beg, she can tell me why in the hell I shouldn't kill him. Why I shouldn't kill this runt she should never have had. This whining little baby she had to replace *me*.

"Then she has to watch me gut him like a deer, just the way I've wanted to since he was born. I save her for last so she can see. With her? I slice her wrists so she bleeds out slow. So I can watch her die, inch by inch."

"I was wrong. You hated her most."

"She threw my father away. She took him away from me. She tried to replace him and me with Stuben, with his ugly little spawn. She deserved to see them dead and to know she caused it. She's the reason why."

Willow gestured with her cup. "I could be set up for the school the next morning, before anybody knew they were dead. I could make history."

"Because you know the school, the routine, when students start arriving."

"I guarantee I could have taken down three, maybe four dozen targets before they managed to lock it down. Recalibrate, take out maybe a dozen a couple blocks over to add some confusion, and then? Cops, reporters, parents, idiots who just want to look — plenty of them would be in range. I'd have a clean hundred before I broke it down. Nobody's ever done that many alone, at that distance. But I could."

"Making you the best."

"I am the best. That would just be the mark in history."

"Your father wouldn't have gone for it."

"I could've brought him around if everything had gone the way we wanted with his agenda. I do his, I get mine. It's fair. He was weak, and this was making him strong again. I'd even have given him a year or two in Alaska for it. But I deserved mine."

Eve waited a long beat. Color had flashed in Willow's face, as it had in her father's. But hers was both rage and pride. It wasn't madness in her eyes — not the kind that didn't know right from wrong. It was the kind that didn't give a damn.

"You're saying that conspiring with your father, you killed the twenty-five people named during this Interview, and had planned to kill others, also named herein."

"That's right, and I'm not saying it all again."

"That won't be necessary. You've also stated that you, individually, planned to murder Zoe Younger, Lincoln Stuben, and Zach Stuben — additionally torturing Younger and Zach Stuben before ending their lives."

"Yeah, yeah, yeah. Wasn't I clear enough? I can plan all I want."

"You additionally stated you planned to attack Hillary Rodham Clinton High School and other areas in its vicinity in the hopes of killing one hundred people."

"World record. You cost me the world record. Being a cop's a dangerous job. Something bad could happen to you, like a year from now. Or, say *three* years from now." Willow laughed into her fizzy. "Three's a good number."

"You think so? How about I pay you a visit, let's say three and a half years from now. In your cage on Omega."

"I won't be there. You, all of you, you're so stupid. You're all morons."

Now she threw back her head and laughed loud and long.

"You wanted me to confess to all this? No problem. I *want* you to know what I did. Write it up, shout it out. I deserve getting credit for what I did, what I can do. And in under three years, when I turn eighteen, I walk out."

"Is that so?" Eve tipped back in her chair. "How do you figure?"

"I *heard* you, you idiots. My father made a deal. He puts me first, and he made a deal. He'd tell you all this shit, and you try me as a minor. I'm out at eighteen, because, hey, I'm just a kid."

"So you think you can cold-bloodedly murder — with premeditation — twenty-five people, injure scores of others, plot to murder — what was that number? Oh, yeah — one hundred more, and walk away free in under three years."

"Burns your skinny ass, doesn't it? You put all that time into finding me, got banged up pretty good, too. You had cops all over me, but I still racked them up. But you needed my father to find me, and he looks out for me. So I do under three in some lame juvenile facility, then I'm out. It burns your ass."

"One of the things about being a cop is understanding it's the job to apprehend criminals, to gather evidence, which is then given to someone like Reo who carries the ball from there."

"Yeah, and people like her?" Willow shot a finger at Reo. "It's all about the deal, the quick fix, the easy way. She didn't want to put me on the stand anyway. Boo-hoo, I'm only fifteen. I was misled." All but dancing in the chair, Willow howled with laughter. "I would *kill* on the stand with that bit. It's almost too bad I won't get the chance to drown a bunch of bleeding hearts on the jury with my teenage tears."

"Yeah, that would be a show," Eve agreed. "It's one I'm looking forward to, because you're right, Willow, you're dead on the mark. It would burn my ass for you to do what you've done, be what you are, and walk out at eighteen to do it all over again. If that were the case."

"You made the deal," Willow said to Reo.

"I did."

"Then how are you going to stop me? Bitch."

"I don't have to. You stopped yourself — with some help from your father." Eve held up her wounded hand, gave it a study, and said, with a smile, "Ow."

"You want to tag on assault on a cop? Go ahead. It's all in the same deal."

"Yeah, it is. Reo, maybe you should explain the deal to her."

"Happy to." Reo opened her briefcase, took out a hard copy of the agreement. "You're free to look this over yourself. The prosecuting attorney for the city of New York agreed to try one Willow Mackie as a minor for all crimes committed *before* the signing of said agreement on the following conditions. One, that information given by Reginald Mackie led to the arrest of the aforesaid Willow Mackie. Secondly, the agreement would become void, all terms, in the event Willow Mackie killed or injured any person or persons subsequent to the filing of the agreement."

"That's bullshit. She attacked me. I was defending myself."

"Lieutenant Dallas incurred injuries at your hand during the course of your arrest. You resisted arrest, assaulted police officers — that's armed assault, by the way — and, in fact, confessed in this Interview the intent to kill Lieutenant Dallas."

"Ow," Eve said again. "In addition, the information your father gave us led us to a dead end. He said nothing regarding the townhouse where you were located, therefore none of the terms of the deal were met."

"You set me up, it's entrapment — and none of this bullshit in here will hold up. I *heard* you arguing about how you couldn't try me as an adult because of the deal."

"Really?" Reo shifted to Eve, blue eyes open and sincere. "I don't believe we mentioned the deal — already voided prior to this Interview — or any of the terms within. On the record."

"Nope. Sure didn't. Why would we? It didn't apply. You're going down — bitch — for twenty-five counts of

411

murder, for conspiracy to murder, for multiple assaults with a deadly. Then there's attempted murder on a police officer, assault with a deadly on same. There's possession of illegal weapons, possession and use of false identification. And the record will show, in your own words, your intent to murder your family and others.

"I see a hundred years — maybe more — of life in a cage on Omega. The sun's not going to shine for you again, Willow."

"It'll never happen." But for the first time, fear lit in Willow's eyes. "I'm fifteen. You're not going to lock me up forever when I'm only fifteen."

"Keep thinking that — and maybe touch base with Rayleen Straffo if you see her on Omega. She was ten when I closed the cage door on her. You guys should really hit it off."

"I know my rights! I know my rights! None of this Interview is valid. I'm a minor. Where's my child services representative?"

"You never asked for one — and . . . " Reo took another document out of her briefcase. "We obtained your mother's permission to interview you."

"She can't speak for me."

"Legally, she can. Of course, if you'd asked for a representative, or a lawyer, one would have been provided for you."

Reo folded her hands neatly on her briefcase. "Willow Mackie, you have confessed, on this record, in detail, to the charges Lieutenant Dallas listed. There are more to add. Given the vicious and violent nature of your crimes, you will be held to account for them as an adult."

"I want a lawyer. Now. I want a rep from child services."

"Do you have a lawyer you wish to contact?"

"I don't know any fucking lawyers. Get me one, and I mean now."

"Arrangements will be made to obtain legal counsel for you, and though you are considered an adult in these matters, child services will be contacted. Do you have anything to add?"

"Fuck you. Fuck all of you. I'm going to fucking *end* all of you."

"Well then." Reo rose.

"Peabody, have the prisoner returned to her cell. Interview end." Eve got to her feet. "It's the plushest accommodation you're going to have for the next century."

"I'll find a way." Though her eyes burned with hate, with rage, and stayed steady on Eve's, her hands trembled.

"You locked your own door," Eve said, and walked out.

Eve went straight to her office. She wanted coffee. Actually, she wanted a really big, really stiff drink, but coffee would do.

Reo followed her in. "I've got to deal with the next steps of this, but I wanted to say, before I do, you played her perfectly in there."

"Wasn't hard. She wanted to brag, wanted to rub it all in my face — or authority's face. I just gave her the platform. Lock her up tight, Reo, tight and long."

"You can count on me."

"I am."

Alone, she turned to the board, to the dead.

"You've given them justice," Mira said from the doorway.

"I brought her in. The rest is up to Reo and the courts."

"You've given them justice," Mira repeated. "And saved unknown others from ending up on your board. You convinced her to reveal herself — and believe me, Eve, that record will be studied by psychiatrists, by law enforcement, by legal minds for decades."

"I barely had to bait her, she was so primed to show off how smart she is, how much better she is."

"You never lost control, and never let her see you were in control throughout. Her narcissism, her utter disregard for any semblance of a moral code, her need to be first, and her enjoyment of the kill, it came through so clearly. Some will argue her adolescence and her father's influence drove her to do the unspeakable.

"It won't fly," Mira added as Eve spun around. "She's calculating, organized, intelligent. She's a psychopath, and one who was given permission by a parent to embrace her desire to kill. I can promise you I'll tear down any attempt by her lawyer to build her as a misguided teenager, coerced and manipulated by her father. Trust me on that."

Count on Reo. Trust Mira. "I do. I do, and that'll help me sleep tonight."

"You should go home, get started on that."

"Yeah, working toward that."

But before she could get out of her office, Whitney walked in.

"Good job, Lieutenant."

"Thank you, sir."

"You locked her up with her own words, but that doesn't negate the work that went into getting her in the box. Today, at least, the city's a safer place. I need you in the media center in ten."

She literally felt everything in her sag. "Yes, sir."

"I'd take this off you if I could. But the fact is, the people of New York deserve to hear from the primary of the investigation that identified and apprehended the two people who terrorized them for nearly a week.

"Turn that around," he added. "In under a week you and your team identified and apprehended two people who, if still at large, would surely be responsible for more deaths. Chief Tibbie and I will both attend, but we agree the statement comes from you."

"Yes, sir."

"Then get the hell out of here, Dallas, and get some ice on that eye."

When she went out to the bullpen, she saw Roarke talking with Lowenbaum beside Peabody's desk. Lowenbaum broke off, stepped to her, held out a hand.

"Thanks."

"Back at you."

"Buy you a drink?"

"Media conference, then I'm going to sleep for a couple years. After that."

"Deal."

She turned to Roarke, shoved a hand through her hair. "It's going to be a little while longer. We've got a media conference, then I'll deal with the paperwork, and we can go."

"I'll be here when you're done."

"Peabody, let's get this over with."

"I'm skipping the media deal. I'm finishing the paperwork. I want to go home, too," Peabody said before Eve could object. "They don't need me in the media center, and I need to tie this up. I really need to tie it up and put it away."

Eve looked at her partner's tired face, hollow eyes. "Okay. Good work, Peabody."

"Good work all around."

With a nod, Eve headed out to give New York a face, such as it was.

CHAPTER
TWENTY-ONE

The media circus could have been worse. She'd had worse. Since Kyung, the media liaison — who wasn't an asshole — told her to use her own words and judgment, she gave what she felt was a straightforward statement.

"Through the efforts of the NYPSD, its officers and technicians, two individuals have been identified, apprehended, and charged with the twenty-five murders and numerous injuries incurred as a result of the attacks at Wollman Rink, Times Square, and Madison Square Garden. Reginald Mackie and his daughter, Willow Mackie, have confessed to these crimes, and as the investigation also uncovered their plans to target others, confessed to same."

Of course that wasn't enough — it never seemed to be enough. She answered questions, some salient, some stupendously stupid. She answered those that targeted Willow's age.

"Yes, Willow Mackie is fifteen. At fifteen she killed twenty-five people in cold blood. The investigation uncovered her plan to kill more, including her own mother and her seven-year-old half brother. Due to the nature of her crimes, she will be tried as an adult."

When pressed, she gave a bare-bones summary of Willow's arrest, then had to pull back a flash of temper when one of the reporters shouted out:

"My information is Willow Mackie was injured during her arrest. Was this retaliation for allegedly killing a cop?"

"Have you ever had a flash grenade tossed in your general direction? No? Ever had somebody in full body armor firing a laser rifle, a handheld, a blaster at you? Missed those, too? Every member of the team involved in apprehending the individual charged with twenty-five murders, including Officer Kevin Russo, put their lives at risk to protect and serve. Every member of the team acted and reacted in a lawful and appropriate matter to the threat, as the record of the arrest will show. Now if you — "

"Follow-up!" Nadine called out, interrupting what would likely have been an unwise assessment of the previous reporter's intelligence. "Lieutenant Dallas, did you incur your very visible injuries during the arrest of Willow Mackie?"

"She objected, violently, to being arrested."

"Would that include what appears to be a severe gash on your hand? Did she also have a knife?"

"Yes, and yes. I guess I forgot to ask if any of you have ever had someone try to slit your throat with a combat knife. She missed. If any of you want to play up the angle of her age, like we should sympathize, just make sure you include the names of the twenty-five. Ellissa Wyman, Brent Michaelson . . . " she began, and named every one.

418

"That's all you get."

"One moment, Lieutenant." Tibbie stepped forward, gave the entire room the hard eye until everyone settled. "I have personally reviewed recordings taken from Lieutenant Dallas, Detective Peabody, Lieutenant Lowenbaum, and others during the confrontation and arrest of Willow Mackie. Lieutenant Dallas, Detective Peabody, and a civilian consultant all received direct strikes deployed by Willow Mackie, and were spared serious injury only due to their body armor."

He allowed just a hint of temper to show as he turned the hard eye on the original questioner.

"Age doesn't matter a whole hell of a lot, in my opinion, when you're armed with laser rifles, flash grenades, and you know how to use them. More, if you use them to strike at civilians, at police officers, and rack up kills like trophies. Lieutenant Dallas and her team risked their lives today, as they do every day, to save yours, to save your spouses, your sons and daughters, your friends and neighbors. If anyone wishes to question the necessary actions of the courageous men and women who risked all to stop that unconscionable number at twenty-five, talk to me.

"Lieutenant Dallas, you're dismissed, with gratitude."

"Sir."

She got out, got the hell out, pitifully grateful Roarke was right there waiting for her.

In the car, she put her head back, closed her eyes. "There'll be others who'll pull that."

"If you mean using her age to pump up a story, or the fact that she got a few bumps during the arrest, yes,

I expect so. Just as I know they'll be drowned out. Put it away, darling."

"Tibble was pissed. You don't see that every day."

"The fact he was, and let it show, has impact. You knew all twenty-five names."

"Some things stick with you."

He let her rest, hoped she slept, but she shifted, sat up as he drove through the gates.

"You're going to want me to eat, but I feel a little off. I don't know if I can deal with food."

"Maybe a little soup. It'll help you sleep."

Maybe, she thought, but . . . "Don't tranq it."

"I won't."

She leaned on him as they walked to the front door, leaned as exhaustion crept back inch by inch. Because it's done, she told herself. Because it's over.

Summerset and Galahad stood in the foyer, as they might after any workday. But it wasn't any day. She could have pulled out an insult, to make it more ordinary, but Summerset had wrestled with his own trauma.

She didn't have it in her.

Apparently, neither did he.

He scanned her face, the bruises, but didn't smirk or comment.

"Will you let me tend to your injuries, Lieutenant?"

"I just want to sleep."

He nodded, looked at Roarke. "Are you hurt?"

"No. You look better."

"I'm fine. We've had quiet times, the cat and I. Now you'll have your own. There's chicken soup, with

420

noodles. I thought soothing would be best after this day."

"Thanks for that." Roarke wrapped an arm around Eve's waist, turned her toward the stairs.

"Lieutenant?"

She glanced back, so tired now she nearly floated. "Evil doesn't have an age."

"No. No, it really doesn't."

She thought briefly of her home office, of checking on the paperwork, but couldn't do it. Not now, not yet.

"Just an hour down," she told Roarke as they turned into the bedroom. "Then I'll think about food and the rest. Just an hour down first."

"I could use that myself."

The cat leaped on the bed as they undressed, bumped his head against her side as she crawled into bed. She gave him a couple of strokes, found it comforting. More comforting yet when he curled his tubby body into the small of her back.

And perfect, finally perfect, when Roarke slid in beside her, drew her close.

She ached, everywhere, from the bruises, from fatigue, from the headache drumming behind her eyes.

But held between two loves, she slept.

And slept straight through until the first narrow break of dawn.

Disoriented, she stared over to where Roarke sat — not in business mode, but elegantly casual, working by the light of his PPC.

The cat had taken over Roarke's spot on the bed, stretched out luxuriously.

Eve started to speak, found her throat bitterly dry. "What?" she managed. "What time?"

"Early." Roarke set aside his PPC, rose. "Lights on ten percent. That eye's more colorful, but we'll work on it now. Let's have a look at the rest."

He whipped the covers off.

"Hey!"

"As I suspected. You've quite an assortment. We'll wand you, and try the jet tub."

"Coffee. Just coffee."

"Not just, but that as well. Maybe some scrambled eggs and toast to start, see how that settles."

"I'm not sick." She sat up, winced. "Maybe sore."

"So the wand, the jets, the food. Otherwise I'll devil you into taking a blocker, and we'd both rather I didn't have to."

She couldn't argue with that. Besides, the healing wand eased some of the soreness, and the tub — along with whatever he put in the water — helped more.

And the coffee helped everything.

She ate the eggs, which settled fine. In fact they woke up her appetite. "Now I'm starving."

He turned to her, caught her face in his hand, kissed her. Long, soft, deep.

"Well, that's not what I was hungry for. But now that you mention it, I think I'm up to it."

"We'll give those bruises a little longer to heal." But he kept her face framed in his hands, kissed her again. "I'm just glad to see you."

"Where did I go?"

422

"Darling Eve, you had grief behind your eyes. So much grief and fatigue. It's gone now."

"I just needed sleep. And you. And the cat." She let out a long breath. "And this."

Now he pressed his lips to her forehead. "There's one more thing you might want. Come with me."

"I was thinking I want pancakes."

"We can get to that." He pulled her to the elevator and in. Programmed the destination manually.

"A swim would be good," she considered. "Might help work out the stiffness."

When the doors opened she was, for the second time that morning, disoriented. "How many rooms do you . . . "

She trailed off as her gaze arrowed in on the wide U, studded with controls, the sleek leather chair in its curve.

"Command center. Holy shit, holy shit!"

It was, sort of, like walking into the design he'd shown her only days before. The walls painted that quiet, easy color that wasn't exactly green, wasn't exactly gray. And the absolute magnificence of her new workstation, an entire wall of screens.

"Did I sleep for a week?"

"You've been out of the office, so to speak, for a few days. And the crew took advantage. Double shifts. There are still some details, some work, but it's up and running."

"That?" She pointed at the big, wide U of deep — maybe *commanding* — brown with its flecks and veins of dark green and that not-quite-green base for an array of controls. "That's up and running?"

"I figured that would be your priority. Test it out."

She beelined for it, absolutely delighting him. Ran a hand over the stone, studied the controls. "How do I . . . " She laid her hand on a palm screen.

It hummed, but did nothing.

"You haven't told it what to do, have you?" Amused, Roarke joined her.

"Like . . . Open operations?"

The command center came to life, controls flashing on, glinting like jewels — the sort of jewels she appreciated most.

Operations open, Dallas, Lieutenant Eve.

"Holy shit," she said again. "Just like that."

"I had a bit of time this morning. It'll take a bit more to transfer everything to your comfort zone, but yes, just like that."

"Okay, open file, Mackie, Willow."

Accessing. Where would you like the data displayed?

"Wall screen."

As she hadn't designated one section, the entire wall filled with data.

"Wow. Ah, display final report by Peabody, Detective Delia. She finished it," Eve noted when it flashed on. "She wrote it up, filed it. Done."

Roarke kissed the top of her head. "Done."

424

"Wait." She dropped into the chair, a chair of rich forest-green leather, said, "*Ahh*." Swiveled. "Oh, this is *it*. Seriously it. The redhead with the tits and the boots knows her stuff. I could play with this all day. I'll need to play with this all day to get up to speed. What else can it — "

"Everything you need. But you might want to take a glance, at least, at the rest."

She swiveled again, surveyed the room.

The seating area worried her a little. It looked entirely too comfortable with its long, low sofa in forest-shadows green. But not fancy or frilly, even with a couple of pillows tossed on it. A new sleep chair, which Galahad had claimed already.

She rose, wandered, found her board — she only had to roll it out of the slot in the wall.

A kitchen area, updated big-time — shiny, yes, but simple.

And simple again, an arrangement of floating shelves — probably real wood, she mused — holding some of her useless but prized things.

The stuffed Galahad Roarke had given her, the statue of the goddess was a gift from Peabody's mother, a sheriff's badge, a fancy magnifying glass, a photograph of her and Roarke taken when they'd been banged up some after an arrest, and smiling at each other.

He'd added art — or the designer had — which hadn't been run by her. But . . . how could she argue with the framed city scapes? Her city.

Their city.

She frowned at the thick green plastic boards over what was obviously a wide hole in the side of the room. "What happened there?"

"It's more what's happening. As I said, there are details yet. This is something extra. When it's done, the dining area goes in front of what will be glass. You open the glass and you'll be able to step out onto a small terrace. I thought you'd enjoy that. We'd enjoy eating here with the glass open in fine weather."

We, she thought. He'd designed the old office for her.

This one was for them.

"You were right, and not just because it looks really good. You were right because it's my space, sure, but it's for both of us. You were right, it was time."

"Remember you said that when we start on the bedroom."

"Not going to think about that. This is much too frosty. Now I need to start playing with my command center."

"I'll give you some pointers, then leave you to it for a couple hours. That's about what we have before we need to leave for Bella's party."

"The what?" Already halfway across the room, she stopped, turned on her heel. "Oh, but . . . Look, don't you think we could skip that? I mean, bruised up, tired out, saved New York? She's not going to notice or care if we're around. She's one."

"I know as little as you about the mind of a one-year-old. But I know Mavis."

"Crap, crap, crap. We have to go." Shoving at her hair, Eve sent the command center a look of longing. "Okay. So we go for, say, an hour, ninety minutes tops, then we come back. Take that swim. We can have pool sex."

"That sounds like a bribe." Considering, amusement clear, he nodded. "I'm very susceptible to the right kind of bribe. I believe we have a deal."

"Solid." She headed straight back to command.

She got her two hours, found it exhilarating and amazing. The comp was so quick, it all but anticipated her commands, the screen images so clear she almost felt she could walk into them.

The holo functions would take her a while to get a steady handle on, but even now she could see using them to put herself back into a crime scene, or bring a wit, a consultant, a potential suspect right into her space.

In all her wildest dreams, she could never have imagined having so much tech right at her fingertips. Even though it meant actually dealing with tech.

But the best, the abso-ult, as Mavis would say, was discovering the mini unit that allowed her to program coffee right at her command center.

That little bonus had her doing a mental happy dance even as they left for Bella's party.

"It's going to be really exceptional pool sex."

Roarke slid behind the wheel. "Is it now?"

She yanked him to her, gave him a hard kiss. "Better stick to the shallow end, because we could drown. And even then."

"Life's full of risks. And we are the brave."

"An hour, ninety minutes tops, right?"

"For pool sex?"

Laughing, she punched his shoulder.

She decided a Sunday afternoon drive downtown didn't completely suck. Closed case, long sleep, hot food — and a command center. Life could be a lot worse.

Maybe it would be the first first birthday party she'd ever attended, but how bad could it be?

Better not think about it.

"You're sure the present deal got there?" she asked as he maneuvered into a parking place.

"I am."

"I just don't want to screw up, be those people who forgot the present for the kid."

"Delivered yesterday, and stowed away by Leonardo."

"Okay. I bet there are going to be others there."

"I certainly hope so."

"No, I mean *others*. The others who crawl or walk like drunks with their hands waving, or zip around like Bella."

"Ah, as in children. I'm sure you're right."

"Why do they stare? They're always staring. Like dolls," she said as they walked into the building. "Or sharks."

"I have no idea, but now I'll likely worry about it."

"Join the club."

She took the stairs as she had countless times before Roarke, to the apartment that had once been hers. To the apartment, she thought, that, like her home office, no longer remotely resembled what had been hers.

She was a lot more than okay with that.

"Start the clock," she told Roarke, and knocked.

The door swung open into noise, into color, into movement.

Balloons, streamers, flying . . . unicorns, fairies, and a rainbow-colored dragon.

All this lived behind the nearly seven-foot black man in a black vest over a red skin shirt. He grinned widely.

"Hey there, skinny white girl."

"Hey back, large black man."

She accepted the hug that had her eyeballing the long red feather that curled down from his earlobe.

How many first birthday parties had the owner/ bouncer of a sex club on the guest list?

Then again, Mavis.

"Hey, Roarke."

"Crack. Good to see you."

"Cak, Cak, Cak," came the call from behind him.

He turned, caught Bella on the fly. And the birthday girl, the pretty little golden-haired sprite in a frothy, sparkly pink dress and sparkly shoes that flashed with lights, nestled in the arms bulging with biceps and tattoos.

She whispered something in his ear that made him throw back his head and laugh.

When he turned around, Bella's eyes widened with delight. "Das! Ork!"

She launched herself at Eve, who managed not to fumble the pass. "Yeah, hey, happy birthday."

Wiggling with glee, Bella launched into one of her incomprehensible monologues, then stopped. Her eyes filled with concern, sympathy, sorrow.

"What?" Instantly, sweat pooled at the base of Eve's spine. "What did I do?"

"Boo." It was heartfelt, as Bella touched her fingers to the fading bruise under Eve's eye.

"Yeah, that's what I said."

Very carefully, Bella leaned in to touch her lips to the same spot, smiled, babbled.

"She says it'll be all better."

Eve glanced at Crack. "How the hell do you know what she's saying?"

"I be bilingual."

"You be full of . . . it." Eve remembered to leave off the *sh* in front of the kid. And when she noted Bella had shifted her attention to Roarke with her dipped chin, angled head, flirty smile, Eve saw her chance.

"She wants you. You hold her."

"Well, I — " But Roarke found his arms full of a flirtatious toddler, who latched on, kissed his cheeks, then batted her big blue eyes.

"You're a charmer, aren't you now?" Eve heard him say as she made her escape.

The floor was full of crawlers, toddlers, other little-type people with sticky fingers or drool.

She spotted Peabody and, relieved — even though her partner wore a pink dress with a line of silver frills down the right side — headed toward her.

But was intercepted by the call of her name.

Mavis, in pink (Jesus, so much pink!) skin pants —
or paint? — covered with white stars and a
crotch-skimming dress — or was it a top? — floating
over it in summer sky blue with pink stars, dashed
toward her on blue-and-pink-striped booties with
dizzying heels. Her hair, fountaining on top and
tumbling down the back, blended all the colors of the
spectrum and bounced, just as she did.

She caught Eve in a fierce hug. "You came!"

"Sure."

"I wasn't sure — not with everything juggling and
whacked. Two minutes," she added, then dragged Eve
through the crowd.

Good God, Summerset! He appeared to be having a
conversation with some kid who barely came to his
bony knees.

And the Miras. She really wanted to get a good look
at Dennis Mira, just to make sure he was all right. But
Mavis kept dragging her until they stood in the
symphonic rainbow that was Mavis and Leonardo's
bedroom.

"We didn't get a chance to huddle much after the
Nightmare at the Garden. I knew you'd come that
time. I knew you'd come, and we'd all get through. I
finally fell asleep, and when . . . " With a shake of her
head that sent the fairies dangling from her ears
whirling, Mavis grabbed onto Eve again. "I was scared,
so scared. I knew Bella was okay, home with the sitter.
But I was scared if something happened to me and
Leonardo . . . She wouldn't have us."

"She's got you. She always will."

"When I saw you, I stopped being scared. Today's for happy. For really happy. My baby's first birthday party."

"Looks like, and sounds like, a hell of a party."

"Wait until you see the cake. Ariel made it. It's a fairy castle. With unicorns."

"Naturally. Did you invite everyone you know?"

"Only the ones who count. Let's get drinks. Lots of drinks."

Eve got a drink, and managed to pretty much avoid Trina — especially when she noticed the hairdresser giving her hair *that* look. She saw Dennis Mira's dreamy smile as he sat right on the floor to play some game with a gaggle of kids.

She watched McNab gallop around in his airboots with some other kid plastered to his back, who shrieked as if being stabbed — a sound everyone else appeared to assume meant pleasure. Garnet DeWinter was smiling down at some visually stunning midsized kid who talked earnestly to Mira.

Leonardo, a shiny, dome-shaped party hat on his long copper hair, beamed at his girls, manning the bar in a tunic the color of sapphires.

Louise and Charles — late to the party. Doctors and cops, Eve thought, and saw Roarke talking to Feeney. Doctors, cops, and criminals — reformed. Bouncers and ex-LCs. E-geeks and fashion designers.

And a serious boatload of kids.

She didn't know everyone, but she knew a good chunk. Her people as much as Mavis's. Like it or not.

Chaos got real when the time came for Bella to rip into the gifts.

"Where the hell are they going to put them all?"

Roarke slid an arm around Eve's waist. "They'll find a way."

Maybe, Eve thought, but certainly at the moment the kid was ridiculously thrilled with everything.

"Looks like we're up," Roarke said as Leonardo signaled. He slipped away with Leonardo into another part of the apartment.

Together they carried out an enormous box of glittery pink and silver.

"I'm told this is a magic box," Roarke said to Bella, who stared at it with huge eyes. "And you've only to pull that ribbon there to see what's inside."

With Mavis's help, Bella pulled the long pink ribbon. The box collapsed outward to reveal the contents.

She'd wanted a dollhouse, according to Peabody — and Mavis had confirmed. And since Roarke had been in charge . . .

Like the home he'd built for himself, it was more castle than house. And in this case, all girl. Pink and white and pretty with its turrets and drawbridges, its arched windows and fussy balconies.

Eve didn't get it, just didn't get the concept of giving dolls a place where they could gather to plot. But she got Bella's reaction, and couldn't deny the little squeeze of her own heart.

Bella gasped, put her fingers to her lips, her eyes saucer wide with shock. Mavis murmured to her, and those eyes went shiny as she looked up at Roarke, over at Eve.

Then another girl squealed and rushed forward.

Bella's shiny eyes went hot and fierce, her teeth showed. Eve was prepared to see a long, forked tongue shoot out between them.

Obviously imagining the same, the squealer stopped dead, and backed up.

Shiny eyes returned, and Bella toddled to Eve. When Bella started to lift her arms, Eve took the safer course and crouched down.

"Das," Bella said with a world of meaning in the single syllable. Her arms went around Eve, and she swayed in the hug — as her mother often did. "Das," she said again, and held out a hand for Roarke. "Ork. Das. Ta. Ta. Ta."

Whatever she said after was beyond Eve's scope, but the emotion was crystal. Pure joy, deep gratitude.

"Glad you like it."

"Ove. Ove ou."

Bella let out a long sigh, then sparkled as she danced in place. Whirling, she charged the dollhouse, applauded, poked at it, pulled out a throne-like chair, and hooted with laughter.

"I'd say it's a hit," Eve said.

Then was struck when Bella looked over, smiled, and held out a hand to the squealer. An invitation to play.

A lot going on in that head, Eve realized, and everywhere else, too. A gift deeply wished for — let me take a minute here, sister. The thanks to the people who'd granted the wish, done with charm and

434

sweetness. Another moment to celebrate, to have it for herself. Then a willingness to share it, to have someone enjoy it with her.

Nature, nurture, what the hell. The nature part was a lot of risk, a gamble, often the luck of the draw. Nurture could be kind or cruel, smart or insane — and still.

But here was a kid, with just one year under her belt. Sweet, innocent — but not stupid. Iron willed but compassionate. Already with her own sense of . . . style, Eve supposed. Her own little agenda.

How did all that get in there?

"You guys hit that one out of the park." Peabody, sipping some frothy pink concoction, stepped up beside Eve to watch Bella and some of her friends with the dollhouse. "It's abso-mag, and when the place clears out some, I'm getting a turn with it."

She took another sip. "It's a good day."

"It's holding its own," Eve began. And her communicator sounded. "Shit. Shit."

She switched to text — too many people — and read the message. "Shit again. I've got to go."

"We catch one? We're not on the roll."

"No, it's Willow Mackie. Some issues."

"Let me tell McNab."

"No, you stay. It's just cleanup. If it turns into more, I'll tag you. Crap. Tell Mavis I'm sorry." She glanced around, saw Roarke had already fetched their coats. "Tell her — tell her I'll tag her later."

She grabbed her coat from Roarke, got out before any questions could delay her.

"What have you got?"

"A uniform in the hospital, a CS rep in hysterics, and people who'd better have a damn good explanation. We're going in hot," she added. "Because I am pissed."

Epilogue

As the communication had come from Officer Shelby, Eve ordered her to go to the garage and wait. When they pulled in, Shelby stood beside Eve's designated slot as if guarding it from invaders.

"Lieutenant, I apologize for contacting you on your free day."

"Forget it. Status."

"The prisoner is contained. She had some minor injuries, has been treated."

"I want her transferred to Rikers today, put in maximum security." And for now, Eve intended to go to the confinement area of Central herself. "The injured officer?"

"He should have arrived at the hospital by now, sir. The MTs indicated while his injuries were serious, they weren't life threatening."

"The ones I give him may be. How the hell did she get her hands on a weapon? And what the hell are you doing here, Shelby? You're not in uniform."

"No, sir, I'm not on the roll. I came in to meet Mary Kate — that is Franco, the nurse practitioner. She had morning duty at the infirmary. We're friends, sir, and we were going to see a vid later. I was going down when I heard the altercation."

In the elevator, Eve ordered containment level, swiped her code to allow it.

"Spell it out."

"Sir. Upon hearing the sounds of an altercation, I withdrew my service weapon from my bag and entered the infirmary. Officer Minx was down, bleeding from wounds on the face and the body. The adult female identified subsequently as Jessica Gromer, the CS rep assigned to the prisoner, was also on the floor, screaming. NP Franco was attempting to defend herself as the prisoner advanced on her with a scalpel. She — Franco — had grabbed a pressure syringe and, ah, a bedpan, sir. I called out to the prisoner to drop her weapon, at which time she attempted to grab Franco, I assume as cover or for a hostage, but Franco held her off. The prisoner then attempted to charge me, at which time I deployed my weapon, stunning her."

Shelby cleared her throat. "I secured the prisoner while Franco immediately moved to Officer Minx to assess and treat his injuries. I did demand, in harsh terms, for CS rep Gromer to stop screaming. Gromer made it very clear once we had the situation under control she would report me for same."

"What were the harsh terms, Officer?"

"Ah, sir, I believe I may have, in the heat of the moment, told her to shut the fuck up or I'd stun her, too."

438

"Good. Your lieutenant advises you not to give another thought to any bullshit report filed by obvious moron Gromer."

"Thank you, Lieutenant."

"What was Willow Mackie doing in the infirmary?"

"Sir, I questioned both Gromer — who was not initially cooperative — and Franco, as Officer Minx needed to be transported. I haven't yet written up my report."

"Spell it out, Officer, write it later."

Eve stepped off, nodded to the guard on the steel door of the containment area.

"The prisoner had availed herself of the rep from CS, who, apparently sympathetic to her age and situation, has already filed an objection regarding her classification as an adult."

"That's going nowhere. Keep going."

"During their interview, the prisoner claimed to be in pain from injuries incurred during arrest — resulting from police brutality."

"Uh-huh. And?"

"The prisoner collapsed, stated she couldn't breathe. The rep called for assistance, and Officer Minx escorted the prisoner and, by her request, the rep to the infirmary. Franco instructed Officer Minx to help the prisoner onto the exam table and restrain her to it, at which time Gromer argued that the prisoner was in pain, and only a child, and should be treated with more care and compassion. The prisoner stumbled forward, as if dizzy or light-headed, knocking over a tray of tools. Pitched forward again, making sounds of acute pain when Officer Minx attempted to assist. From the statements it would appear, at this time, the prisoner grabbed a scalpel from the drawer of the counter — though neither Gromer nor Franco saw the move. But when Minx again went to assist, she slashed his face. She nearly got his eye, sir, then stabbed him — his throat, his chest — kicked him back and down, then turned on Franco. It was, sir, about this time that I entered the room."

"Okay. Good work, Officer. Hold here."

She went to the cop on the door, and though they knew each other, offered her badge for scanning. "Log us in. Dallas, Shelby, and Roarke."

"Who you going to pay a Sunday visit to?"

"The Mackies. Both of them."

He logged them in, gave Eve their sectors and cell numbers.

He opened the door — palm plate, retina scan, security swipe, and a code that changed twice daily.

Inside, more cops, another scan, another door.

It wasn't Rikers, Eve thought, but it wasn't a pink-and-white dollhouse, either.

Through that door, and into the cages lining the sidewalls.

And plenty of people in them. Some grouped together in more basic holding. Others, in one- or two-person cages, waiting for transfer elsewhere. A few waiting for their turn before a judge on Monday morning.

For the hard cases, like Willow Mackie, there was yet one more door. The cop on this eyed Eve, eyed Shelby. "How's Minx?"

"They said he'd be okay," Shelby told him, and he shook his head.

"Barely out of the Academy. Needs a year or two on the beat, in Traffic, in a cube before they plug them down here. She's third cage, left."

Eve walked down to where Willow sprawled on the single bunk in a cage. It held a toilet — no lid — bolted to the floor and a small sink bolted to the wall.

"I don't have to talk to you."

"Not interested in anything you have to say," Eve returned. "Just wanted a look before you take up housekeeping at Rikers — later today."

"I'm not going there."

"You don't seem to get your days of choices are finished. Officer, I also wanted you to have a look at someone you've helped put where she belongs."

"CS is getting me out. Gromer told me. And when I get out — "

"Gromer's going to be reprimanded, if she's lucky. And if I get my way, she'll be out of a job come tomorrow. And you will now be further charged with attempted murder of a police officer, with assault with a deadly on same, with attempting to escape, with attempted assault with a deadly on a medical. Just adds weight.

"Rikers max security until trial — you just bought that. And, oh boy, they're going to love you there. Fresh, really fresh meat."

"I'll get out!" Tears leaped into Willow's eyes as she shoved to her feet. "I'll get out, and I'll come for you."

"Now I'm bored."

Satisfied, Eve signaled to Shelby, to Roarke, and walked away with Willow's curses echoing.

"Go on up, Officer. Write it up, and file. Then find your friend and go to the vids. You did good today."

"Thanks, Lieutenant. Thank you for the opportunity."

"I put you in Homicide. I didn't put you in that infirmary. The psychopath back there gave you the opportunity, and you handled it. Dismissed."

"Yes, sir."

"You choose well," Roarke murmured when Shelby headed out.

Eve gave him a fierce smile. "I like to think so. One more stop."

More steel doors, more scans, then Eve stood outside the cage holding Reginald Mackie. He didn't sprawl on the bunk like his daughter, but paced, back and forth, from wall to wall.

She imagined him pacing a cage for the rest of his life.

"Has word traveled down here that we took your daughter alive?"

He stopped pacing, turned, stared at her with his ruined eyes. "You can't try her as an adult. We had a deal."

"Terms were not met, not even close to met. Let me be the first to pass along the fact that she just tried an escape — used the infirmary, an idiot CS rep, and a green officer. The officer is now in the hospital, with his face slashed, with stab wounds. She's going to Rikers, Mackie, and there she'll stay until her trial. Then it's Omega for the next century. Give or take a few years."

"I helped you."

"You didn't. She wasn't where you said, where you probably really thought she'd be. She was at your ex-wife's, lying in wait. And on the record, she bragged about how she intended to kill her stepfather, then gut her brother while she made their mother watch. Then she'd finish her. She wanted to rack up a hundred bodies at the school. Kids, teachers, parents, bystanders. Didn't matter as long as she hit the number.

"That's what you spawned, Mackie. I figure maybe she was born wrong. Maybe she had that twist in her right from the jump. But you nurtured it. You stoked it, educated it, brought it along. She had choices, sure, but you made the choices she made easy for her. You made them righteous."

She felt nothing for him when he began to weep. Nothing.

"I want you to think about that for the rest of your life."

When she walked away, his sobs echoed as Willow's curses had.

"We are done down here now?" Roarke asked her.

"Absolutely."

"There's good news, as this place is starting to make me twitchy."

"Not a cage that could hold you, ace."

"I'd rather never find out."

"I just have to go up, make the arrangements for her transfer, and I should contact Whitney, just bring him up to speed. Then we're done."

As they moved back — the correct way, in his opinion — through the doors, he ran a hand down her back.

"On home then?"

She started to nod — home sounded excellent — then she thought: Choices. To kill, to train to kill. To move into trouble, or turn away. To share a precious new gift. To give thanks.

Wherever you came from, however you grew up, it always came down to the choices you made. Even when you only had one year on the planet.

She made one of her own, and took his hand.

"Let's go back to the party."

"Voluntarily?" he said, making her laugh.

"Let's go back to the weird and the happy. Let's go have some fucking birthday cake."

He made a choice of his own, cupped her chin, and kissed her. "That sounds absolutely perfect."

They rode up, away from the cages, from the curses, the tears, from those who chose to shed blood. And made their way back to the weird and the happy.